Stranger

Dennis Royer

PublishAmerica
Baltimore

First printing

This book is a work of fiction. Names, characters, places, and incidents are products of the author's imagination or are used fictitiously. Any resemblance to actual events or locales or persons, living or dead, is entirely coincidental.

ISBN: 1-59286-433-3
PUBLISHED BY PUBLISHAMERICA BOOK PUBLISHERS
www.publishamerica.com
Baltimore

TO

Beth,
for enduring all of the late nights while I spent time with the keyboard.

ACKNOWLEDGMENTS

I would like to extend special thanks to Jane and Allen Flenner for their continuing support. Also, thank you, Lina Martin, for your enthusiasm!

For my FRIEND, KATHY
ENJOY!

Dennis Royer

PROLOGUE

"All legends are based in fact," Pedro protested.

His friend and classmate, Luis, countered, "We're anthropologists. This is what we do."

Pedro and Luis were in the process of completing their graduate work from Manaus University in Brazil. They were on semester break, and Luis had talked Pedro into going on an adventure.

"The stories about an isolated queendom told by the indigenous Serra Dos Carajas tribes are consistent with legends from the other native people in the region. These could be the original Amazons, Pedro, and nobody has investigated whether or not the tales are true."

"You mean nobody has returned alive," Pedro corrected him.

"More than likely any men finding their way in would not want to come back," Luis said. "Think of what it would do for our careers if we actually did find something. Professor Stamos would be proud of us."

Luis was talking big, but he also had his doubts. "At least we get to enjoy the outdoors for a week."

"You know, I usually like to go camping where there are at least a few other people around," Pedro confessed. "What are we going to do if a jaguar decides to dine on us? Did you pack the rifles?"

"Yep, and I brought along plenty of ammo, too."

The two of them rode in Pedro's Jeep to the town of Altamira near the confluence of the Iriri with the Xingu River. They replenished their supplies and were enjoying a final cooked meal and brew at a local cantina.

"I thought we were going to travel light," Pedro continued with his complaining. "Look at all of this stuff, bedrolls, food, water, lanterns, and rifles. This is a lot for a six day camping trip."

"This is traveling light," laughed Luis. "We're not bringing our textbooks are we?"

Pedro finished his beer and motioned to the waitress for a refill.

"Do you think it's possible that Stamos has been looking in the wrong place all of these years?" Luis mentioned while sipping his brew. "The man has spent his entire life studying the legends and lore of Amazons. Why would he dismiss the stories told by the Serra Dos Carajas people?"

Pedro wrapped both hands around his glass and stared at it in deep thought. His voice trailed off low while thinking aloud. "Misdirection. If I were them and had survived for centuries out there in the jungle, I wouldn't want to be found. I would want fame seekers to be looking somewhere else."

Luis laughed. "Are you saying that these primitive women hatched an elaborate scheme? Would they plant evidence of themselves a thousand kilometers from here in the Tefé region just to throw off the professor and his colleagues? To what end, Pedro, what is their sinister plan?"

"Maybe they just want to be left alone," Pedro answered, "Maybe a stray hunter happened to venture out too far and stumbled onto something that he wasn't supposed to see. It could have given birth to these newer legends."

"Uh," Luis grunted, waving his right hand while drinking with his left.

Pedro appeared hurt. "Don't reject the whole idea."

Luis smacked his empty glass down onto the table. "I reject nothing," he said with a stern expression. "I'm the one that talked you into making this trip, remember? It's just that I respect Professor Stamos. You saw his expression when we told him what we were going to do this week. He gave us a look that implied we were wasting our time."

"Was it that?" asked Pedro. "To me it seemed his expression was puzzled, like he was trying to remember something that he forgot about long ago."

"You could be right, but he had no encouraging words for us, did he?" Luis finished both his glass and the conversation. When the waitress noticed, she walked over with a pitcher. Luis waved his hand over the top signaling that he had enough.

The next morning they headed south out of Altamira. There were a few ranches in the area, some rubber plantations, and a few nickel mines. After 200 kilometers, all signs of civilization ended, and Pedro and Luis found themselves deep in the jungle. The road turned into an overgrown one-lane trail. After another 70 kilometers, it became too dense for the Jeep. Pedro parked at the base of a large tree as close as possible to the river. They knew that getting lost was not a possibility, since they were going to follow the river upstream.

By the end of the second day, Pedro and Luis were both tired. Their progress turned out to be much slower than anticipated. Vegetation was dense, growing all the way to the edge of the riverbank. Neither of them got much sleep as spooky jungle noises kept them wired.

Sitting around the small campfire the second night, Luis considered aborting the hike. Pedro was trying his best to keep his friend's morale high.

"Come on, Luis, we were prepared to trek onward for a full three days before turning back. Why don't we stick to that plan?"

"No problem, we just don't seem to be getting anywhere. This vegetation is fighting us every step. I bet we haven't covered more than 15 kilometers each day."

"Maybe not, Luis, but by the end of the day tomorrow, by your reckoning, we will have penetrated this jungle up to about 50 kilometers. That's a real accomplishment. We may even get lucky and find ourselves sleeping in a city of women. Wouldn't that be worth an extra day of battling this jungle?"

"Pedro, you paint a great picture, but the next time you'll see a woman is when we return to that cantina in Altamira."

Pedro prevailed. The following day the vegetation thinned, but hiking remained difficult. The river was climbing in elevation toward the mountains, and the ground was rockier. The change in terrain was a welcome diversion to the monotonous jungle. As the altitude increased, the humidity seemed to wane. That evening, the two of them mentally prepared to begin the three-day return trip back to civilization.

"This is disappointing, Luis. We've seen hardly any exotic animals or birds, much less wild women."

"We sure didn't get very far, either. It makes me wish that we had a few days more."

"Yep, I guess the Amazon ladies are safe for a while longer," Pedro answered as he yawned. "It's their loss."

The next morning as they turned back down the river, Pedro expressed a thought. "You know, we're probably going to make much better time going out since it's mostly downhill. We cleared a pretty good path on the way up, too."

"So what are you thinking?"

"Well, I thought that we could probably hike upstream a few more hours. What do you say?"

"Not a chance," Luis blurted out. He noticed Pedro's expression change. "What is it?"

Pedro pointed to the ground a few feet in front of them. They walked cautiously to the spot and looked down.

"Footprints!" exclaimed Luis, "bare footprints."

"I didn't see them yesterday when we passed this place, did you?" Pedro panted.

"No, these are fresh prints, and they are coming out of the water. See how the current is eroding away that impression at the water's edge?"

"How old do you make them to be?" questioned Pedro.

"I would say no more than ten minutes. Look, they go up the bank and into the overgrowth. I didn't notice before, but it looks like that is a trail."

"Luis, let's follow it for few minutes and see where it goes."

"Whoever it is will not be far ahead. I'd feel better if we unshouldered these rifles first."

"I'll not argue with you about that. You stay about ten paces behind. We shouldn't be too bunched up in case there is some sort of ambush."

They pressed slowly through the undergrowth and followed the trail. It made a loop ending near where they camped.

"What's going on here?" Luis whispered. "Are we following, or are we being followed?"

"I don't know," Pedro responded. "The way I figure it we can wait here until our mystery guest shows himself, or we can proceed cautiously down the trail."

"There is one other option."

"What's that?"

"We can cross over the river and maybe see where our visitor came from. The trail may be clearer over there."

"Okay," Pedro said.

Luis looked at him. "Okay, what?"

"Let's go over to the other side," Pedro said as if annoyed.

Luis checked the chamber in his rifle. "From these prints it's easy to see that there is only one of him, and we have rifles. I guess we could check it out."

The river was no more than a knee deep and about twelve meters wide. Luis went first. Pedro followed but kept glancing back over his shoulder. Luis was correct. On the other side, they found the footprints entering the river off a more clearly defined trail. It angled up into an adjacent mountain.

They looked at each other, thinking.

Luis spoke first. "I know that we should be leaving, but like you said, it shouldn't take us as long to make the return trip. I must admit that this is irresistible."

Pedro agreed, "I suppose we would regret it if we didn't see this through."

The trail was deceiving. It went on for many kilometers up the mountain. In their excitement, Pedro and Luis gave little thought to the time they spent in their diversion. At midday they stopped.

As Luis munched on some jerky, he noted for Pedro, "I figure it to be another hour to the summit. Once there, we can have a good look around."

Pedro shook his backpack. "We have plenty of extra food," he said. "I'm concerned about fresh water. The higher we go, the less likely it is that we'll find a spring to refill these canteens. Do you think we should come back at some future time, better equipped to follow up on this?"

"Why later? I hope we can get some answers now," Luis objected. "Our mystery person may be from some undiscovered tribe."

"Then again it could be a coincidence," Pedro offered. "He could just be a native hunter."

"Nah, there are no known tribes around this area. By the way, you keep saying 'he.' Those footprints weren't very big. Have you considered the possibility?"

Pedro didn't laugh. "That's all I've been thinking about since we started up this mountain."

"Let's move on," Luis advised as he started to walk away. "We'll be able to see a greater distance once we reach the top."

The trail didn't go to the top. After another hour on foot, it descended winding around toward the backside of the mountain away from the river. Much to their relief, Pedro and Luis found a fresh water spring and were able to fill their canteens. At this lower elevation, the jungle once again became dense and dark. The trail narrowed, and Luis led the way single file. At a low point, they arrived at another small stream and stopped to rest.

"We have about two hours until dark," Luis reported after looking at his watch.

"Let's go on another hour and then look for a place to camp," Pedro suggested as he looked behind him on the trail. "This is going to prove to be a wasted day, isn't it?"

"I should say not," Luis corrected him. "We did see footprints, didn't we? It wasn't a mirage. Also, somebody cut these trails. Maybe we will not meet up with anyone, but there can be no doubt that we've made an important discovery."

Pedro removed the boot from his right foot and began massaging his toes. "Yeah, you're right. I'm just disappointed that we don't have anything more to show for our effort."

The two of them walked on. The trail ascended another smaller hill for about two kilometers. At the summit, Luis strained his eyes.

"Is that smoke that I see off in the distance?" he asked.

Pedro peered in the same direction as Luis. "It looks that way to me," he concurred. "If we follow the trail, it should take us right to it."

They went on cautiously. It was starting to get dark as they approached their goal. Pedro held out his arm and stopped Luis. "Is that food I smell?" he wondered while sniffing the air.

"After eating camping rations it smells great," Luis whispered.

"I don't think there's anyone here."

"Somebody had to make that fire. Keep that rifle pointed in front of you."

The two of them sneaked closer. Luis wasn't sure if he could believe what he was seeing and smelling. As he reached out to touch the roasting meat, a rustling sound erupted around them. In an instant, a dozen women with arrows nocked surrounded Luis and Pedro. They wore hemp capes and leather headbands.

The leader made an up and down motion with her fully drawn bow. Luis and Pedro got the message and lowered their rifles to the ground.

The ones standing directly on the trail parted as a more important looking woman entered the light of the fire. She was athletic but not particularly attractive.

In perfect Portuguese, this one looked at them and said, "I suggest you eat and drink. Get some sleep. We have a long journey tomorrow." She turned and started to walk away.

The two men looked at each other dumbfounded before Luis spoke up, "Excuse me, we are anthropology students exploring this area. My name is Luis, and this is Pedro. Can you tell me please, what is your tribe?"

The woman stopped, turned around, and walked up to Luis within an arm length of his face. She spoke in a low tone.

"I don't care who you are, or why you have come here. All you need to know for now is that you will never again leave this land." After a short pause, she continued expressionless. "As I said, eat, drink, and get some sleep. We have a long journey tomorrow."

CHAPTER 1

Baltimore, Maryland — 6 months later

My dream last night was unsettling. Actually, it was too vivid to be a dream. It was more like a vision.

I recall a bell. It resonated with deep harmonious tones, beckoning me to approach.

"Where have you been?" a gruff old woman demanded. "The Mistress is waiting for you upstairs. You're late, and she is going to be angry."

"I don't know your Mistress," I remember saying to her in a frantic tone. The woman started to laugh.

Suddenly, she pointed off into the distance and ran away. I heard the approaching clip clop sound of horse's hooves and the laughter of a baby. An old open top coach glided in toward me piloted by an infant baby boy. I noticed that the coach was not real, but rather from a circus carousel. The horses bobbed up and down on their poles while pulling the imaginary rig. A subtle white light surrounded it. The passenger was a stunning young woman with long, wheat-colored hair.

She studied me in silence for some time. The baby was delighted. I became distressed as he laid my heart bare. Sensing my discomfort, their probing ceased. The woman gazed at me with a genuine look of concern. She spoke only this one sentence.

"Is your will strong enough?"

Feeling ashamed and unworthy of being in her presence, I heard myself mutter a soft, "probably not."

She nodded as if approving of my answer. The coach and mannequin horses with the angel and the baby slowly started to drift backwards and away.

"Who are you?" I shouted as the coach ascended out of sight among the clouds. She told me her name. I repeated it to myself, but now I can't remember it. Somehow, I don't think I was meant to.

*****

"Dream girl, huh?" Sharon snorted as she slid the bacon and eggs onto his plate. Although she didn't enjoy getting up at four in the morning, this special treatment, preparing Derek's favorite breakfast, was for his birthday. "I suppose instead of bacon from her it would have been passionate kisses."

"Oh, jealous of a dream now are we?" Derek teased her while enjoying the aroma of the eagerly anticipated meal. "Here I am being a sensitive guy sharing my innermost feelings, and you throw it back in my face."

"Yeah, what could she possibly have that I don't, birthday boy?" With that question she untied the sash around her housecoat letting it hang open just enough to tease Derek as she flitted about the kitchen.

This was Derek Dunbar's thirty-third birthday and his debut as "Captain" at TransGlobal Airlines. Today was his first flight as head pilot, and he wanted to arrive extra early to check out the equipment.

"You know, Derek," Sharon said in a more serious tone, "I know there have been other women, I mean...before me. We've had seven great years together, but it seems that they keep coming on to you wherever we go. You're just too damn good looking. Do you ever think about wanting someone else?"

"It's your job to keep me wore out, so I don't have the energy for anyone else."

Insecurity was typical of Sharon but not Derek, yet troubling thoughts bothered him. *What's with these dreams I've been having? My life has been easy. Sharon is right, women constantly fawn over me. I'm in great physical shape for a thirty-three year old man. I feel like I'm nineteen.*

Smiling at Sharon while sipping his coffee, Derek thought it strange that he'd never been sick a day in his life, not even so much as a cold. He resorted to faking minor maladies from time to time so as not to appear abnormal to his friends.

Derek breezed through college with straight "A"s, followed by a four-year hitch in the Air Force where he was one of the chosen few to receive pilot training. After completing his service obligation, TransGlobal hired him. Other than the miserable start that Derek had as a child and the tragic death of his adoptive parents, he had been blessed.

Last summer, at his college tenth year class reunion, even though he and all his buddies were in their mid-thirties, signs of aging appeared on them. Some sported a hint of grey and a few wrinkles, while others grew beer bellies. Yet, there were whispers, mostly from the women, about how Derek still looked the same as when he graduated.

Maybe I am somehow a freak, the thought raced through his subconscious. *Now who's the insecure one?* his sense of reason countered. *Still, sometimes I feel different, above them all, a stranger among humankind*. Even more disturbing was the perception that there were others like him, just a blink of a feeling from time to time.

"Hey, you really are far off," breathed Sharon. "Are you even noticing me?"

"Are you kidding?" Derek asked as he snapped back to reality.

Derek met Sharon McGee during his last year in the Air Force while stationed at Nellis Air Force base. She was a student finishing an Art degree from the University of Nevada, Las Vegas. She was right. There had been others, but at this point in his life, Derek welcomed a stable relationship. The death of his parents made him realize that life was too precious to waste. After dating a few times, he asked Sharon to move in. She had been with him ever since.

Their townhouse in suburban Baltimore was modest given their substantial combined income, but neither one of them especially cared to assume the responsibilities of owning a showy estate. Instead, they banked their money. Besides cooking, which was one of Sharon's talents, she was not really the "domestic" type. She would rather spend her time at the health club.

Sharon worked for Burnham, Croft, and Dane Architects. Although a rather good graphic artist, some of her insecurity was based on the notion that she had never been given the big break, a chance to have her work used in conjunction with a major project. The firm's matriarch, Lisa Dane, the only surviving member of the original founding triumvirate, repeatedly snubbed her work.

Unexpectedly, she laid it on Derek. "Mr. Boggs, my department head, just can't understand it. My drawings of the Market Square restoration project are dazzling. He told me that it's some of the best work he's seen, sure to be a hit with the City Planning Commission. Ms. Dane chose Deb's stuff instead. I wonder what 'favors' she performed for Lisa."

Sharon's reference was to Debra Seals, one of her co-workers.

For years it was suspected that Lisa Dane was gay. One night, Boggs returned to the office late, around eleven, to retrieve a forgotten asthma inhaler. Noticing the light on in the boss's office, he sneaked up to the open door. He caught Dane and one the younger female staffers "in the act." They didn't notice him, and he made a quick exit, once again forgetting the inhaler.

"Look, hon, stick it out a while longer to make the resume look good, and then you can tell that Dane bitch to kiss off. There are other firms that will appreciate your work."

"Well, Derek, when my belly is full with our baby, I can quit for a year or two."

This was one other source of insecurity for Sharon. Seven years of near constant sex and never so much as a one day late menstrual cycle. She wanted a baby.

Although Derek was convinced that Sharon loved him, whenever the subject of marriage would enter into the conversation, she always seemed uneasy and evasive. He sensed that it was their inability to produce children that caused her to avoid the subject. The results of testing bore out that he was the one with the problem.

"It's amazing, Mr. Dunbar," he could still hear the stinging words of the doctor. "You are an intact and healthy male, yet the test shows that it is not just a low sperm count, but no sperm count. Don't fret; it has to be a kluge at the lab. See my receptionist to schedule another test."

He never did. This fueled the insecurity in both of them.

"Really, I've got to get going, Sharon. I promise that when I return from Frankfurt the day after tomorrow, we'll try like we've never tried before!"

"I'm going to hold you to that," were her final words as he headed out.

It was still dark and too early even for the baggage crew as Derek began a slow walk around the wide body aircraft. He'd always taken the pre-flight physical inspection seriously. This being his first flight as captain made him even more determined that everything would go well.

TransGlobal was in the habit of naming all of the planes in their fleet. These names were painted on both sides of the nose of each bird just below the cockpit windows. The marketing department decided that it added a more romantic touch, something the customers would remember with fondness. It was an idea borrowed from the cruise line industry. Everyone remembers sailing on the "Titan of the Pacific" or "Queen Mary," but no one remembers a trip on "Flight 38." The name of this plane was *Adventurer*. Derek noticed with curiosity that the letters "urer" of the name on the port side seemed faded to the point where he could not read it.

"Hmmm," he muttered to himself. "Are you ready to go today, Ms. Advent?" Derek started to feel uneasy like someone was there, watching. He hadn't noticed anyone in the immediate area when he passed through the security gate onto the tarmac.

"Probably nothing," he concluded. "Just a case of pre-flight jitters."

From the wheels directly behind him under the port wing, Derek heard a rustling sound. This was too obvious to be an overactive imagination.

"Hey, is that you, Sanchez?" Derek asked. He was referring to Juan Sanchez, the lead mechanic for TransGlobal at Baltimore-Washington International Airport. Juan told Derek that he would meet him early for a briefing session on some of the specific idiosyncrasies of *Adventurer*.

Silence.

"Juan, I thought we were going to meet in the pilot's lounge over some coffee," Derek offered as he walked toward the wheels. Although still quite dark, a shadowy figure dropped from the wheel well and darted toward a nearby fuel truck. Now, Derek realized that something definitely was not normal. His adrenaline began to quicken.

"Who the hell is that? Stop." Derek began to give chase.

Realizing that he could not get away, the shadowy figure reeled around and flashed a blade, squared up, and stood ready to defend.

"Who are you; what do you want?" Derek repeated and approached with caution. He was scared but also livid at this intruder.

Nothing but heavy breathing came from the person in the shadow of the fuel truck.

"Look, pal, if you don't want me to take that blade from you and stick it up your ass, you better start talking." Derek made an imposing figure given his size and build, and he was trying his hardest to intimidate the intruder.

A raspy voice emerged from the shadows, "Señor Dunbar, the Mistress from afar orders me to kill so that you will come down to her. I will not kill you. I'm going to kill the bitch."

Derek now understood that he was obviously dealing with a nut case, probably very dangerous. He became enraged at the thought that this little asshole had done something to his plane. In a fit of anger, he lunged and slammed the intruder's hand against the frame of the tanker. The hand went limp sending the blade flying under the truck. Pulling him out into the illumination of a nearby building light, Derek saw the intruder to be a skinny, slimy punk. He knocked the punk to the ground and with his hands around a scrawny neck began dashing his head against the tarmac repeatedly yelling and slamming with each syllable.

"What...have...you...done...to...this...plane?"

"What...have...you...done...to...this...plane?"

"What...have...you...done...to...this...plane?"

"Señor Dunbar, please stop, you are killing him," Juan Sanchez begged as he grabbed Derek around the waist. Juan had just arrived at the scene as the fracas began. A nearby airport security cruiser closed in with sirens and lights flashing. It took the two officers in the car plus Sanchez to subdue Derek. Another few moments and the slime ball could have been dead. As it was, the back of his head was bleeding profusely, and his wrist was badly bruised from where Derek slammed it against the tanker.

"I must have Nino, give me Nino," the pathetic bleeding man screamed as he lunged for the blade now resting harmlessly under the truck. Sanchez was able to grab him by the ankles and pull the man back just as his hand was about to seize the blade.

"No, you don't," blurted Sanchez. "Who are you? What is your name?"

"Give me Nino, I must have Nino," the punk repeated.

At this point Derek began to regain control. He marched over to the punk and began interrogating in his most menacing tone, "You heard the man, who are you?"

"First, give me Nino, I must have Nino," the punk shot a sideways glance at the blade still under the truck.

"Okay, Nino, what the hell are you doing here, what did you do to the landing gear, and why did you threaten me with that blade?"

"I'm not Nino. I'm Blaze. Give me Nino."

"Señor Dunbar, I think he means the knife's name is Nino," offered Sanchez. He asked in Spanish, "Is that your name, Blaze?"

Blaze said nothing but continued to stare under the truck.

One of the security guards retrieved the blade and placed it in a plastic "EVIDENCE" bag. He moved toward the police cruiser with the intention of stashing it in the glove box for safekeeping. Blaze began screaming and sobbing with a sickening, piercing voice.

"Give me back my dagger. GIVE ME NINO."

"Yeah, I'll give you Nino all right," Derek began to feel his temper rise again at the irritating screams and sobs.

"That's enough, Dunbar," warned the other security guard. "We'll handle it from here." He grabbed Blaze and escorted him to the cruiser. Blaze was very willing, because that was where his beloved Nino was.

As they drove away with the perpetrator, Derek's thoughts turned once again to the possibility of sabotage. "We need to call in the bomb squad,

Juan, and go over this bird with a fine tooth comb. I'd start with the port landing gear. That's where I found the asshole."

"Señor Dunbar, there is no need. I spotted him on the security camera. I saw him drive in on that baggage caddy just before you arrived. When he hid from you in the wheel well, I thought something was fishy, so I called security. He really didn't have time to do anything."

Sanchez reconsidered his words after noticing Derek's demeanor was still one of suspicion. "Just the same, I will personally inspect that wheel well for you in case he did something with that dagger."

"Thanks, Juan," Derek felt somewhat relieved. "Come on, I'll buy the coffee. Let's have that briefing. I still want to get this flight off of the ground on time."

Derek was now only concerned about focusing on the flight, yet in his subconscious he was anything but at peace with himself. There was something odd about Blaze, and the words he spewed were a riddle nagging at Derek's mind.

"The Mistress from afar ordered me to kill. I'm going to kill the bitch."

This means something, his mind was telling him. "Juan, I'm gonna deal with this Blaze thing later. Right now let's plan on getting *Adventurer* in the air."

"Sí, Señor Dunbar, you buy the coffee. Make mine hi-test. It's going to be a long day."

The takeoff was uneventful and perfect. Over the Atlantic and half-way to Frankfurt, Derek was surprised to find himself all but bored.

Imagine this, he mused to himself. *My big day, and I could easily take a nap.* Of course, he knew all along that it would likely be this way. Derek had been second in command long enough to know that once underway, the eight-hour flight really posed no challenge until time for approach.

"I guess it's like most other things in life, all hype and no real substance."

"What was that, Captain?" asked Joel Washington, the flight's co-pilot.

Derek was startled that he thought aloud. "Nothing, Washington, just going over some procedures to myself."

My ass, Washington thought. *I'm seven years Derek's senior and this young upstart somehow muscled his way into the captain's chair ahead of me. How did he do it, who the hell does he know at Corporate? This son-of-a-bitch, I'm the one that showed him the ropes when he first came here green from the Air Force.*

Derek didn't know that Joel Washington hated him. Joel was ambitious and wasn't about to let anyone stand in his way. During the weeks after the announcement that Derek was promoted to the top spot, Joel let the hatred well up inside him like a poison, slowly eating away at his soul. All the while slapping Derek on the back and hosting a promotion party for his long time "friend," Joel was blinded by a hate that reflected his own lack of self-esteem. Washington now longed for the scheme about to unfold that would destroy Derek's career with TransGlobal.

The truth was that TransGlobal management promoted Derek over Joel, because he was simply a better pilot and had a better rapport with the staff and especially with the customers. He was well liked. Joel, although a good technical pilot, just didn't possess Derek's knack or quite his skill level. They also noticed that in key relationship skills, Washington was often short with the flight crew and didn't seem friendly enough with the public.

The panel reviewing his performance noted in his promotional denial that, "Joel, although a fine technical pilot, is not ready to assume a Captaincy, as his leadership abilities are not yet fully developed."

All of this was lost on Washington. He was blinded by his bitterness toward the man that beat him out.

By now Derek was upset with himself at how sleepy he had become. Of course, what he wasn't aware of was that Joel Washington had spiked Derek's coffee with a double dose of a mysterious drug. Joel got the white powdery substance from a special courier. It was Cobo, a highly effective central nervous system depressant. As Derek floated away into unconsciousness, Joel allowed himself to smile for the first time in weeks. His plan to destroy Derek Dunbar had officially begun.

Security at BWI airport held the man-punk, Blaze, in a conference room. It was one of those secret little windowless rooms off the main concourse marked, "Authorized Personnel Only." Passengers always glance curiously as they walk by these rooms when seemingly important people with chain-bedecked key cards unlock and enter, or when someone suddenly emerges from one of these mysterious places.

Officer Grace Jamison and her supervisor, Manny Cotrell, were weary and out of patience. They had been grilling Blaze for the past four hours about the nature and intent of his security breach. They were especially curious as to how he was able to gain access to the tarmac area. He looked like a mummy with his head wound wrapped from the beating he suffered at the hands of Derek Dunbar. The bandages extended from the pulpy mess at the back of his head all the way around covering his forehead. His eyes and ears were free. Despite trying various forms of persuasion, threat, reason, and outright begging, they were getting nowhere.

"One more time Mister, uh, er, Blaze, please be reasonable. Why did you threaten Captain Dunbar with this dagger?" Officer Jamison stuttered the question between slurps of her coffee. She picked up the dagger and plinked it down again on the tabletop. Blaze's eyes sparkled as he eyed it.

"Mistress from afar orders me to kill her," Blaze repeated the same answer over and over again as if in some mantra like trance.

"Come on, you sniveling moron," Supervisor Cotrell blurted with nerves snapping and losing his composure. "We've been over this time and again. Derek Dunbar is a 'he,' not a 'her.' You went after him. Who is this mistress?"

"Hold on," Officer Jamison interjected. "Look, we're getting nowhere with this nut case. Don't you think it's time we turned him over to the feds?"

"Yeah, I was thinking the same thing," Supervisor Cotrell agreed as he gave Blaze a menacing stare. "You had your chance to tell us. We're the nice guys. Now the big bad FBI will have at you." Blaze was oblivious. His mind was a fog, and he had a wrenching headache. It was the result of the head slamming by Derek, but it was also compounded by his desire to finish the job for his Mistress. He could still hear her parting words as they played repeatedly in his mind.

"Blaze, finish your mission. I command it. Then you may have me."

No police could compare to the terror of his Mistress's wrath, and no reward could possibly be greater than the promise of a sexual treat from her.

"Jamison, keep an eye on him, but keep your distance. I'm gonna go and call this one in."

"No need to worry, sir." Officer Jamison patted the butt of her Browning 10mm service handgun. "He isn't going anywhere."

With a click, Manny Cottrell opened the door and emerged into the terminal. A woman with a burgundy Washington Redskins sweatshirt happened to be walking by, pushing a baby carriage. She jerked her head in predictable fashion at the click and gave a curious blank stare into the little room. It was a stare that Cotrell and Jamison were accustomed to, and they no longer noticed. She picked up the pace as the sight of the half-wrapped Blaze startled her.

What the woman didn't see were handcuffs. BWI Airport Security several years ago started using heavy gauge plastic ties to bind the wrists of troublemakers instead of metal cuffs. This, they were told, would draw less attention from customers, some of whom were already anxious about flying. These ties were the ratchet type, one-way only binders that could be tightened but never loosened. They had to be cut to be removed. Although highly effective, they were vulnerable, as Officer Jamison would soon discover.

She observed that Blaze had been fixedly staring at the door with an empty stupid look. She let her mind wander a bit while waiting for her boss to return.

Sergeant Grace Jamison, Lieutenant Grace Jamison, hell, Commissioner Grace Jamison, she mused to herself contemplating how many years it would take to reach such a plateau. Yesterday, she completed her third interview with the Maryland State Police. They were visibly impressed with her and with the experience that she acquired as special officer for BWI. Being a black female would also go a long way toward satisfying their EEO requirements. Grace was a shoo-in for a job.

"I could do better than monkeying with perps the likes of you," she spit out in Blaze's direction.

Blaze stared at the door, waiting for an opportunity to get on with his task.

Jamison had to turn her back to Blaze in order to reach for the coffee pot.

"Oh, Mistress, please give me pleasure. You will give me pleasure." Blaze muttered to himself. "Do it quickly. This situation is dangerous. It can stop me from pleasing the Mistress."

Jamison was rather burly for a woman, and Blaze was a skinny, slimy punk. Being alone in the room with him did not threaten her. He was bound, the dagger was way out of reach at the other end of the table, and she had her Browning. She was confident that there would be no way this empty-headed wimp could possibly get the drop on her.

Wrong. Blaze was highly motivated. The pleasure/fear paradox playing out inside his crazed mind was the sustaining force of his life. He could not fail. The searing pain wrought of failure could not be endured. The sensual joy that would result by pleasing his Mistress had to be achieved.

No one on Earth was better at understanding human nature than the Mistress. No one was better at manipulating men to do her will.

Jamison was still day dreaming about her potential rise to commissioner while pouring her coffee. It was a momentary distraction. As the voice inside his head commanded Blaze to act, he leaped to his feet, kicking over the chair. Although bound at the wrists, his sinewy legs sprang like a frog, and in one hop, he was on top of the table.

"What the..." Jamison started as she snapped back into reality. Too late. Blaze dived head first into her stomach launching Jamison backwards against the wall. The force did not knock her unconscious, but it left her momentarily dumbstruck and dazed.

"Nino," Blaze sighed as if being reunited with a long lost lover. He grabbed the dagger and managed to use his fingertips to slip the blade between the strand around his wrist. With a quick sawing motion, the plastic snapped and his arms were free.

Jamison started to regain some composure and moved her hand to the Browning. "Freeze," was the only word she could muster. She was still partially dazed and still in a sitting position. This word would be the last spoken by Grace Jamison.

Blaze lunged, aiming Nino squarely at the middle of her chest. Instinctively, Officer Jamison raised her arm to block the assault. This action deflected Blaze's own forearm which was then driven upward resulting in the blade being plunged directly into Jamison's left eye. The entire blade penetrated up to the hilt, through the eye and into the brain. Death was instantaneous.

Blaze slowly backed away, Nino in hand, watching the red blood turn a pinkish color upon mixing with vitreous humor and pieces of gray matter.

At that moment, Manny Cotrell returned and opened the door knocking Blaze backward. It took Cotrell a full five seconds for his brain to process the sight. Spread out before him was the hideously disfigured body of his dead subordinate.

Before Cotrell could react, before he could even think, Blaze reeled around from behind the door and allowed Nino to strike again. This time the blade found its home in Supervisor Cotrell's adam's apple.

Gurgling, but unable to scream, he slumped forward. Blaze pulled the man into a position behind the door and made a quick exit. The door echoed the distinctive click as it shut. Nobody was in the immediate vicinity, so nobody had the opportunity to cast a curious glance into the shambles. Blaze tucked Nino under his shirt and left through the lower level of the terminal by catching a ride on the "long term parking shuttle - blue route."

Manny Cotrell drowned when his own blood filled his lungs.

CHAPTER 2

Near Jerusalem — 70 A.D.

Sara was startled by what she thought was a scream coming from the encampment.

It's probably just a bird, she concluded.

The background noise created by the small rapids in the stream was enough to muffle any distant sound. The camp was about ten minutes away by foot. Sara awoke early that morning before the rising of the sun. She was desirous of some private time to bathe before resuming the dusty journey to the city. Although she never caught anyone, she sensed that certain men in her party slipped nearby to ogle her during normal announced periods of bathing with the other women. This earlier, private time would be sure to disappoint those with wandering eyes and improper desires.

At seventeen, Sara had developed into an exceptional beauty, taller and more exotically featured than the other women in the region. She was blessed with smooth olive skin, long legs, brilliant hazel eyes, and pouty lips. Her long dark hair hung past the middle of her back and flowed sensuously when she moved. She infatuated even older men. Sara's suitors were now becoming more assertive with Eleazar, but he was staunch about holding onto her a few months longer until her eighteenth birthday. It was at that time that her contract would expire.

Sara was an indentured servant in the household of Eleazar of Bethezuba, an arrangement that was sealed while she was an infant, abandoned in the courtyard of the town's temple. The elders gave the infant to Eleazar to raise until she was of marrying age. This was in return for her services in the household. He was the wealthiest merchant in Bethezuba and of means to deal with another mouth to feed. A kindly man, Eleazar provided for all of her needs and intended to help her find a proper husband at the conclusion of the period of the indenture.

Ascending the trail back to camp, she heard what sounded like the thundering hooves of horses echoing away from the distant sunrise. Upon approach, she was able to discern the bawling of Mary's baby.

So, that's it, she thought, relieved that she was able to finally determine the source of the disturbance.

Mary was Eleazar's daughter, a few years older than Sara was and also very pretty. She was married to a farmer and had given birth during the past winter to a male child that she named Stephen. It was a tragic time for Mary, as she was already facing widowhood. Her husband died of a pestilence that swept through the region a few months prior to the birth.

This was also the time of the Roman conquest of Judea. The region had come under siege, and the smaller villages were no longer safe. A period of lawlessness developed as organized brigands began to sack smaller settlements, unguarded by men folk who were off fighting the advancing Roman horde. As a result, Eleazar, his wife, daughter, grandchild, and Sara joined with six other families from Bethezuba in an exodus to Jerusalem. There they all hoped to escape the conflict by taking refuge behind the safety of that magnificent city's legendary fortress walls. Unfortunately, roving gangs were all too aware that the many caravans of pilgrims on the road to Jerusalem carried with them their riches and valuables. Their method of attack included the classic surprise ambush: kill everyone and carry off the booty. Hit and run, be gone within minutes and without a trace.

"They still sleep, sir," reported a scout. He was called "Crook" because of a bent nose. The leader named Ben asked about the number of livestock and if anyone was seen leaving the camp. Crook hadn't noticed Sara's departure to bathe as she stealthily made her way to the stream before he got there.

"What about guards?" queried Ben.

"The one they appointed to keep the early morning watch did not take his job seriously. I found him asleep. He still sleeps, permanently," scoffed Crook with a gleeful glint in his eye.

"How did you do it this time, fool?" Ben continued with disdain. "The last time you slit a guard's throat, the whole camp woke to the wheezing and gurgling of that poor bastard. We lost the element of surprise."

"It was easy," bragged Crook. "I approached him from behind, covered his mouth with my left hand, and plunged my dagger into the middle of his chest. He only made a little noise from the kicking and twitching, but it was quickly over. I dragged him away."

Ben was uncomfortable with Crook's apparent pleasure with killing and with his stupidity. *Blood lust and dull wittedness, a dangerous combination,* he thought to himself. Slapping Crook in the face, he spouted, "Idiot, hiding the body was a waste of time. Anyone noticing all of the spilt blood at the scene will immediately know what has happened."

Crook cowered away.

Observing that dawn was now breaking, Ben understood that urgency was at hand.

"That's it, let's be quick about it," he ordered as his band mounted their horses. "I want this done before others awake and gather their wits about them."

Mary awoke with a start at the sound of approaching hooves. Fearing for the child, she hid her sleeping baby under a pile of soiled linens.

Eleazar threw on a mantle and grabbed his sword. Turning to his wife and Mary, he motioned them to remain quiet. The baby, still asleep, did not stir.

"Do you know where Sara is?" he whispered to Mary.

"Nay, father, she was here in the tent when I retired last evening, but I didn't hear her leave. Do you think that it's her causing that commotion outside with those horses?" At first, Eleazar was unable to distinguish the riders in the semi darkness of the new dawn. The vanguard had ridden past his tent to the end of the encampment to keep the victims hemmed in from both ends. Crook and Ben, along with a half dozen others, approached the tents nearest to Eleazar.

"Can I be of service to you travelers?" offered Eleazar, keeping a firm grip on his sword. A hollow feeling grew in the pit of his stomach as the men ignored him. He heard one of them, the apparent leader, order his subordinate.

"Remember, Crook, kill them all quickly, we don't have the time to dally here."

"I'm taking the best looking of the women with me this time," Crook sneered.

"Yeah, and if her screaming and fighting slow us up, I'm going to have to kill both her and you," Ben cautioned him.

Crook and Ben moved on Eleazar while the five remaining bandits at the rear descended on the neighboring tents. Eleazar fought valiantly in defense of his family but was easily overcome by the two. As he lay dying, his last thoughts were of Sara and where she may be hiding. He died before he could hear the screams of his wife.

Crook immediately spied Mary and was pleased at having already found a worthy trophy in this, the first tent. He menaced her with a small dagger.

Mary screamed. Startled, Crook dropped the dagger and made a fist.

"You'll be coming with me," he snapped at Mary as he struck her unconscious with a blow across the jaw. Forgetting about the dagger, he snatched Mary, throwing her over a shoulder.

Ever wary, Ben had stationed a watchman on the hill overlooking the back trail just before the attack. At that moment, this watchman burst into the tent.

"Ben, Crook, a large army is coming. It must be a Roman legion. Their dust covers the entire rising sun and horizon. They can't be more than a few minutes out."

"Go get the others," Ben barked to both Crook and the watchman. "I'm going to see for myself."

The sun had now completely risen. Ben squinted as he left the relative darkness of the tent and rode back the trail to the lookout point. From a small rise in the road, he could detect the cloud obstructing the red sky of the dawn. Dismounting, he prostrated himself on the ground, listening and feeling the vibrations. This was no small group of riders, not exactly a legion, but much larger than a scouting party.

He rode back to the camp at a full gallop and ordered the party to leave the livestock unmolested and to not burn the tents.

"We must not attract even more attention. Grab what you can carry in your hands only, and let us ride."

The band was in a foul mood having to leave their booty in such haste.

Sara walked unsuspecting toward the camp. Mary's baby had finally begun to cry, undiscovered in his hiding place. As she grew nearer, Sara heard no other sounds and began to sense that something was terribly wrong. She detected a crumpled form lying near the entrance to her tent.

"So much blood," she thought she heard herself say. Gently, Sara rolled the body over. "Eleazar," she swooned. "Dear Father and Master, what have they done to you?" Cautiously she entered the tent. To her right lay the dead body of Eleazar's wife. Sara began to cry. She was drawn to the sobs of the baby. Uncovering the infant, she lifted him over her head and wondered. "What strangeness is this? Eleazar and my lady murdered, but baby Stephen is unmolested. Where is Mary?"

As Sara glanced over to the spot where Mary had retired the evening before, she noticed the blood-stained dagger. Surmising that Mary had been wounded and had left the tent for help, Sara carried the crying baby out into the morning air and began to shout.

"Mary, Mary, Anyone."

Stillness greeted her. The change in temperature and cool morning air distracted baby Stephen. He stopped crying. Mary began to inspect all of the six other family tents. Death greeted her at every threshold. Not a single soul was alive, and there was no sign of Mary. Dazed, she wandered back into her own tent and sat on Mary's bedding beside the dagger. She wept while rocking the infant. It was in this position that they found her. Oblivious to the approach of riders, Sara's mind shut down unable to grasp the scope of what she had just witnessed.

The riders were not Romans. This was a large detachment from the Idumaean army. They were racing toward the defense of Jerusalem. With a hand motion, their leader halted the army, dismounted, and wandered toward the encampment to investigate what appeared to be a hastily abandoned scene.

"What is this?" he asked his lieutenant. "Here I see livestock roaming unattended, strewn debris, and the stench of much blood."

His subordinate checked his approach. "Sir, let me investigate this for you. If I do not reemerge from any of these tents, saturate them with arrows."

"Go ahead, but I doubt if any of us are in danger here."

All the tents were carefully checked. The soldier returned sickened and choking. He reported, "A young maiden and child are in the second tent. Everyone else is slaughtered. Judging from the lack of flies, I would say this happened less than half an hour ago."

"Strange," the leader breathed. "A maiden with a child you say, spared while all others are murdered? What is the meaning behind this?" He gazed at and circled Eleazar's body prior to entering the tent. The man kneeled before Sara, put his hand under her chin, and lifted her face so that her gaze met his.

"My name is Simon bar Gioras. I command a large army. We are going to Jerusalem to make our last stand against the Romans. You are safe. Now, pretty maiden, tell me please what has happened here?"

Sara thought for a moment. *It is all happening so fast. I'm safe but in a sorrowful state. Eleazar was soon going to free me, and I was ready to begin a life unfettered by my debt. Eleazar and his family have been so kind to me, and I love all of them just as I would have loved my own flesh and blood parents. Mary is every bit a sister to me as a sibling by blood. Now they are all gone. I am still an indentured servant. Is this man, Simon, going to let me go? Will he take my word for it that as a slave girl I was soon to be freed?*

In desperation, an idea began to take root in Sara's mind. A glimmer of hope born out of this desperation seized her, and she began to relate to Simon what had happened during the past hour. The story changed.

"The baby and I traveled in the predawn darkness down to yonder pool to bathe," she lamented. "I discovered this carnage after we returned. The man and woman you see here are my mother and father."

"The bandits along these roads are a pestilence to unprotected travelers during these times. Your father and the others were fools to attempt such a trip. The invading Romans would have treated you better than these, your own countrymen." Simon's temper rose in response to his pity for the lovely storyteller. "Tell me, what is your name?"

Sara paused, continued to hold Stephen in her arms, and rose to her feet. Gazing straight into the eyes of Simon bar Gioras she proclaimed, "My name is Mary. I am the daughter of Eleazar, well-known merchant from the city of Bethezuba. This is my son, Stephen."

"Well, Mary," declared Simon still held by her gaze. "By fate or ill fortune your family and fellow travelers are all dead. Being the survivor and a citizen of this land, all of these possessions, the livestock, and anything of value are now yours. My men will help you gather these things together and they will bury the dead. I must insist for your own safety that you accompany me to Jerusalem. After that, I entreat you to remain a guest under my care. The women in our main fortification would be pleased to help you with Stephen."

"I have no choice but to consent," Mary replied. "I am grateful for your offer, especially since it has been made by one so kind and handsome."

From that moment, Simon entertained the hope that she would possibly become his mistress. He was completely smitten by her. From the look in his eyes, Sara knew that her lies had been successful and that her manipulation of him was complete. As he turned to give commands to his men, Sara glanced at the dagger remaining at her right side. She shifted Stephen to her left hand and examined the blade. It was a plain thing with a dull blade and handle made from bone.

Not worth much, she thought, *but it may yet serve as some small defense for me at a later time.*

The second day after their departure, Sara, Simon, and the Idumaean detachment came into view of Jerusalem. The walled fortress stretched around a majestic hill and was crowned with a magnificent temple.

"So this is the legendary city!" she exclaimed to Simon. "It is a monument to the power of man."

"Nay, my lady," corrected Simon, "It stands as a monument to the power of God. Its mere existence is a dire threat to the Roman Empire. It is not only a safe haven, but also a sacred stronghold representing all that we believe. Jerusalem is the city of our fathers and our fathers' fathers. A great day of sorrow it will be if this great city falls."

"Do you believe that it can withstand the Romans?" Sara asked with concern.

"In the temple courtyard, there is food enough to feed all of the inhabitants for years. There are natural springs for water, and the great walls are formidable. We have a large army. These Idumaeans are part of the main force. Our ally, John of Gischala, commands many men and guards the temple grounds. If Jerusalem falls, the Romans will possess all of Judea. It is a great prize for them, and they are highly motivated to take us."

"So, if our forces stay together and stay strong, we shall prevail?" asked Mary.

Looking suddenly troubled, Simon replied, "Ah, that is a source of much personal concern. You say, 'if our forces stay together.' Can they do this if such a siege results in a test of wills? Already one of our citizens, named Eleazar, son of the late prince Simon has gathered to himself 2,400 men. They are camping with John's forces inside of the inner temple walls and are fomenting an offensive strike against the Romans. Fools, the approaching legions will cut them to pieces. Our only hope is to defend and hold the city. It is in this defensive strategy that we hold the advantage. If Eleazar succeeds in convincing more men to follow him in this offensive folly, it will leave us too weakened to make a final defense."

"And if the city is breached, what will the Romans do to us?" Sara asked.

"For me, it would mean death as I would fight to the last. The same holds true for those that follow me. For you, you would be a shining jewel that any man will gladly possess. If you survive the onslaught, most likely one of the officers would claim you and return you to his home in Rome as a trophy of great value."

Rome, she thought to herself. *Rome, capital of the world, greater than even this magnificent city. Why, if by fate I were born into such a situation instead of being the orphan and slave that I am, I know that I surely could become a queen.*

Within her, Sara resolved that she would cling to this Simon for the status and protection that it could afford her. She was also hopeful that the invaders would prevail and that she would survive. Sara wanted to go to Rome!

As they entered through the main gate to the city, one of Simon's couriers met him and with a troubled demeanor drew him aside. Sara noticed a change in Simon's disposition as they conversed out of an earshot. Simon motioned for her to approach.

He confided to her, "Four Roman legions are encamped two days out. Praise God for our good fortune. Had we lingered any longer we could have been cut off from the city. As it is, it may be too late. Eleazar has assembled a great force near the temple and they are making ready to ride on an intercept course. John has called for me to meet with him as soon as possible. We must take Eleazar to task and prevent him from leading forces out of the city."

"Please, Simon, I must go with you," entreated Sara. "Maybe I can help you to persuade Eleazar."

Simon roared with laughter. "Truly, Mary, you amuse me. With your beauty there are many things that you could persuade a man to do."

Sara, of course, had discovered this all too well.

Simon continued, "I believe that you could even coax the sun to give up its light to you. Fortunately, my desire to preserve you alive is stronger. It is my duty to keep you and Stephen safely hidden under my protection until this time of trouble passes. When that day finally comes, we will share many happier times together."

He assigned a dozen soldiers to escort Sara and Stephen to a home inside a more protected inner wall. This home belonged to Cornelius, a cousin of Simon. He had recently died in battle leaving the empty house to Simon's care. Sara was to make this her dwelling. Being further inside the city, it was much safer than the garrison found just inside the outer wall. Simon did not see Sara again for many weeks, although he sent other women from his family to ensure that she was well provided for and protected.

Stephen was inconsolable and sobbed the entire night. Even as an infant, he knew that Sara was not his mother, and he missed Mary. Sara tried to comfort the boy, but no matter what she did, he would not respond. As her patience waned, she began to despise the child. She leaned over his bed and spoke to him as if he could understand.

"A fine prop you serve for my designs, and I will mother you where it serves my purpose. If this wailing all the night long is to be your demand for payment, I tell you that your price is too high. Beware, little man, an abandoned orphan during these difficult times would result in your certain ill fortune. Rejoice instead in our partnership as untenable to you as it may seem to be."

At daybreak, Stephen spent his energy and fell into a deep sleep.

"Finally," sighed a relieved Sara. "The boy sleeps, but I have no rest.

This house is suffocating. I must leave the confines of this place and wander in the cool morning air. Maybe upon my return I will be able to finally retire."

She gave no thought to leaving the infant alone and crossed the threshold into the morning light. Sara looked up to the peak of the mount and marveled at the glory of the temple. The apparition attracted her, and she soon found herself at the main gate of the temple wall. As she approached, a clamor arose from the street behind her, and the gate to the temple wall was opened. Sara stepped aside as a company of soldiers on horseback ascended toward the gate. They appeared to be tired. The leader of the company motioned the riders to halt and asked the gate sentry of any news.

"The priest, Matthias, continues to protest our presence on his temple grounds and becomes more agitated daily. Other than this, the night passed without incident."

The leader replied, "We will not need the old man much longer. The people of this city are sheep, and his presence calms them. Let him be bellicose for a little while longer, but be of cheer. During our night patrol, we discovered that the Romans are on the march and will soon surround the city. A call to arms will cause these people to forget their priest. Survival will be their motivation, and they will cry out for a strong leader."

All of the men in the company began to cheer at the prospect. Until now, none of them took notice of Sara as she stood at the side of the road. She became bewildered and was unable to control the fear rising within her.

"Romans are soon to lay siege, and you men are happy? Have you no fear of death?"

A sudden silence fell over the company and their leader swung his horse around to gaze down on Sara.

"Why what have we here? In my weariness from the long ride and the bed that waits, I failed to notice our outspoken spectator. Tell me of yourself."

Sara fell into her false role and replied, "I am Mary, newly arrived refugee from the city of Bethezuba. Not being from this place, I assure you, sir, that I am no sheep. Furthermore, your priest means nothing to me. I am fascinated, however, by the man that I see before me. Are the words of boldness that I have heard uttered from your lips an attempt to reassure your own fear and the fear of your men, or do you indeed have a grand design in how to defeat this Roman pestilence that has despoiled our land?"

Sensing opportunity, she added this one thing. "Could it be that you are really as brilliant as you are handsome? What am I to call you, the man that is to be our hero?"

Stunned by her boldness and now conscious of her great beauty, he was rendered speechless for some time. Finally, he provided an explanation.

"Mary of Bethezuba, it has been too long since I have been in the presence of one that is both so fair and so bold. If you were from Jerusalem, you would already know that I am Eleazar, son of Simon, Prince of the city. You would also know that I have no fear except that this great city may fall due to the inactivity of the citizenry and their willingness to befriend these Roman defilers. I assure you, dear maiden, that this will not happen. I do have a grand design that has already been set into motion. In the end, I will drive this plague all the way back to Rome. I will defeat that city and make it my western capital. We will not wait for some legendary savior from God to deliver us as the priest promises. I am that man, and the time for the end of our suffering is now."

Now it was Sara's turn to be astounded. Just three days ago, she was an indentured servant, a mere slave. By fate, she had been able to assume the role of a woman of means, and now she stumbled onto a man that had the drive and ambition to possibly defeat a world empire. Sara understood that she could use this man to enable her to acquire a power far beyond her expectations.

"Prince Eleazar you say?" she began to weep. "Excuse these tears, my lord. My father was also named Eleazar. I mourn his death at the hands of bandits just a few days ago. It happened as we fled to this last great fortress."

Wiping away her tears and peering directly into his eyes she spoke, "I am grateful to have met one as brave as you. Your optimism provides me with comfort and a hope that the death of my father will be avenged."

With both pity and longing, he was held trapped in her gaze. "Are you alone?" he asked.

Sara remembered Stephen but quickly dismissed any concern for him. "Yes, my lord," she replied. "I was rescued along the way by the Idumaean forces riding with Simon bar Gioras. He helped me to retrieve my property and livestock and arranged for me to move into the house abandoned by his dead cousin, Cornelius."

"Simon," interrupted Eleazar. At the mention of this name, his countenance fell and he began to look stern and threatening.

Sara understood his unspoken thoughts and knew how to recapture his mood.

"Yes, Simon bar Gioras," she spoke as if giving no care to his reaction. "He was kind to me, yet I suppose that he would have aided any such unfortunate soul in my predicament. After he saw to my needs, he rode off. I don't suspect that I will see him again, although I will be dealing with his representative in the payment of rent for the use of Cornelius's house."

"That pig," sneered Eleazar. "It sounds as if he is taking advantage of your misfortune. He did not rescue you. He seeks only to find a tenant for his property."

Sara countered, "Be that as it may, I now have a roof over my head, and now that I have met you, some hope as to a more promising future."

At that, Eleazar made further inquiry. "Why is it that you wander here under the shadow of this temple gate so early in the morning?"

"I could not sleep and needed a refreshing walk."

"What kept you from sleeping?"

"Grief over my lost father," she replied without skipping a beat. "But now after the exertion of walking up this mount, I find myself tired and hungry."

"I, too, am tired," sighed Eleazar, "and hungry from patrolling all night."

Taking the bait so cleverly placed before him he offered, "It would please me, Mary, if you would take a morning meal with me. I promise that if you do so, I will tell you more of the great victory that I have planned. Afterwards, I will see you safely to your house where you can finally rest."

"Nothing would please me more," she replied. "Although," here she paused, "I fear that I will be too weary to make the return trip. I've been through a lot the past few days. Perhaps, you could find me a secure place to rest for a while before returning."

Perhaps, indeed, thought Eleazar to himself.

While they dined, Eleazar explained about a great meeting that he had planned with Matthias the priest, Simon, and John of Gischala. "These men control vast armies within the city and must be convinced to support my cause."

"What if they resist?" she probed. "Will you still be able to carry out your plan?"

With a gleam in his eye and a smirk, Eleazar whispered, "They cannot resist. They may try, but I have already mastered this situation. They will be forced to fight."

After further discussion, Sara feigned exhaustion. As with all other men that met Sara, Eleazar was an utter victim to her youth, beauty, and charm. He leaned over, and taking her face in his hands, he made his pitch, "Mary," he said, "A woman such as you I would make my queen. There is none other in this city with such grace and magnificence. Stay with me today to take your rest. Otherwise, I will be unable to clear my mind of thinking about you."

So it was that Sara, pretending to be Mary, seventeen, soon to be eighteen, lay with a man for the first time.

Afterwards, staring at the ceiling, she was filled with wonder and thought to herself, *Is this all there is to getting what I want? Can men be so easily manipulated? Is it really this simple?* Entertaining doubt, she rolled over and gently breathed, "Eleazar?"

"Yes, Mary?"

"What you said earlier about me being a queen. Were you trifling with me in an attempt to get me into your bed?"

Eleazar embraced her. "Mary, I knew from the moment that I laid eyes on you that you were special. Now I am deeply in love with you. Really, how could it be otherwise? Yes, Mary, if you will have me as your man, than you will be my queen."

Mary slept a deep and satisfying sleep.

At mid-morning she awoke and found that Eleazar was gone. After dressing, one of the maids of the household met her.

"Eleazar had to make ready for the great council today," she explained. "He wishes to call on you again soon after these matters have been resolved, and he asks that you watch for him to come for you. I am to escort you home if that is your wish."

"That will not be necessary. I am well rested and look forward to the walk. Please inform Eleazar that I eagerly await his visit."

"Be assured that I will get the message to him," the maid guaranteed.

Sara began the walk back to her house contemplating her future.

Baby Stephen dreamed of rocking in his mother's arms. His instincts revealed to him that this woman holding him was not his mother, yet he was not troubled. Cooing, he looked up at her and beheld the face of an angel bathed in white. He smiled in awe. Her presence brought him much comfort. What he could not discern was that the angel was weeping.

"Dear child," the angel sobbed, "I'm sorry. This one proves too powerful. I am unable to protect you from what awaits. Take some solace for now. It will be painful for only a little while longer. You may then enter undisturbed into your final rest."

Stephen woke upon Sara's return. It was now high noon. He was hungry and began to cry.

Sara smiled, "Cry until you die for all I care. I am a queen, and you are only an orphan."

He calmed down as she fed him.

Sara began to entertain thoughts as to how she could unload herself of this burden. She also dreamed about how powerful she would be as the woman of a conquering king.

CHAPTER 3

This time the scene was different. A sensual breeze tickled an uncut grass field creating long flowing waves that eventually disappeared over the horizon. As the intoxication of the moment climaxed, Derek felt a presence. It was the angel whose name he could not remember. The infant was not with her this time. He felt happy to encounter her again so soon.

She spoke softly, "Beware, Derek, not all things are as they appear, and not all things must happen as they should."

In an instant, there was death. The field of grass became souls, not blown by the wind, but rather fleeing as if from a great conflagration. The stench of smoke invaded his lungs.

"Save us," the voices rang.

The angel took his hand which immediately transformed them to a more serene place and a different level of consciousness.

"Why is it that I couldn't help?" he questioned.

She sighed and then told him, "You cannot help at present, for they are not like you, and you are not like them. They can never be what you are, but you may someday be what they are."

"What do you mean? I don't understand," he heard himself think. The trance that this angel held him in was pleasurable, but he was growing disturbed at her endless riddles.

Sensing his attitude shift, she went on to counsel, "This is exactly what I mean, my son. You must choose the path to your destination. It can only be chosen by you."

He felt shame, and her "my son" made him think of the mother Derek never knew. She died giving birth to him, a Jane Doe who wandered into Baltimore City Hospital. She provided all of the necessary information, all of which was falsified. The woman was a real unknown as was his natural father.

He recalled Kyle and Anita Dunbar who adopted Derek, providing a loving home and upbringing. They, too, tragically died in an auto accident during his 29th year. Sharon was now all that he had. He was free to focus all of his love and attention toward her, yet he was unable to give her the thing she wanted most, a child.

Somehow hearing these thoughts compelled the angel to continue, "Remember all of these things. You may be able to draw upon them in their time. Remember this above all, you must not kill her. In the instant that you kill her, the prize will be lost to you. You will become the catalyst around which a great event will unfold. You will be guided along, but again remember, her death must not occur at your hands. It is possible that she may yet be redeemed."

In a distance, Derek heard an infant begin to wail. It was the baby boy, and he was crying for his mother.

The angel vanished, casting Derek into a state of confusion. He was slowly waking up. A new voice, ominous and far away whispered into his ear, "Come to me."

As the approaching dawn begins to overtake the darkness of a long night, Derek Dunbar began to rejoin the world. Holding on to the final threads of a drug-induced dream sleep, a clue was presented to him.

"The Mistress from afar ordered me to kill. I'm going to kill the bitch."

"Not all things are as they appear."

Derek snapped awake to a gripping fear.

"Blaze never intended to do anything to *Adventurer*. It's Sharon, he's come to kill Sharon, but why?"

"I've got to get to a phone, where am I? Ooh, my head," Derek winced as he tried to concentrate through the mental fog and his throbbing temples. The confusion grew as he realized that he was no longer in *Adventurer's* cockpit. It became clear that he was in a hospital bed.

"Herr Dunbar, Welcome back," a high, thin voice floated from near the entrance door to the room. "My name is Doctor Steiner. We've been worried about you."

"What happened, where am I?" was all Derek could muster.

"You're in Frankfurt's Rhein Main Hospital, and as to what happened, I was hoping that you could tell me, Herr Dunbar."

"*Adventurer*, I was piloting TransGlobal Flight 38 from BWI. We were cruising, I got tired, and that's all I remember. Is the plane safe? How did I get here?"

Ignoring those questions, Doctor Steiner offered up a few of his own. "Herr Dunbar, do you have a drug habit? Were you celebrating the fact that this was your first flight as captain?"

"Where the hell are you getting this from?" quipped Derek.

"Hey, big boy, calm down," came the voice of Joel Washington. He had been sitting in the visitor's chair beside the window at the opposite end of the room. "The doc here is just trying to get to the bottom of this."

Derek hadn't noticed Joel until now. If he did, he would have seen a big, bright smile across his countenance. Joel was thrilled that his plan was going so well.

"Hey, Joel, it's good to see a familiar face. What do you mean? Get to the bottom of what?"

"It's like this Derek, old pal. Over the middle of the Atlantic Ocean, you drop off to never-never land leaving me to hold the bag, *Adventurer* that is. You scared the shit out of me. None of us could wake you."

"What happened?" Derek began to cloud over again.

"Don't worry," answered Washington. "She was in capable hands. It was a flawless landing. And now, it looks like I am going to be in seat number 1."

"What happened?" Derek repeated, "I mean, what happened to me?"

"Isn't it obvious, fly boy?" snarled Washington. "You're busted, caught with the goods in your flight bag and stupid enough to sample your own poison. You arrogant son-of-a-bitch, your entire future is in front of you, and you blow it on a stinking drug deal."

Derek was trying desperately to drink all of this in. It made no sense to him.

Joel Washington continued with the onslaught. "Well, you really blew it, old boy. Now complicity in a double homicide is added to the heap."

Washington lowered his tone as if to seek empathy with Derek. "Hey man, what were you thinking? Why didn't you come to me if you were in some kind of trouble? You know we've been friends for a long time." He was absolutely beside himself with glee. It was just too good seeing Derek on his back in bed, helpless, with that twisted look of confusion in his eyes.

Of course, he knew that the tests administered by Dr. Steiner would show traces of downers in Derek's blood. Cobo mimics sedatives in the blood, although the former is unknown in the northern hemisphere. It is also much more dynamic of a drug. It came close to killing Derek.

"That's enough for now, Herr Washington," Dr. Steiner reminded. "The polizei are outside and also want to speak with Herr Dunbar."

"Later," said Washington as he exited the room. In the lobby, he found a public phone. "I would like to place a call to Baltimore in the USA," Joel

Washington annunciated in his best German.

Joel dictated the number to the operator, and after a few moments, the phone rang.

"Hello?"

"Elyria?" asked Washington.

"Yes," a husky female voice floated over the miles to Joel Washington. "What is the news?" she asked in businesslike fashion.

"We've got him right where we want him." Washington related the sequence of events and went on. "By the way, your operative, Blaze, the one that supplied me with the stuff, I got him through the security door using my badge, and he screwed up. The dumb shit got caught and murdered two cops. I had it handled. I planted the stuff in Dunbar's flight bag. What did you need him for?"

Elyria shot back, "That is none of your concern, Señor Washington. The mission is complete. Our alliance has now run its course, and there is no longer need for further communication between us. Your payment has been wired. We will never speak again."

Click.

"Well excuuuuse me," Washington thought aloud while walking away. He wondered about the first time he received that out-of-the-blue phone call from the mysterious Elyria.

Who is she, and how could she possibly know about my ill feelings toward Dunbar? She took an awful risk approaching me about such a plan. Then again our only contact was that disposable cell phone number. I never met her in person. Even if I would have notified the police, nothing could have been done about it.

His mood changed as he thought about how well the plan had gone despite the serious situation with Blaze. "Well, that's not my problem," he muttered under his breath. "Nothing can link that little grease ball to me, but everything points directly back to my good buddy, Derek." There was an extra spring in Joel Washington's step as he contemplated not only the destruction of Derek Dunbar, but also the irony that he was paid handsomely for his participation in something that he gladly would have done for free.

What Elyria didn't tell Joel Washington was that Blaze had three distinct tasks. He was to deliver a kilo of cobo to Joel, pursuant to their prearranged plan. Elyria would leave nothing to chance, so she also instructed Blaze to plant a small quantity in the baggage compartment. It would be mixed in with other articles of clothing and tagged with Captain Derek Dunbar's name.

This never happened, because Blaze was caught. That duffel would not be discovered for many months in its hiding place. It was carefully stuffed under the driver's seat of the baggage caddy. His final task was to kill Sharon McGee. He and Elyria were to return as quickly as possible to Casa Cobo. Frankly, neither the Mistress nor Elyria cared much if Blaze returned. He was just another drone, a man programmed to do the dirty work.

Elyria supervised Blaze. She didn't control his mind like the Mistress did, but she could keep him on track by goading him into having sex with her. While inside her, Elyria would whisper to him how much more pleasurable it would be for him when he completed his task and was able to return to the Mistress. While he groaned on top of her thinking about the Mistress, Elyria would be fantasizing about Derek Dunbar.

With all of the attention that Elyria paid to Derek, she failed to supply Blaze with a good photograph of Sharon. Elyria figured that Blaze would be resourceful enough to figure out Sharon's identity at the appropriate moment.

Elyria punched the buttons on her phone. Thousands of miles away in a cantina at the edge of the Amazon rainforest, a phone rang. It happened to be the same cantina where two male students were last seen six months earlier. Teresa, the manager answered.

"It's for you, Gloria. There's good news from up north," Teresa informed her.

Gloria hoisted the receiver to her ear. She managed to get out a, "Hello?" For the next few minutes, she said nothing, but intently listened to the voice of her comrade thousands of miles away at the other end of the phone.

As soon as the conversation ended, Gloria drove away south. No lines of communication existed directly into primitive Casa Cobo. Everything was relayed in person from the cantina, the closest point of civilization to the hidden tribe. Gloria's mission now was to provide all of the details to the Mistress. She was one of the Mistress's intricate network of operatives, a Shadow Woman, the highest rank attainable in the tribal organization. Several hours later Gloria parked her vehicle in a hidden spot, slipped out of her civilized garb, and changed into her familiar, comfortable hemp outfit.

It was many days by foot through the dense rain forest to the hidden realm of Casa Cobo. Gloria's finely tuned, athletic body was in perfect condition for jungle travel. She moved like a cat.

Wonderful, the Mistress thought to herself after hearing the report. *Soon Derek will be rushing into my arms. I merely need to eliminate his reasons to exist and he will flee to me*, she pondered knowingly. *I've already taken his livelihood, his reputation, and destroyed his ego. Only one thing now remains, the weak, mortal Sharon-bitch.*

Yes, how well I know these humans, the Mistress thought. She was so full of herself.

"Burnham, Croft, and Dane Agency," the receptionist answered in a most official tone.

"Please connect me with Sharon McGee," Derek spoke from Police Headquarters in Frankfurt, Germany. By now, he had collected his wits and was released from the hospital into the custody of the German police. This was his one phone call.

"Derek, you hunk of man, is that you," she mused.

"Yeah, Katy."

Kathleen Miller had heard Derek's voice many times before, and of course, Sharon was always bragging about him. Although they never met, Katy and Derek became friends because of their phone conversations.

"Look, Katy, I really need to talk to Sharon right away. It's important, and I don't have much time."

Hurt by his abruptness, she shot back, "Well, you have a good day, too. I'll put you right through."

"Sharon McGee speaking."

"Hi, hon, it's Derek."

"Hey, cowboy."

Derek told her all that transpired to that point, but he left out the incident concerning Blaze.

"My God," she gasped after taking it all in. "What are you going to do?"

"I don't know yet. The Germans are gunning for me, TransGlobal is furious, and the FAA has pulled my license. In a few minutes the police are going to have at me in interrogation.

"Listen, Sharon, some sort of treachery is happening here. I haven't figured it out yet, but somehow you may be victimized too. I need you to do something for me."

"What?" she breathed.

"Don't go home tonight. Stay at the Best Western Hotel at the airport. You know the one that I mean. It's where we used to rendezvous."

"Yeah, I know," she answered, "but, why?"

"I have a bad feeling about all of this. Please, do it for me."

"Okay," was all she could say. "You will call me later, right?"

"Of course, as soon as I can. I'll call the Best Western."

They exchanged "I love yous," assurances to each other that they would be careful, and the conversation ended.

Sharon started to weep and wandered into Lisa Dane's office to announce that she wasn't feeling well and was going to take the rest of the day off. Debra Seals and Ms. Dane were leaning over a drafting table reviewing a set of plans.

After Sharon left and the door closed, Debra scoffed, "What a weak little girl. No wonder she always loses."

"Now, now, my dear," replied Ms. Dane. "We can't all be as magnificent as you," she said as she gently stroked Debra's cheek.

Sharon checked into the BWI Airport Best Western and turned on the TV. "Damn, nothing but talk shows," she said aloud while flipping through the channels. Sitting at the edge of the bed, she picked up the phone and caressed it in her lap.

"Please call soon," she spoke to the phone.

The interrogation continued. The German police allowed U.S. FAA officials to be present, but they would not allow them to ask any questions of Derek. This was their show, and it had the makings of a high profile, international incident that they wanted to keep under their own strict control.

"Okay, Herr Dunbar," the interrogating officer quipped. "Shall we take it from the top and go through this one more time?" It really wasn't a question, but rather a statement of fact.

"You arranged for a drug pick up in the early morning hours from this courier named, er, what was his name, Herr Dunbar?"

"Blaze," Derek said in an impatient tone. "You already know that the name this guy referred to himself is Blaze. I never saw him before, and I never talked to him before, and I don't know a thing about drugs."

"Oh, I see, Herr Dunbar." The German now began to stroke his chin as he paced the room. "Perhaps you can explain why it is that he tried to slash you with a dagger, and why it is you tried to beat him to death against the tarmac. Were you trying to keep him from talking?"

"About what?" retorted Derek.

"About the kilo of that powder that we found in your carry-on flight bag," the German shouted back. "And about the traces of the drug that Doctor Steiner found in your blood after your in-flight siesta," he now taunted.

This was too much for Derek. He leaped from the chair.

"Look, pal, I don't know what you are talking about so either charge me with something, or let me go."

"As you wish, Herr Dunbar, I hereby arrest you for possession of a controlled substance with the intent to distribute. I also charge you with reckless endangerment, piloting a commercial aircraft while intoxicated. When we are through with you, the American authorities want to charge you with complicity in the murder of two police officers at BWI airport."

"Yeah, yeah," snarled Derek. "Go ahead and read me my rights."

The German official smiled. "Let me remind you where you are. This is not America, and you have no rights here, Herr Dunbar."

Shit, thought Derek, now defeated. He was beginning to experience another headache.

"May I contact the American embassy?" he asked while holding his head.

Like a hound chasing game, Blaze had a one-track mind. Only one mission remained. He had to find the one to kill as ordered by his Mistress.

His head ached as his puny mind executed each step in the preprogrammed mission. Stealing a map of Baltimore from a newsstand, Blaze made his way to a prearranged meeting point with Elyria. He was able to travel silently and unmolested through the city. The way he looked, everyone steered clear of him. A pathetic figure he appeared to be, slimy and grimy, long black greasy hair wrapped in blood soaked linen.

He found Elyria. She was annoyed with him for being so sloppy. "The Mistress will be very unhappy," she chided him. "I figured that you had completely failed. I would have had to find this woman and kill her myself. Do you know what would have happened to you if I would've had to do this?"

"I got away, didn't I?" he sniffled. "Look what they did to my head. I fought well."

"You're very fortunate, Blaze. Fail again, and she will never allow you to return to Casa Cobo. You will be completely cut off," Elyria said making a cutting motion with her hand in the direction of his crotch.

"Don't tell her. Please, don't tell her," he whined sounding like a little boy.

"You have one more chance, Blaze. You can still carry out your mission. She and I both will be pleased. Do it right this time, and I will not have to tell her. You do want to please us don't you, Blaze?"

She took his hands and placed them on her breasts.

"It feels nice doesn't it, Blaze? The faster you are done with this, the quicker we can go home. Wouldn't you rather be feeling the Mistress this way?"

"Mistress," he spoke softly while fondling her.

Elyria dropped Blaze at the building of Burnham, Croft, and Dane around six. Most of the staff had gone home for the evening. She remained hidden nearby in the parking garage to monitor Blaze's progress. His head ached fiercely.

I must find her, but do not be seen, he remembered the instructions given him by Elyria. *Hide and kill, hide and kill.*

Blaze wandered unnoticed into the office parking garage. There was a recess in the wall around the backside of the elevator shaft. He hid there waiting for his opportunity.

Blaze did not have to wait long. Boggs was a workaholic, and it was customary for him to stay later than his subordinates. This upset his wife who frequently had to call and remind him to come home. This was one of those nights. In a hurry, Boggs was trying to make a quick exit. His wife asked him to stop for cigarettes. She was out. From experience, he knew that without them, he would have to hurry. If the delay was too long, she would transform into a bitch from hell as the nicotine withdrawal began. Mrs. Boggs was a two pack a dayer, and it already had been since four o'clock that she had a smoke.

Damn, disgusting habit, he thought to himself. *She really needs to quit, or get some therapy.*

Ding.

The chime of the elevator door interrupted his thoughts as it opened at garage level.

Paying no attention and deep in thought, he exited and began to feel for the car keys in his pocket. As he unlocked the car door, Boggs felt a tap at his shoulder. Turning around, he was surprised by a punch to the stomach and a follow up slam to the jaw. Boggs crumbled to the ground.

Working quickly, Blaze dragged the unconscious Boggs around to the backside of the elevator and began to strip off his clothes. When Boggs emerged from the elevator, Blaze noticed that he was about his size and build. Understanding that his garb would be too conspicuous for the fancy office, Blaze made the snap decision to steal the suit that Boggs was wearing.

As Blaze hurried to discard his own clothes, Boggs started to groan. He regained consciousness. He was puzzled when he saw the other man wearing his clothes, and the trauma of the incident began to induce an asthma attack. Gasping for air, Boggs reached out at Blaze. He was groping for the inhaler located in the inside pocket of the suit coat.

"Silence," glowered Blaze. He looked around to make sure nobody else had entered the area. The victim's moans and gasping became louder. This further annoyed Blaze but gave him an idea. He ripped off the bloody bandage that had been wrapped around his head and stuffed it into Boggs's mouth. He held Boggs's nostrils shut. After a few wild kicks in the air, Boggs became forever silent.

Blaze wrestled the car keys from the victim's clenched fingers and decided to hide the body in the trunk of the car. It would be much safer there than behind the elevator. He dragged the body feet first and smiled thinking, *Blaze is very smart. I throttled the loud man. This is good. No blood to worry about.*

Clunk, the trunk lid sounded as Blaze turned the key. With some struggle, he lifted the dead weight over the lip of the trunk. Boggs's head thudded when it hit the floor.

As Blaze reached up to close the lid, he spied a set of golf clubs and a ball cap. He winced as he felt the back of his head. It was still oozing blood. Realizing that this would be a real attention grabber, he picked up the ball cap.

"Birdie," he spoke softly, noticing the Baltimore Oriole insignia. Adjusting the plastic band at the back of the cap to its loosest position, he gingerly set it on his head. It did not entirely cover his wound. Blaze was pleased nonetheless, thinking himself to be very resourceful.

Ding.

The door of the elevator opened.

Blaze slammed the trunk lid shut and spun around to face the elevator door.

Debra Seals emerged carrying a purse over her right shoulder and a tube containing plans in her left hand. After taking six steps, she noticed him.

Look at this weirdo, she chuckled to herself. *Pushing the fashion envelope with a designer business suit topped with that silly ball cap. And what's with that greasy hair?*

Blaze started toward her, and Debra instinctively picked up the pace.

"Halt," he blurted out. "Señorita Sharon?"

Debra did not respond and kept on walking toward her car.

"Señorita Sharon? You, Señorita Sharon?" he asked while feeling in his belt for Nino.

She reached the car door and spun around.

"That's close enough," she sputtered. "I'm going to get in my car now and drive away. Come any closer, and I'll scream loud enough to wake the dead."

This stopped Blaze. He wasn't near enough to lunge at her and certainly didn't want to invite anyone else to this party. He also didn't know if this was the right woman.

Trying another tactic, he smiled and said in broken English, "Please, señorita, I will not hurt you. I need to find Sharon. It's very important. Are you Sharon?"

"No," she said still on her guard. "If you're talking about Sharon McGee, I think she might have left early, but if not, she would be on the fifth floor."

"Fifth?" Blaze repeated a bit confused due to his aching head. It dawned on him, "Ah, cinco. Gracias, señorita."

Debra dove into her car and locked the doors. Her heart was pounding, and she felt a little guilty.

Shit, why did I tell this slimy jerk the floor that I work on? she thought, upset at herself. Driving away, she glanced in her rearview mirror and noticed Blaze jogging in the direction of the elevator. She considered whether he really was looking for Sharon McGee.

This guy would scare the crap out of her. I'd actually like to be there to see that.

Snapping back from this daydream, she became serious again.

Damn, where are the cops when you need them? Tomorrow I'm going to see Lisa to bitch about this. She turned on the radio hoping the tunes would calm her down.

Blaze wasn't quite sure what to do next. As he rode up to the fifth floor, he tried to formulate a plan. *Even with these stolen clothes, I stick out. People are going to be uneasy when they see me. I'll just tell them that it is important for me to find Sharon McGee.*

Blaze felt under the suit coat for Nino. It was secure in his belt.

Ding.

He slowly exited the elevator wide-eyed and ready for anything. Nobody was around. The entire office was dim. Blaze's head ached with greater intensity as his eyes adjusted.

"Michael Thiel," he read on a nameplate in front of the nearest cubicle. Blaze realized that he struck pay dirt. He would wander around checking the names on all of the cubicles and offices until he found the right one. The elevator was located roughly near the middle of the office, so he decided to check everything along the wall on his left first. Making his way back along the windows, Blaze remained unsuccessful. As he started working the right side of the office, he noticed one of the cubicles was well lit. The nameplate was labeled, "Sharon McGee."

Looking over his shoulder first, Blaze reached down and caressed the hilt of Nino. Crouching down, he entered Sharon's workspace. Nobody was there. Since she left in the middle of the day, Sharon didn't think about turning off her light. She had a lot on her mind and was in a hurry.

"The light is on, she is still here," Blaze mumbled under his breath.

He decided to take a chance and stood on Sharon's worktable to get a better look at the entire area. The only other source of brighter light seemed to be coming from the crack under the door of the corner office.

Maybe she is in there, he thought.

As he got down from the table, he noticed a framed picture on Sharon's desk. It was an eight by ten print of Sharon and Derek from his class reunion.

Very pretty, he thought as he fingered the glass in front of her face. *Yes, pretty, but not like the Mistress*.

Thinking about the Mistress caused Blaze to get moving again. He removed the photo from the frame, folded it, and stuffed it in his front trouser pocket. Now that he knew nobody else was in sight, he moved directly to the office door. Placing his ear against it, Blaze listened.

"I didn't think Debra was ever going to leave," he heard a woman's voice say.

"Are you sure nobody else is out there? I'm certain I heard the elevator a little while ago." This second woman's voice was higher and more unsteady.

"Relax, Katy, everything is okay."

"What about the cleaning people?"

"They never start in our office before ten o'clock."

Blaze, find her, kill her, the voice droned on in his aching head. He reached down and gently turned the knob. It offered no resistance. Ever so slowly, he eased the door ajar to get a better look.

For an instant, he witnessed Lisa Dane and Katherine Miller sitting beside each other on the sofa in Lisa's office. Katy had her eyes closed. She was naked above the waist, and Lisa was fondling her breasts. The door creaked and they both jerked their heads in his direction.

Caught, Blaze realized there was no longer a reason to keep up his pretense.

He finished opening the door and walked right in.

"Sharon McGee?" he asked.

"Who the bloody hell are you?" yelled Lisa Dane.

Katy screamed.

"Shut up, shut up," screeched Blaze. The scream ignited the pain in his throbbing head like a bolt of lightning. His hands went up and covered his ears.

Katy grabbed her blouse, held it tightly against her bare breasts in an attempt to cover them, and cowered against the far arm of the sofa.

Lisa Dane sprang into action. She jumped into the corner where her golf bag was standing and yanked out the putter. Holding it over her head, she ran toward Blaze with the intent of pounding him into the ground. The scene resembled a lumberjack getting ready to split a log with an axe.

Blaze reacted as she brought the club down. He rolled out of the way and brought out Nino. Lisa started to raise the club over her head again. On the way up, Blaze darted in and slashed her deep across the midsection. Lisa dropped the club and fell down to the floor into a sitting position. She moaned as she held both hands over the gash.

Blaze studied her face. It did not resemble the likeness of the woman in the picture that he stole from Sharon's cubicle. This one was older and not as soft looking.

He turned his attention to Katy. She still sat on the sofa curled in a fetal ball and shaking. She was too petrified to continue screaming.

Blaze couldn't be sure. This one looked like the image on the picture. She was young and pretty, but the hair wasn't quite right. He wanted to be sure.

"Sharon McGee?" he asked while pointing Nino at her.

Katy quivered and could only shake her head no.

Blaze wasn't convinced. "Sharon McGee?" he asked again in a more menacing tone.

Silence.

Blaze walked over and put the tip of the blade against her throat. Katy kept hold of the blouse covering her breasts but moved her eyes in the direction of the dagger. Blaze grabbed her by the hair with his other hand.

"Wait," she barely got it out. "Are you looking for Sharon McGee?"

"Are you Sharon?" Blaze inquired.

"No. I'm not Sharon. Please don't kill me, and I'll tell you where you can find her."

Blaze stood back a bit. "Where is Sharon?"

Katy had been bored that day and decided to eavesdrop on the conversation between Sharon and Derek. Instead of transferring the call to Sharon's extension, she pressed the "conference call" button on the PBX and listened in. She heard everything, including the part about Sharon going to the Best Western.

Blaze grew impatient at what seemed like a long delay and backhanded her across the face. Katy yelped and fell over from the force of it.

"Where is Sharon McGee?"

"Hotel," she coughed. "Best West..." In that instant, Katy's survival instincts kicked in. She knew that Blaze would kill her once she had given up the information that he was seeking. He couldn't take the chance that she would call ahead to warn Sharon.

"It's very difficult to find, don't kill me, please," she begged. "I will take you to her. Without me you will never find her."

CHAPTER 4

Josephus was a Jewish man captured by the Romans and eventually befriended by General Titus, son of the Emperor Vespasian and commander of the legions in Galilee. Titus understood that the taking of Jerusalem would involve a long and costly campaign, yet necessary in order to secure complete victory over the region. During their many years together, Titus developed trust in Josephus and often sought out his advice. He had no desire to spill more blood than necessary and would rather have the city surrender instead of resist the inevitable conquest. The two of them and their scouting party rested on a summit overlooking the distant city.

With a sigh, Titus said, "Josephus, I admire your people for fighting. If the circumstances were reversed, I suppose that I, too, would savagely defend my home."

"No, you wouldn't," interrupted Josephus. "You are much too practical a man. Common sense would prevail. Just as the strongest of Rome's galleons could not survive a mighty sea tempest, you would know in your heart that resistance would result in the unnecessary death of you and your family. No, my friend, you would set your pride aside and capitulate."

"Perhaps," replied the general, "if cool heads such as yours exist, maybe there is a way that I could spare this city. Rome has no desire to turn this place into ashes and dust, nor does it serve our Empire to create another river of blood. My father needs taxpayers, not more graveyards."

"See how well you prove my point about being practical," mused Josephus. "For my part, I have family and friends in the city. It would grieve me to lose them unnecessarily."

"And that would grieve me, too," agreed Titus. "I am tired of the killing. I call on you to use your best skills of persuasiveness to make them understand. They must lay down their arms, pledge allegiance to the Emperor, and allow an occupation force. Not one soul needs to die here. After this is accomplished we can go home."

"My Lord, for the sake of my family, I will make my best effort. I fear, however that it will be to no avail. The most radical of our element remains in this city, and they exert great power over the armies and populace."

"May your God be with you," said Titus as he rode away. "You have two days until our legions arrive."

Eleazar, son of Simon, agreed to host the gathering. While in preparation for the meeting he thought to himself, *I must convince my peers and the citizenry to join with me. With my 2,400 men I could successfully launch hit and run style strikes against the legions using the mountains as cover. If I could only convince the Idumaeans and the men under Simon and John, we could launch a full frontal assault against the Roman hosts. Surely these invaders far from their own lands and weary of the many months of fighting and sleeping on the hard ground would be dispirited when faced with such a challenge. A glorious victory over the Romans, and they will crown me King of Jerusalem and all of Judea.*

If he could not convince the others outright with his words, he had a fall back plan that would force them into action.

The meeting was held in the temple. John arrived with an entourage of two dozen bodyguards. Simon escorted Josephus, under a flag of truce, along with a contingent of Idumaeans. Matthias, the high priest of the temple, sat under the shade of a large tree in the temple courtyard. Being an older man, his three sons waited on him and saw to his comfort. Eleazar paced behind Matthias. John, sitting across from Matthias, was quietly conversing with him as Simon and Josephus approached. These two sat beside John and fixed their gaze on the fidgeting Eleazar.

During the several seconds of silence that followed, Josephus felt himself tighten as he studied Eleazar's countenance. *The face of a madman*, he thought to himself. *If this one prevails, my mission will fail.* He decided to take the initiative.

"My name is Josephus," he said looking directly at Eleazar. "I am a Galilean that was captured during the Roman occupation. I am no friend of Rome, yet by fate I have the fortune, for good or ill, to serve the son of Vespasian, the Emperor. It is he, General Titus, that has sent me to address you in our own language and to bear a witness to you of both his generosity and of the great cruelty of the forces that soon surround this city."

"Enough," raged Eleazar drawing his sword. "How dare you presume to lecture us on the deeds of our enemy. As a citizen of this land you should have taken the opportunity to kill this Titus, if as you say, you have been close to him. Instead, you slither in here to undermine our will to fight. Traitor, let me send a message back to your lord, your disemboweled body stuffed with your head."

As he stepped toward Josephus, Simon raised his own sword scolding him, "This man is under my protection. Whether he is a traitor or patriot is yet to be established. I want to hear the words of this Titus, if for no other reason than it may expose some weakness that we can use against him."

Matthias rose with his sons and shrieked, "This is the house of God. Haven't we suffered enough at the hands of our enemies without your actions bringing further disrespect? Think, men, we are all brothers in the faith here."

John finished this train of thought. "Indeed, look, Eleazar, Titus laughs at us as we do his work for him. Go ahead, kill us all. It will be less of an effort than for his soldiers to defeat this great city."

In this short exchange, Eleazar already sensed that he would not win them over. "So it is by force after all," he contemplated. A nod served as an acknowledgment to the captain of the guard to execute the backup plan. The captain quietly gathered to himself a few chosen men, and they set about their task.

Eleazar sheathed his sword and changed his tone. He wanted to let them all talk for as long as they wanted while his plan was set into motion. "Tell us," he started looking at Josephus. "What of Titus, your master?"

"It is uncomplicated," Josephus began again, motioning to them all. "Lay down your arms and allow the Roman forces to enter. You will taste of the generosity of Titus. Everyone will be spared and you will keep your wives, children, and property. Is this not the wise course of action?

"I am no traitor," he said now addressing Eleazar. "A patriot does not throw away the lives of his friends and family needlessly. No, he accepts a temporary defeat and awaits the time for deliverance from his enemies when the advantage is more fully in his favor."

"Yes, but you assume that we could not win this battle now," John interjected. "We have a large combined force. I agree that it would be folly to oppose four Roman legions in open battle. However, we could outlast a siege. With the natural cisterns for water and the great storehouses of food, we would prevail for many years in comfort within these walls. As a defensive force, we would be formidable. Even if they should breach, only a few could enter at a time, and we will cut them down. Soon their resolve will wither, and they will return to their land."

"Respectfully, John, you are mistaken," Josephus countered. "Titus will simply rotate out his legions and bring in fresh troops. You may hold for a year or two, but eventually your food will run out. In desperation, you will fight. On that day, you will suffer under the wrath and cruelty of the enemy storm. The Roman horde will raze this city. This sacred temple will be torn down, all your men will be slain without mercy, and your women and children will be marched away as slaves. This simple choice is before you. Accept a temporary defeat, and live to cast these invaders out later, or resist now and be destroyed. Choose wisely."

Josephus understood that Simon, John, and Matthias were not as brash and emotional as Eleazar. His perfunctory statements were all that would be necessary to reach these men. Glancing over at Eleazar, he suspected that no words could reach past his screen of emotion and into his ability to reason.

Eleazar returned the glance of Josephus with a smile. He was waiting.

They debated the issue further for most of an hour until there was nothing left to say. Matthias spoke, "I have no armies at my command, but as high priest I am charged with caring for the spiritual needs of this city. To me the choice is clear."

Struggling to stand, Matthias's sons helped him to his feet and remained by his side. "The days have passed since I've influenced men over such affairs, yet I now entreat you with urgency. Heed the words of Josephus. After hearing them for myself, I am convinced of their truthfulness and of his honor. It took great courage for him to appear before us. He could easily have been indifferent and continued to abide with Titus."

As he spoke, Matthias was interrupted by a commotion to his right. Several of the soldiers went peering over the temple wall into the city.

"It is true, sir, I see smoke," yelled one of the guards. "It appears to be coming from the great granary storehouse in the east of the city."

Another soldier galloped in from the gate. After a minute he gained his breath and reported to Eleazar, "Sir, the storehouses, in the east, west, north, and south, all of the great storehouses of food, they are all ablaze."

"What treachery is this?" asked Simon as he turned to John. "Come, we must gather our troops and save what we can."

Simon bar Gioras, John of Gischala, Josephus, and all of their contingent raced out of the temple leaving behind Eleazar with his troops and Matthias with his three sons.

After they had passed, Eleazar let loose with a long roar of laughter. "Yes, run, run, and fight those flames. You are already too late. Do you fools want to talk some more or do you now want to fight for your life?" He danced gleefully as his men closed in around Matthias. His sons wore no weapons.

"What is this that you have done?" demanded Matthias.

"Motivation, my dear priest. When we have driven these Roman bastards from our lands, even John and Simon will understand that I have been right about this. There will be no temporary surrender. I have now seen to it."

"This changes nothing," Matthias shouted. "John and Simon can still influence their men to lay down their weapons. We cannot allow this temple to be defiled."

"No, old man," corrected Eleazar with a disrespectful tone. "We cannot allow foolish priests like you to continue to meddle into military affairs. For centuries, talk of your God and of his deliverance of us out of enemy hands have held back our forefathers from becoming a mighty nation. Now it is my turn. When this is finished, all the peoples everywhere will bow down and worship me. I will become, Eleazar the Great, conqueror of the Roman dogs, emancipator of the lands of Abraham."

Drawing his sword, Eleazar stared menacingly at Matthias. "Bow down, priest. Worship me, your new God and savior."

"Blasphemy," Matthias wailed. "Get out of this temple. Go, and may God forgive you."

"I don't think so." Eleazar motioned to his archers and they proceeded to shoot down Matthias's three sons to death in front of his eyes. Matthias crumbled to the ground in shock.

Grabbing Matthias by the hair, Eleazar knelt down, and while staring directly into the eyes of the priest, he whispered, "Centuries we will no longer wait. Go now to your God. Proclaim my coming, and warn him to stay out of my way."

Eleazar, son of Simon, personally executed Matthias, high priest of Jerusalem.

The conflagration overwhelmed any efforts to save the food stores. All of the granaries were utterly destroyed. The devastation was complete.

Josephus pleaded in agony. "Simon, this is not by the hands of Titus. He may have spies in the city, but this is not what he wants. There is no Roman treachery in this terrible thing that has occurred."

"You are not suspect, my friend," consoled Simon. "I know that even if the Romans had done such a thing, you would never allow yourself to be complicit in such a deed."

"My family and friends reside within these walls, and now I have lost hope that they or any of us will survive," Josephus lamented.

In reply, Simon countered, "No one is dead yet. The people must now understand that there is only one way. Go, Josephus, return to Titus and sue for peace. I will do everything in my power, if that is enough, to calm my armies. I will also try to make John see the futility in a continued challenge. It is only Eleazar and his zealots that I fear. John and I must find a way to stop him before he brings us to ruin. If there is treachery in what has occurred here today, I suspect that it may be by his hands and not by the Romans."

"I cannot help them with their current predicament," growled Titus to Josephus. "We have food enough for our men, but the citizenry must provide for themselves. What did they prove by destroying their own stores? This is madness. Nothing that I have done should have caused them to do such a thing."

Josephus explained, "There remains within the city only one fractious element intent on resisting. It is these zealots who performed this cowardly deed. If they wanted to fight and die for some greater glory, I would have tried to persuade them to face your legions openly on the field of battle. Yet, they hide behind their women and children, forcing you to smite the entire city. You would not do so to these innocents due to the madness of these few men, would you? The vast majority wants peace."

"The demands remain the same," reiterated Titus. "They must lay down their arms, allow an orderly occupation, and pay tribute to the Emperor. Tomorrow you will go with my tribune, Nicanor, and his company to the city gate. There you will demand entry. Ask the leaders to assemble in front of Nicanor and pledge their allegiance to Rome. Upon entry, a processing camp will be assembled for all of the families to be counted, taxed, and for them to hand over their arms."

"Eleazar will not comply," Josephus reminded. "His forces are small, but they remain fiercely opposed to such an arrangement."

Titus snapped back, "This matter must be handled internally by the others. Either they will succeed or the city will be lost. The surrender must be complete and by all factions."

"You would not destroy the entire city because of these few?" Josephus pleaded again.

"I have already spoken my terms," Titus sternly replied. "I am capable of great mercy, but my first consideration is to the safety of my men and to Rome. Josephus, do not presume much more due to our friendship. Now go and make ready."

At dawn, Josephus joined the assembly of Nicanor and his three hundred men and marched up to the main gate just outside of bowshot. Simon and John met the night before to make plans for the surrender. They agreed that their forces would keep Eleazar and his zealots confined within the temple walls and act as a buffer between him and the occupying Romans. In time, they would deal with him. John concluded that Eleazar would have to be killed. They were discussing how this was to be accomplished when they were brought word of the approach of Josephus and Nicanor.

One of Simon's closest lieutenants was a man named Castor who did not agree with the surrender. The Romans had killed his father and brother during the taking of his home city of Caesarea. Castor was blinded to all reason by his lust for revenge. Unknown to Simon, he had defected several months earlier to the camp of Eleazar. During their meeting, Eleazar convinced Castor that since he was of high rank and trusted by Simon that he should return as a spy. His task was to quietly foment dissension among Simon's men. Now, he knew that a fateful moment was approaching and that action must be taken to prevent the occupation of Jerusalem.

Thinking quickly, turning to Simon he volunteered, "Sir, you and John have met this entire night and must certainly be weary. Allow me to meet the approaching riders at the gate and extend hospitality to them in your name. When you are rested and refreshed, you and John may descend along with the rest of our troops. This would be a more proper, showy entrance for you to parlay with our visitors."

"I appreciate your offer, Castor. I am tired and have no desire to meet these emissaries of our new master until I have rested and my mental ability is restored. Take only a small number, say ten men with you, and inform the riders that we will formally hand over the city at noon. This should give us enough time to properly prepare and to align some of our soldiers to keep Eleazar hemmed in."

Castor quickly selected ten men that he had previously recruited and who entertained the same desires for revenge. They proceeded to the main gate and relieved the current guards after informing them of Simon's wishes.

"Well, Josephus, these are your people," said Nicanor. "What do you think? Is it safe for all of us to ride right up to the gate, or should just one of us approach to measure their true resolve?"

"Unless Eleazar has prevailed against Simon, all should go well," replied Josephus. "On the other hand, they would expect us to be cautious. Let me approach alone. I will ask the captain of the guard to summon Simon."

Josephus spurred his mount into a slow cantor and approached the gate. A voice from the battlement shouted down, "Brave rider, there is no need to test us. Our orders are to allow your band to pass on unmolested into the city."

"On whose authority do you act?" asked Josephus.

"On authority of my master, Simon bar Gioras and his ally, John of Gischala. They rest for now but have instructed us to entertain you until they arrive at noon."

Relieved, Josephus shouted, "Open the gate as a sign to those behind me that all is well. I will motion for them to approach."

Castor nodded to the captain at the gate to comply. The captain hesitated.

"Sir," he spoke softly, "There are only ten of us. If they enter, we will quickly be overwhelmed."

Castor answered, "They will not enter. Watch me. I will hide behind this battlement and draw my bow. I will let it fly at their leader as soon as they are close enough. When this happens, close the gate at once. None of the others will enter, but we will kill several more before they realize it is a trap."

Josephus raised his left arm and waved for Nicanor to approach. Being vigilant, Nicanor rode with ten men in the vanguard. He commanded the rest of them to ride in ten at a time until they would all pass through the gate.

Josephus entered and stopped to speak with the gatekeeper. As the first wave approached, he noticed the man start to shake and continue to glance up at the battlement. Alarmed, he sternly charged the man, "Our civilization hangs in the balance during these next few moments. Do you wish our people to survive or die? If you know something, tell me now."

The gatekeeper retorted, "I don't know about which civilization you speak of. My people are descendants of Abraham. God has made a covenant with us that we will endure in this promised land forever. If any are to die here in the next few moments, it will be you and your hosts, Roman lap dog."

He hurled a large stone at Josephus and scored a glancing blow to the forehead. When Josephus flinched, his horse was startled and reared on hind legs throwing him to the ground. His body fell backwards through the gate and rolled on the ground in view of Nicanor.

With great anger Castor shouted, "Fool, they are not yet in good range. Couldn't you control yourself a few moments longer?" In his rage he let loose an arrow that pierced the middle of the gatekeeper's chest.

Nicanor waved off his company and ordered a retreat. Josephus, regaining his senses, threw himself on his horse and flew after them. Castor had time for one final, near impossible shot. Aiming high, he shot in the direction of Nicanor. By chance, the arrow found its way and penetrated through the back of Nicanor's right shoulder. Although the wound was not mortal, it was inspirational for the defenders.

"Guided by the hand of God, a sign of sure victory," shouted Castor. His remaining nine men cheered loudly and began to sing in celebration.

Word of what happened quickly spread throughout the city. The populace had accepted that they were going to be occupied, but now this news emboldened them. They spilled out into the streets and in great jubilation held up Castor and his men as heroes.

Sensing that the timing was right, Eleazar rallied his men for battle. The assembly gathered near the same tree where Matthias and his sons were slain. A tarp covered their bodies. Eleazar stood on top of this tarp and made a motivational appeal.

"For centuries our people have been tossed about as leaves in the wind, being in subjection to one group of enemies after another. Empires have come and empires have gone. First the Egyptians, then the Babylonians, then the Persians, and now these Romans, each empire exacting an ever greater toll from our people and our lands. During all of this time, what have our priests told us? 'Be patient,' they said. Pointing to the scriptures, they mutter for us to wait for God to deliver a savior. Have these priests succeeded in driving our enemies out?"

With one voice, the assembly shouted a resounding, "No."

"Has their promised savior yet to appear before us?" continued Eleazar.

Again, the throng answered, "No."

Continuing the harangue, he further taunted, "Has the Galilean that was crucified some forty years ago delivered us?"

"No, no, no," they all began to chant.

Raising his hand to quiet the assembly he continued, "By your own testimony I judge that these priests have been false. They are the ones who have been the real oppressors and traitors to our people and to our God. The verdict for their treachery is death."

He jumped down from the tarp and grabbed the edge. While pulling it aside to expose the bodies of the high priest and his sons, he flatly stated in a normal tone of voice, "The sentence has already been carried out." Many of the assembled began to murmur in fear but dared not openly say anything.

The shock value provided by this display is exactly what Eleazar had hoped for. The men were terrified of his resolve. Now was the time to declare himself. "These false prophets have led us all astray. You need not fear me, for I understand the power they used to hold on to you. I, too, was a victim of their lies, but now their falsehood has been revealed."

After a pause, Eleazar began his summation. "Surely if these priests were from God, I would have been struck down for killing Matthias. If these priests were from God, he would not have allowed the flames to consume our great storehouses. If these priests were from God, he would not have guided the arrow of Castor over such a remarkable distance. It found its mark, the back of a Roman tribune who now probably lies dead."

With that statement, a great cheer arose among the troops.

"And surely, if all of this were not approved by God, I would not now be standing here before you. Friends, these signs prove it. Our deliverance is now at hand. I am the chosen one, your deliverer, and savior. Cast off your yoke of servitude and follow me. Take part in this great day of liberation and victory over the Romans. We are the new and everlasting empire."

In a frenzy, all of Eleazar's 2,400 men and hundreds more of the assembled citizens that were influenced by his eloquence waved their swords and standards in the air cheering, singing, and dancing. Eleazar mounted his horse and led them down from the temple in an unstoppable wave toward the outer gates of the city. Turning to Castor, he yelled loudly to be heard above the throng, "Lead them on outside of the walls, I must delay for a few moments but will join you on the field of battle." He turned aside and rode to the house of Cornelius yearning to see Sara.

John of Gischala gathered his men and began a march to the temple to stop Eleazar. It was too late. Waves of soldiers led by Castor descended upon them. Many of John's own men, inspired by the show of force and now hopeful of victory, defected and rode on with the zealots.

Simon's leadership also proved ineffective. Many of his soldiers and some of the Idumaeans fell in behind Castor. The passion of the moment and the pent up frustration of living for centuries under foreign rule blinded them. Simon and a few of his faithful soldiers made a stand at the main gate.

As Castor approached, Simon shouted out to him, "You have ridden with me in many campaigns as a loyal lieutenant. What is this that you now betray me and our people?"

"God has provided a great sign to me today," he yelled back. "With my own arrow, I turned back a tribune of Titus and sent that traitor, Josephus, to flight. Victory will be ours. Join us."

Castor soon passed out of an earshot pushed along by the sea of men marching to battle. Simon wandered too close to a galloping horse and was accidentally knocked to the ground. His men dragged him out of harm's way.

CHAPTER 5

Derek sat brooding in his holding cell. Desperately trying to piece together in his mind the events of the past day, he could find no answers. Blaze, the drug blackout, the dreams, and the murders in Baltimore made no sense. His mind churned while playing out the scenes. He kept wondering whether these matters were all somehow related. Even more frightening were the thoughts that Sharon was involved and also in some danger.

Derek heard the metallic slide and clunk of the opening outer cell door. He strained at the echo of hard-heeled shoes striking the tile floor as they walked toward his cell. A well-dressed man in a navy blue, pin-striped suit stopped in front of his cell door. The guard accompanying the man motioned Derek to stand back as he unlocked the door to the cell. The two visitors said something to each other in German, and the guard locked the cell door and walked away.

"Derek Dunbar?" the man asked.

"That's me," Derek responded with a suspicious look in his eye. "Who are you?"

"Relax, Derek," the man said. "My name is Klaus Hall. I have been retained by the U.S. Embassy to represent you against the charges filed by the German authorities."

"You're a lawyer?"

"Yes, maybe we had better sit," the man said while drawing a chair over from the wall.

"I'm afraid I don't understand, why would the embassy send a lawyer? Are you on their payroll?"

Mr. Hall answered, "Not exactly. Your embassy requests that I represent you in the same manner as what you would call a public defender. I work for the German government. Requests such as this from your ambassador are routine in cases such as yours. My guess is that they assume that you do not have your own legal counsel in this country. Are they correct, Mr. Dunbar?"

Derek leaned back on the chair and locked his fingers around the back of his head. After taking a deep breath he looked up at the ceiling and groaned. "That's right. I have no German lawyer. I never thought that I would need one over here." Derek lowered his gaze and stared directly into the eyes of Mr. Hall. "In my country, a public defender isn't worth shit. All of the good lawyers make big money in private practice. A P.D. usually ends up as a P.D., because he washes out."

Derek walked over to the cell door and asked, "Are you any good?"

Klaus Hall remained motionless in the chair as he responded. "Mr. Dunbar, if you were a German, I suppose that I would be insulted by that question. Your observation about public defenders is not entirely accurate. I am well known in Frankfurt as a very successful advocate for my clients."

Derek did not move and said nothing.

"On the other hand," Mr. Hall said as he slid his chair back to stand. "If you would prefer the services of someone else, there are several other options available to you."

"Okay, wait," Derek acquiesced as he turned around to face Mr. Hall. "Don't take offense. This is a difficult situation, and I'm pretty stressed out. What should I do? I mean, what is going to happen to me?"

Mr. Hall took his seat again and motioned Derek to sit. He complied.

"Mr. Dunbar, you are facing multiple charges here in Germany. These will need to be addressed first. After resolving these matters, you will most likely be released into the custody of your own country. I can help you with the drug and endangerment charges brought against you here in this country. After that, you will need to retain an American attorney to assist you with the more serious charges that await you in the State of Maryland. Let's concentrate on just the German charges for now."

After a pause, Mr. Hall continued with a grin. "Mr. Dunbar, there is one element of truth in what you said earlier while castigating public defenders."

"Yeah, what's that?"

"How do you Americans say it? I believe it is, 'you get what you pay for.' I can represent you very well given our current arrangement. If, however you desire certain extra attention, you are an airplane pilot and very well off. I'm sure we can make additional arrangements to accommodate your needs."

"Okay, I get it," Derek chimed in. "Look, Mr. Hall, I want you to do whatever it takes. You understand me? Do whatever it takes."

"Understood, Derek, may I call you that?"

Derek nodded his approval.

He told Klaus about everything, minus the details of his dreams. While talking through the events in sequence, he was once again at a loss as to how the drugs came into his possession and how he managed to get them into his body.

When Derek concluded, Klaus looked back over his notes. "Derek, there are two components to this story that I find very interesting. First, you said that this mechanic, Juan Sanchez, told you that he saw Blaze on the security camera drive the baggage cart to the plane just prior to your arrival. Is this correct?"

"Yes, he also told me that he didn't see Blaze carrying anything."

"Good. If this man, Sanchez, corroborates this, it will eliminate the connection between you and Blaze in any drug transaction."

"How so? They may say that we could have made a deal earlier and that the stuff was already in my flight bag."

"True, but unlikely. I could press the point about why Blaze would seek you out at a time after such a deal was already transacted. Logically, he would be long gone. No, Derek, I can make the case that this incident with Blaze is random, at least where any drug deal between you and him would be concerned."

Derek felt a glimmer of hope, but he also understood that with Blaze something deeper was going on. He remained puzzled and asked, "What about the second thing that you find interesting?"

Klaus leaned over and frowned. "You said that your lady friend, Sharon, made your breakfast."

"That's right, but I fail to see any connection."

Klaus interrupted Derek's train of thought, "You had some coffee with this Mr. Sanchez, right?"

"Yes, I bought it. Where are you going with this?"

"If you did not voluntarily take any drugs, someone had to slip it to you in something that you ate or drank. Think, Derek, did you eat or drink anything else?"

Derek's mind was swimming. *The coffee that I bought for the meeting with Sanchez never left my hand. I was nervous over the incident with Blaze and drank it down. Was there anything else? After take off, after engaging the autopilot, I drank another cup of coffee. That's right, I really didn't want any but decided to be polite by accepting a cup that had already been prepared for me.*

Suddenly things started to fall into place. *The sudden drowsiness occurred after I drank that coffee. I was accused of wrongdoing by my friend and co-*

pilot while helpless in a hospital room. I beat him to the captain's chair. He didn't say so, but I can sense that Joel resents me for that. That's it. That has to be it.

Derek's eyes grew wild, and he bolted upright out of his chair. The suddenness of it startled Klaus. He shrank back.

"Joel Washington!" Derek cried. "Joel is the one behind all of this."

"Settle down, Derek," chided Klaus. "Tell me what you are thinking."

Derek laid it out for him. Klaus smiled.

"What do you think of your public defender now, Derek?" he joked.

They both started to laugh. The comic relief was a welcome wave of pleasure for Derek. He was grateful for Klaus's efforts.

"Well, I still don't know how good a lawyer you are," Derek said, "but you make a great therapist. I haven't laughed like that since this whole incident began."

"That's a start," Klaus said faking a frown. Standing up and walking to the door he continued, "I will get a hold of this Juan Sanchez for a statement. I suppose you would be willing to pay for his trip to testify on your behalf?"

"I said to do whatever it takes, remember?"

"Good. Next I will find your Mr. Washington. A conversation with him should prove to be fascinating."

"You do that," affirmed Derek. He thought about Sharon and became troubled again.

"Klaus, when can I get out of here?"

"I can't say for sure, Derek, but our conversation has given me a lot to work with. It should go well for you."

"Am I going to be able to make some phone calls?"

"No, Derek, you are allowed visitors but no phone calls."

"In that case, I need some of that 'extra attention' from you that we discussed earlier."

Klaus now was very attentive and begged Derek to speak his mind.

"It's my lady friend, Sharon. I'm spooked by Blaze escaping, and I have a hunch that he is going to go after her."

"What makes you think that?"

"There is some plan in the works to have me discredited, or worse. If we end up pressing Joel Washington and things go badly for him, she would be a natural target for any others that may be involved in this."

Klaus thought about this for some time and asked, "What is it exactly that you want me to do for you?"

Derek didn't know whom he could trust, or how deep this scheme went. He realized that Sharon wouldn't stay holed up in the Best Western for very long without a phone call from him. He also regretted now that he didn't say anything to her about Blaze.

"Klaus, I want you to get a hold of Juan Sanchez as soon as you leave here, I mean as soon as you walk out this door. Give him a message for me."

"Sure, Derek, and what's the message?"

"Ask him to phone Sharon. She's at the Best Western at the airport. Have him escort her back to our house and pack her things. Ask him to tell her to bring as much cash as she can, and tell them to get on the first flight here to Frankfurt."

"Will she trust him enough to do as he says?"

"She better," Derek hoped. "I really believe her life may be in danger."

Lisa Dane hung on although slumped over with pain. She was badly cut along her gut. She watched as Blaze marched Katy Miller out at knifepoint. Ms. Dane held her left hand over the wound and used her right hand to pull herself along the carpet toward her goal, the desk phone. Every movement was a struggle, but in a few minutes, she had reached the desk. The phone cord was run up through the floor and inside of a channel that attached to the top of the desk. There was no way for her to pull the phone down to her. She was going to have to get up.

Lisa Dane refused to cry. She was in pain, but she was also angry and determined. *I outlived Paul Burnham and Roger Croft to rise to the top of this company*, she thought to herself. *I'll be damned if after all of that, I allow myself to go out this way.*

Lisa grabbed the edge of her desk and using all of her resolve, she pulled herself up. Screaming, she crumbled into a sitting position.

Breathing heavily, she reached over with her right hand and grabbed the lip of her desk. Ever so slowly, Lisa managed to pull her chair to the desk. The phone was now in reach. Not daring to let go of her stomach with her left hand, she punched the speaker button and dialed 911.

Help is on the way, she thought to herself. *I'm going to make it.*

Juan Sanchez answered the phone in his office and made his statement to Klaus Hall. It completely corroborated Derek's story. He also agreed to travel to Germany to help his friend. Klaus informed him of Derek's wishes concerning Sharon.

"You are sure, Señor Hall? He wants me to pack up Señorita Sharon and bring her to him?"

"He is emphatic about this," the voice at the other end of the phone demanded.

The Best Western is only ten minutes from here, he thought as he headed for his car. *I hope this lady listens to what I have to say.*

"She's in this hotel," Katy stated looking over at Blaze. Blaze made Katy drive Boggs's car but kept the point of Nino pressed against her side with his left hand. "One of us needs to go in to the front desk and find out what room she is in."

Now Blaze had a problem. If he killed Katy Miller now, he could finish the job himself. He didn't know, though, if this woman was lying to him. Maybe Sharon wasn't at this hotel. Another alternative was to march into the hotel with Katy close at his side. If she bolted into a crowd of people, he would not be able to do much. He had to make a decision.

"Park the car," he barked. Katy pulled into the nearest spot. Without saying a word, Blaze took the keys, got out of the car, and walked around to her door. Opening it for her, he ordered, "Get out and put on your overcoat."

Shaking, she put on the coat and grabbed her purse.

"No, leave that here," Blaze said. He snatched the purse and threw it onto the front seat. He stood at Katy's left side and reached his right arm under her coat grabbing at her belt.

"Just like lovers we will walk side by side," he said leering at her. "Remember, señorita, Nino is near. If you try and shout or run, it will strike out at you and slit that pretty throat." He dragged his left index finder across her exposed throat in demonstration.

Katy shuddered.

There was only one attendant working the desk. Blaze started to perspire as he anxiously waited for her to finish checking in the businessman that was in the line in front of them. Katy Miller stood there stiff as stone.

"Here are your keys, Mr. Austin. Drive your vehicle around the left side of the building and park anywhere on the outer ring. Use the entrance marked "C" and take the stairs to the second floor. Do you need help with your bags?"

Blaze breathed a heavy sigh of relief when the man finally left. The two of them stepped up to the counter. Blaze looked at Katy and tugged at her belt, signaling that she should do the talking.

Katy smiled, but the edges of her lips were trembling.

"How can I help you?" the young lady behind the desk asked.

"Um, we are supposed to meet Sharon McGee here. Can you tell me what room she is in?"

The lady punched a few keystrokes into her computer and a puzzled look crossed her face.

"McGee you said?" she asked. "I don't seem to be able to find anyone by that name in our system."

Katy's heart started beating so hard that she could feel it in her throat. Her waist tightened as Blaze pulled harder on her belt. She could hardly breathe. *Could I be wrong?* she thought to herself. *I thought sure that Derek told her to come here to the Best Western at the airport.*

"Are you sure, Miss? Could you please look again?" Katy pleaded.

The desk clerk started fiddling with the keyboard. After what seemed to be an eternity, the puzzled look turned into a smile. "Ah, here it is!" she said. "I'm sorry, I must have misspelled the name the first time. That's Sharon McGee, right? I have her listed in room 302. That's all the way at the end of the building. Take the stairs to the third floor. It's the first room on the right."

They started for Sharon's room as Juan Sanchez pulled up to the front door. He left the motor running as he hopped up the steps and walked to the front desk. "Hello there, miss," Juan greeted the desk clerk. "There is a lady staying here by the name of Sharon McGee. I would like to call her from this desk phone if that is okay with you. Can you give me her extension?"

Surprised by his request, the clerk said, "302, just dial 302. She is a popular lady tonight. Do you know that other couple that just walked out of here? They are on their way up to see her."

Juan considered her response. *That attorney told me that I was the only one that knew she was here. At least that is what I thought he said.*

"Are you sure, miss?" Juan asked. "They asked for Ms. McGee?"

"That's a fact," the desk clerk confirmed. She wasn't very busy and welcomed a chance to chitchat. "They're a strange couple. She's tall and pretty but looked a bit shook up, as if she just stepped off a roller coaster ride. Now that guy that was holding onto her, he didn't say a word. He is a Hispanic looking fella, dressed to the nines in that suit, but he probably hasn't washed his hair in a month. He sure looked strange in that baseball cap."

Warning bells sounded in Juan's head.

"You say it was a Hispanic man with long greasy hair? Did you notice if he had a head wound?"

68

"Why now that you mention it, I did notice what I thought was a bloody spot soaking through the back of his hat. I dismissed it as my overactive imagination."

Juan interrupted by pounding his fist on the table and shouting.

"Get on your phone and call the police. Do it now. Tell them that the man who killed the two airport security personnel is in Room 302. Hurry."

The desk clerk turned white and reeled around to do as Juan had commanded.

Juan knew that he would not be able to catch Blaze and the woman in time. He picked up the receiver of the house phone and punched 302.

Sharon was brushing her teeth when the phone rang. It startled her. Quickly she rinsed her mouth and jumped onto the bed. Sharon reached over to the phone located on the nightstand and picked it up on the fourth ring.

"Hello?"

"Is this Sharon?"

"Yes, this is Sharon."

"Sharon, listen to me. My name is Juan Sanchez. You don't know me. Your man, Derek, asked me to call you."

"Derek?" How is he? Can I speak with him?"

"Listen to me," he said as firmly as he could without yelling. "Do as I say. Do not answer your door. A man and a woman are on their way up to see you right now. If the man gets in, he is going to kill you."

"What?"

"Do not open your door. The police are on their way, and I will be there in about one minute. Do not open your door."

Juan dropped the receiver and sprang out of the lobby. Turning the corner, he raced the length of the building.

At that instant, there was a soft rap at the door. Sharon remained sprawled out across the bed, frozen in fear.

"Again," Blaze ordered while pressing Nino against Katy's liver. "Get her to open the door."

Another rap, this time a little harder.

"Sharon?" a familiar voice on the other side of the door inquired. "Sharon, it's Katy Miller. I need to talk with you. Can you let me in?"

She sat up on the bed and considered to herself. *Katy Miller, how could this be? How is it that all of these people know where I am hiding? I didn't tell anyone. It must be Derek. Derek called work and probably asked Katy to get a message to me. But why is she here? Why didn't she just call me from*

69

work? What about that strange man, Juan? He said that a man and woman were going to knock. What man? All of these thoughts raced through her head.

"Katy?" asked Sharon, "Are you alone?"

Blaze nodded his head and motioned for her to speak.

"It's just me, Sharon," Katy said. Her nerve finally failed her, and she began to sob. "Sharon, please let me in. I have to talk with you."

Sharon walked over to the door and looked through the peephole. She saw Katy crying. Eyeliner was running down her cheek. What she didn't see was Blaze standing a few feet away out of range of the peephole.

Katy, she thought to herself. *I wonder what this is all about? Maybe it's about Derek. That's it. Something is wrong with Derek, and Katy knows about it. She's upset. That's why she's crying. Whatever it is, she wanted to tell me in person and not over the phone.*

Panicking, Sharon fumbled the dead bolt. It clicked, and she opened the door.

"Derek," she said. "Katy, tell me. What's happened to Derek?"

"I'm sorry," Katy gushed. "Sharon, I'm so sorry."

The next sequence of events happened quickly. Blaze jumped over and knocked Katy out of the way. She tripped and fell to the ground. Blaze grabbed Nino from his pocket and held it ready to strike.

"For my Mistress!" he exclaimed. Just as he was about to plunge the dagger into Sharon, Juan Sanchez cleared the corner.

"Blaze," he screamed. This was enough to make Blaze hesitate. He spun around to find out who had yelled his name. At the same time, Juan dove head first into Blaze's midsection. The force drove them back. Blaze tripped over Katy, and the two men fell on top of her. Blaze struck the back of his already battered head on the floor. He screamed and momentarily blacked out. Juan grabbed at the dagger in Blaze's hand and threw it back down the hall toward the stairwell.

"Run," he screamed at the two women. "My car is running outside the main lobby. Get in and lock the doors until I return or the police arrive."

Sharon sprang into action. She helped Katy to get up. Holding hands, they raced to the stairwell. As they got there, Sharon bent down and picked up the dagger.

"If anyone comes after us, at least we'll have this," she said to Katy.

Katy limped by her side and slowed. She started repeating, "I'm sorry, Sharon. He was going to kill me. I had to lead him here. I'm sorry."

Sharon grabbed both of Katy's shoulders and shook her.

"Snap out of it!" she yelled. "We're not safe yet. Come on." Sharon grabbed Katy's hand and led her down the steps to the main level and out the door. They ran toward the lobby and the waiting car.

In the meantime, Juan tried to restrain Blaze by straddling him and pinning his arms to the floor. Ignoring his pain, Blaze thrashed his legs wildly and threw Juan off balance. He heaved his body upward and bucked Juan off to the side, slamming him against the corridor wall. Unleashed, Blaze sprang to his feet and turned to run after Sharon. Juan reached up from his prone position on the floor and made a last second shoe string tackle. Blaze fell.

Jumping on top, the two of them rolled into Sharon's room. Blaze kicked at Juan as he attempted to stand. One of the blows caught Juan in the jaw. It staggered him. Blaze picked up a lamp and brought it down in the direction of Juan's head. Juan ducked to the side, and the blow went wide. The momentum of the attempted strike caused Blaze to stumble face first onto the bed.

Juan grabbed the lamp's electric cord and looped it around Blaze's throat. He pulled it tight with all of his strength. When Blaze started thrashing, Juan began to knee him in the kidney. Weakening, Blaze began to fade. Juan felt him go limp and released his grip. Gasping for air, Juan's heart was still pounding as he popped through the door to the outside at the bottom of the stairwell.

Three police cars screeched to a halt in front of him. The flashing lights caused Juan to wince. He sat on the ground at the entrance and pointed up.

"Third floor," he said hoarsely. "He's up there in 302."

With guns drawn, two officers ran by. They burst through the door and up the steps. As they rounded the landing on the second floor, the officers were met by a scream.

Holding the lamp over his head, Blaze motioned them back.

"Nino," he cried. "That bitch stole my Nino. I'll smash her to a pulpy mess." He lunged down the steps, screeching wildly with the lamp held high over his head.

The two officers looked at each other. Turning to face Blaze who was now charging them like a raging bull, they opened fire emptying their semi-automatic handguns into him. Blaze folded in half and fell at the officers' feet. During the last second, as the life force drained out of him, Blaze's thoughts turned to his Mistress. He died smiling.

CHAPTER 6

Eleazar rode to the house of Cornelius and boldly entered unannounced. "Mary," he spoke, "where are you?"

"Eleazar?" she asked emerging from the room where Stephen was playing. "The whole city is shaking, and there is a great uproar. Are we under attack?"

Laughing, he embraced her and exclaimed, "No, my dear, it is the Romans that find themselves under attack. We ride today, for you!"

"For me? What do you mean?"

"When we laid together the other day, I can't explain it, but I fell completely under your power. Never has making love so completely absorbed me in such ecstasy. No longer do I do what I do for my own glory only. The greater part of my inspiration is to grant you your desires. I go now to make you a queen, but first I must lay with you again. Now."

Sara was totally bewildered but yielded to his advance. He carried her into the bedroom and was startled by the infant's presence.

"Hello, little man," he said.

Reading the questioning look on Eleazar's face, she explained, "His mother has taken ill, and I agreed to watch him for a while."

"Well," he addressed the boy, "since this isn't your mother, I don't suppose you will mind when I make love with this pretty lady. Watch well, little man, and learn."

He ravaged her body while Sara pondered his words about being 'completely absorbed in ecstasy.' She did vaguely remember something. Before when Eleazar filled her, Sara experienced a strange sensation for a fleeting moment that almost went unnoticed. Being her first time with a man, she was unsure of herself and detached from her physical feelings. Now she was curious and felt more at ease. As he slid into her, Sara explored her consciousness to rediscover this strange feeling.

She concentrated.

In a few moments, something primal filled her. From the depths of her bosom, a spark of energy sprang into life and kindled at the base of her spine.

Stephen watched them with a blank expression. Being an infant, he had not yet developed the ability to think in a language. The closest translation to what he experienced at that moment would be, "Pretty colors."

Nerve endings exploded as the surge cascaded along Sara's spine toward her brain. The pace of the rush quickened, and as it reached her neck she felt on fire. The swell burst into Sara's brain, and her entire body seized. At that moment, she redirected her mind toward Eleazar and felt his power enter into her. Her orgasmic blast arced across into Eleazar's body and racked his brain. He screamed.

Lying beside her, Eleazar's spent body quivered with spasms. Minutes later he regained control and hoarsely spoke, "What was that? What did you do to me?"

"It was sex, silly," she giggled in a girlish manner. "It felt nice."

"No," he coughed and gasped for air. "It was much more than that. You had my soul in your grasp. If you wanted to you could have crushed me. I could be dead."

Sara laughed, "It was that good for you?" In her heart, though, she knew that he spoke the truth. It was both frightening and thrilling.

Eleazar got dressed and began to look differently at Sara. He realized that she now fully controlled him. He needed her. Sexual contact with her was an overwhelming narcotic. He had to have her again soon. She owned him. She controlled him. When she turned her mind toward him, she could place whatever thought she wanted into his head. He stood staring at her. Eleazar resembled a dog awaiting instructions from his master. She walked over and kissed him. He tingled. Staring into his eyes, she softly spoke, "Go Eleazar, make me a queen."

After Eleazar departed, Sara walked outside and looked up at the temple. Closing her eyes, she reached out with her mind. *Who am I?*

Across the city dwelled a woman named Helena originally from Adiabene. She was a queen there, but migrated to Jerusalem with her husband and converted to the Jewish faith. Thinking about the chaos that was occurring, she was suddenly jolted out of her meditation.

"By the grace of God," she started in alarm. "I thought I felt it before, but now I know for sure. There is another one of us here, one with more power than I ever felt before. Could this one be the source of the madness that grips this city?"

Closing her eyes, Helena projected a simple thought, *Come to me.*

Sara felt something touch her mind. Her eyes popped open, and she fell to the ground paralyzed with fear.

"So, I am not alone," she mumbled to herself unable to understand the intentions of the mind that probed hers.

John was riding his horse down a side street when he spied Eleazar on the main road making for the gate. He pursued at a full gallop but did not overtake Eleazar until he passed through the gate and out of the city.

"Eleazar, son of Simon, stop. I would have a word with you," gasped John as he pulled along side.

Eleazar paid no attention. He was unaware that John was even there.

Go Eleazar, make me a queen. The refrain played over and over in his head. Nothing else mattered. He needed to prevail and return as soon as he could to her bed.

After several attempts to shout him down, John, in desperation, rode as close as possible to the other rider and threw himself into Eleazar. John grabbed him around the torso, and they both tumbled to the ground. Their horses, now unburdened and without guidance, stood idly by.

With his concentration broken and smarting from the fall, Eleazar glared at John. "What is the meaning of this?" he snorted.

"That is my question for you," John responded.

"I have no time to parlay. Castor is in temporary command of my men, and I must rejoin them to lead the attack."

"Eleazar, look at me and answer my questions," demanded John. "The high priest, Matthias, is dead. The granaries have been destroyed. A Roman tribune has been ambushed and our friend, Josephus, has been turned away. Are you responsible for these misdeeds?"

Wanting to get away as quickly as possible, he blurted out, "Yes, yes, yes, and yes again. I commanded all of these things to occur. Now get out of my way."

As he tried to pass, John struck him in the face and knocked Eleazar to the ground.

John further demanded, "What gives you the right to cause these things to occur? What madness has blinded you to this folly? It is because of you that a generation will be lost and a way of life destroyed."

"What gives me the right?" Eleazar shouted back. Wiping blood from his nose he continued, "I take the right. It is mine from God. You cowards would allow these Romans to dance unopposed into our land when we have a chance to strike them down. Either get out of my way, join with me, or die. This parlay is over."

John let him pass, and they both reached their horses at the same time. Eleazar mounted. John grabbed his spear and cried, "Eleazar."

As Eleazar turned in response, John impaled him through the chest.

Eleazar grabbed at the base of the shaft and feeling hot blood gush through the wound, he fell to the ground. "My queen," were his last words.

John rode back to the city to join with Simon to prepare for a final defense.

Castor waited a full day for Eleazar. When Eleazar did not appear, he took command of the army and led the attack. They killed thousands of Romans, but thousands more were in reserve. Not a single one of the soldiers from Jerusalem survived. The Romans destroyed them all in that single day.

Six weeks passed and Jerusalem was in the death throes of a city gripped by famine. Not only were the inhabitants without food, but they also became void of any sense of morality. Class distinctions had vanished. The poor had no food, and the rich were running out of food with no hope of replenishment. Their gold and silver could buy them nothing, because the markets were empty. Any stores that were laid up in private homes were now either exhausted or plundered by mobs desperate for nourishment.

In the early stages, the sick and elderly died. As was the custom, they were grieved for and buried by their families. Now, death was everywhere and even the pretense of grief by the living had ended. Emotions dried up. Entire families died together too weak to care for those that fell before them. Many took their own lives when the suffering became too great. Corpses filled the side alleys, and the stench drove away even the rats.

By this time, many men had abandoned their posts. Some organized into gangs and raided homes of any that they suspected were holding back on food.

Simon gathered up Sara and Stephen during the third week of the siege, and he moved them into a private room inside his garrison. He did this, because they were no longer safe living alone in his dead cousin's house. During the final weeks, all of the livestock that she inherited from her adopted father and from the six slain families had been butchered for food or doled out to feed Simon's men. Simon gave away all of her belongings to buy the continuing loyalty of his closest troops. One large trunk remained that held her clothing, blankets, and other necessary items. Sara held on to the dagger left behind by Crook during the attack on her family.

During the fifth and sixth weeks, the food ration became even more meager and inadequate. Sara was in misery at the agony of her hunger, but little Stephen fared well. Two goats were spared and allowed to graze on the grass that remained in the garrison courtyard. From these, Stephen and some of the other infants under Simon's protection had milk.

Sara became deeply depressed. All of her hopes and dreams had been smashed. Eleazar, the man who would make her a queen, had failed her. Her inheritance was depleted, and this city that was to be her refuge was crumbling. Worse, the fools that were protecting the city would not give up.

I'm going to die here, she thought to herself. *If only I could stay alive until the Romans breach these walls, I may have a chance. As it is, I started my journey to this place as a poor slave, and now I will meet my end destitute and starved.*

As the stench of the dead bodies penetrated the garrison, Simon and his men decided to take turns in shifts to dispose of the corpses. They gathered them up into carts and dumped them over the outer wall into a ravine adjacent to the city. They poured oil out into the ravine and set the bodies ablaze. After some days of doing this, they had burned thousands of bodies and a great black smoke hung over Jerusalem as a further sign of impending doom.

Titus had been working with his engineers in building war machines, catapults, battering rams, and siege towers. To keep the soldiers busy he had them construct a great earthen ramp all the way up to within a bow shot of the city walls. Now he ordered them to move the catapults up to the edge of the ramp. From here, they would begin the bombardment of the city walls with great boulders.

While inspecting these works, Titus noticed the pall over the city and sent for Josephus.

"I must allow them one more opportunity to resign themselves. Surely, some would now have cooler heads. Can we convince them and avoid further carnage?"

"We can try, my lord," responded Josephus. "Do not expect much. Those that are willing to walk away and freely declare themselves as your subjects would be shot in the back by the zealots before they traveled ten paces from the city wall." He sighed and went on, "It pains me to suggest it, but the greatest mercy you could grant them would be to take the city as quickly as possible and destroy the element that holds the good people in fear."

Titus pondered these words and rebutted, "Your way may prove to be true, but it would involve great loss of life on both sides. Josephus, since I have been in this land, I have grown fearful of your God. I must prove myself innocent of the spilled blood in this, his capital city. We will make them another offer."

Josephus thought for a while and formulated a plan. "Perhaps there is a way. If I could somehow smuggle myself into the city under the cover of darkness, I would seek out Simon and John, leaders of the two reasonable factions. I do not know if they are alive, but if by chance they are, I could make your final appeal to them."

It was with a heavy heart that Simon approached Sara's door. The two goats that provided nourishment for the infants had been slaughtered. His men had been without food for too long and they could no longer bear the hunger. In their distress, they disobeyed Simon's orders to spare these last two goats for the sake of the children. Taking pity on them, Simon could not bring himself to punish the men.

Sara was completely wretched in both mind and body. Although emaciated, Simon still marveled at her beauty. *Another time and place, and I could have loved you,* he thought to himself.

"Unless we are delivered by some divine providence, I fear that Stephen has eaten his last meal," Simon told her as he detailed the situation.

Sara only nodded. She was too weakened in her spirit to engage in much conversation. Glancing at the ceiling, she thought about the nagging and never ceasing wails as the boy would beg for food up to his death. Still silent, she contemplated how it would be easier if she would escape by dying first. Sara hated the burden of caring for this child and ceased having feelings for him long ago. *If only the bandits would have carried him off,* she thought.

After several minutes of waiting for some response from her, Simon gave way to tears. He embraced Sara and gently stroking her hair said, "Forgive me, I have failed you and your son. To see you die here in the bloom of your youth along with Stephen is too much for me to bear. If I could only make it right for you."

Sara stopped him by pressing her index finger against his lips. "It is not your doing, Simon," she interjected. "Thank you for all that you have done. Now go, and be at peace. You have many burdens other than Stephen and me. I forgive you. The boy and I will die together remembering your kindness to us."

Simon embraced her one last time, and then he left her alone.

Stephen remained quiet that night despite not having been fed. Sara, tortured with the pain of a starved body consuming itself from within, fell into a troubled sleep. Her mind reached up from the depths of her despair, and she experienced a terrible nightmare.

The rapids of a mighty river tossed Sara about. In the distance, she heard the roar of a great cataract. It summoned her.

"Sarrrrrra, Sarrrrrra," the waters hissed. "Do not fight. Give in to the current and allow it to lead you home, Sarrrrrra, Sarrrrrra." The vibrations rattled at the teeth in her skull. Fearing for her life, she began to struggle to reach the shore. The harder she fought, the more determined the current pulled at her. A voice floating above her head caught Sara's attention.

"Don't be a fool," it roared. "The waters deceive you. Grab at the branch and save yourself."

"Where are you?" Sara screeched as she choked on the foam in the churning waves. "Save me," she pleaded.

"Grab at the branch and save yourself," the resonating voice commanded. Its tenor was deep and savage.

"I cannot see," she shrieked.

"Sarrrrrra, Sarrrrrra," the cataract continued to hiss.

"Take it and live," the voice boomed.

She heard the sound of laughter, and suddenly Sara was transported back to her childhood. Sara and her sister, Mary, found themselves chasing a bird to the edge of the woods.

"Look, Mary, it's getting away," she heard herself say as a small child.

"Don't worry, Sara," Mary giggled back in exuberance. "I'll go into the trees and scare it back out to you. Wait a minute. Oh yes, look; there it is up in that branch. It is in the nest."

Mary being older and somewhat taller began to climb the tree. Stretching out, she pushed at the base of the branch, and it began to bend down toward Sara who remained on the ground.

The bird flew away.

"Take the branch, Sara," Mary appealed. "See if there are babies in the nest."

Mary grunted little girl grunts as she struggled out onto the limb. The further she pulled her body toward the end of the limb, the more it bent. As it descended, Sara's face was now level with the edge of the nest. She stood on tiptoes to peer in.

"Come on, Sara, take the branch," Mary implored. "Are there babies in the nest, little birdie babies?"

Looking into the base of the cup shaped structure, Sara found no birdies.

There were no eggs, only some tiny bones and maggots. As she stared at them, the maggots began to crawl around into patterns, and they used their bodies to make letters. Sara watched with wonder as the letters formed one by one. When they stopped moving, their fat white bodies had formed themselves into two words. They spelled:

P R E T T Y   C O L O R S

Little Sara backed away in disgust. "No, I wouldn't be able to do that."

"What do you mean, orphan bitch?" little Mary's voice now sounded vile and contemptuous. "I climbed up here and gave you this chance. Now, take the branch."

"No, I can't possibly do that," Sara reaffirmed.

"Take the branch," commanded Mary.

Sara's dream ripped her back into the rapids. The voice above her boomed in a continuous taunt. "Grab at the branch, grab at the branch, grab at the branch and live."

"NO," she screamed and covered her ears with her hands. She began to sink under the water.

"Sarrrrra, Sarrrrrra," the rapids hissed.

Her lungs now on fire, Sara longed desperately for a sweet breath of air, a breath of life. Kicking madly with her legs, she fought up from the depths with all her will. Kicking and fighting with her last ounce of strength, Sara breached the surface. Gasping, she stretched out and her fingertips brushed the edge of the branch.

"Sarrrrra, Sarrrrrra," the rapids now lamented.

Sara awoke with a start. Wide eyed and terrified, she slobbered onto her bedding. After regaining her senses, she crawled over to her chest, opened it, and lifted out the dagger. Making her way back to the bed, Sara sat and inverted the blade in her hands, pointing it toward her chest. She was insane with hunger.

Stephen awoke and began to wail.

"There is nothing left of my soul to forgive," she resigned herself.

In the middle of the night, Josephus crept alone along the city side of the ravine. Feeling his way through the burned bodies was a living nightmare. He managed to preserve his sanity by concentrating on the lives that he was trying to preserve. He decided to take this less guarded route. His goal was a small door in the wall that was used to draw water from a pool at the upper source of the gulley. Josephus prayed that it would be unguarded. He sensed that they would pay no heed to this potential weakness, because no serious attack could be launched from such a narrow place. He approached the door as quietly as he could and pressed his ear against it.

There was no sound. Josephus exerted pressure against the surface, and it gave way. He backed up expecting some kind of response. There was nothing.

Far too few survived to patrol the entire city. He arrived at Simon's enclave as the sun rose. The half dozen guards at the garrison door were all asleep. He could easily have slipped by, but decided to wake the captain of the guard.

"Josephus," he yawned, "Am I dreaming or dead?"

Lifting a sack from his back, Josephus spilled the contents onto the ground. There were eight loaves of bread. The captain's eyes opened wide, and he began to cry.

"It is an apparition here to taunt me at my impending death," he sobbed.

"No, friend," corrected Josephus. "It is real. Eat. I bring news from General Titus. Does Simon yet live?"

The rest of the guards woke as they heard the conversation and spying the bread, they descended on it like ravenous wolves. The captain, with his mouth stuffed full, looked up at Josephus. With thankful eyes, he pointed into the courtyard.

Simon embraced Josephus and felt him all over to make sure he was not dreaming. Josephus helped Simon to sit and proceeded to inform him of all the details concerning these many weeks and how Titus had been moved to make this final appeal to the residents of the city.

"We will not be able to escape. The zealots will cut us down," grieved Simon.

"You still have a loyal following of men," corrected Josephus. "Few would be so bold as to attack a squad with numbers as large as yours."

Filled with hope, Simon considered it. "Many of us will die before nightfall. We are in our last hours of life. Starvation takes us."

"Josephus," Simon continued. "If we are to make this brave attempt, it must be now, God help us."

"Surely, though, you have enough for one last ration, don't you?" asked Josephus.

"No, my friend. There is nothing but the leather from our sandals."

"But you must be mistaken, I smelled cooking in your kitchen as I passed on my way to your quarters."

Simon laughed, choking on his own phlegm, and he coughed in spasms. Josephus handed him some water.

"You are well fed I see," Simon said poking at Josephus's stomach. "But it seems that you are the one suffering from hallucinations and not me."

"No, I smelled cooking. Knowing you as I do, you likely gave all that you own to your men and are denying yourself some nourishment. Come, let me help you. We can go and see for ourselves."

Josephus led Simon to the threshold of the kitchen.

"Blessed God," exclaimed Simon. "Am I mad or do I, too, share in your hallucination? I smell food."

"Let's go in and see," Josephus said leading the way.

The kitchen was merely a room with an open roof. Pots, bowls, and other utensils were stacked on shelves along an adjacent wall. The stove was in the middle of the floor. It was a simple stone circle with a bronze grate. The remains of a fire glowed in the circle and some soiled utensils laid at the side of the stove. A wooden dining table was set up near the far wall.

As they crossed into the room, Simon and Josephus saw a beautiful young maiden sitting at the table. She had a grease-smeared face and was gobbling down the last scraps of what appeared to be a fine meal. She stabbed at the last piece with her dagger and looking up at them, belched.

"Oops," she giggled and with a twinkle in her eye put her hand over her mouth.

Holding out the dagger with the last mouthful dangling off the end, she offered it to the men. Josephus reached out, but she hastily jerked it back.

"Sorry," she said, "all gone!" She folded her full lips around the morsel at the end of the dagger and sensuously sucked it off.

The show froze both men.

Tucking the dagger back into her garment, the maiden stood up and excused herself. As she made her way to the door, Simon grabbed her by the arm.

"What is this mystery?" he uttered. "What have you done?"

Angrily she yanked her arm out of his hunger-weakened grasp.

"Pretty colors!" she sang out in a child's voice.

She burst into hysterical laughter and ran out into the courtyard, through the gate, and up the street. With newfound strength from the nourishment coursing through her body, she ran laughing and singing. The maiden made her way up and through the second wall toward the temple gate. In time, she fell down out of breath. After several minutes of silent thought, the maiden began to sob. Removing the dagger from her garment, she prepared to take her own life.

"Should I stop her?" asked Josephus as Sara left the courtyard.

Clutching at his chest, Simon voiced, "Let her go. Her soul is lost."

The remainder of Simon's men along with their households and relatives totaled several hundred souls. Josephus was correct. This was too large a party for anyone to stop. They helped each other along and carried some of the weaker ones. They marched straight down to the main gate and ordered it open. Josephus explained to the guards what was going on and of Titus's offer. All of them dropped their weapons and joined the refugees.

Josephus wished that he could call on the homes of his family and the rest of his other friends, but they were scattered about the city and there was too little time.

If they survive, he thought to himself, *Titus promised me that he would spare them.*

Titus met them at the edge of the earthworks and shouted out with joy at Josephus's accomplishment. He ordered a great feast to be held for all of those with Simon. It was a happy time for Simon and his party. Their suffering was over, and this sad chapter in their lives had ended.

CHAPTER 7

Derek slept in his jail cell. He dreamed that he was adrift in an open sea. Holding on to a plank in an attempt to stay afloat, he was cold and scared. It was a moonless night, pitch black.

"Help, help, can anyone hear me?" he hollered. Scanning the horizon in all directions, he concentrated with all of his might. Helplessly bobbing up and down in the current, he was forlorn. Suddenly, he thought he saw a flashing light. Derek renewed his concentration in the direction where he thought he saw it. There it was again! The light resembled the lamp from a lighthouse, sweeping the sea as a welcome beacon.

"Over here," he cried out. "I'm over here."

The lamp listened and swung in Derek's direction. The beam came to a rest in front of him. A shining path shimmered on the water. It was a line connecting the two points with Derek at one end and the lighthouse on the other end.

Derek heard a voice. "There you are," it said.

"I'm over here. Send someone out to pluck me out of these waters."

"Follow the path," the voice said. "You can see it, can't you? Don't fight against the current. Follow the path. Come to me."

"Who are you?"

"You know the way," Derek heard waking up from his sleep.

"Come to me," sighed the voice, and Derek's eyes popped open.

He sat at the side of his bed holding his head in his hands. "No more," he pleaded. "I can't take more of this. I'm losing my mind."

After the police finished interrogating them, Juan walked over to the two waiting women.

"Let me take you ladies home," he offered.

"My car is still at the office," Katy sniffled. "Please take me there, and I'll drive myself home."

"My car is here at the hotel," Sharon added.

Sharon rode with Juan as he took Katy back to the office.

"You sure you don't want us to follow you home?" Sharon wanted to give her a second chance.

"No, thanks, I'm gonna be okay now."

After shutting the door, Katy motioned for Sharon to roll down the window.

Katy smiled for the first time that evening, "Hey, Sharon, don't look for me at work tomorrow. I need a day off."

"No shit," said Sharon. "Don't look for me either."

Juan waited until Katy safely left the parking garage before driving off.

"Derek wants you to come to him."

"Did he say why?"

"He thinks you are in danger and feels safer if you would get away from here."

Sharon pondered these words for a while and asked, "Blaze is dead. Don't you think the danger is passed?"

"I don't know," Juan replied. "As far as I know, Blaze acted alone, but there is a possibility that there is more to this."

"What does Derek want me to do?"

"He wants you to clean out the bank accounts and the two of us are to take the first flight to Frankfurt."

"That's crazy!" she blurted out.

"It's not crazy," he admonished her. "I don't know you or how long you've been Derek's girlfriend. What I do know is that I have worked with Derek ever since he started with TransGlobal. He is a good man, very centered. I know that he wouldn't ask you to do something this radical unless he had good reasons. Sharon, he's scared. I believe that you should do as he says."

"Maybe I should try and talk to him. Did that lawyer give you a telephone number?"

"That's part of the problem. The authorities over there will not let you call him. You can only visit him in person."

Sharon thought some more and asked, "What else does Derek want me to do?"

"He told me that I am not supposed to let you leave my sight. We're supposed to go to your house so you can pack your things and get your passport. It's late. We have to wait until the banks open tomorrow."

Hesitating, Juan continued, "Sharon, if you trust me, I will stay in the house with you overnight."

"Derek trusts you. That's good enough for me."

They sat at the kitchen table. Sharon wanted to drink some warm milk to calm her nerves before retiring. Juan joined her. She looked at him, questioning, "Juan, why are you being so kind to us?"

"It's like I said," he explained, "Derek is a good man. Most pilots don't give us maintenance guys the time of day. With egos as big as theirs, we aren't worth their time. Don't think I'm trying to cry 'victim' here, but they are especially hard on me, being Hispanic. My work is always scrutinized. It's like they don't trust me."

Juan took a break from talking to slurp some of his warm milk.

He went on, "From day one, Derek was never like that. He always puts in a good word for us guys. He buys us dinner and jokes around with us. He respects me as a human being. I'm honored to be able to help him in this time of difficulty. Derek is my friend. I know that he would do the same for me. I have a lot of accumulated leave time, so TransGlobal will not mind my taking some of it now."

Juan stopped again to finish drinking down his cup.

"One more thing, Sharon."

She looked at Juan waiting for his response.

"If you have any doubts about his involvement in this drug thing, I can tell you flat out, there is no way. I don't know exactly what has happened, but I do know that Derek would never get involved in anything like that."

Sharon reached over and grabbed his hand.

"Thank you, Juan. You really are Derek's friend, and mine too."

After a few seconds, she withdrew her hand and looked at the clock.

"Do you think I should call TransGlobal reservations and book our flights for tomorrow?"

"No, Sharon, after what happened today, you have to assume that we will be monitored by the police. If they picked up on a move like that, it would cast all kinds of suspicions. They may intercept and stop us. It's best to go directly to the ticket counter. If we're lucky, we will already be in Germany before they find out about the ticket purchase."

Sharon yawned. "This milk is doing the trick. I'm going to bed."

Juan watched as she shut the bedroom door behind her.

I don't know what Derek's waiting for, he thought. *Why doesn't he marry this woman?*

Klaus Hall had no trouble finding Joel Washington. Most pilots stayed at the swank Frankfurt Royale Resort near the airport. Joel was in the bar drinking heavily and buying rounds of beer for the flight crew. It was a real party atmosphere for Joel. The crew wasn't very excited, but they didn't turn down his generosity.

Klaus decided to hang back within an earshot and observe this show. It seemed inappropriate to him that Joel should be in such a festive mood.

"I knew it from the time he put on the uniform that the guy was a phoney baloney," Joel slurred. He was hanging all over Anne Sprague, one of the female flight attendants. She didn't particularly care for his advances but decided to give him a little latitude for now.

"I thought he was your friend," she said.

"Friend, shmrend, that son-of-a-bitch stabbed me in the back. He's the one that kept me from the pilot's seat. That smooth-talking bastard, he talked his way right around me, he did."

Anne stared at the wall behind him as if daydreaming. She mumbled, "Poor Derek, he was always so nice to me. I had no idea he was involved in anything like this. I mean, Jesus, drugs."

"Don't waste any of your sympathy on him," Joel said as he put his arm around her.

Anne removed Joel's arm and continued the conversation. "Really, Joel, he treated us all okay. Don't you feel bad for him at all?"

"Yeah, I feel bad that I didn't do anything to him earlier."

"What do you mean, Joel? If you knew something before, why didn't you go to management?"

"Management!" he scoffed and put his arm around her again. "Management wouldn't buy anything I told them. Hell, they promoted him instead of me. Nope, I had to fix him myself."

Anne removed Joel's arm again and asked, "What do you mean 'fix him yourself'?"

Klaus perked up and thought, *Yes, Herr Washington, what do you mean?*

Joel winked at her and tried again with his arm. "Let's just say that a certain other party has it in for him. They arranged a little scenario that got him right where I wanted him. I just took advantage of the situation. Let's just say that the certain other party appreciated my putting him in his place and rewarded me handsomely. Not that I needed to be rewarded, but hell if they wanted to throw money at me, I'd be a fool not to take it."

This time she more aggressively removed his arm. The force of it caused his wrist to bang against the back of the stool.

"You mean a police sting? You set him up?"

"Hey, Anne," Joel winced as he massaged his wrist. "You ought to treat me a little better. I could be really nice to you, you know."

"Yeah, right," she said.

"No, I mean it. You know those paintings that they have for sale here in the lobby? I noticed you admiring them. I could buy one for you, see."

He reached into his pocket, pulled out a wad of Euros, and flashed them at her.

"Put that away," she shrieked and glanced about nervously. "You know better than to flash money around in a public place."

"Don't worry about it, baby. There's plenty more where that came from. I told you that they rewarded me handsomely. Let's go see about those paintings."

Anne sighed. "Okay, you said it yourself. If you want to throw money at me, I'd be a fool not to take it. Right after that though, you need to get to your room. Oh, and I mean alone. I want you to get a good night's sleep. Remember, you need to fly us home tomorrow."

"That's the spirit," he beamed and put his arm around her again. This time she let him. They walked out together.

"Fascinating!" Klaus said under his breath. He downed the rest of his beer and thunked the empty glass down on the table.

CHAPTER 8

As Sara prepared to plunge the blade into her chest, she experienced an odd sensation. Involuntarily her hand opened and the dagger dropped harmlessly to the ground. Gazing up from where she sat, Sara saw a woman standing over her. A full-length garment covered the woman. When she let down her hood, Sara saw that the woman was stunning. Her every movement oozed with polished refinement. This was a woman of class and nobility. The woman extended her arms and taking Sara by the hands helped her up. Looking into Sara's eyes, their minds locked.

"Hello, my dear," the woman said. "So, I have found you at last." In a sterner voice she continued, "Look at this city. Have you played any role in this madness?" Inspecting Sara further, the woman went on to say as if talking to herself, "Why look at this one, so young and so ravishing. Is it possible that she does not yet know?"

Baffled, Sara asked, "Who are you?"

"My name is Helena of Adiabene. What is yours?"

"Mary of Bethezuba, daughter of Eleazar."

"Your name?" Helena forcefully repeated.

Sara lowered her head in shame with full realization that with this woman the ruse would not work. "Sara," she said. "My name is Sara, and I am a slave girl."

"Yes, your name is Sara, dear girl, but you are hardly a slave."

Looking up again, Sara beseeched Helena, "Who am I?"

Locking minds with Sara, Helena probed her consciousness and laughed, "By God! You really don't know, do you?"

Taking Sara by the hand, she led her away. "Come child, I have many things to teach you, but first we must get out of the street before you drive any more men into even greater madness."

Sara picked up her dagger, stashed it away, and allowed herself to be led.

Helena led Sara to the corner where an alley intersected the main road. Peering up and down the street, she checked whether anyone was watching.

Feeling secure, they darted around the corner and down the alley.

"My house is the large structure on the other side of the alley," Helena pointed out to Sara. "It is abandoned, and I now dwell inconspicuously down this alley in the rear of an old storehouse."

Helena led Sara through the old store. The door had been smashed and the place was completely looted. They looped through a maze of debris and into a small closet disguised as a privy.

"An unassuming appearance is the key to survival. That is your first lesson," Helena said as she lifted a trap door disguised by a layer of dirt. They descended about four meters by means of a rope ladder into a good-sized underground room. Helena lit an oil lamp and with an attached rope pulled the trap door closed.

Sara looked around. A small pool fed by a spring bubbled in the far corner of the room. It drained into an overflow that led into a lower opening. Nearby, a tight-fitting door covered a pit. This was a toilet. It also somehow drained away. The area nearest the ladder contained a large elevated platform. Sara surmised that this served as a bed, since layers of blankets covered it. There were various wooden tables and chairs. The place was somewhat damp, but not uncomfortable.

In disbelief, she noticed that the entire adjacent wall held shelving. The shelves contained dry goods and lots of food, food enough for a few people to survive for months.

Noticing the longing in Sara's eyes, Helena nodded to her. "Go ahead and help yourself. You will have to get used to eating raw or cold, water-soaked grain. It provides decent enough nourishment. We cannot build a cooking fire in this place. There isn't enough air circulating."

Sara used a stone hammer to smash some corn. She filled a bowl with water from the spring and added the kernels. It made a primitive gruel. She ate it greedily. Along with the meal that she had an hour earlier, Sara now felt sated for the first time in weeks.

Helena sat on the bed with her legs crossed and observed Sara closely.

"How did you find this place?" Sara asked.

"My husband built it long ago," Helena replied. "When the Babylonians laid siege to the city, he constructed this room as a hiding place. It has been a place of refuge for me many times."

"The Babylonians?" asked Sara. "You mean the Romans, right?"

"No, the Babylonians."

Sara laughed. "The Babylonians conquered Jerusalem half a millennium ago. You are barely older than I am, maybe twenty-five years of age."

"Lesson number two, Sara," Helena said flatly. "Appearances can be deceiving."

Sara waved off the comment and continued her inquiry, "Where is your husband?"

"You mean the one that built this place? Dead, he's long ago dead."

"Obviously you are a lady of great means. Where are your servants and the others of your household?"

Helena looked down at her hands resting on her lap. "When things got bad up there," she pointed, "I released all of my servants. I informed them that I was going to move in with other relatives. After they had all gone, I moved into this place. Here we will remain safe until the storm above passes."

Sara pressed, "But what about your other family, and your children? You do have children, don't you?"

Helena smiled and responded, "Other family? Like you, I am an orphan. There are no others. And children," she snickered, "Sara, our kind cannot have children."

Startled by her response, Sara grew defensive. "How do you know that I am an orphan? You seem to know a great deal more about me than you should."

"Relax, Sara," Helena said in a soothing voice. "Long ago it was necessary for someone to explain many things to me. Now, by fate it is my turn to explain these things to you. I was just as frightened then as you are now. There are many days yet that we will need to hide here. During that time, I will open a wondrous new world of possibilities for you. I suspect that for some time now you have known that you are a different kind of woman. Sara, let me tell you that you have no idea how different you actually are."

Sara was shocked, but in her heart, she discerned that everything that this woman was telling her was true. After a few moments, Sara's thoughts began to return to the past few weeks. She recalled all that she had experienced and the terrible thing she had just done a few hours earlier. Sara became despondent.

Helena looked into Sara's mind. "Don't think about that," she said. "Just like any other creature, we do what we must to survive. Don't look back."

Like any other creature, those words hung in Sara's mind. "We are evil, aren't we?" she asked looking away from Helena's face.

Helena looked down again at her hands and answered, "Yes, Sara, we have been born of evil and are capable of doing horrible things." After a pause she continued, "But sometimes we do great good. It is a matter of choice and the exercise of control over our power."

Still looking away, Sara meekly asked, "But mostly we do evil things?"

Helena continued to look down. "Yes, mostly we are evil."

Moments passed, and Helena lifted her head. "Look at me, Sara."

With moist eyes, Sara gazed in her direction, and Helena finished the conversation. "In the end, it is possible for God to redeem us, but that path is hard, so very, very, hard."

"Wine, more wine," directed Crook as he clapped his hands at Mary, "and be sure you fill the goblets of Ben and Jesse, too." Intoxicated, he groaned as he stood up and walked away to relieve himself.

The four of them were all that was left of the original gang of thieves. When the Romans surrounded Jerusalem, all activity in the region stopped. No travelers ventured either to or from the city. Refugees that had previously fled to the mountains stayed gathered in numbers too great for bandits to invade. Business was bad. The rest of the bunch slowly wandered off destined to other lands where they could reform anew and continue their scavenging ways.

Ben was the toughest of the bunch and savvy. During his life, he committed despicable acts. Now, getting older, he began to question whether it was all worthwhile. Approaching forty, he was growing tired. The sum of all his deeds had done nothing to bring him fulfillment.

The three men were eating an evening meal and contemplating what to do next.

"This place is dead," moaned Jesse. "There is no more opportunity for us here. Ben, I've been thinking about it and believe that it is time for me to finally move on. I wish you would reconsider and ride out with me."

Ben sighed, "I know, old friend. I can't blame you and the others for leaving. We held a good bunch together for a long time. It's been profitable."

"It can be that way again," Jesse said with a devilish look in his eye. "Let's go south. There is great wealth in the regions along the coast."

Ben interrupted him, "No, Jesse, I've been thinking too. I've been a thief and murderer all of my life. It is all that I know, but look at us. What do we have? Sure, there is a nice tidy sum of gold, enough to last us for quite a few years, no doubt, and we have fine horses. But we also have broken bones and deep scars."

"What are you saying?" asked Jesse.

"I'm retiring," replied Ben. "I'll take my share and start doing some trading with those Romans down there. There are many things in these mountains that they could use. There is game here and herbs for medicines. I might even build a house in an out of the way place. As a matter of fact, this spot right here could be suitable enough."

Jesse roared with laughter, "You, Ben the Brigand, most fearsome of highwaymen, becoming an honest man? Next thing you'll tell me is that you will want to keep a woman."

Mary arrived at that moment and refilled their cups with wine.

"I've been giving that some thought, too," Ben responded, leering at Mary.

"I would rather die," she said is an expressionless tone. "You killed my father and murdered my mother right in front of my eyes."

"Who says that you have any choice in the matter?" Ben growled.

"Bastard," she spat back and jerked her head in the direction of Crook. "I'm no comfort to him. When he lies on top of me, I just go limp. When he orders me around, I just go through the motions. It would be the same way with you. Some day he will grow tired of me and kill me. It doesn't matter; I'm ready to die. I consider myself dead already. My life ended back there the day you men marauded through our camp." Throwing the pitcher down on the ground, she ran back to her tent.

At first, Ben resented that Crook toted Mary around, but he rationalized that she was his property just like any other booty stolen from his victims. In time, though, he started to grow fond of her. She was nice to look at. Now, he began to feel protective toward her and hated it when Crook mistreated her. Crook beat her often, just to make himself feel more of a man.

Jesse noticed the far away look in Ben's eye and cautioned, "Be careful, Ben. You know he is a mad man and crafty, too."

"I know," Ben said, "I should have dealt with him long ago. The showdown between us is coming."

The next morning Jesse assembled his belongings and his share of their plunder and made ready to ride out.

"Good bye, Jesse," winked Ben. "And, oh yeah, one more thing. When you find a new gang and get to raiding again, if you ever run across me out there on the road, remember our friendship and kill me quickly. I don't want to linger any, this life's been hard enough."

Jesse laughed, "I'll keep that in mind, just don't you resist when that day comes." Looking down at Crook and looking back again at Ben he said, "You watch yourself, Ben."

He kicked at his horse and rode away.

The two of them watched until the dust faded. Crook slapped Ben on the back and exclaimed, "Well, it looks like it's down to just you and me now!" Turning aside, he started to dance like a wild man. When he fell down out of breath, he started laughing and rolling. Finally, with a sidelong look he jumped up.

"Where's my woman?" he taunted loud enough for Mary to hear. "It's time for the two of us to celebrate."

Within a few days, the inner wall was demolished and the Romans had only one more obstacle, the temple. The city was sacked and a great pile of goods was assembled for the trip back to Rome. The zealots that continued to fight were killed, but the soldiers that surrendered were treated the same as the civilians. All of these prisoners were gathered into a camp near the edge of the city. Here they were fed and remained unmolested. Josephus was once again called to appear before Titus.

"I know that it pains you to see what is happening here, Josephus. Your people are defeated and the city of your God is despoiled. You probably despise me for all of this, but search your heart and you must agree with me that it is of their doing. It did not have to be this way. Now I ask once again for your service. I ask this so that you can help me to spare more of your people."

"My lord, how can I despise the man that has kept his word with me. It is with great joy that I have been reunited with my family. Also, I have been able to save many of my friends. Your generosity in setting them free is a deed that I will remember you for all the days of my life. I will gladly do as you ask of me. How is it that I may continue to serve you?"

"There are two things," Titus explained. "First, go the temple. Many of your fellow citizens have retreated to within those walls. Go down to the prison camp and find some of your citizens that are well known. Ask them to accompany you to the temple, and offer them as proof to those inside that we mean them no physical harm.

"My lord, you said that there were two things. What is it that you further desire?"

"Sit, Josephus, and drink some wine with me." Titus motioned a manservant to bring over a pitcher and goblets.

"This is going to be difficult for you," Titus murmured as he handed a cup to his friend. "The intentions of my father have been from the beginning to spare this city. You are well aware of the original terms for surrender that you, yourself, delivered to them. The situation is that they did not surrender. They resisted. As a result, many thousands of lives have been lost on both sides."

Titus took a drink and went on. "The fact of the matter is that your people have lost. This makes things much different, and now there is a price that must be paid for their disobedience."

Both men stopped for a moment to enjoy a sip of some more wine. Josephus encouraged Titus, "Please go on, what is the price that you are seeking?"

Titus set down his cup. "Josephus, when you go down to the camp to gather those well-known citizens that I spoke of, I also want you to spread the word among the people. They are not going to be temporary prisoners. I want you to tell them to eat and become strong. They will be marching back to Rome."

"As slaves, my lord?"

"Yes, Josephus, as slaves. They will never see this land again. All that will remain are those that you purchased with your service to me and those fortunate souls that fled to the mountains before we trapped them in this place. Jerusalem will become a Roman garrison."

"What of those that are too far gone or those women about to give birth?" Josephus's voice now became more desperate.

"We will be as accommodating as possible, but it will be a long and difficult journey." Titus grew serious. "Josephus, have them prepare well. My men are longing to get home and are short on patience. The pace will be fast. Those that cannot or will not keep up will either be killed or left to die."

Helena and Sara spent several days in the underground room. During that time, Sara learned many things from her mentor. At first, she found her origins to be disturbing, but this soon gave way to a joy that she had not experienced for some time. Sara had a new sense of purpose and a new life.

"When you found me, Helena, I was about to take my own life. Now I can't wait to get out of here so that I can live again."

"Patience, Sara. The storm rages above. What a waste it would be to be killed after just being newly reborn with the knowledge that I've presented to you."

The next day, Sara continued to press Helena, "How much longer until we can leave this place? I must see the sun again."

Helena relented, "We can go up for a short period of time. I emerge every few days to check on the destruction and to decide when it may become safe to abandon this hiding place. It was during one of those times that we found each other. If I had it in my power, I would persuade you to stay here. It is more difficult for two to move with stealth."

"I will not stay here," stressed Sara.

"I know. We must be very careful. Before we go, you must listen to my advice. If they discover us, they may kill us outright. You now know of the effect we have on men. It is possible that they will take and abuse us until we die. During times such as these, there is no morality. Here, take this garment and cover yourself from head to toe."

Sara received a grimy and soiled sackcloth from Helena's hand. "You would have me wear this?" she whined.

"Remember how I appeared when you first saw me. Stay concealed and do not draw attention to yourself. The trip will not be far."

"Where are we going?" asked Sara.

"To my house at the intersection of the alley with the main road."

"The one that you pointed out to me when we came here?"

"Yes, we can enter through a hidden side door and climb up to the roof. We can lay behind the parapet and observe for a short time what is happening."

"And to enjoy some sunshine," Sara said raising her arms in the air and looking up at the dark ceiling.

They made it to the roof of Helena's old mansion without incident and looked about the city. All was quiet. The only activity they could detect was coming from the temple mount.

"It's almost over," Helena said. "Another couple of weeks in hiding, and we will be able to get out of here."

"Another couple of weeks," Sara squawked. "I can't abide another day in that hole."

Helena looked over Sara's shoulder. Sara noticed that her expression changed. "Well, my dear, you may get your wish," Helena said staring.

Sara turned to see why Helena was startled. Six Roman soldiers were standing on the roof of a home three doors away. It was uphill in elevation from Helena's house, so the soldiers could easily see them hiding. They were caught.

CHAPTER 9

Everything was coming unraveled. Elyria followed Blaze as he made Katy drive him to the motel. She was surprised to witness Sharon run out of the place with Katy. The strange man that had interfered was a mystery to her. She groaned to herself when they removed Blaze's covered body. Elyria faced her worst fear. Blaze had failed, and now she had to make new choices.

Elyria knew what was expected of her. She was a Shadow Woman, independent, confident, and sworn to the cause. The Mistress would want her to finish the job by herself, as unpleasant as that might be.

There really is no option, she thought. *I must kill this woman myself. If only the Mistress would have sent a second man along with Blaze.* She remembered why this was not possible.

Men are just commodities to her, and good ones are rare, she recalled. Elyria pondered with disdain that the Mistress seemed to keep most of the good-looking ones. *She uses them up so quickly after only a few love-making sessions.*

Wasteful, she thought. *Why can't the Mistress let me love one like this Derek Dunbar? I could settle down and provide many children to serve the Mistress with a man like that.*

Elyria allowed these thoughts to swirl in her mind. *No, the Mistress wants him. She is trying to make Derek go to her. I do not know how or why, but the death of his woman is a key component to making it happen.*

Elyria kept her distance while she followed Juan and Sharon.

Sharon thought about how it was only two days ago that she made the same breakfast for Derek. Now the eggs were for her and Juan.

"I was so self absorbed after what happened last night, Juan, that I forgot to ask about your family. Are you married? I hope that nobody is worried about why you didn't come home last night."

Juan looked off in the distance. "My wife, Mrs. Sanchez, died two years ago. It was cancer."

"Oh, I'm sorry," Sharon expressed as she looked away. "You're a young man. That must have been difficult for you."

Juan still maintained that far away look in his eye, "I think about her every day. We were very happy, yet I regret that we didn't try to have children sooner. Actually, Sharon, it was my fault. I'm the one that wanted to wait. Now, I have no one."

"What about other family?" Sharon asked.

"My sister and her family live in Torreon in Mexico. Other than that, I have some cousins that live in the Chicago area. There are no other relations around here, but I have many friends, like your man, Derek."

Sharon smiled. "I'm your friend now, too, Juan."

He smiled back. "I'm a lucky man."

Sharon remained curious about Juan. Wanting to know more, she decided to press him a bit further.

"Juan, how did you end up here in Baltimore? You are far away from the rest of your family."

"Just like Derek, I was in the U.S. Air Force," he replied. "My father was Mexican, but my mother was born in Brownsville, Texas. She met my father in Torreon while on a mission for the church. They fell in love and got married. I chose to become an American citizen. My sister married her childhood sweetheart and decided to stay in Mexico. After high school, I joined the Air Force, and they trained me to be an airplane maintenance man. Later, I got a job with TransGlobal, and they assigned me here to Baltimore."

Juan paused a moment to wipe the corner of his mouth. Looking up he asked, "Sharon, is it possible for me to have some more eggs?"

"Of course," she said with a smile. She picked up his plate and walked into the kitchen.

Juan raised his voice a bit so that she could hear him.

"Sharon, now that I've told you my story, maybe you can indulge me with one of my questions."

Sharon was cracking two more eggs over the skillet as she acknowledged Juan.

"Sure. What do you want to know?"

Juan felt a little uncomfortable but decided that they had become familiar enough with each other for him to pry.

"Derek and you," he said gingerly. "He talks about you all of the time. It's obvious to me that the guy is crazy in love with you. Did you ever think about making a family and maybe getting married?"

Sharon continued stirring the eggs in the skillet and didn't answer Juan for a long time. Juan shuffled in his seat with discomfort.

Go ahead and put your foot in your mouth, he thought. *Obviously I crossed the line with that question.*

Sharon sighed and continued working with the eggs.

"You opened up to me, Juan, so that's a fair question for you to ask."

He quickly jumped in. "Please, Sharon, if I am treading in territory where you would rather not go, forget it. I'm just trying to make conversation. Excuse me for being so nosy."

"Stop it, silly!" Sharon said as she turned around and smiled at him. "Friends can comfortably share their feelings with one another." Turning back to continue working, Sharon went on, "It's not really such a big deal."

Juan waited, more uncomfortable than ever. He sensed that although Sharon said it was no big deal, her voice betrayed her.

"We've been trying to make a family, Juan," she lamented. "The two of us together are a sex machine, but somehow we can't make it happen."

Juan blushed. This was more than he wanted to know.

Sharon continued. "We've been talking about marriage."

Sharon took the eggs off the stove and slid them onto his plate. She returned to the dining room and set them down in front of Juan. Sharon sat and finished her orange juice. As Juan started to eat, she watched him. Driven by an impulse, Sharon shared with him something that she never said aloud before.

"Juan, I'm almost thirty now and concerned. If we haven't been able to make a baby after all of these years together, I'm afraid that it isn't going to happen. It's just not fair. I don't know what to do."

He set down his fork and gazed into her eyes.

"Sharon, do you love him?"

"With all my heart," she replied.

"Listen carefully," he said. "I already told you about the regrets that I have. My wife is dead. We didn't have a family, because I didn't want one. Don't you make the same mistake in reverse. If Derek wants to marry you, don't hold your inability to make a baby as some sort of sign that you should keep him waiting."

Sharon broke eye contact with Juan and looked down. He didn't let this stop him.

"Did you ever consider that maybe if you got married that it would take the pressure off of both of you? Then, maybe it would be easier to make a baby."

She looked up somewhat startled.

"I never thought about it that way."

"Well, I'm happy that we had the opportunity to have this conversation. Maybe in some small way I've been able to help you."

The smile returned to Sharon's face, and she recommended to him, "Maybe you missed your true calling, Juan. You should be a priest instead of a technician."

Juan burst into laughter. "Me, a priest! Hell, no."

After breakfast, Sharon finished packing her suitcase. As she was about to snap closed the lid, she glanced down at the pile of clothes from the night before. Sharon remembered the dagger. She buried it in the pile under her bra. Picking it up, she inspected it closely. There were a few flecks of dried blood, but otherwise it was in good shape.

This thing is really old, she thought to herself. *I've never seen metal like this before. It's dull and not shiny. Maybe I ought to hold on to it.*

Sharon had second thoughts. *Nah, I don't want to be lugging this thing to Europe.* She threw it back down on top of the pile and started to close her suitcase again.

Sharon found that she couldn't bring herself to snap it shut. Something was compelling her to reconsider taking the dagger.

"Oh, okay," she remarked. Sharon picked it up and tucked it in between some jeans and a sweater.

"Can I give you a hand with anything?" Juan yelled in from the kitchen.

"I guess so," she answered. "You know us women. I have the world's largest suitcase. If you can take it out to the car, I can handle my carry-on bag."

Sharon and Juan walked into the main terminal just before lunch. On the ride over, Juan suggested that they should avoid TransGlobal for this trip. He knew too many people, and they wanted to keep their plans as secret as possible. Juan also advised that they should use a credit card for their flights. Last minute ticket purchases using cash always aroused suspicion. He explained that this fit the profile of drug dealers and terrorists.

Sharon and Juan approached the Lufthansa counter.

"Two round trip tickets to Frankfurt on today's flight?" the attendant asked. "Yes, we have seats available, but it's going to be expensive. Are you sure that you want to do this?"

"No," said Sharon trying to appear somber. "A good friend of ours is being buried tomorrow. It was an auto accident. I hate to fly but need to be there for his family."

"Oh, I'm so sorry to hear that," the attendant said with genuine concern. "Of course, let me punch this up for you right away."

After they passed through security, Juan looked amused at Sharon.

"That was pretty good back there," he chuckled. "You nailed it. That attendant wasn't the least bit suspicious."

CHAPTER 10

Mary howled as Crook belted her across the mouth. "Bitch," he screamed at her. "This stew is tepid. I said I wanted it to be hot."

"Fix it for yourself, bastard," Mary cried as she held a hand up to cradle her swollen jaw.

"I'll fix it all right," he grunted. "Right after I fix you." Ripping away her robe, he threw her down on the ground naked.

Ben was camping nearby and decided that the time had come. "This is it," he said to himself. He entered Crook's tent and found him groaning on top of her. Ben grabbed him by the hair on the back of his head and dragged him off Mary and onto the ground. Mary quickly covered herself and scampered into a corner.

"What is the meaning of this?" Crook was furious.

"Pick up your sword, Crook. One of us is going to die here."

"Since when do you care what I do with my property?" he said with a hurt voice. "It's never bothered you before." Crook looked back and forth between Ben and Mary.

"Oh, so that's it," he laughed. "Hey, this is no problem. I will gladly share the woman with you. Go ahead, I'll have my turn again with her later."

"Your sword, Crook," Ben demanded.

Realizing now that this ran much deeper than the woman, Crook grew hostile. "So this is the way it is going to be? Well then, die. After that, I'll kill this bitch. When I dig a hole to bury the two of you, I'll throw her in first. That's the only way you're going to end up on top of her." Crook picked up his sword and charged at Ben.

They spilled out of the tent and fell to the ground with swords flailing. With his free hand, Ben grabbed Crook around the neck and squeezed while fending off sword blows with his own sword hand. Being the more powerful of the two, Ben could have prevailed in this tactic, but he was unable to neutralize Crook's other hand. Crook used it to dig a thumb into Ben's eye. With a cry of pain, Ben released his grasp on Crook's throat and rolled out of the way. Crook's agility and determination surprised Ben. Crook sprang up and ran over to where Ben had rolled and started to laugh. With both hands, he raised his sword over his head with the blade pointed down. He made ready to plunge it into Ben's chest. Ben watched Crook's eyes. At the moment Crook plunged, Ben noticed his pupils dilate, and he quickly rolled out of harm's way.

Crook was caught off balance for an instant as he struggled to yank the sword from the ground. This was all Ben needed. Still lying on his stomach, Ben rolled toward Crook and with a backhand slash gashed open Crook's side at ribs. Both men sprang up. At first, Crook wasn't aware what happened, but then he felt the pain. His hand automatically felt for the wound. Pulling it back, he saw red.

Wailing, he raised his sword again and charged. Ben ducked as Crook swung wildly and thrust his own blade into Crook's other side as he passed.

Now unable to stand, Crook fell to the ground with blood pumping from both of his sides. He looked up as Ben was about to deal the finishing blow.

"Not the throat, you know how you hate that gurgling sound," Crook laughed and choked.

"Don't worry," said Ben as he plunged the blade through Crook's chest. "I learn from my mistakes, too."

It took a minute for Ben to recover. After regaining his breath, he wandered into Mary's tent.

"He's dead," Ben told her.

"I don't care," she sniffled. "It's only trading one dog for another."

Ben walked over, sat beside Mary, and took her by the hand. She flinched.

"Not all dogs are mean," he said in a soft tone. Releasing her hand, he told her, "You are free. If you want to go, go. Before you do, though, perhaps you might want to hear me out."

At this, she raised her eyes but said nothing.

"Yes, I killed your mother and father. For this I expect nothing but hatred from you. I must pay this price. I demand nothing else from you. You are not my domestic slave, nor are you my sexual slave. I leave you in peace.

"As for me, my days of killing are finished. I will not lift this sword again unless it is in defense. I have sufficient means to begin a new life, one that is strange to me, but one that my belly now needs. I will begin to trade with these Romans, the new masters of this land.

"As for you, you have been raised as a pampered lamb. It is a wild and dangerous place out there for a woman alone such as you, and you have no place to go. I know that right now you don't care if you live or die, but if you stay for a while, I tell you that you will live. On your own, you are no hunter. What will you eat? How will you find your way?

"Hear this promise that I make to you. Stay with me in your own tent unmolested until Jerusalem falls. After this occurs, I will journey down from these mountains with the purpose of establishing trade. At that time, you can accompany me. When you reach civilization, I will turn you loose and give you half of my silver. I will keep the other half and all of my gold. This doesn't buy back your mother and father, but it will allow you to start a new life more to your liking."

The next day Ben awoke and looked to see if Mary was still around. He smiled as he spied her gathering wood for a fire. When they sat to eat their morning meal, no words passed between them until they both finished.

Mary gazed off toward the horizon and said, "I have a son. I also have an adopted sister." She proceeded to relate the events of the day of their meeting. Mary told him how she hid the boy and of the mystery of Sara's disappearance. When finished she sobbed, "My only reason for living now is to try and discover what happened to Stephen and to hold onto the hope that Sara lived and found him."

Pity was a new emotion for Ben, and he wasn't sure if he liked it all that much. Nevertheless, the story moved him. He took her hand. This time she didn't flinch.

"Mary," he said, "if you want me to, I will try and help you find your baby and your sister. The chances are not good. The people in this land have been widely scattered if they are not dead."

Mary understood that it would take a miracle.

"This place isn't all that bad," Sara announced. "They treat us decent, give us food, and we have all this sunshine." She looked up and dropped her hood just enough to allow the warmth to caress her face.

"Don't be too eager," corrected Helena. "In a little while, you could be some centurion's whore."

"That would be at his peril, wouldn't it," snickered Sara.

"Hush, remember the things that I taught to you. If you want to survive, you would control yourself in a situation like that, and..."

"I know, I know," Sara interrupted, feigning annoyance. "An unassuming appearance is the key to survival."

A few hours later, a great commotion arose near the eastern side of the compound. Sara talked Helena into sneaking over to the scene so that they could see what was going on. As they got closer, the women noticed a company of soldiers accompanied by a Jewish man. He seemed to be calling a few of the people out of the crowd.

"What are they doing?" Sara wondered.

"I don't know," replied Helena, "but off to the side I see they have brought out Philippe, the physician, and Dorcas, the tentmaker, and look there is old Marcus, the judge. Sara, these are all people well known in Jerusalem. Something is going to happen."

The soldiers helped the Jewish man up onto a platform so that he could more easily see all of the detainees. When Helena saw who it was, she squeezed Sara's hand and exclaimed, "Our way out, Sara. Praise God, we have a way out!"

She tore off her hood and began to jump up and down waving her arms and yelling to be heard above the din of the crowd. "Josephus, Josephus, over here, over here."

"Not very unassuming are you?" Sara joked.

It worked. Josephus pointed to Helena and the soldiers ordered a lane to be opened so that she could pass through.

"Come on," she screeched and grabbed Sara's hand.

As they approached the platform, Helena felt resistance build in her mind and turned to look at Sara. She was ashen.

"That man," Sara gasped, "I can't let him see me. He was there in the kitchen with Simon."

"Hush," Helena said understanding. "You are in a full covering now. Keep silent and keep your hood on. Pretend that you are my maidservant."

The crowd locked Sara in as they converged in the lane behind her. She approached the platform with great trepidation.

"Queen Helena of Adiabene," shouted Josephus as he embraced her. "I am thankful that you are still alive. A sad day it would be if a flower such as you were to disappear from the living. Let me look at you."

Josephus had not seen Helena for five years. His good friend, Andrew, had convinced this stunning woman to marry him, leave her homeland, and convert to Judaism. Josephus felt guilty, because he was abnormally jealous of Andrew's good fortune in finding and marrying such a beautiful woman. The effect that she had on him was unsettling. If he could have found her first, it would have been he that may have plucked this rose. Looking at her again, he was troubled. How could this woman remain as ravishing now as she was five years ago, despite the passing years and despite the siege?

Helena sensed that he was troubled. So did a frightened Sara.

"Josephus, dear friend," she whispered and gave him a kiss. He went numb, and his mind opened. "What you are thinking isn't all that important, is it?"

"No, why no it's not," he cried out forgetting his thoughts. "I'm just so grateful to be able to see you again."

Looking down at Sara, he asked, "Helena, who have we here?"

Sara shuddered.

"This poor child is my maidservant. She is mute and very afraid given the current events. I have grown quite fond of her. She is like a sister to me, and she has no one else."

"Beautiful and charitable as well, you are quite a woman, Helena." Josephus looked more closely at Sara and became troubled again.

"There is something familiar about this one," he said. Looking her in the face he asked, "Child, have we met before? Please lower your hood so that I can see you better."

Helena thrust herself between them, embraced Josephus and gave him another long kiss.

"I'm so grateful to see you again, too. These are trying times, are they not? The Romans have plundered all of our wealth, have they not? They can't steal our friendship with one another, can they? What you are thinking right now isn't all that important after all, is it?"

"Of course not," droned Josephus completely forgetting about Sara.

Astounding, thought Sara, *and she thinks that I'm the one that is powerful.*

"Helena," he said. "Titus has given me the power to set my friends free. You and your maidservant are free to go, but I was wondering if you would consent to assist me with a great mission to save some of our people."

"How is it that I can help?"

Josephus informed her of the plan to allay the fears of the last holdouts by appearing in front of them unharmed. She gladly consented.

They were loaded onto a wagon with the others and began the trip up the mount toward the temple.

"Did he say 'Queen' Helena?" asked Sara.

"That is a story for another time," she replied.

"Why are we doing this? We could have walked away free," Sara groaned.

"Remember our first conversation, Sara. I told you that sometimes we are capable of doing good things. These opportunities should be taken when presented." Helena's voice trailed off, "For the sake of our souls."

"For the sake of our souls," Sara repeated.

What appeared to be an entire legion of the Roman army surrounded the temple. Sara had never seen so many men. The poor people on the inside were wailing with hunger and fear. One by one, the friends in the wagon stood up outside the gate and entreated those on the inside to give up. Helena took her turn and Josephus spoke last. As he finished, the gate to the temple wall opened and the crowd began to shuffle out. Sara gasped as she witnessed their pitiful condition, so gaunt and wasted. They could scarcely walk.

As the crowd inside the temple thinned, a contingent of the army rode in to begin securing the area. One of the last surviving priests stood defiantly across the opening to the sanctuary.

"As I live, you will not enter this sacred place," he challenged.

A centurion rode up. "That's fine, elder," he said. "Maybe you would rather see it burned." He grabbed a torch and tossed it through the opening. The flames leaped into the air as the torch ignited the sanctuary screens. The sight of the fire caused the remaining stragglers to panic, and they rushed the temple gates.

"They attack," yelled the centurion. This rekindled the passions of the soldiers, and they became uncontrollable. Storming in, they set fire to the rest of the sanctuary and trampled down the stragglers.

Witnessing this from their cart on the outside, Josephus was horrified but was powerless to stop them. Sara began to cry and buried her face in her hands.

"Doing good," murmured Helena. "It can be such a fragile thing."

A week later, the army and the captured slaves began their long trek back to Rome. Josephus called on Helena prior to their departure.

"I am duty bound to go with Titus to Rome," he told her. "You are free and may go where you wish. You can even stay here."

"There are now too many painful memories here. After Andrew died, I lost any further reason to remain. No, Josephus, I'm returning to my homeland. We will follow behind the forces and the slaves and under your protection, that is, if you will permit us."

"No, I will not permit it," he was obstinate. "You will follow nobody. I insist that you and your maidservant ride in one of our provision wagons. I'm sure that I can arrange at least this much for you."

"Your generosity is undeserved. Thank you. We will never forget your kindness."

Josephus smiled and felt warm all over.

The wagon was a little cramped, but it offered some degree of privacy and a place off the ground for Sara and Helena to sleep at night. To keep the trip from becoming too boring for Sara, Helena told her wondrous stories from many far away lands. She also continued to provide wise counsel to Sara.

Four days after leaving Jerusalem, they met up with a caravan of merchants during one of their meal stops. Sara and Helena decided to try to purchase some meat, as they grew tired of constantly eating grain. When they drew near to the caravan, Sara spied a woman. It was Mary. At once Sara's heart bounded with joy, and she began to run toward her. After a few steps, Sara stopped cold as she remembered the terrible evil that she committed. Helena caught up to her.

"Sara, listen to me. You are no longer the naive young girl that I found ready to kill herself. You know now that you are much more. In your life there will be many challenges, and you will have to bear many burdens. This is only the first of many. I cannot help you with this. You choose whether to ignore your sister or go to her. Either way, take the experience to heart and grow with it."

Sara looked again at Mary and sensed that her spirit was in great pain.

"I can't stand to see her like this," she whispered. "I don't know if I have it in me to always turn away from doing bad things, Helena, but this time, this one time, I will try and do good."

"Sara?" asked Mary. "Sara, is that you?"

"Yes, sister, by some miracle of God we see each other again."

"Ben," Mary gasped, "Ben, the impossible has happened."

He came running from a neighboring wagon with a hand on his sword. "What is it, Mary, some trouble?"

"Ben, it is my sister." The two girls fell into each other's embrace and wept for some time in the joy at finding each other. Mary's thoughts turned toward her son.

"Sara, my son, Stephen. Did you find him? Is he alive?"

Sara's face turned down. She struggled, "Mary, in the city, there was a great famine. It was horrible. Many of us lost our minds." She broke down and could not go on.

Mary looked at her and remained calm, "He's dead?"

Sara began to weep bitterly. It was a cleansing for her soul. "He did not suffer, Mary. I swear to you, he did not suffer. I was there and…" This is all that she could get out between sobs.

"Hush child," Mary said as she tenderly held onto Sara. "Don't suffer so on my account. I finished grieving for him long ago. It was only by the slimmest of hopes that I yearned for him to be alive. Now that I know for sure that he is dead, the wondering is finished. My spirit is once again free. I lost my poor boy, but my sister I have gained back. Sara, Ben has provided for me for some time. We can stay with him for some time more and then start over."

Sara allowed Mary to hold her for some time until the Roman hosts began to move again. Sara was running short on time, and she was faced with the further burden of once again breaking Mary's heart.

"Mary, you know that we are not sisters by blood. I will always love you, but now that I've been alone, I have found out some things about myself. Things are, well, they are different from before."

"What do you mean?" Mary protested. "I've never considered you anything other than my sister. It doesn't matter that it's not by blood."

Reaching into her soul for strength, Sara stopped her. "Mary, I can't stay with you."

"But, where will you go?" Mary's eyes began to well up.

"Rome, I'm going to Rome."

"You are not a slave to them, are you?"

"No, not to the Romans, but Mary there are other forces. Please, I cannot explain."

"Well, then I will come with you," Mary cried in desperation.

"You can't, Mary," Sara said trying to be strong. "Look, you are with a fine man that loves you. Can't you see it in his eyes? Now that we have met and had a chance to soothe each other's pain, the circle is complete. You have a new life, and I am also doomed to mine."

They both cried.

"Sara?" asked Mary. "Will I ever see you again?"

Sara looked down and turned to walk away. After a few steps, Mary spoke again.

"Sara, wait."

She couldn't bear to turn around. Sara knew that if she did, she would not be able to refuse her again. She kept walking, but Mary ran around in front of her.

"Do you know what day this is, Sara?"

"No, Mary."

"It is the twentieth day of Lous. Eighteen years ago this day you were found abandoned in the courtyard of Bethezuba. Sara, your period of an indenture has now expired. You are free."

They embraced one final time.

"Good bye, Sara," Mary said. "May you find your way to whatever it is that you are looking for."

"Thank you, Mary. Go with God, and be forever happy."

Mary watched Sara walk away and eventually meet up with another woman along the way. The two walked together into the crowd of wagons and disappeared.

"My promise is still valid," said Ben as he offered Mary a sack of silver. "You can go with her, but believe me when I tell you that it would grieve me greatly."

Mary pushed the hand away that held the bag and grabbed onto his other hand. She gazed into his eyes. Ben saw a glow in her that he had never seen before.

"Ben," she said, "let's go home."

"Bravo!" Helena clapped her hands as Sara approached her. "Well done, Sara."

As they walked away, Sara was shaking. When they got back to their wagon, she looked off in the distance. "Helena," she said. "You are right. That path is so very, very hard."

"Yes, it is, isn't it? Take heart, Sara, you made it through, and I doubt if you will ever find the path quite that hard again."

As the weeks passed, the great party cleared the Mediterranean Sea that until now always blocked their way on the west. They turned toward Rome. Again, after some time, they crossed into Byzantium and made for Macedonia.

One morning Sara woke and found Helena packing her clothing and some stores for a journey.

"What is this, Helena, where are you going?"

"Home," she said and pointed south.

"But I thought that you were going to Rome with me."

"That is where your destiny awaits you, Sara, not mine. I have a Greek heritage, on my mother's side of course. It is too long since I've smelled the sea air and watched the sun both rise and set over those islands. There is where I will begin anew."

Sara jumped down off the wagon in protest. "You can't leave. Who will teach me, what shall I do?"

"Dear Sara, I've taught you everything that you need to know. It is now time for you to face alone the trials that life puts in front of you. That is our curse. You passed a great test back there in Judea. Now, as a teacher, I feel comfortable about releasing you, my student. You have it within you to judge great matters for yourself. Also, Sara, you are growing. Your power runs deep, it frightens me."

"I would never hurt you, Helena. I owe you my life."

"Examine yourself, Sara. I think that you already know that our kind cannot stay together for long periods. A struggling of sorts would develop between us."

"We will never meet again, will we?" Sara asked with her head bowed down.

"This I do not know. It is my hope that someday we will. Then it will be your turn to tell me some great stories." Seeing that Sara remained dejected, Helena continued, "Sara, there is one thing that we now share with each other that you may use when you become too downhearted."

"I know, it's a kind of signature," Sara said.

"You can touch me anytime, even over great distances."

The wagons pulled away and Sara sat alone watching as Helena faded from view. When she could see her no more, Sara decided to try. She closed her eyes and reached out. After a few seconds passed, she became alarmed. Then like a gentle breeze, a sense of well-being passed over her. Helena had touched her back.

Smiling, Sara knew that everything was now going to be all right. Turning to the west, she thought about the awesome life that she was now about to begin. Joy filled her heart.

After a few minutes, a soldier rode up to her. He appeared to be of great importance.

"Young woman, weren't there two of you here before?" he asked.

"It's okay," Sara said. "She has gone to her home. Now there is just me."

"So what is your name, maiden?"

She let loose her hood and removed her outer mantle. The rider was stunned into silence.

"My name is Sara, kind sir. Thanks for being concerned about me. What is your name, and why is it that men salute when they pass?"

"My name is Nicanor, maiden, and men salute me, because I am a Tribune."

No less than a Tribune! Sara thought to herself as she flashed him her most beautiful smile.

CHAPTER 11

Tabitha Carr lived in a moderately sized estate near Barcelona, Spain. Her dwelling occupied the second and third floors of the home, while her business occupied the first floor. Tabitha was an antique dealer specializing in fine art and old original manuscripts.

The American made regular visits to this part of the world, but this time he seemed to be lingering for an unusually long time. It was none of her business, but she was troubled by the amount of force generated from his mental energy. Tabitha seemed especially sensitive to him.

"Enough already," she mumbled to herself. Tabitha wondered if she should reveal herself to him.

She sighed, "He is desperately searching. One of us should help him. Werner is a man, so he can't feel him as strongly as I can. Other than Werner, I guess that I am closest."

Tabitha made herself some tea and sat at a small table in her living room.

"Well, here it goes. Let me see if I can comfort this American with a nice, soft kiss."

She closed her eyes. Tabitha was experienced and had a lot of self-control. She was able to summon up just the right amount of psychic energy to send out a gentle nudge.

The wave went north.

Derek Dunbar paced the holding cell waiting for Klaus Hall.

"Where the hell is he?" he said. There was no one else there to hear him. It was mid-afternoon and still no word had come from Derek's lawyer. He especially wanted to find out if Sharon was safe. Derek walked over to the bars and clutched them with both hands. He turned his head to peer down the corridor toward the main door at the end of the hall. There was little activity. He was expecting Klaus to enter at any moment.

Still grasping the bars, Derek closed his eyes and hung his head.

I really miss my Sharon, he thought.

Suddenly Derek felt a warmth flow through him. It reminded him of his dreams. It was the same kind of feeling that accompanied the haunting 'come to me' command. This time though the feeling seemed more benign.

"No," he cried out. "I'm not sleeping. Maybe I really am losing my mind, but I refuse to let this bother me during my waking hours."

Derek was an emotional mess. Given what he experienced the past few days, he was confused, frightened, angry, and frustrated all at the same time. He was spoiling for a fight.

Closing his eyes, Derek clamped his mind around this feeling that was now waning. He pushed hard.

"You want me to come? Where are you? Show me. Who the hell are you, and who am I?"

The emotional release felt good to Derek, so he ratcheted it up to a higher level. The recent events flooded over him. He exerted all of his energy. Derek didn't realize, but he was screaming at the top of his lungs.

"Where...are...you?"

"Who...am...I?"

"What...have...you...done...to...this...plane?"

"Where...is...that...asshole...Klaus?"

"Sharon?"

A country away, in Barcelona, Spain, Tabitha was writhing on the floor of her living room. The table was lying on its side and the teacup had shattered from the fall. She was experiencing convulsions.

"God, please stop," she was screaming. "Release me, please stop." Tabitha's mind was exploding.

Derek felt a sharp pain in his stomach. He fell to the floor limp. When Derek refused the commands of the guards to stop his screaming, the supervisor zapped him with a stun gun. The jolt caused Derek to break his concentration. He lay there incapacitated.

Tabitha pulled herself up into a sitting position. Wiping her nose, she felt a warm trickle of blood against the back of her hand. She could barely breathe.

"Just like her," she gasped. "There's two of them now. God save us."

A few minutes later, Klaus Hall stood over Derek who was still on the floor. Klaus walked over and sat on the chair next to Derek's cot. He waited.

Derek started to pull himself together. Pushing up on his knees, he grabbed the bars of the cell. Using them for support, Derek hoisted himself to his feet. He was still a bit unsteady and shuffled over to the cot. Derek collapsed onto it and covered his eyes with his arm.

"I guess I really caused a commotion," he groaned.

Klaus didn't say anything and continued to stare at him.

"This is one of the lowest points of my life. There's nothing I can do for myself while I am in this cage. Klaus, the frustration is getting to me. I actually think that I am going out of my mind. It's the real deal. There are strange dreams, feelings like someone else is inside my head, and voices." Derek removed his arm from his eyes and waved his hand in front of him. "Klaus, you've got to get me out of here."

"Mr. Dunbar," Klaus spoke in a low deliberate tone. "You make my job more difficult than it already is. This 'cage' that you are referring to represents special treatment. The Ambassador at your embassy asked our government to make sure that you are comfortable. Assurances were given that despite the seriousness of the charges, you would be a model prisoner. The police commandant went through a lot of trouble to arrange these accommodations for you."

Klaus stood and walked up to the door. He rubbed his wedding ring against one of the bars. It was subconscious on his part, as he was deep in thought.

"Derek, you are making your Ambassador look bad. In the process, you are also embarrassing yourself."

He turned around to face Derek who was still prone on the cot.

"Now, what was that outburst all about?"

Derek managed to roll up into a sitting position.

"It's like I told you. I'm going crazy in here. Don't they have anything like 'bail' here in Germany?"

"Not until your hearing, Derek"

"When will that be?"

Klaus ignored Derek. He thumbed through a notepad that he had been carrying and fired off a few questions of his own.

"Derek, how well do you know a woman named Anne Sprague?"

"Annie?" Derek repeated. "She's a regular on my flight crew. Why are you asking about her?"

Once again, Klaus ignored Derek's question and pressed on, "Would she come and visit you if I asked her to?"

"I guess so. Sure, we get along really well." Actually, Derek knew that Annie had a huge crush on him, just like most other women.

"Does she 'get along' well enough with you that she would risk some discomfort for you?"

Derek stiffened. "What are you getting at? How is Annie involved in any of this?"

Klaus explained to Derek about the encounter at the Royale the night before.

"Police?" Derek questioned. "Why would Washington and the police set me up?"

"It's not us," Klaus said. "I have contacts on the force. Nobody has ever heard of you. If it is a set up, your American police force is behind it."

Derek shook his head. "No, no, no, I don't buy it. This is way beyond the realm of possibility. Are you sure he said it was a police sting?"

"No, Derek, Anne Sprague is the one that reached that conclusion. Joel Washington told her that he was working with 'certain interested parties.' Who could this be?"

Derek stared straight at Klaus. "I honestly don't know."

Klaus walked back over to the chair and turned it around. He sat on it backwards facing Derek.

"This is where Anne can help your case. She is a good-looking lady. Your Mr. Washington seems to be trying very hard to seduce her. Do you believe that you can persuade her to play along?"

"You mean try and get Joel to talk?" Derek asked.

"Exactly."

"Suppose that I can enlist her to do this. What good would it do? It would be great if we knew what was going on, but would her testimony be valid enough in your court system to free me?"

"It would be," Klaus said with a devilish grin. "It would hold up in court if we could get her to, how do you say it in America? Wear a wire."

Derek perked up but did no allow himself to become too hopeful.

"She likes me, Klaus, but this would be asking a lot from her. Going public would ruin her career. Who would want to work with her again? Nobody would trust her."

"Not necessarily," Klaus rebutted. "You could help her. After it is all over, you can give her a big kiss in front of the news media and announce how loyal she has been in helping her friends and her company root out a criminal in their midst."

"You're right, Klaus, that might sell, but it still is a big risk for her."

"That is why I want her to visit you in person. A request like this should come directly from you."

"Yeah, set it up," Derek said, not too convincingly. He suddenly realized that he had another concern. "Sharon?" he asked. "What can you tell me about Sharon and Juan?"

"I did manage to contact your Mr. Sanchez. He left a message at my office about an hour ago. They are at BWI airport right now and are scheduled to arrive at Rhein Main Airport early tomorrow morning."

"Thank God," Derek breathed a sigh of relief. "Did you detain Joel Washington?"

"Not yet. If Ms. Sprague agrees to help us, we should allow him to go. He will be back, right?"

"Next week," Derek said. "Our flight crew rotates into this assignment every Sunday."

"Good, that will give us time enough to make all of the necessary arrangements."

"And if Anne doesn't agree?" Derek considered.

"I will have Mr. Washington brought in for questioning immediately."

Derek looked down at his watch. "You better hurry, Klaus, they return to Baltimore in six hours."

Sharon and Juan boarded and buckled themselves in. Juan occupied the window seat on the port side of the wide body aircraft, while Sharon sat beside him in the middle seat. The aisle seat remained empty. Sharon wasn't lying to the ticket attendant. She did not particularly care to fly and gladly yielded the window seat to Juan. Nervously fumbling through the seat pocket in front of her, she carefully inventoried the contents. There was a *SkyMall* magazine, the Lufthansa marketing magazine, a customs declaration form, a sick bag, and an emergency procedure instruction card printed in twelve different languages. Eyeing the seat pocket in front of the still vacant aisle seat, she proceeded to inventory its contents as well. Nothing different was there.

Sharon looked at her watch and said to herself almost inaudibly, "It's ten minutes after scheduled departure, when are we going to push back?"

Juan heard her and smiled, "If it helps you can root through my seat pocket."

"Sorry, Juan," she remarked. "I guess I'm a little nervous. I hate these long flights, and this one hasn't even started yet. We will be in the air for eight hours, right?"

"Yes, give or take a half hour. Sharon, this isn't so bad. It's an all-night flight. Just ask for a stiff drink when they bring the beverage cart. You'll sleep like a baby."

"I sincerely doubt that," chuckled Sharon.

A voice boomed over the intercom. "Ladies and Gentlemen, please excuse the delay. A connecting flight from Knoxville was running late, and we have been holding for several passengers. That flight has arrived and those passengers should be boarding shortly."

A man appeared wearing reading glasses. He was straining to compare the seat number printed on his boarding pass with the overhead label.

"21C, that's the aisle seat here, right?" he asked.

Sharon looked up at him and smiled. "Yep, this is it."

"Great," he sighed out of breath.

Sharon noticed that he was perspiring. "I guess you were on that Knoxville flight, huh?"

"That's right. I thought for sure that I wouldn't make this connection in time. I almost knocked a few people down running to get here. Wouldn't you know that they parked us way over in Terminal A?"

The man was struggling to stow his bag in the overhead bin.

"Geez, when you're one of the last ones to board there isn't very much room left, is there?"

Sharon welcomed the diversion to talk with this gentleman. It took her mind off the long flight ahead. "Do you want me to buzz the stewardess to help you find a place for that?"

"No thanks, I believe it's squeezed in here good." He pushed the overhead door shut. The man took his seat beside Sharon and buckled himself in. He proceeded to speak incessantly.

"Did you ever notice how those overhead compartments make that distinctive clicking sound when you latch them? I don't suppose there is anything else that makes a sound quite like that. Did you also ever notice how everyone seated nearby loves to watch when people open and close those doors? They sound like 'tick' when you unlatch them and 'click' when you latch them again. Tick, click, tick, click," the man repeated and started to chuckle.

He smacked his forehead with his right palm. "Geez, where are my manners. I'm sorry, miss. My name is Hank Kimball. Not the one from *Green Acres* fame, although you're too young to know about that anyway."

He reached over to shake Sharon's hand. She gave him hers. He pumped her arm in three or four short, staccato shakes. He quickly let go and started talking again.

"Here's another thing about folks on an airplane. They all worry about who will be sitting beside them. I'll bet you were probably hoping that it wouldn't be some fat guy with a gut that would spill out over the armrest. As for me, my biggest bugaboo is a woman with a screaming baby. Can you imagine, 'wah, wah, wah,' for this entire eight-hour trip? I tell you that I sure am relieved that it is a nice-looking young lady."

Mr. Kimball stopped and smacked his forehead again.

"Geez, there I go again. I'm sorry, miss. I didn't even give you a chance to tell me your name."

"Sharon McGee," she offered, "and I'm relieved to be sitting beside such a gifted conversationalist. You can save me from being bored these many hours."

What a pleasant man, she thought.

He's an air head, thought Juan.

This time Sharon jumped in before he could continue. "What brings you from Knoxville to Baltimore to Germany, Mr. Kimball?"

"Cuckoos!" he exclaimed.

"Huh?" Sharon stared at him blankly.

"Cuckoos," he repeated. "You know, like in clocks. I own a tourist shop in Gatlinburg that specializes in German curiosities, like cuckoo clocks, nutcrackers, Hummel figures, and such. Actually, it's a thriving business. People come from miles around, because they know my stuff is authentic. It's all made by real German craftsmen."

He continued, "Sharon, this is a business trip for me. Geez, I hope it's okay for me to call you Sharon. Once we get to Frankfurt, I'll be driving down to Freiburg. That's deep in the heart of the Black Forest. The best cuckoos in the world are made there. I'm going to buy them up. What do you think about that, Sharon?"

"Well, I don't know a whole lot about German curiosities, Mr. Kimball."

"Ah, ah, call me Hank."

"Okay, Hank, I'll bet you are a great salesperson."

"I'm not bad, no siree. It's easy to be a salesperson if you know the secret. Do you want to know my secret, Sharon?"

"Sure."

"Observation, you have to be a skilled observer. When you get good enough at that, you can discover the hot buttons in people that make them want to buy."

"Oh?" Sharon asked hinting for him to continue.

"Geez, it's one of my favorite things to do, observing that is. I suppose it's sort of a hobby of mine. That's how I was able to tell you about the overhead compartment doors and the way people think about who is going to sit beside them."

"That's really interesting," Sharon loved this entertainment. "Tell me more."

"Okay, Sharon. You know this whole time I've been observing you. I bet I can tell you a lot about yourself."

"Give it a try," she responded eagerly.

"Well for starters, did you notice that I've been calling you, 'miss'? That one was easy, no ring," he said pointing at her hands. "My guess is that the gentleman beside you is not your boyfriend. If he were, he would be a whole lot more uncomfortable at my being so forward with you. How am I doing so far?"

"I'm not married," Sharon acknowledged. "Juan is a good friend of mine, but you're right, we are not intimate, if that is what you mean."

"Hello, Juan, my name is Hank Kimball," he said and reached his hand across in front of Sharon.

Juan reluctantly took it and with an effort managed to speak the obligatory, "Pleased to meet you, Hank."

"Juan, I'm in the process of telling Sharon something about herself based on my observations."

"Yeah, I heard," Juan said stoically. He was jealous that Sharon was so captivated by this guy.

Hank continued, "Now, as I was saying, you are single, and Juan is not your boyfriend. You will recall that I was relieved to be sitting beside such a 'nice-looking lady?' Since you are so pretty, my guess is that you probably do have a boyfriend and that you are probably on your way to visit him. Is he in the armed forces, stationed somewhere in Germany?"

"That's pretty good," gasped Sharon. "I am on my way to visit my boyfriend. His name is Derek. The only thing you got wrong is that he is not in the service. He's an airline pilot."

"Geez, a pilot! I would have never guessed that."

"I can't wait to see him," Sharon sighed.

"Now that I could have told you," laughed Hank.

The conversation paused when the plane pushed back and the head flight attendant read the safety instructions. Minutes later they were in the air.

Hank looked over at Sharon. She was glancing through the *SkyMall* magazine.

"One more thing, Sharon."

"Yes, Hank?"

"You have a look about you. You're worried about something."

Sharon smiled. "I swear, Hank, you would make a great detective."

"Geez," he responded and looked away.

CHAPTER 12

Trujillo, Spain — 1539

Gonzalo wiped his eyes and read the letter one more time to himself.

> *"To Gonzalo Pizarro of Trujillo, brother of Governor Francisco Pizarro. Emperor Charles V requires your immediate presence in Madrid on a matter of grave importance to the Empire. Please make haste with the bearer of this letter, Friar Gaspar de Carvajal."*

The friar noticed Gonzalo's puzzled expression.

"You will notice that it bears the official seal," he pointed out to Gonzalo.

"I don't doubt the authenticity," squirmed Gonzalo. "It's just that I can't understand what the Emperor could want with me? How does he even know me?"

Gaspar laughed, "You are too modest. Everyone in Spain knows of the famous Pizarro family. Your brother, Francisco, has distinguished himself as conqueror of the Incas. The gold that he sent back from Lima fills the treasuries of our Emperor from floor to ceiling. Your cousin, Orellana, has also done well as governor in Guayaquil."

"My cousin, Orellana," mused Gonzalo with fondness. "We are the same age. I have not seen him or my brother in twelve long years." He continued to recall, "It seems like only yesterday that we played together as children."

"Yes, but these are happier times are they not?" asked Gaspar. "The Moslem hoard has been driven from our shores, and our fame as a nation has blossomed under Charles's rule."

Gonzalo nodded, "Everyone may know my family on account of my brother and cousin, but I have played a lesser part. They are the ones sending gold from the new world. As for me, I've never been away from Spain. My assignment has been in the enforcement of the Papal Bull. Again, how is it that the Emperor summons me?"

"The reestablishment of Christianity is every bit as important to Spain as a galleon filled with gold," Gaspar told him. "Consider the success of your assignment with the same honor as that of the success of your brother and cousin. As to your question, I have no insight as to why Charles wishes to see us. I know only that I received the same invitation two days ago. My letter ordered that I was to seek you out and travel with you to Madrid. It appears, Gonzalo, that you and I are bound together in some purpose that will be revealed to us in due time."

Gonzalo gazed around at the land belonging to the estate of his family. Gaspar perceived what he was thinking.

"You're still a young man, Gonzalo. If Spain requires more of you, consider it a privilege to be of service. You will have plenty of time for all of this later."

Gonzalo sighed, "If we leave now, we will reach Madrid tomorrow afternoon."

Two female sextons entered the catacombs deep beneath the Cathedral of Grenada. One carried a tray of food and water. The other bore fresh clothing and an empty bucket. They stopped before a heavy iron door at the end of a hallway. The older of the two women nodded to the soldier guarding the door. He removed a key from beneath his breastplate, unlocked and removed an external lock. The older woman unhinged a hasp that revealed another inner lock embedded inside the door. She took a separate key and turned it in the lock. With a sharp click, it released a bolt from inside the wall. The two women entered. The guard waited until he heard the internal bolt move into place and then refastened the outer lock.

The two women found themselves in an antechamber. A small worktable was pushed against the right wall. Another locked door awaited them at the opposite end of the room.

"This is a frightening place," Juana shuddered as Esther checked the oil in the lamp.

"You get used to it," Esther said. "I've ministered to her for the past year. You will soon take my place after you are fully trained."

"I still don't understand," objected Juana. "We are sextons. How is it that we are providing for this prisoner in the next room? This cathedral is a strange place for a prisoner, isn't it?"

Esther scolded her, "Don't question it. Father Rey has ordered this arrangement."

"But what about the rumors?" Juana asked. "I've heard that she is a witch."

"I don't know," Esther said matter-of-factly. "Father Rey instructs that she is no danger to other women as long as we follow the rules. Only women may see to her needs. As a precaution we do not speak with her, and we do not stare at her."

Juana looked at the door at the end of the hall. "I've heard that she is very old and that she has been locked up in there for a long time. Some even say that she has been locked in there for generations."

Esther laughed. "So much for rumors. You will soon see for yourself that she is quite young, younger than you, and very pretty."

"If she is so young, what could she have done? Why is she a prisoner?" inquired Juana.

"We don't speak of it," replied Esther. "That is Father Rey's business, and it's best if you keep your nose out of it."

Esther pulled out the keys and walked over to the door at the end of the hall. Juana followed. Esther slid the key into the lock. Before disengaging the bolt, she turned and placed a hand on Juana's arm.

"Remember," Esther told her. "She's quite insane."

The governmental palace in Madrid was functional rather than ornate. Gonzalo was more impressed with the garrison of soldiers guarding the grounds.

"They are disciplined and intense," he said to Gaspar.

Gaspar chuckled, "More colorful than the prosecutors that you rode with?"

"Definitely," replied Gonzalo. "These troops carry themselves well."

"You are looking at the finest in the Empire," said Gaspar. "This is the garrison from Habsburg. They travel everywhere with Charles. It's his version of a praetorian guard."

Gaspar handed the two letters to the captain of the guard. He saluted smartly and motioned for them to follow.

The captain led them into the palace and down a long corridor to a waiting area. He motioned them to sit and handed the letters back to Gaspar. Without a word, he turned and returned to his duties.

A few moments later, a young squire approached them.

"Your visit is eagerly anticipated," he told them politely. "I am to show you to your quarters where you can refresh yourselves. Your audience with the Emperor will be this evening after dinner."

The two of them were led to a large room with a roman bath. In the recesses of the wall were two feather beds trimmed in gold. The squire bowed and took his leave.

"These are considered 'quarters?'" remarked Gonzalo.

"Probably better than what your brother and cousin are used to," snickered Gaspar as he began to undress. "I'm going to jump into that bath."

After a period, the squire returned and led them to a banquet hall. About forty other men were already assembled there. They appeared to be soldiers. One of them looked hard at Gonzalo and approached him.

"Are you a Pizarro?" he asked.

"I am Gonzalo Pizarro, brother of Francisco."

The man laughed and slapped him on the arm.

"Francisco's little brother!" he exclaimed. "Yes, I can clearly see the family resemblance. My name is Sanchez de Vargas. These are my men."

"You know my brother?" Gonzalo asked excitedly. "What news do you have from him? I have seen neither him nor my cousin Orellana in twelve years."

"I don't know about your cousin, but your brother is fat and happy in Lima," laughed Sanchez.

"When did you return? Why are you here? Is my brother coming home?" Gonzalo fired away with the questions.

"Whoa, one at a time, young one," Sanchez said as he continued to laugh. "My men and I returned six months ago with Captain Pinzon of the Nina. He is the elderly gentleman standing at the wine cask. We are here because of an order that we received from Charles. Your brother remains in Lima at present. Before I answer any more questions, let's eat."

While Gonzalo and Sanchez conversed, Gaspar found Father Rey of Grenada. The two of them engaged in quiet conversation.

During dinner, Gonzalo listened with rapt attention to the stories and jokes that the men told of the new world. Shortly after they had eaten their fill, an armed contingent of the Habsburg guards entered the banquet hall and stationed themselves between the guests and the far end of the hall.

The room fell silent. Gaspar poked Gonzalo while the squire entered ahead of an entourage of attendants.

"Well, Gonzalo," he said. "We are about to find out what this mystery is all about."

"Please rise," the squire's voice boomed and reverberated through the banquet hall.

Sanchez and his men looked at each other and stood along with Gaspar and Gonzalo.

The squire smiled and spoke. "Please bow down for Charles the Fifth, King of Spain, Holy Roman Emperor, Protector of the Pope, and secular head of the Catholic Church."

Charles entered from directly behind the squire. He was dressed casually and demanded no further homage. He walked over and stood at the end of the banquet table.

"Sit," he commanded them. "Welcome, fellow countrymen. Thank you for responding to my request. All of you have been summoned to learn of an extraordinary quest that I am about to lay before you."

Charles stopped and took a drink from a golden goblet. It was a dramatic pause to hold the attention of the assembled men.

"Before we begin, I must invite in our other visitor. Friar Gaspar, would you kindly walk over to the door from where you entered this great hall. I would like you to assist our visitor."

Gaspar complied and made his way to the end of the room. All eyes followed his every footstep. Charles wore a grin. As Gaspar approached the door, Charles looked over and nodded to the squire.

The young squire's voice boomed once again.

"Our special guest, Bishop of Rome, Vicar of Jesus Christ, Successor of St. Peter, Primate of Italy, and Supreme Pontiff of the Universal Church, Pope Paul the Third."

The man entered the room.

"Friar Gaspar de Carvajal of Extremadura, Spain," he said. "I've heard many good things about you. It pleases me to meet you at last."

Gaspar kissed the Pope's hand and began to weep. He had never met the Pontiff before and his emotions overcame him. Pope Paul gathered him up and led him to his place at the table. The Pontiff took his seat beside Charles. Gonzalo, Sanchez, and all of the other assembled soldiers stared in awe. They were in the presence of the two most powerful men in the world.

The woman watched as Esther and Juana entered the room that made up her whole life. She knew Esther but had never seen the other one before. She noticed that Juana was trembling.

"Don't be afraid," the woman said to Juana. "I would never harm you. I just want to talk. Nobody will talk to me. Will you please talk to me?"

Juana looked at her with pity. *She's barely a woman*, Juana thought to herself.

"What is your name, maiden?" Juana asked.

Esther slapped Juana with a fierce backhand across the face. Juana screamed and fell to the floor.

"Nobody talks to her," bellowed Esther. "The next time I will tell Father Rey, and he will have you beaten. Do you understand?"

Juana nodded while holding her cheek.

The woman sat beside Juana and groveled.

"God bless you," she sobbed. "Thank you for talking to me. I can't remember when the last time..."

Before she could finish, Esther kicked the woman.

"Get away from her," she ordered.

The woman yelped and crawled away.

"There was no need to do that," Juana screeched. "She is just a young woman."

"Shut up," Esther retorted. "You don't know what you are dealing with. Empty her chamber pot, and let's get out of here."

The woman couldn't contain herself. She wanted to answer Juana.

"I've used many names in many places," she said. "The name first given to me was Sara. You can call me Sara."

Juana looked over at Esther. In defiance of Esther, she quickly glanced back over at the woman and repeated once, "Sara."

"That's enough," Esther chided. "Let's go."

Sara watched as the two of them disappeared behind the door. She heard the lock engage. Moments later she heard the unlocking and relocking of the door at the far end of the anteroom. Sara would not see them again until the next day. It was once a day, every day, and all the time. Year after year it was this way, decade after decade. Nobody talked to her and nobody touched her. She longed for companionship, even the simplest of conversations, or one gentle touch.

Sara sat in the middle of the floor of her prison, legs crossed, and rocking back and forth. Soon she began to sing to herself.

"Pockets full of posies, pockets full of posies.

Aschew, aschew, they all fall down dead anyway.

Long before the buboes come."

Emperor Charles leaned over and spoke softly to Sanchez de Vargas. "You should dismiss your men for the time being. What we are about to discuss should be heard only by the principals gathered here."

Sanchez immediately dispatched his men to their quarters. Charles motioned his Habsburg soldiers to leave the hall. They saluted smartly and marched away.

Charles looked over at Pope Paul as if asking for approval. The Pontiff nodded at him. Charles motioned for all in the remaining party to approach.

"Come closer men, and sit by us," he directed them.

Pope Paul and Emperor Charles sat at the end of the table. Father Rey took a seat beside the Pontiff and Friar Gaspar next to the Father.

On the other side, Sanchez sat beside the Emperor, then Captain Pinzon, and finally Gonzalo took his place directly across from Gaspar.

Before anyone spoke, the attending squire filled everyone's goblets with fine wine.

Pope Paul blessed the gathering. Charles clasped his hands together and let them lay on the table in front of him. He stretched out his back against the chair and sat erect. "I know the deeds of everyone at this table," he began. "You are all noble and worthy citizens of this great Empire and of the church. All of you have proven yourselves unquestionably loyal."

Charles started around the table with Captain Pinzon.

"Captain Vicente Yanez Pinzon the Third, your grandfather, piloted the Nina with Christopher Columbus. You have faithfully carried on in his tradition. The Nina sails again with you at the helm. How many trips to the new world have you completed for Spain?"

"The return from Lima with General de Vargas completes my second voyage," Pinzon replied proudly.

"Yes, and both trips you have returned heavily laden with the treasures of the conquered Incas while taking nothing for yourself," Charles added. He looked at Sanchez.

"General Sanchez de Vargas, you and your men have served well in the conquest of the new world."

Vargas smiled and put an arm around Gonzalo. "It has been my pleasure to fight side-by-side with this man's brother, the great Francisco Pizarro."

Gonzalo was embarrassed and bowed his head. He gazed up and exclaimed, "My lord, these are all great men in this room. I do not belong in this company, as I have done little in your service."

"What?" Charles asked with an amused expression. "As a prosecutor, it is my understanding that you assisted greatly in driving the pagan influences out of this land. Is this not the case?"

"Why yes, my lord," Gonzalo struggled. "This is a small thing compared to the deeds of these great men or of my brother."

Pope Paul interrupted at this point. "My son, your service to God in this matter is of even greater importance than the military victories enjoyed by your peers," he corrected Gonzalo.

The Emperor added to this while laughing. "Young man, you will be tested soon enough just as these other men have been tested."

Finally, Charles recognized Gaspar. "Friar Gaspar, the Pontiff suggests to me that your zeal for the church is renowned. Are you ready to reach out and serve in an even greater capacity?"

"My life is committed to God, my Lord. I will go where needed."

While Charles spoke with Gaspar, Pope Paul leaned over and whispered to Father Rey, "Do you know why you are here?"

"There can be only one reason," Father Rey responded.

"Does she yet live?"

"Yes, your Excellency. She has been well taken care of as the church has commanded."

The Pontiff noticed Gonzalo staring at their whispers and stopped Father Rey before he could say more.

Emperor Charles now became more serious as he neared the point of disclosing to all of them the purpose of the meeting.

"All of us are men, great men. What needs to be discussed here is of grievous concern to our way of life. Since this is such a weighty matter, let us drop all formalities for the purpose of this meeting and speak to each other not as kings and priests but as men."

Charles clapped his hands. The attending squire hurried into the room with a large scroll and handed it to the Emperor. Charles untied the scroll and rolled it out onto the table in front of them.

"Behold," he said while waving his hand over the scroll, "The Holy Roman Empire." It was a map of the world. Shaded on the map were all of the lands under the rule of Spain.

Charles pointed to the area of Europe and began to explain to them. "I inherited the Spanish Empire from my maternal grandparents, the great King Ferdinand and Queen Isabel. Due to my mother's marriage, the responsibility for the Habsburg Empire also passed to me at the death of my grandfather, Maximilian."

He pointed to the South American continent on the map. "The Treaty of Tordesillas signed with our neighbors, the Portuguese, greatly expanded our holdings in the new world. Men, we are the masters of the world. Blessed by

God we have been able to spread Christianity and uproot the pagan influences that threaten our civilization. We have also been able to keep invading forces from our distant lands. Finally, let us not forget that we have just completed a major war with the Moslems."

General Sanchez de Vargas sprang up and while holding his goblet in the air exclaimed, "Great is the might of our Empire under God and his Emperor."

Gonzalo and Captain Pinzon applauded.

Charles waved them off. "Men, this brings me to the point of this meeting. A decade from now, it pains me to say that our citizens will look back on these days and lament, 'Great *was* the might of our Empire under God and his Emperor.'"

Murmuring broke out between them moving Gonzalo to speak. "My lord, surely you cannot mean that the Empire is in any danger. At the very least, nothing can threaten us during the next ten years. We've conquered all of our enemies. We have the mightiest naval armada in the world. Who stands against us?"

Charles answered him with a grim expression. "They all do, young one. Do you not think that the Britons or the Moslems or the Norsemen or the Mongols test our resolve every day? We are in a constant struggle. This world continues to be governed by the aggressors. It is precisely due to the size of our Empire that we are now most vulnerable."

"As this Empire stands or falls, so does the Catholic Church," Pope Paul charged them.

"Then the Empire must never fall," added Gaspar.

"Think men," Charles began again. "Is it easier to defend one castle from invaders, or is it easier to defend the entire realm?"

"Why it is easy to defend a castle, my lord," spoke General de Vargas. "All of the military resources can be concentrated within the safety of the walls. Without those walls, the resources become spread throughout the countryside. The forces can be breached at their weak points."

"The same is true of our Empire," Charles told them. "General de Vargas is correct. Our resources are spread thin; we have many troops to pay and to feed. We also have many ships to maintain. Men, the royal treasuries are on the verge of bankruptcy. We cannot sustain what we now have."

This was a shocking revelation. Captain Pinzon blurted out, "The gold and riches won with the lives of our men — what has become of it?"

Pope Paul jumped to the defense of Charles. "Spent, my son, all in defense of the church. Your struggle has been valiant, but your two ship loads did nothing but purchase a few more months, maybe a year of time."

Using his military mind, General de Vargas quickly realized the alternatives and informed the gathering. "We have two choices. Either we find new means of paying for our present defenses, or we cede some of our lands. Our Empire could be collapsed into a more financially manageable state."

"That is not an option," rebuked Pope Paul. "God has given us these lands so that we may spread Christianity. It is our destiny to maintain what we have and even expand the Empire."

"Then we must find the financial means," General de Vargas concluded.

Silence filled the room. Each of them were lost in their own thoughts. Charles looked up and had a strange glimmer in his eye. They looked at him as he said to them, "The means exists."

"Go on, my lord," requested a curious Gaspar.

"Friar Gaspar?" Charles asked. "Have you ever heard of the legend of El Dorado?"

Gonzalo rolled his eyes. "A myth, my Lord, a story for children and for soldiers to entertain their wives. A city filled with more gold than my brother reclaimed from the great Incan realm of Machu Pichu. Surely after all of the searches for this place, you do not believe that it actually exists, do you?"

Captain Pinzon stood up horrified at the outburst. "Silence, you young fool," he shouted. "Nobody addresses the Emperor with such disrespect."

Charles roared with laughter. "Sit, Pinzon. Did I not say that for this meeting we would address each other as men and not as kings?"

He glanced at Gonzalo and said, "I admire your fiery spirit, Master Pizarro. Indeed, you are correct. More fortunes have been spent looking for the mythical city than the fortunes contained in the city itself."

He continued to address all of them. "Men, allow me to enlighten you. As you know, young Master Pizarro has two famous relatives in the new world. His brother, Francisco Pizarro, rules as Governor in Lima. Lieutenant General Francisco Orellana, cousin of our young friend, is Governor in Guayaquil. They have both sent independent reports back to me concerning this El Dorado. Through their examinations of the many tribes native to the new world, they have been able to discover that El Dorado is not a place. Men, El Dorado is a man, a living breathing man."

Pope Paul stood and took over from this point. "It is not exactly a man, but rather a very old creature, an abomination to God. The tribes all tell the same tale of an ancient wise man, youthful in appearance and spry. He has hoarded gold and treasures over the period of centuries. More riches than have been accounted for in all the treasuries of the world. They all tell the same story. Find the man, subdue him, and you will have found the treasure."

"Why has this man not been found?" Gonzalo asked. "What makes him so elusive?"

"Remember what the Pontiff told you," replied Charles. "He is ancient and wise. It is easy for him to elude God's children."

Father Rey had been quiet to this point. Now, he suddenly had a moment of enlightenment. "Of course," he cried. "He would be able to elude a mortal man, but one of his own kind…" He looked over at the Pontiff.

"That's right, my son," Pope Paul confirmed his suspicions. "An abomination can be found by another abomination. Will she do it?"

"By my reckoning the church has held her prisoner in Grenada Cathedral since ordered by Pope Clement the Sixth in 1348. It's been one hundred and ninety one years. She will do anything for freedom; however, the isolation has turned her mad."

"Can you get through to her?" asked the Pontiff. "Tell her that it is for the church of God, and it is an opportunity for her to save her soul."

"Excellency, as you are no doubt aware, this one has no soul," Father Rey pointed out.

"Exactly," the Pontiff agreed. "God will not punish us for deceiving her. She does not exist in His eyes."

"Excellency?" Friar Gaspar questioned. "What are these strange things of which you speak?"

"Not now, Gaspar," answered Father Rey. "We will speak no more of this for now. Pay attention to the master plan of our Emperor."

Charles continued as if the side conversation among the three holy men did not happen. "I am charging each of you to take part in a holy crusade to find and conquer this man, El Dorado. Return the great treasure that he controls to Spain. By all accounts the load will fill an entire armada and will sustain the Empire for a generation."

"Where do we begin?" asked a confounded Gonzalo.

Charles explained the plan. "Tomorrow morning, General de Vargas and his men will accompany Captain Pinzon to the port of Malaga to prepare a waiting fleet of ships. Captain Pinzon, the Nina is once again at your disposal."

"Gonzalo, you will go with Friar Gaspar and Father Rey to Grenada Cathedral. He will turn a prisoner over to your care. Pay attention to me, Gonzalo, beware. Do exactly with this one as the Father instructs. Do not deviate, and do not fail me.

"Father Rey is to remain at Grenada. Gonzalo, you and Friar Gaspar are to escort the prisoner to Malaga where you will meet up with Pinzon on the Nina. Then set sail at once for Lima."

"Lima!" Gonzalo shouted. "You are sending me to my brother?"

"Yes, young friend," replied Charles. "This is only the beginning. You need to inform your brother of our plans. I want you to go to Guayaquil and also inform your cousin. I want him to supply General de Vargas and his men for a great journey inland. Sanchez will command his men, but you and Gaspar will be the guides. Your prisoner will show you the way.

"After you find what we are seeking, return to Guayaquil. Captain Pinzon will be waiting for you there with the fleet. He will return the bounty to me."

Charles started to laugh again. "Gonzalo, if your mission is successful, I will appoint you Governor of Quito. You will be more famous than either your brother or your cousin."

"After that, what are we to do with this, El Dorado and the prisoner?" Gonzalo asked.

Charles couldn't stop laughing. "I told you, didn't I? You will be governor. They are completely at your disposal. Do with them as you wish."

"No," interrupted Father Rey. "You should kill both of them."

"Am I to return to Spain?" asked Friar Gaspar.

"Absolutely not," Charles told him. "We need a zealous man like you in the new world. I want you to remain with Gonzalo in Quito. At the direction of His Excellency, I have decided to name you as Archbishop of New Andalusia."

Gaspar and Gonzalo were both reeling as they returned to their quarters.

"I'm troubled," Gonzalo confessed to Gaspar. "The fate of the Empire hangs on the cooperation of one prisoner. What are we to do?"

Gaspar recalled the conversation between Pope Paul and Father Rey. He struggled with the meaning of it. "Things are at work here of which I have limited knowledge," he admitted to Gonzalo. "I fear that once we leave this place tomorrow, we will never see it again."

CHAPTER 13

Anne Sprague was sleeping in her room at the Frankfurt Royale when she was awakened by a crisp rat-tat-tat at her door. She debated to herself whether to ignore the interruption. She glanced at the big red numerals of the digital alarm clock on the nightstand.

Four and a half hours until we take off, she thought. *I need to get some more sleep.* Just as she drifted back into unconsciousness, Anne heard another rat-tat-tat. This time it was executed with a bit more assertiveness.

Shit, she thought. *I hope this isn't Joel. I told him that he couldn't get into my pants just by buying me one lousy painting.*

A voice interrupted her thoughts. It was muffled as it carried through the hotel room door.

"Fraulein Sprague? Your friend, Derek Dunbar, sent me to see you. Are you in?"

"Derek?" she repeated as she snapped awake. "Just a minute." The Royale supplied all of their guests with long, white, terry cloth bathrobes. Anne jumped up and grabbed the robe off its peg behind the bathroom door. She tied the sash in the front while walking to the door.

Anne felt somewhat uncomfortable about the situation. She saw a well-dressed, pleasant-appearing man through the peephole.

"Did you say that you are Derek's friend?" she inquired.

"Actually, Fraulein Sprague, I am Derek's attorney." After a short pause he quickly added, "and his friend."

"What do you want?" she asked still reluctant to open the door.

"Derek has asked me to give you a message."

"What's the message?"

"Please, Fraulein Sprague, it is too difficult to speak with you this way. Would you please let me in?"

"I just got out of bed."

Sensing her discomfort, Klaus suggested an alternative.

"Please excuse me. Of course, you do not know me. Would you feel more secure if we could meet in ten minutes down at the hotel bar? Please, it is very important."

"Make it twenty minutes," she replied. "I want to shower first."

"As you wish," he acquiesced. "I will be waiting for you."

Anne watched through the peephole as he disappeared.

This is mysterious, she thought. Then a smile crossed her face. *Derek needs me for something. Now there is a man that I would happily allow to share my bed. All he would have to do is ask. He wouldn't even have to buy me a painting.*

Anne decided to go ahead and get dressed up in her uniform and pack for the return trip. She gave up getting any additional sleep and sensed that her meeting with this mysterious attorney friend of Derek's would probably take some time.

Klaus watched as she entered the bar. Anne had her carry-on bag in tow. It was a handsome, black leather valet with shiny, silver wheels. The left wheel was stiff and made an annoying "eek, eek, eek" sound. She didn't see him at first, so Klaus waved his hand to get her attention. Anne walked over, sat at his table, and retracted the telescoping handle on the bag.

Klaus pushed his business card across the table.

"Please accept my apologies for disturbing you. I know that you will be leaving soon, but the situation is urgent. Otherwise, I would not have bothered you in your room."

Anne studied his card. Written in German, it did not mean much to her, but she sensed that the man was legitimate.

"I understand," she spoke. "Tell me about Derek. How can I help him?"

"He has a personal favor to ask of you. I know what it is, but it is weighty enough that he would like to talk to you in person. As you may know, he is being detained at a local police station not far from here. Would you kindly consent to allow me to drive you there?"

Anne was still unsure and gave him a suspicious look.

"Ravioli," blurted Klaus.

She gave him an even stranger look.

"Derek told me that you might be hesitant to get into a car with a strange man, so he told me to tell you that he always selects ravioli as his in-flight meal. He also tells you to leave the parsley on top. He likes to eat the parsley."

Anne began to feel more at ease.

"Did he tell you about the special treatment?"

"Why yes, Fraulein Sprague. You always cut the ravioli squares for him ahead of time so that they cool down faster."

Anne chuckled, "I wouldn't do that for just any man, Mr. Hall. He's special. If Derek wouldn't already have a woman, he wouldn't stand a chance. I'd spoil him in ways he couldn't possibly imagine."

Now Klaus started to feel ill at ease. He cut her off.

"I'm glad that you are so fond of him. He needs your help."

"Well, let's get going," Anne ordered as she looked at her watch. "Time is growing short."

Klaus Hall took pride in his professionalism as a lawyer, but he couldn't help dwelling on Anne Sprague's good looks. As they walked to his car, the old Beatles tune invaded his mind.

Something in the way she moves, he thought. He succumbed to his urge to flirt with her.

"Derek sure was right," he stated.

Anne turned to look at him. "What was Derek right about?"

"You have the most beautiful deep green eyes!"

"Derek said that?" she asked surprised.

"Well, no," Klaus replied suddenly embarrassed. "I'm sure though that he thinks so."

"Really!" she teased him.

Klaus was upset. He was in deep and seriously wanted to extricate himself.

"I'm sorry, Fraulein Sprague. I shouldn't have said that. It was inappropriate and unprofessional. Please except my apology once again."

"Nonsense, Mr. Hall. Feel free to compliment me anytime."

American women, are they always so informal? Klaus thought.

German men, are they always so uptight? Anne thought.

The valet didn't think anything. It just rolled along serenading both of them to the sound of "eek, eek, eek."

The trip to the police station was a short ten minutes. During the ride, Anne thought about what Derek could possibly want with her. Like everyone else, she was frightened when he passed out on the flight from BWI. She remained unconvinced that he was involved with drugs. The story Joel Washington told cast even more doubt in her mind about Derek's guilt in the matter. Anne knew from experience that Derek possessed unwavering self-control. He wouldn't let anything interfere with his ability to safely pilot his passengers and crew to their destination. He also wouldn't allow any of her advances to crack his loyalty to Sharon. She entertained the thought that this time it might be somehow different.

He needs me, she thought to herself.

The intrigue involved with meeting him this way, and all of the rumors surrounding the incident, excited her. Unconsciously, Anne removed a mirror from her purse to check her hair and make up.

"The mirror on the back side of the sun visor has a light," Klaus said trying to be helpful.

"Thanks," replied Anne. She decided that everything was properly in place and snapped her purse shut.

Derek heard two sets of feet clip clopping against the hard floor as they approached his cell. He stood to greet his visitors.

"Hello, Annie, thanks for coming. Klaus, thanks for escorting her to me."

"Glad to be of service, as always," Klaus bowed slightly.

Anne inspected Derek. He was understandably disheveled. His face was wrinkled from worrying, but in her eyes this made him appear even more rugged and masculine. When the guard unlocked the door and allowed them to enter, Anne walked right up to Derek and hugged him. He welcomed this outpouring of warmth from her and was reluctant to let her go.

Klaus pulled the chair out from under the table. He spun it around and sat on it backwards, repeating this behavior from his previous visit.

Derek pulled away from Anne but kept hold of her hand. It felt warm and comforting. They sat on the cot side by side.

"I came as soon as I could, Derek. I'm so glad that you asked for me. You know that I'll do whatever I can to help you."

"Annie, I appreciate that more than you can know, but you better listen to what I have to ask first."

Derek broke eye contact with Anne and looked over at Klaus.

"Did you tell her about what you heard?" he asked.

"Not yet," Klaus answered. "Now that we are together, we can proceed."

Klaus related about how he found Joel Washington at the bar and how he had eavesdropped into the conversations between Anne and Joel. Still holding her hand, Derek felt it tense up as Klaus described how she left the bar with Joel.

"Derek, I want you to know that nothing happened between Joel and me."

He looked at her and smiled, "Of course nothing happened. You're much too classy a lady to allow yourself to sink to the level of a Joel Washington."

After a pause he went on, "Just the same, you should've let him buy you one of those paintings."

Anne laughed, "My thoughts exactly."

Klaus cleared his throat, and they both looked his way.

"Fraulein Sprague, the German authorities have assured me that Derek has not been the subject of any investigation. It is unlikely that the Americans would have initiated any undercover sting on foreign soil. We are of the opinion that Joel Washington and maybe other persons are trying to discredit Derek."

Anne looked from Klaus to Derek. The pause became uncomfortably long, and she became defensive. She pulled her hand from Derek and expressed with horror, "You don't think that I'm involved?"

"Of course not, Fraulein Sprague," assured Klaus. "Obviously Joel would not have been speaking with you in this manner if you were already part of the plan."

Derek sighed. He wished there was a way that he could take hold of Anne's hand again.

"Annie, Klaus thinks that Washington wants you really badly."

"Yeah, that's obvious," Anne said as she rolled her eyes in disdain.

"He also thinks that Washington was on the verge of blabbing to you the whole story about what really is going down with me."

"I suppose that's possible. He had been drinking pretty heavy."

Anne thought about the probability that Joel would confide in her. It dawned on her what she supposed that Derek was going to ask her to do. Anne's heart ached. She would do just about anything to help Derek, but she was hurt that he was actually expecting her to become a whore.

"You, you want me to sleep with him?" her voice shook.

Derek was shocked, "What are you talking about?"

Anne grabbed a tissue from her purse and wiped her eyes.

"It sounds to me like you want me to get him drunk and take him to bed in order to get him to talk," she sniffled.

Not a bad idea, Klaus considered to himself.

"Hell no!" Derek stated forcefully. He reached over and once again took her hand. Squeezing it, Derek commanded, "Annie, look at me."

She looked up. A few feet away, Klaus noticed how beautifully her moist green eyes sparkled.

"Annie, I have no right to ask that, and I wouldn't. You mean a lot to me. You're a dear friend."

Anne saw from his eyes that Derek meant every word. She was touched.

The scene also moved Klaus, but he wanted to get them back on track.

"Fraulein Sprague, no gentleman would ever ask something so disgusting from a woman. We want you to get him drunk, yes. We want you to stay in the security of a public place, like the bar of the Royale Hotel. If you could get him to reveal to you what he has done to Derek, we could capture it on tape. This evidence would free Derek."

"You want me to set him up, just like he set up Derek?" she asked Klaus, wanting to make sure that she fully understood his intentions.

"It would help me out, Annie," Derek pleaded. "The choice is yours. I promise that I will not think less of you if you are uncomfortable with this."

Anne squeezed Derek's hand and then let go.

"Mr. Hall, can I speak privately with Derek?"

"Of course." Klaus immediately stood and motioned for the guard. "Call me when I can return."

After Klaus walked out of the holding area, Anne stood and walked over to the table.

Derek remained seated on the cot. She had her back turned to him and began to tap on the table top with her right index finger.

"Derek," she breathed almost in a whisper. "I'm twenty-nine years old. I've had my share of relationships with men. All of them were pretty much disasters. I don't know. Maybe I try too hard and just expect too much out of a relationship."

Derek got up, walked over to Anne, and put his arms around her from behind. He spoke softly into her ear.

"Annie, there is no need for you to feel insecure. I've known you for the past two of those twenty-nine years. Not only are you drop-dead gorgeous, but also you're a kind and giving soul. Any man that allows a relationship with you to become a disaster isn't much of a man."

Anne slipped around inside his arms and faced him. They were now locked in a hug. She laid her head against his chest. Very gently, she began to rock her stomach back and forth against where it touched his groin.

"You're a man that wouldn't allow a relationship with me to become a disaster, would you?"

Derek felt himself respond to her stimulation. She was soothing and warm. The sweet smell of her hair added to his pleasure. He fought the urge to push harder into her touch, but at the same time, he didn't let her go.

"If circumstances were different, Annie," he began.

"I love you, Derek," she admitted. "I've loved you for a long time."

He continued to hold onto her. Many thoughts raced through Derek's mind.

I know you do, he thought to himself. *All of you do. I can see it in every woman's eyes. It's been that way since puberty. It was great back then. With barely a glance, I was able to convince all of you to make love with me. Why? What is it that makes you want to throw yourselves at me? I'm not a kid anymore. I've torn apart the hearts of so many of you. I see all of your faces in my nightmares. I can't do this to you anymore. That's why I've settled down with Sharon, just Sharon. She's my one and only. But what about this woman of my dreams that wants me to come to her? She is real, isn't she? Or am I losing my mind? No, she's real. I can feel her. She needs me. She is consumed with her need for me. Why? I'm afraid of her, aren't I?*

All the while Derek was daydreaming, Anne increased the pressure of her rocking against him. With eyes closed and her head still resting on his chest, Anne felt Derek achieve a full erection. She longed to lay with him, even if it had to be on this jailhouse cot.

Derek's daydream ended as he realized what was happening. He allowed himself to continue in the warm embrace for a while. Tenderly, Derek began to unfold himself from the embrace. Maintaining his hold on both of Anne's hands, he looked into her pretty eyes.

"I love you too, Annie," he finally told her. "It's just that Sharon is my first love. I need to remain loyal to her. Please understand."

"I know, Derek," she smiled while blinking back tears. "You don't have to explain."

They talked for some time, and then Derek summoned Klaus Hall to return.

"I'm going to help Derek," Anne announced to Klaus. "What specifically do you want me to do?"

"Continue being friendly with this Joel Washington," he answered her. "Let me drive you back to the airport. Go home. In a few days you will return, and we will have all of the arrangements made."

"Annie, if you have second thoughts about this…"

"I know," she interrupted Derek, "I'm going to do this for you, don't worry."

"I'm not worried about me. I'm worried about you," fretted Derek.

"I'll be just fine. We'll be in a public place. Klaus will not let anyone hurt me."

"You can count on that for sure," interjected Klaus.

The guard opened the door to let them out.

"Good bye for now, Derek," Anne smiled and blew him a kiss.

As she walked down the hall, Derek grabbed Klaus's arm.

"Klaus, I hope we're doing the right thing. She's very fragile."

He laughed, "My dear Mr. Dunbar, you just feel that way because you have feelings for her. We always want to protect those we love. I believe that you will find that she is actually a very strong woman."

Before Klaus Hall walked away, he reassured Derek. "I'm afraid that I've developed feelings for her too. Really, what man wouldn't," he laughed. "She's very pretty, isn't she? I will protect her.

"We both better be careful," he joked. "I wouldn't want to make Mrs. Hall jealous, and I'm sure you feel the same way about your Sharon. You will see her tomorrow. I will bring her to you right away after her plane lands. Get a good night's sleep."

Derek was once again alone in his cell. "A good night's sleep?" he asked of the walls. "If only it were possible."

CHAPTER 14

Sara slept in her prison in the catacombs and dreamed of a time long ago.

Leon was a merchant from Grenada. He traveled the great overland trade route from Europe to Asia. Leon found Sara at a market in Constantinople. She was telling a story to little children while their parents shopped. She glanced over to the doorway and was startled to see him standing there.

Sara jumped and grabbed the robe lying at her side. She completely covered herself and walked over to speak with the man.

"Many pardons," she apologized while gazing at the ground. "I wasn't expecting anyone to return so soon. Which one of these little ones is yours?"

"You are of Iberian descent, are you not?" he asked her.

"No, sir, I was born in Judea," she replied.

"There is no need for you to cover yourself in front of me. I am a Christian, and besides, it is such a waste. You are striking."

Sara guessed that he was not there to retrieve a child. "It is out of respect for those who are not Christian," she informed him. "I make my living by watching children from many tribes and religions while their parents shop. How is it that I may be of service to you?"

"Two things," he told her. "First, have you seen a goat run by here? It got away from me. It was to feed me for the long journey back to Spain."

"Poor thing," Sara joked with him. "Wouldn't you run?"

"Animals are meant to be eaten, aren't they?" he asked.

She no longer felt like joking. "What is the other thing you want of me?" she inquired never once looking up from the ground.

"Your name?" he requested.

"In your language, I am called Sara."

"Sara," he repeated. "Look at me."

"No, sir, one of my other customers might come. If they are Moslem, they will take offense."

"I thought you told me that you weren't expecting anyone soon?"

"One of the parents might cut their shopping short and return…"

"Sara," he stopped her. "Look at me."

"Please, no," she beseeched him.

He reached down and gently lifted her chin.

"Don't," she begged.

Their eyes met. He stared into them for a full minute of time and let go of her chin.

"Yes, very pretty," he shrugged. "Well, I'll be looking for that goat now. Good bye."

As he walked out the door, Sara was dumbstruck. *How could this be? This man invites torment and willingly walks away?* she thought to herself.

"Wait," she yelled.

"Yes," he responded.

She didn't know what to say. "Your name?" she inquired. "I wish to know the name of the handsome man that gazed into my eyes. You did gaze, didn't you? You are not blind, are you?"

He could hardly contain himself. "Leon is my name. I gazed deeply into those stunning eyes, and no, I am not blind. Good bye, maiden."

One of the children started crying, and she had to let the man go.

"Sorry that I left you alone, little ones. Where was I in telling you the story?"

She started again with the children. Leon hid from view outside the door and peeked back in at her. He watched in wonder at how well Sara held the attention of these children, marveling at her poise and beauty. Dropping the charade, Leon closed his eyes and reached out to her.

Sara stopped talking to the children in mid-sentence, stood up, and stared at the doorway. Their eyes locked again.

Leon smiled. "Hello, Sara, I am truly blessed to be able to make your acquaintance."

She walked over and playfully punched him in the arm. All of the children laughed. "You tricked me," she giggled. "I thought that perhaps the curse was lifted from me."

He held both of her hands and kissed Sara on the forehead. "Oh, no, maiden, I am completely under your spell."

They embraced.

The children squealed with delight and clapped their hands.

That evening they met in Leon's tent.

"You are a natural with those children," Leon observed.

"I'm fond of all the little ones," Sara explained. "They bring me much joy. It is a great way to make a living."

"Are you paid well for being a baby sitter?"

"I wouldn't say that I am well paid, but I make enough to live comfortably. Anyway, I consider myself much more than a baby sitter. There are times when I make a real difference in one of their lives. It provides me with a sense of purpose. Helping them, Leon, can be rewarding. Also, these little ones are not affected by the dreaded curse. I can look at and touch them without fear of causing them pain."

Leon studied her for some time. "Sara, you could be so much more."

"I already have been," she told him. "I've led lives that most women could only dream about. It's a hollow existence, Leon. It's too easy to get what I want by destroying men. The challenge is to enrich their lives. This in turn makes me feel good. I'm happier now than I ever was as a queen. Besides, this simpler life with the children is atonement for things that I have done in the past that I am not proud of."

"To what end?" he argued. "Someday you and I will both die. In that moment, it is over. Why not ravage this existence of theirs?"

Sara looked down and paused in deep thought. "Leon, I believe that there is hope for us, otherwise we would feel no pain."

"Don't confuse emotional pain with passion," he corrected her.

"You aren't very old, right?" she asked of him.

He glanced suspiciously at her and asked, "What do you mean by that?"

"After many lifetimes, one reaches a certain level of understanding. Men and women live and grow old and die. In time, they are forgotten while we remain. It is frustrating, Leon. When we don't show signs of age, they begin to wonder about us. Then we always have to run far away and start over. It is too tiring to live a high life. Better it is to remain anonymous in the shadows. A modest life, Leon, is a happier one. You, too, will learn this in time."

"Apparently there is much that I have yet to learn," he lamented. He studied her some more. "Sara, exactly how old are you, anyway?"

She laughed at him. "Leon, you do have much to learn. Never ask a lady that question."

He grew serious. "Will you teach me?"

She contemplated her own coming of age and the tutelage that she received from Helena. "Looking back at my life, I believe that my teacher released me too soon. I made some terribly painful mistakes. Perhaps I can spare you some of that pain."

"That settles it," Leon clapped his hands. "Tomorrow we begin the trip back to Grenada."

"Not so fast," she stopped him. "If you want me to teach you, you are going to have to linger here with me."

Sara felt pity at the disappointed look that crossed his handsome face.

"My goods," he argued. "Spices and silk will make me a rich man. I have to get back. Can't you travel to Grenada and stay with me for some time? You can always return."

"I could," she considered, "but aren't you forgetting about something?" Sara held up the robe that was crumpled up beside her. "In the Moslem world, my life is considerably easier. There are no prying eyes. I am commanded by law to stay covered and to always look down. There is great freedom in that for me."

Leon was dejected and sighed, "I understand."

Sara considered the thrill it would be for her to spend time with Leon. She didn't want to let go either. "You would have to protect me," Sara told him.

Leon looked at her but said nothing. He waited for Sara to explain.

"Can you keep me hidden away in your household? I could remain covered so far as it is the custom in your land."

"That should not be much of a problem," Leon confirmed. "The Moslem influence remains firmly entrenched in Spain."

"Great," she giggled. "Now it is time for your first lesson."

"I am your humble student," Leon bowed low.

"The males of our kind don't get used up during sex with the females of our kind."

"So I have been told," he informed her.

"I don't do that to human men anymore," she said with a grin. "It's been a long time, Leon, too long."

"Teach me!" he commanded.

Sara held onto Leon as they laid together after making love. He was facing away from her, and she pressed tightly against him. She heard him ask, "Sara, what is the greatest lesson that you have learned?"

"My," she exhaled on the back of his neck. "Such a heavy question?"

After pondering his request, she began to blink back tears. "Never fall in love with one of them. They grow old. It hurts to watch them fade."

Leon felt the stream from one of Sara's tears running down his shoulder.

She does feel emotional pain, he realized with astonishment. *Could it be that we do have souls?* he considered to himself.

Sara continued to dream while she slept in her prison. She dreamed of a happy year with Leon in Grenada. They both developed deep feelings for each other and began to ponder the possibility of staying together indefinitely. Sara's influence over Leon was apparent. He became a kinder man, helpful to his friends and neighbors. Instead of accumulating the riches he received from his trade, Leon gave much of it away. He even found some measure of happiness in doing so.

Sara stirred in her sleep as the dream she was having turned bad. She recalled in her mind the day it started. They were having a conversation about how Leon would have to figure a way to extricate himself from this life in a few years. He had grown too popular.

One of the neighbor children that Sara adored burst into their home. "Mummy doesn't feel well," the little boy said and started to cry.

Sara picked him up. "Don't cry," she told the little boy. "Let's go and visit your mummy and cheer her up." The boy felt hot to Sara. She put a hand to his forehead.

"Leon, he's burning up," Sara told him quietly.

He became alarmed. "I'd better come with you."

They found the boy's mother to be delirious. She was perspiring heavily.

"Bring me some water, Leon," Sara charged him. She lifted the woman's arm and noticed large black bruises along the inside of her upper arm.

Leon returned with the water, and Sara showed him the bruises.

"Buboes," Leon muttered. "Sara, it's the Black Death."

The year was 1348 and the plague decimated the population of Europe. Sara had seen nothing like it since the great Jerusalem famine. Bodies were piled high in the streets. The living were too sick to mourn for the dead. Corpses were gathered into horse drawn wagons and buried in mass graves.

The stench was so great that people carried posies with them. When it became overwhelming, they would sniff the small flowers to cover the smell. The people also believed that sniffing these flowers strengthened them against the disease.

The pattern was the same. First came the fever, then the black bubonic bruises along the lymph nodes, then delirium, and finally death. The sick flocked to the great cathedral of Grenada, but soon there were no priests available to administer last rights. They were all dead. Sara and Leon toiled in the cathedral helping to make the dying ones more comfortable. They were counted among the half of the population that survived. No one took notice, until it got worse.

After the first wave passed, a deadlier pneumonic form of the disease seized the land. This one passed from person to person by coughing and sneezing. Death took them so quickly that the black bruises never even had a chance to appear. The mortality rate was greater than 95%.

Once again, Sara and Leon assisted in the cathedral. It became a quarantine zone. The sick were driven into the great building. None emerged unless carried out dead. A ring of soldiers under the command of Bishop Arturo Bolivar surrounded the grounds. Archers killed anyone attempting to leave in order to protect the rest of the citizenry. In time, this wave also passed.

Sara and Leon watched helplessly as the last of their patients died. They were alone in the cathedral. When they appeared together at the entrance, Bishop Bolivar ordered them to remain. After ten days had passed, he was convinced that Sara and Leon were no threat. They were allowed to leave.

Sara tossed more violently in her sleep as she recalled the tumult that followed.

Interpreting the survival of Sara and Leon as a sign of God's grace, Bishop Bolivar sent word of the account to Pope Clement in Rome. In time, the Pontiff summoned the Bishop to obtain a detailed accounting of the events.

Clement expressed enthusiasm about the significance of this miracle, but he also had some reservations. Finally, he confided in the Bishop about his uncertainties.

"Arturo, the significance of your accounting concerning this young miracle couple is not lost on me. If these two were truly blessed by God in reward for their courage while ministering to the sick, it would serve as a source of inspiration for generations. On the other hand, we must be sure that there is no other explanation."

"I was there, your Excellency," reassured Arturo. "No other soul escaped the pestilence. Those in their care sneezed and coughed in the same rooms as the couple. Surely it is only by divine providence that these two have survived."

The Pontiff led the Bishop to a side room filled with many ancient manuscripts. He unlocked and opened one old dusty chest and withdrew several scrolls. Arturo watched as the Pontiff unrolled the dozen or so old documents.

"Arturo, these scrolls are drawings of people. Please examine them, and tell me if any of these drawings resemble the likeness of your man and woman from Grenada."

The bishop did not understand this request but carefully inspected the drawings. The third scroll was a drawing of Sara. None of the scrolls resembled Leon.

"Excellency!" Arturo exclaimed. "There is no mistaking that this drawing is of the young woman. The artist has captured her features to perfection. Look at the eyes and the hair. How did you come to possess this? What is this mystery?"

Clement groaned and placed a hand on Arturo's shoulder.

"My fears are proven true," he uttered to Arturo. "This is no miracle but rather a mockery. It is the abomination."

Arturo studied the Pontiff for some further explanation. Clement removed the hand from his shoulder and spoke, "Read the description."

Unrolling the scroll, Arturo found near the margin some text written in Latin. It read, "Wife of Nicanor, a distinguished Tribune of Rome. This woman was observed in the city for 72 years after his death. She disappeared Anno Domini 164."

Now even more puzzled, Arturo looked at the Pontiff with questioning eyes.

"Throughout human history they appear from time to time," the Pontiff explained. "When suspected by the church, their likeness and actions are recorded. This woman could not remain a young maiden forever if she were human. She should have died centuries ago.

"Return to Grenada," Clement ordered. "If these two can still be found, remove them to the cathedral for examination. They are to be kept there for study or until such time that the Church may find a use for them."

Her infatuation with Rome led an inexperienced Sara to linger there too long. She ignored Helena's advice about leading an unassuming life.

Sara moaned while sleeping and dreaming.

It was late in the year. The cold weather had pushed the plague into remission. Leon held Sara closely as they slept. A company of soldiers led by Bishop Arturo Bolivar burst into the home violating their sleep. Sara and Leon snapped awake, wide-eyed and fearful.

The Bishop walked into their chamber, unrolled a parchment, and read from the edict. "By order of his Excellency, Pope Clement the Sixth, the two subjects known as Leon and Sara are to be removed to Grenada Cathedral where they are to be examined under the eyes of God."

Arturo looked at the soldiers and made a motion for them to grab Sara and Leon.

Leon jumped up and grabbed the sword from its place near the bed. Sara grabbed her ancient dagger but held it behind her back.

"What is the meaning of this?" Leon demanded in a threatening manner. "Have we not proven ourselves as faithful subjects, ministering to those in need in the very place that you would now take us?"

Sara urgently begged him, "Leon, there are too many. Do not resist. We will find another way."

They moved in, and Leon began to fight them off.

Sara had not overtly used her powers on mortal men for centuries, since it always caused harm. Now in desperation, she made an appeal to Arturo.

"Father Bolivar, look at me!" she cried above the noise of Leon's struggle. "This is not what you want, is it? Order them to stop fighting."

He looked away and held a crucifix between them.

"I've been warned about your witchery," he shouted. "Get behind me, Satan."

Leon pierced the stomach of one of the soldiers and gashed the arm of another. They both fell down screaming. All restraint by the other soldiers vanished. They closed in on Leon. He felt cold metal bite at his thigh. During the rush, one of the men slipped and fell to the floor. From his position, he was able to slice at Leon above the knee. The pain caused Leon to momentarily lose his concentration. The others punctured him throughout his body.

While this was happening, Arturo approached Sara. She held out the dagger in defense, but he easily grabbed it away and threw her to the ground. He bound Sara's hands and blindfolded her so that she could no longer make eye contact.

Sara did not see Leon die, but she felt his last mental touch as he sent it out to her. By the time she was able to acknowledge it, Leon was already dead.

The dream climaxed, and Sara awoke. She sat anguished on the edge of her bed.

Sara moaned, "An eternity I would languish here if I could have you back, Leon, my love."

Sara lost her will to achieve salvation. The kindness shown her by the young sexton, Juana, offered a spark of hope, but the dream of Leon and of his death crushed her spirit once again.

"I am not the evil," Sara told herself. "Leon and I helped and comforted them. In return, they killed my sweet man and imposed this purgatory on me.

"Curse them all," she wailed. "If I survive and escape this place, I will use all of my powers to conquer and dominate them."

*****

Gonzalo was troubled as they prepared for the journey from Madrid to Grenada. Charles was a man that he had idolized all of his life, a man in whose name he fought and would have given his life. Now in Gonzalo's mind, the Emperor had proven himself a foolish dreamer. As he rode along side Friar Gaspar, Gonzalo felt compelled to share his thoughts.

"Gaspar, what are we doing?" he inquired. "Charles actually believes in legends spouted by heathens? We blindly go along with this madness and agree to lead an impossible quest? Is this some sort of twisted test of our character? Does he expect us to resist?"

Gaspar thought about what Charles was asking and replied, "No, this is no test of our loyalty. Many powerful men were at that meeting along with the Pontiff. It was too elaborate to be merely a scheme. I believe the Emperor is sincere in what he is asking us to do."

"It seems so unreal," Gonzalo responded. "Think of it. The Empire is in financial difficulty. The future of our way of life depends on the ability of a strange prisoner to lead us to a mythical man hidden away in the new world."

Gaspar reassured him, "I do not doubt the Emperor's sincerity, Gonzalo, but know that I am of the same mind as you are. I have my doubts. Did you overhear the strange conversation between the Pontiff and Father Rey about our prisoner?"

"Nothing that I could understand," answered Gonzalo. "There were many things said and implied that I could not understand. Gaspar, I do not know these men well, but I do know my brother. I can't wait until we see him again. He is a person that is not given to nonsense. If there is any truth to this, he will be able to provide a clear explanation."

"I have not lost my faith in our Pontiff, either," added Gaspar. "He has entrusted Father Rey with some knowledge that has not yet been told to us. Perhaps, there are certain facts that they did not wish to reveal to the others."

"Then the key to this mystery lies with the good Father," Gonzalo summarized. "We are away from the others now. Let's ask him about it."

Later that morning, the three men, Gonzalo Pizarro, Friar Gaspar de Carvajal, and Father Rey set out on horseback for Grenada. The Father noticed the anticipation in the eyes of the other two and thought about how he could explain the story of Sara. Finally, about mid-day, Gonzalo's patience had reached its limit.

"Father Rey," he barked. "Many things were said at the meeting last night.

The one thing requiring an immediate explanation would be the reason behind why Friar Gaspar and I are accompanying you to Grenada. Who is this prisoner, and what special powers will assist us in our quest?"

The Father glanced around to make sure that they were alone on the road. He began to explain. "You must understand that what I am going to relate must remain locked forever within you. A select few of us possess this knowledge — the Pontiff, the Emperor, and a number of clergy. Now the ring is expanded to include the two of you. Gonzalo, you have the privilege of being the only living of the laity to learn of this sacred secret."

Gonzalo was unimpressed. He had his fill of secrets and fantastic stories. "What makes this secret so sacred?" he asked mockingly.

Father Rey tolerated the impertinence of the young soldier and went on to explain. "This knowledge is too frightening for the masses. It would shake their faith in the authority of the Pontiff and his Holy Emperor. Legitimate miracles would begin to be questioned. Gonzalo, this is not the stuff for those unlearned in the scriptures."

"I see," Gonzalo smirked. "Ignorance is bliss."

Friar Gaspar started to become caught up in the words of the Father and asked him to continue.

"Since the time of Christ, the Christian Church has been tracking an abomination that dwells on this Earth alongside of God's children. Their numbers now are very few. We have lost track of them all, except for the one that we hold prisoner and this El Dorado."

Father Rey paused to allow what he had just said to sink in. He continued. "Your prisoner is a woman. She is ancient and possesses great power, particularly over men. She can use these powers to help you find El Dorado. The women sextons of the cathedral care for her. No man sees her. I have gazed at her only one time and for a brief moment. Despite her age, she remains an irresistible temptress. There are strict rules that must be followed while she remains alive and under your care."

Gonzalo was amused. *A sexy old woman!* he thought to himself before turning his attention back to the Father.

"The power comes from her mind, but the weapon is her eyes. Now that we have a fixed purpose for this one, we will upon our arrival immediately pluck out her eyes. This will greatly reduce her threat to you."

"Will she survive that?" asked Gaspar. "You said she is an old woman."

"She has the strength to endure it," confirmed the Father. "I will release her to you after she heals. Listen to me, Gaspar and Gonzalo, she will remain a risk to you even after this procedure. You must follow my instructions."

Father Rey paused again to be sure they were listening to him.

"While in your charge," he continued, "I will send one of the sextons, a woman, with you to continue to care for her. Keep them isolated to the best of your ability. You should initiate all communications by using the sexton as an intermediary. If it becomes necessary to speak with her in person, only do so with the two of you together and with the sexton at your side. You will be able to stop each other if one of you should happen to fall under her spell. Under no circumstances should you allow yourselves to remain alone in her presence. It would be ruinous to our quest."

Friar Gaspar said nothing in response. He was deep in thought considering the improbable.

Gonzalo questioned his own sanity for allowing himself to even consider this folly. After a few moments he asked the Father, "What is this woman's name, and how is it that she became your prisoner?"

Without hesitation, Father Rey spoke, "The creature calls herself Sara. She was captured by the forces under Pope Clement the Sixth during the time of the great plague."

"The great plague!" gasped Gonzalo. "That was two hundred years ago."

Father Rey interrupted him, "We have records of her long before that time. This woman is at least fifteen hundred years old."

Gonzalo stopped his horse and dismounted. He walked over to the side of the road and stared off into the distance. He didn't know whether to laugh or cry. The two holy men remained mounted and waited for him. Gaspar grabbed the reins of Gonzalo's horse. Finally, Gonzalo turned and began a tirade.

"An Emperor possesses a mind filled with fantasies. Our Empire has no means of support. There exists a new world filled with dreams of an old man and his gold. A Pope plays along with these delusions, and now you spin tales of an ageless witch. With all due respect, Father Rey, and make no mistake, very little respect for you remains within me, I am going home."

With that Gonzalo took the reins of his horse from Friar Gaspar, mounted, and began to ride in the opposite direction away from them.

Father Rey shouted at him. "Gonzalo Pizarro, you are under direct command from Emperor Charles the Fifth and his Excellency Pope Paul the Third. Do you disobey their command and betray their trust in you?"

Gonzalo ignored him and continued to ride away.

Friar Gaspar grabbed the Father's arm and sought confirmation of what he had just concluded, "She is a product of the Great Rebellion, isn't she?"

Father Rey nodded.

"Stay here, Father, I will ride and bring him back."

A few minutes later, Friar Gaspar caught up with Gonzalo.

"Hold up, Gonzalo," the friar pleaded as he rode alongside. "I told Father Rey to wait for us. Let's talk about this."

"What is there to talk about," groaned Gonzalo. "Do you know how I feel right now? All of the great men that I've admired since I was a boy have proven to be fools. The idea of a just and noble Holy Roman Empire is all lost to me, Friar. During the past day, all of it has been dashed to pieces. They live in a fantasy world. How can I believe in anything anymore?"

"Hear me out, Gonzalo," the friar beseeched him again. "Please stop."

Out of deference to his friend, Gonzalo complied and reined in his horse. Both men looked at each other.

"You've heard it all the same as I have," Gonzalo said. "You don't believe any of it, do you?"

The friar stalled for a moment while thinking. He offered his opinion. "I don't know what to believe about this," he admitted to Gonzalo with sincerity. "This much I do know for sure. While men can fail us, God does not. There are a number of things for you to consider before you act so rashly."

Gonzalo responded, "The only thing I want to consider right now is the shortest route home, or maybe I will also consider how to wake up from this nightmare."

"What home will you go to?" the friar reminded him. "Father Rey is right, you know. You are under direct order from the most powerful men on Earth. It is not your decision to abandon this quest. How long do you think Charles will allow you to dwell in peace before, in his wrath, he descends upon you with all of his military might? Next week at this time, you will be dead."

"Then I will go into exile," Gonzalo blurted out.

"That is what they are already asking you to do," prompted Gaspar. "What better place to exile yourself than the new world, far away from the wrath of Charles and under the protective arm of your brother? Look, Gonzalo, continue with this, even if it is a pretense on your part to fulfill your duty. Anything can happen along the way."

"What you are saying, good Friar, is that I have no choice. I am to be exiled from my home as either a loyal soldier or as a disobedient criminal."

"Unfortunately, this is true," confirmed Gaspar. "Not only is it true for you, but also for me. Remember that I am bound by the same command."

"Destiny takes us together to the new world, doesn't it, Gaspar?"

"Either destiny or God's will, Gonzalo. If indeed your heroes have been touched in the mind, or if some other evil is at work, maybe it has fallen on us to make it right."

"Saving the Holy Empire is a crushing burden," lamented Gonzalo.

"I will help you to bear it, friend," assured the friar. "Let us ride."

The two of them returned to a waiting Father Rey. They did not speak of the quest again until they reached Grenada.

Juana was now responsible for the care of Sara. She had a kind heart and a great deal of sympathy for Sara. In defiance of Esther's training and of the orders from the church, Juana began to have conversations with her.

"Sara, I have some news for you," Juana whispered to her with delight.

Sara barely acknowledged. Although she welcomed the outpouring of kindness from Juana, she was totally broken. The dream caused her to relive one of the most painful experiences in her life.

"Father Rey ordered me to draw water for your bath early this week. You are going to receive visitors, Sara. I believe that some men will be coming to speak with you."

"Men," Sara murmured. Her face turned fearful, and she began to cry. "Juana, they are coming to torture me. Please help me."

"Hush, child," Juana tried to console her. "The Father would not let anything like that happen to you. You are in the house of God."

"No, you don't understand," Sara sobbed. "When I was first brought here, in the name of God, they violated me in unspeakable ways, probing with objects and cutting me. They never mortally wounded me, but they tortured me to study how I healed. It went on like that for years before they lost interest in me."

Juana didn't believe her. Although she pitied Sara, she was convinced of her madness. Juana thought that Father Rey kept Sara to allow her tortured mind to heal.

"Come, Sara, I will fill this pool with hot water. You can relax and enjoy a soothing bath."

Sara could not be calmed. "Please, Juana," she begged. "When I was brought here, they stashed my personal belongings in a sack. These items could still be in a chest in the anteroom."

"Why yes they are, Sara," smiled Juana. She was pleased that Sara had turned her attention away from the pending visitors. "Esther showed me the sack. She told me to take good care of those things because of their historical value."

"Juana, one of the items in that sack is an old dagger. Please, retrieve it from there and come back and kill me."

"Don't speak of such things, Sara. I could never hurt you."

"Bring it to me, and I will kill myself. I wish to die rather than be violated again. Juana, you have no idea how painful it was. Please, bring the dagger to me."

Juana was touched and began to blink back tears. *Poor tortured soul*, she thought.

CHAPTER 15

Elyria came very close to failing her mission. She followed Juan to the BWI Airport long-term parking lot and carefully tailed them on foot to the shuttle stop. Sharon and Juan were the last two to fit onto the already full shuttle. A distraught Elyria was left behind to wait for the next ride. The terminal was busy, and Elyria had no idea where they could be. She sat on a bench in the terminal and tried to think it through.

This man helping Sharon McGee appears to be a friend. They are traveling together. I observed both of them pack for a lengthy trip. Sharon went to the bank and withdrew a large sum of money. Where could they be going?

As she put it together, Elyria figured that there could be only two logical destinations. Sharon was running away from danger due to the narrow escape with Blaze, or they were fleeing to Germany and Derek. Running away seemed the least likely of these possibilities since Sharon now had a champion at her side. Elyria gambled that the two of them were going to Frankfurt.

Springing from her seat, Elyria ran to the electronic schedule board and homed in on the flights labeled, "International Departures." There were three flights to Frankfurt that afternoon, one each from TransGlobal, Air France, and Lufthansa. Elyria's almost fatal flaw was the assumption that they would choose TransGlobal.

She ran through the terminal to the TransGlobal ticket counter. About fifty people were anxiously waiting in line.

Good, she thought. *They could not have made it to the attendant yet*. Scanning the line, Elyria was unable to find Sharon and the man. She considered whether they could have pre-purchased electronic tickets and would have proceeded directly to the gate.

"No, Sharon's bag is too big. She would have to check it at the ticket counter."

Damn this modern civilization, Elyria cursed to herself. *I long for the jungle and my simple life. This being a Shadow Woman for the Mistress can be burdensome.* She cursed again as she thought of the failure of Blaze and how much more difficult this task had now become.

Air France was the next closest counter. This one was not as crowded, but she couldn't find them here either. *It's possible they could have made it through by now*, she thought.

The Lufthansa line was the shortest. Elyria still did not see them. Assuming that Sharon and the man had cleared the ticket counter, she decided to go ahead and purchase a ticket from Lufthansa. All three flights to Frankfurt departed from the international terminal within two hours of each other, but from different gates. Elyria's plan was to gain entry to the terminal with her ticket and search all three gates for the travelers. If she found them waiting for one of the other flights, Elyria would return, cash in the ticket, and purchase one from the same airline. Worse case scenario was that she would fly to Frankfurt on Lufthansa and try to catch up with Sharon.

She had no idea that they would end at the airport. After dropping Blaze at Sharon's office, Elyria never had an opportunity to return to her rented room. She was carrying no clothing or bags. This would raise suspicion at the ticket counter. Elyria ran through the gift shops in the airport concourse. She purchased a bag, small enough to carry on, but large enough to convince the attendant at the ticket counter that she was a legitimate European traveler.

Next, Elyria purchased an assortment of souvenir tee shirts, sweat pants, a jacket and some personal items. She stuffed them all into the bag and hurried to the Lufthansa counter. This process was taking a great deal of time. She purchased one of the few remaining coach class seats and cleared baggage screening.

Elyria was relieved to spot Sharon on a lounger at the Lufthansa gate. Boarding had already begun. In another few minutes, she never would have known that Sharon was on that particular flight.

After buckling into her seat, Elyria began to unwind. For the first time in the past 24 hours, she could finally get some sleep. She didn't have to maintain a vigil. For at least the next eight hours, Sharon and this strange man were going nowhere.

The uneventful flight to Germany landed at 6:15 a.m. local time. Hank Kimball yawned and glanced over at Sharon.

"Good morning," she greeted him with a smile.

Hank squinted at his watch and groaned. "Quarter after midnight Baltimore time. This is usually about the time that I'm going to bed."

She sympathized with him. "This is one of the reasons that I'm not fond of travel. About the time my body gets used to the new time zone, it's time to return."

"How long will you be visiting your boyfriend?" asked Hank after another long yawn.

"Our return tickets are open ended," Sharon stated as she nudged Juan awake.

They deplaned and queued up in customs. Elyria had already cleared and was discreetly observing them from behind a billboard. After gathering their baggage, Hank, Sharon, and Juan stood together near the rental car counters.

"Can I give you folks a lift?" Hank asked. "I just need to sign out my car over there. I don't have to be in Freiburg until late this afternoon and would be happy to drop you off."

Sharon responded, "That's very kind of you, Hank, but we are expecting a friend to pick us up."

"Well, that's it," Hank said sadly. He extended his hand to Sharon first and then to Juan. "Geez, it sure has been a pleasure spending time with such nice folks. Have a wonderful visit."

"Hank, you drive carefully and have a safe trip." Sharon waved good bye as he walked away.

Sharon and Juan waited some time as the crowd thinned. Klaus Hall figured that the pretty American woman and Latino man should be Sharon and Juan. He approached them and introduced himself.

Juan shook Klaus's hand. Sharon gave him a quick hug.

"Thanks for taking such good care of Derek. When can we see him?"

Klaus glanced at the clock in the lobby. It was 7:30 a.m.

"Visitors are allowed after nine. If you like, Ms. McGee and Mr. Sanchez, we can grab some coffee and a sweet roll. I can fill you in on some details."

"Music to my ears!" declared Juan. "Hopefully I'll be able to take a shower sometime soon. That's what I really need to wake me up."

Klaus considered this and informed Juan, "The Royale check-in time is after three. I assume that is where you would like to stay?"

Sharon looked at Juan and shrugged her shoulders.

Werner Klopp stood staring out of the window in his office. It was eight in the morning and an old friend of his was coming to visit. There was also someone else, the man from America. The buzzing of the desk phone interrupted his thoughts. It was his secretary.

"Sorry to bother you this early, Mr. Klopp. There is a woman here to see you. She calls herself Miss Carr."

"Yes, I'm expecting Miss Carr. Please send her in."

The door opened and the mysterious Miss Carr slowly entered the room. She was dressed in a conservative, navy blue business suit. Her skirt hung well below the knee, and her blouse was hidden beneath a heavy wool blazer. With a sensuous movement, she removed her sunglasses and inserted one of the temples between her loosely closed lips.

Werner took and kissed the back of her gloved hand.

"Hello, Tabitha," he said as his heart began to beat a little faster.

She looked him up and down and responded, "You look absolutely delicious. Let's have sex."

Werner's heart started beating even faster.

"That's my Tabitha," he hummed while she started nibbling at his ear. He gently pushed her away while maintaining eye contact. "How much time do you have? We really need to talk first."

"Sorry, you're right," she sighed. "My return flight is right after lunch." In a more serious tone she admitted, "It's just that, well you have no idea how horny I am. You're a lucky bastard for not having to hold it back."

"I know, I know," Werner interrupted. "It may kill them, but what a way for them to go."

"That's not funny, I don't use them like that anymore. It's despicable, and it bothers my conscience," Tabitha retorted. Werner noticed a quiver in her voice.

"You're serious!" he said. "Just how long has it been, Tabitha?"

"Too long, Werner. I really need you, please?"

"I thought maybe with the two of you in town that you and the American were together."

She smiled and turned her back.

"No, I haven't met him, but he's the reason that I traveled here to see you. I thought that maybe the two of you were cooking something up. Werner, he's dangerous. This one is strong. He scares me."

This time it was Werner whose tone became serious.

"Really?" he asked.

She walked over and peered out the window.

"I've never felt any other man with his kind of strength. Werner, I touched him, and he almost tore my head off in return." Lifting a hand to her brow, Tabitha looked like she was squinting to see something way off in the distance. She continued. "You can bet that she knows about him by now, too."

Werner laughed, "You mean Sara? How long has it been since anyone has seen her? Is she even still alive?"

Tabitha dropped her hand and turned to face him.

"You know she's still alive. Can't you feel her? She is searching, always searching. Now that is a woman with patience, waiting for just the right time."

"Tabitha, if what you say about the American is true, it could mean big trouble for our kind if Sara gets her hooks into him."

"I know," she admitted. "That's why you need to talk with him."

"Me?" Werner asked with an irritating tone.

"I don't think he knows yet," she said.

"It would be much more pleasant for him if you were the one." He winked at her and said, "It could be nice for you, too."

Tabitha responded, "Werner, I told you, he scares me. Given his power, the temptation would be too great. I don't want to turn out like Sara."

"Yes, but you're not of the same stock that she is."

"It doesn't matter. It would eat at me from the inside. I worry about my soul. Werner, I have many regrets, and I'm getting tired, so tired. I keep thinking that there still may be time to make an appeal."

"Tabitha, you know that we are lost souls. It's better to enjoy our existence and not worry too much about that spiritual stuff."

She interrupted him, "Don't say that. We are not entirely without hope."

Noticing that Tabitha was shaking, Werner gave her a hug. He reassured her, "I know, Tabitha. It's all right. I'll be the one to go to the American."

After a few moments, he started to release her. Tabitha immediately stiffened and grabbed Werner tighter. She was trying to pull him down to the floor.

Werner stopped her. She gazed at him with a hurt expression.

"No, not on the floor, never the floor for my Tabitha," he said smiling. "A woman like you deserves so much better. Let me take you to my house. It's not far. We would be completely alone and wouldn't have to worry about the shock wave."

"Shock wave?" she giggled. "It's been such a long time that you'd better prepare for a cosmic storm!"

Hank Kimball stood in line behind Elyria at the rental car counter. He tapped her on the shoulder.

Elyria spun around and stared at him.

Hank spouted, "You know we could save the taxpayers some money if we shared a vehicle. After all, we're on the same mission. There's no sense in both of us going about this separately. How many days do you think it's going to take until we get to the bottom of this? We could keep each other company, in the car that is. Of course, the taxpayers are going to have to spring for separate hotel rooms."

Elyria spoke good English, but this barrage was too much for her to take in. She raised her hand motioning him to stop.

"Who are you, and what do you want?"

Hank smacked the palm of his hand against his forehead.

"Geez, forgive my manners." He reached into his jacket pocket and pulled out a badge and ID. "Special Agent Hank Kimball, FBI."

Elyria grew frightened. She didn't understand what was happening. Hank saw the fear in her eyes and backed away.

"You're CIA or Treasury, aren't you?" he asked her. "I mean you've been following Sharon McGee around. So have I."

Elyria swallowed hard. She intuitively began to consider an escape route.

"Didn't you see me, you following them and me following you? We made a real circus train driving all around Baltimore, didn't we?" he chuckled.

Elyria got the gist of what he was saying and understood that she was in deep trouble. In the jungle where many predators flourished, she was always wary of her back. Here in civilization, she never gave a second thought to someone possibly pursuing her. Here is where she was supposed to be the huntress. There was no denying him. This man knew too much. She had to think of a way out, and fast. Although dangerous, Elyria decided that for the time being, she would play along with him.

"My name is Elyria," she stated and forced a smile.

The Mistress teaches that men will let their guard down when we smile at them, she thought.

Elyria was correct. If Hank Kimball had any doubts about her, they vanished with that smile.

"Please to meet you," he said and shook her hand. "Who are you working for?"

"I am not allowed to say," she shot back at him. "All that I can tell you is that I am a soldier."

Hank was amused. "A soldier, say that's pretty mysterious! You have such an exotic name and accent. Wow, I've never heard anyone from the agencies describe themselves as a soldier." He paused, waiting for some response.

"I can tell you nothing more. I am on a mission," she told him with very little expression.

"A soldier on a mission," he repeated. "Imagine that. I suppose that the mission has something to do with Derek Dunbar? You see, he is the subject of my investigation. I'm supposed to observe his activities and determine if there are any links between him and the murders back in Baltimore. Am I getting warmer, Elyria?"

"I suppose so," she revealed to him nervously.

"Okay, why don't we work together?"

Elyria stared at this man. There was no reason to fear him. She was a Shadow Woman, an Amazon. The Mistress taught her that the desire for sex drives all men. This is what can be used against them.

Maybe given the right opportunity, she pondered, fingering the packet of cobo in her pocket, *this man could be my replacement for Blaze.*

That was it. She picked up her new carry-on bag and stepped out of line. Hank thought for a moment that she was going to run.

"Hey, I didn't mean anything," he fussed. "If you want to go it alone, we can stay out of each other's way."

"You get the car for us," Elyria ordered, cutting him off. She remembered to smile at him.

Before they left, Hank called Washington, D.C. to make his report. The voice at the other end of the line provided the address of the police station where Derek was being held. They received this intelligence from the American consulate.

"Got it!" Hank exclaimed as he waved the paper in the air in front of Elyria. "Why don't we take a little drive over and hang out near where they are keeping good old Derek?"

Elyria was amazed. She made the right choice in playing along with this man. The ways of the Mistress always proved to be true.

The long awaited moment had finally arrived. Derek heard the footsteps of many visitors as they started down the hall toward his holding cell. One of them was running. Sharon stood before him and embraced Derek through the bars. She started fidgeting and glancing nervously at the guard bringing up the rear. When he finally opened the door to the cell, Sharon burst through, and the two of them melted together. Anne's embrace from the night before had been a wonderful respite from his troubles, but this is what Derek really needed.

The four of them sat together and recounted to one another the events of the past few days. Sharon was relieved to hear of Klaus's plan to clear Derek.

"So what's next?" Sharon wanted to know. "How do we get Derek out of here?"

Klaus explained, "This is going to be the hardest part for you, Sharon and Derek. This is only Tuesday morning. Your TransGlobal Flight 38 with Joel Washington and Anne Sprague will not return to Germany until Sunday morning. I'm afraid that we will all have to wait until that time."

"What?" Sharon was shocked. "You mean Derek is stuck in here?"

"I've put off his hearing until after we've had a chance to deal with Joel Washington. It would go worse for Derek if we pushed before we are ready. You must trust me on this, Sharon."

Derek stroked her hair and put a finger up to his mouth.

"Shhh, I'll be okay now, Sharon. You are here and out of harm's way. You can visit me every day. The time will quickly pass."

Looking over at Juan he winked, "You will not mind keeping an eye on her for me a little while longer will you, old friend?"

"I will keep both eyes on her, Señor Dunbar. She is very easy to look at."

"Juan, after all we've been through, don't you think it's time you started to call me Derek? You don't know how much I appreciate your sacrifice in coming here to testify for me, and for caring for Sharon. We both owe you for her life."

Juan blushed, "You would have done the same for me, Derek."

"But you actually did do it, Juan. Thank you."

Elyria worked out the plan. There was enough cobo in the packet that she carried to administer a fatal dose. She needed to find a way to get close enough to Sharon to slip it into a drink. Hank was the key. Sharon knew him. Somehow, she had to convince Hank to help her.

As Klaus Hall drove Sharon and Juan to the Royale, Elyria followed them. Once again, she recalled what she had learned from the Mistress.

"Hank?" she asked. "Since we are going to work together, wouldn't it be more convenient if we actually stayed in the same room? That way if we needed to move quickly, we would be right there."

"I suppose if it wouldn't make you too uncomfortable, that would be a better arrangement." Hank Kimball thought he had just won the lottery. "Nobody has ever told me that I snore," he chuckled.

"Good," she said. "You can pay for the room."

He laughed, "Whatever agency you work for sure has you well trained."
You have no idea, she thought.

Since Sharon and Juan were staying at the Royale, Elyria and Hank decided to stay there as well. Hank had to be careful. He didn't want to be seen and blow his cover. Sharon and Juan didn't know Elyria. Hank sent her in to book their room. He was afraid that he might bump into them and instead chose a side door to enter the building.

Elyria found out from the desk clerk that Juan and Sharon were sharing adjoining rooms, 781 and 782. She and Hank were assigned to room 350.

Hank claimed the double bed closest to the window. Elyria didn't seem to mind one way or the other and began to unpack the few things in her bag. Hank watched her.

I wonder what her story is? he speculated. *She doesn't say much.*

Elyria disappeared into the bathroom for a moment to drop her personal items onto the sink. *We know what he's thinking, don't we?* she mused. *A little cobo later on to keep him compliant.*

Hank sat on the edge of his bed by the window. He crossed his right leg over his left and began playing with the laces on his shoes as he continued thinking.

I've been on stakeouts before with a lot of different people, and I've been on plenty by myself. I guess it's always better to have some company. This is by far the most pleasant situation I've ever been in. Yeah, she's not as pretty as a Sharon McGee is, but she's cute enough. She kind of reminds me of a young Navajo woman.

Hank allowed his thoughts to become base. *Look at how athletic she is. Christ, she could bounce me off the ceiling.* When Elyria reappeared, he decided it was best not to allow himself to become too worked up.

"Say there, Elyria, since the Bureau is springing for the room and the car, why don't we let your company pay for dinner tonight?"

"Sure, Hank," she encouraged. Elyria walked over and sat on her bed directly across from him. Putting her hands between her knees, Elyria bent over slightly toward him.

"You have to trust me, Hank," she appeared to be pleading. "After the terrorist attacks, many secret shadow agencies have been established. This is serious business."

"Terrorism," Hank gasped. "Your company has reason to believe that these events are related to terrorist activities?"

Elyria couldn't believe how gullible this man appeared to be, or was he just toying with her?

"What do you think?" she offered as a safe answer.

At dinner, Hank did most of the talking, as usual. Periodically he would interject a question for her to answer. Elyria was pleased with herself. Every question that Hank asked about her personal life she could rebuff with the "I'm not allowed to tell you" line. She couldn't believe how well she had maneuvered herself into this situation. This had the real potential of making her task much easier.

Before dessert, Hank excused himself to use the men's room. Elyria seized the moment to sprinkle a dose of cobo into his beer. Just enough to open his mind, and enhance his susceptibility to the power of suggestion.

Elyria raised her glass after Hank returned. "To a successful mission," she toasted.

"I'll second that," he agreed as they plinked their glasses together. Hank drank it down.

Later that evening, they both lay on their beds watching the television. Neither one of them understood the language enough to make sense of the broadcast. Elyria got up to brush her teeth and to change into something to sleep in. She looked through the stuff that she purchased at the Baltimore airport. Grabbing an extra long tee shirt, Elyria flitted into the bathroom and slipped it on. She looked at herself in the mirror. The red decal on the white tee shirt read, "Maryland is for crabs." She was wearing nothing underneath. The shirt was just long enough to hide her pelvic area when she lay down.

Elyria nonchalantly walked out of the bathroom and plopped down on the bed. At the sight of her, Hank started having a hard time breathing. She lay on her side facing him and propped her head up on the pillow.

"What do you think they are doing right now?" Elyria asked.

"Huh?"

"Sharon and the rest. What do you think they are doing right now?"

The question temporarily broke his spell. "Sharon is probably in her room. Visiting hours at the jail are over. Derek is probably wishing that she were with him. That guy, Juan, is also probably wishing she were with him."

"Do you wish that she were with you?"

He looked over at her and smiled devilishly. "Actually, I'm happy with the present company."

"Why thank you," she smiled, "but I'm not anywhere near as pretty as Sharon."

"Geez, Elyria, don't sell yourself short. You are plenty pretty."

"Hank, part of my mission involves getting close to Sharon. I suspect that would be of benefit to you as well. You'll help me to figure out a way to do that, right?"

"You can count on it," he answered her.

It was driving Hank nuts that a good-looking, nearly-naked woman was lying six feet away from him. It didn't matter. The cobo made him sleepy. A half hour later, he was snoozing comfortably.

Elyria laughed to herself, reached over, and turned off the light. This first day had gone much better than she could have hoped. Although she was having fun with this man, her thoughts turned serious. She had to remain focused on the main objective. The Mistress wanted Sharon McGee dead, and Elyria was to make this happen.

Hank's contacts were able to keep him informed about Derek's situation. The hearing concerning the criminal charges being brought against Derek by the German government was to occur the following Tuesday. This gave Hank and Elyria a full week of tailing Sharon and Juan. One week didn't seem too bad for Hank. He was used to long and sometimes fruitless stakeouts. To Elyria, it was boring and frustrating. She needed to figure out a way to get to Sharon. Elyria needed the information that Hank was able to provide to her, so she continued to play along.

The routine followed by Sharon and Juan was methodical. Every morning Juan knocked on Sharon's door at eight, and they would eat breakfast together. At ten, they would visit with Derek until lunch. In the afternoon, they would run errands. Sometimes Sharon would work out at the Royale's fitness center. Around three they would visit Derek again for about an hour. Dinner would follow, and then Juan would button Sharon back into her room by eight every night.

On Saturday, Elyria and Hank waited outside of the police station during Sharon and Juan's morning visit with Derek. This is when it dawned on her. Sharon did not go to the fitness center the day before. She felt sure that Sharon would want to work out after lunch. Her pattern was to never go two days without exercising.

This one keeps herself pretty and slender by using machines, she contemplated. *How unnatural and reproachful. These civilized people are so far removed from the earth. They have no concept of the joy in running through the mountains in pursuit of game. This is where the Shadow Women get their strength. I will be waiting for Sharon at this fitness center. It is time that I reveal myself and make friends with her. Then I will kill her.*

Hank dozed as he sat waiting in the car. Elyria forced a smile, reached over, and put a hand on his thigh.

"Hank, it's almost time for lunch."

He jerked awake and looked at his watch.

"Geez, where did the morning go? They should be coming out soon."

"Hank, if they go back to the Royale for lunch, let's do something different. I'm bored of eating in that bar."

"Well, what did you have in mind?"

"This has been a long week of running around. I was hoping that maybe we could order room service. I'd like to nap for about an hour."

During the nights they spent together, Elyria enjoyed teasing Hank, but she always stopped short of openly inviting him between the sheets. She wanted to build his desire for her to the point where he could be controlled with the promise of sexual intercourse.

It was working. Hank thought to himself about Elyria's request, *Hmmm, Elyria, room, nap, bed, in the middle of the day, and I will be there with her.* He said exactly what she knew he would. "Sure, I can go along with that."

"Good," Elyria stated with finality. "You can buy."

After they followed Sharon and Juan back to the Royale, Elyria continued to set her trap.

"Hank, go up to the room and call room service. Just get me a simple salad and sandwich. I'm going to drop by the bar and pick up a bottle of wine for us."

This is getting better and better! Hank thought.

For the second time since they met, Elyria plotted to prepare a cobo cocktail for Hank. This time it was to going to be a little stronger. She wanted to knock Hank out for a period of time, but she didn't want the dose to be fatal for him. If her plan were successful, Sharon McGee would be dead in a few hours, in which case Elyria would have no further need of Hank. If, however, Sharon didn't show up at the fitness center, or if something else went wrong, Elyria would still need him. The intelligence that Hank had access to was invaluable to her.

Elyria considered that this time Hank might suspect that he was drugged. She set things up very carefully so that she would have a plausible explanation. This first glass of wine was not spiked. She held it out.

"Here's to a successful mission, Hank."

"And here's to happy endings," he countered.

They touched glasses and began to sip their wine.

Hank was sitting on his bed and Elyria was lying on hers. They faced each other. Elyria knew that Hank was revved up after sleeping for several nights in the same room with her.

"You know, Hank, we've shared the same space for almost a week now. Anyone who didn't know would swear that we were married."

He chuckled, "Yeah, I guess we have been sort of joined at the hip."

Elyria continued to lead him down the path.

"Sometimes when two people spend such an intense amount of time together, they grow close."

"What do you mean?" Hank responded. He didn't know what to make of this.

"I like you, Hank, probably more than I should, given that we are in a professional relationship. You seem so centered and in control. I'm attracted to that."

Hank downed his drink. *Perfect*, she thought.

"You know what attracts me to you?" he asked. "Other than the fact that you are so obviously good looking."

Elyria teased him, "Stop it, Hank, I may have an athletic body, but to say that I am good looking, say like Sharon McGee, is a real stretch."

"There you go again, selling yourself short," he reminded her.

Elyria got up and fixed a second drink for the two of them. She didn't spike this one either but made sure that his glass was completely full. She only filled hers about one third. While her back was turned, Elyria posed the question.

"Well, what is it?"

"What?" he replied.

Elyria handed him the wine and returned to her place on her own bed.

"What is it that attracts you to me other than the fact that I am so obviously good looking?" she giggled.

Hank sipped some wine.

"It's the mystery, Elyria. I don't know anything about you. You tell me that you work for a covert government agency. You hint that this case may have something to do with terrorism. I've shared everything that I know with you, but you don't give up anything. I find all of that somehow sexy."

"Hank, do you want me to give something up to you?"

"Geez, that would spoil the mystery, wouldn't it?"

"Damn it, Hank, you're too much of a gentleman. Drink that wine and come over here and sit beside me," she ordered.

166

She didn't have to repeat the order. It was all over in about ten minutes. Hank lay beside Elyria. He was warm from the afterglow and from the wine.

Elyria kissed him.

"I'll be right back. I have to use the ladies' room."

He watched as her tight, athletic body disappeared behind the door.

While she was in the bathroom, Hank spoke. "What just happened?"

She reemerged with a smile. "If you don't know, we'll have to do it again so that you can figure it out."

Elyria glanced over at the wine bottle that by now was almost empty. She took Hank's empty glass and filled it. This time she slipped him the cobo.

"Hank, go ahead and finish this little bit for me. It's not much. I'm afraid it will go bad if we let it sit."

At that point, he would have walked a mile barefoot through broken glass. After drinking it down, Hank patted his hand on the bed.

"Geez, are you going to help me figure it out?"

Elyria smiled, got on the bed, and straddled him.

I really did win the lottery, pondered Hank.

After they finished, Elyria faked falling asleep. Hank lay there for a while watching her breathe. He relished the sight of her naked chest heaving up and down with each breath. The cobo was working on him. In another few minutes, he was out.

CHAPTER 16

After the three riders arrived at Grenada Cathedral, they agreed to rest from their journey. They would meet again in the morning for the meeting with Sara. As he reclined in his bed, Gonzalo grew anxious. He dressed and walked to the friar's room.

"Friar Gaspar, are you still awake?" Gonzalo spoke softly as he lightly rapped on the door. A few moments later, he heard a muffled, "Enter, Gonzalo."

The friar could see that his friend was troubled.

"About the old woman," Gonzalo expressed. "If we are to get at the truth concerning any of this, would you not think it more appropriate for the two of us to interview her without the Father."

"I don't follow you," Gaspar said as he rubbed his tired eyes.

"Is it possible that Father Rey being with us would intimidate the prisoner? She must be terribly frightened of him and might say anything in his presence."

"I doubt it, Gonzalo, besides the matter is already settled. We are going together to see her in the morning."

"No, Gaspar, I'm going to see her now," Gonzalo said with determination. "Can you tell me where she would most likely be held?"

"Catacombs," Gaspar said while yawning. "Wait, I will come with you. If you have it in your mind to do such a thing, let us at least heed the Father's words and go together."

Father Rey smiled as he watched the hot iron glow red in the coals. Sara screamed as four female attendants blindfolded her. With an attendant stationed at each of her limbs, they picked up Sara's writhing body and tied her to her bed. She was completely naked. The Father and the attendants invaded her prison room just as she was finished bathing. Juana jumped to Sara's aid, but Esther and two of the other female sextons grabbed and held her immobile.

Juana screamed at the sight of the hot iron. "Forgive me, Sara, I didn't believe you. Father Rey, you are a priest, what is this that you are doing? Please, have mercy on the poor child."

"Shut up," he yelled back at her. "This abomination deserves no mercy. She was damned at birth. For the rest of this witch's miserable life, it will no longer be possible for her to ensnare good men."

Father Rey held the hot iron an inch above Sara's stomach and slowly moved it along her torso, between her bare breasts and around the curve of her neck and chin. Sara felt the searing heat grow closer on her cheek as it approached her blindfolded left eye.

Both Sara and Juana were screaming with every ounce of energy in their bodies. Father Rey's countenance was beaming.

"In the name of the Father, and of the Son, and of the Holy Ghost," he chanted. "Amen."

Father Rey touched the hot iron to the cloth over Sara's eye and prepared to plunge it down into her face. At that moment, he felt a hammer-like blow strike him in the temple. Father Rey fell unconscious against the far wall of Sara's room. Gonzalo and Gaspar burst into the room. It was Friar Gaspar that flew into Father Rey, punching him in the side of the head.

All of the female attendants scurried from the room leaving the men there along with Sara and Juana. The blindfold had caught fire from the hot iron. Juana sprang over to Sara and tore it from her eyes, Sara was physically unharmed, but the shock of the incident had driven her into a catatonic state. It was her only defense against the expected pain. Juana picked up a blanket next to the bed and threw it over Sara's naked body.

Gonzalo and Gaspar stared at Sara. The few moments that she remained exposed profoundly affected the two of them. Juana noticed, reached out, and gently closed the eyelids over Sara's beautiful eyes.

With the spell broken, Gonzalo looked at Juana and asked her, "Who is this maiden?"

"Her name is Sara," Juana choked between sobs. "Please have mercy, don't hurt her. She is terribly anguished."

The two men looked at each other.

"It's not possible," gasped Friar Gaspar. "How could this be the ancient one? She is just a young girl."

"She is not ancient, Friar Gaspar, but you saw her. I think you will agree with me that she is no young girl," Gonzalo corrected him. "I've never seen such a beautiful woman."

They both stared at the curving form under the thin blanket. Friar Gaspar began to have feelings that were forbidden to a priest. He took Gonzalo by the arm and made him turn away.

"Gonzalo, do you begin to understand the danger here? She may not be a witch, but the two of us are very vulnerable to her beauty."

"You, Friar Gaspar!" Gonzalo allowed himself to smile. The friar did not return his smile, and Gonzalo felt compelled to turn around and gaze at her again.

Gaspar pulled at him. "You can't help yourself, can you? You are drawn to her."

"Nonsense," Gonzalo flatly stated. "You think that I could not keep myself from her?"

Gonzalo started to slowly back toward Sara. As Gaspar approached him again, Gonzalo felt himself grow hot with desire for Sara.

"Gonzalo," the friar warned. "Do you notice what you are doing?"

Gonzalo looked down and found his hand on the hilt of his sword. He was ready to draw it against his friend.

"There is something to this, isn't there, Gaspar?" Gonzalo asked ashamed of himself. "Get me out of here."

Juana screamed. Father Rey had regained consciousness and the two men jerked around just in time to see him madly swinging the iron at them. It was still red hot. Gonzalo ducked, but Gaspar took a shot to his arm. It sent him tumbling over backwards. Gonzalo drew his sword.

"Her eyes are her weapons," Father Rey breathed heavily. "The witch's weapons must be removed. Don't you see, I must burn them out." He turned toward Sara.

"Stop," hollered Gonzalo. "Drop that iron, or by God I will cut you in half."

The Father hesitated and let the iron slip away harmlessly to the floor.

"Fine," he said. Raising his voice to Gonzalo, he repeated again, "Fine, you deal with her now. Get this abomination out of my church and be on your way."

Father Rey stormed out of the room.

Gonzalo helped Gaspar to his feet and asked him, "Are you all right?"

"I think so," replied Gaspar as he moved his hurt arm around at the shoulder. "There will be a pretty good bruise, but I'll live."

Gonzalo smiled at his friend. "Excuse my language, Friar, but we are getting the hell out of this place right now."

"God forgive me," Gaspar laughed out loud, "but those are exactly my sentiments, too."

Juana leaned over Sara's body to protect her. Gonzalo sheathed his sword and went over to talk with her.

"You are a good friend to her," Gonzalo told her. "What is your name?"

"I am Juana," she was still sobbing. "I beg you, do not hurt her."

"Enough," Gonzalo said and gently shook her. "The danger has passed. Nobody is going to hurt either you or Sara. The friar and I have come to take her out of this hole. Can you get her ready to travel?"

Juana wiped her eyes in disbelief. "Rescue?" she asked. "You are rescuing her? She will be so happy."

"One more thing," Gonzalo added. "Can you also travel with us for a while? It appears that the friar and I are the ones needing protection."

Juana hurriedly dressed Sara in several layers of clothing and gathered her things. Friar Gaspar carried Sara's personal belongings along with the sack containing the dagger. Sara remained in her catatonic trance so that it became necessary for Gonzalo to carry her out. He dared not look at her face, yet he felt a warm energy emanate from her body as he carried her. It was intoxicating.

"Gaspar, keep talking to me," he requested. "I need to keep my thoughts turned away from her."

Sara thought that she was once again dreaming. There was a cool breeze in her face, something that she had not felt in almost two centuries. She also felt the warmth of a man's body carrying her. Sara relished the dream.

"Leon?" she uttered softly.

"Everything is fine, Sara," Juana answered back. "These men have come to rescue you. You are free, Sara, you are free!"

Sara smiled and fell back to sleep. She felt sure that she was still dreaming.

Joyful tears streamed down her face as Sara felt the warmth of the morning sun against her skin. The songbirds were a sweet symphony to her ears and the smell of fresh air filling her lungs was divine. Juana explained to Sara the events of the previous night.

Before breaking camp, Gonzalo asked Juana if the two women could join them for a meeting. He wanted to ask Sara to wear a blindfold, but didn't have the resolve to ask her to do so. Instead, he and Friar Gaspar decided to avoid eye contact.

Sara sat with her face to the sun. She completed rummaging through all of her old belongings. Sara strapped the old dagger to her waist inside of her outer garments. Juana looked at her with concern.

"Don't fear for me," Sara said as she noticed Juana's expression. "The madness is out of me. I will not harm myself. This dagger is part of me. I've owned it since the beginning."

The two men sat off to the side. Sara noticed their discomfort and guessed that they knew her secret. She started the conversation.

"You men are wise to respect me for what I am. Juana informed me that you have been responsible for my rescue. There is no way that you can possibly gain an understanding of my agony or of how grateful I am to you." Sara paused as her emotions welled up rendering her unable to continue. Juana put an arm around her until she stopped crying.

Gonzalo, ever curious, inquired of her, "Maiden, tell us of yourself. There is much that we do not understand, and much that we need to discover. A great task remains at hand, and we require your guidance."

Now it was Sara that became curious, but she wanted to answer them first before asking questions of her own.

"You already know much," she confirmed. "I have no intention of causing harm to you, my heroes. Understand, though, that I now view all humans as wicked. Never again will I allow myself to be caged. Quite the contrary, it is my intention to enslave humanity or die trying. All that you men know and practice is war and death. You do not have the right to rule yourselves. Do not attempt to restrain me, and the two of you will remain free. From this point onward, I come and go as I please. Men will kill each other for a mere look at me. Women will tremble when they hear of my approach. They will fear for their husbands and the ruin that I will visit upon them. Humanity be damned."

Gonzalo pitied Sara as he listened to her words. *What savagery has this maiden suffered at the hands of that priest that she requires such an emotional release?* he pondered to himself.

"Such ugliness from one so beautiful," Gaspar said. "If you extend loving kindness instead of hate, dearest Sara, it will be returned to you many fold."

Sara laughed. "Loving kindness?" she echoed. "I've tried that course, Friar. I've reached out and given and given and given and now there is no more to give. My repayment has always been misery and the death of those that I love."

"You have great strength, Sara," Gaspar continued to counsel her. "I've been touched by it. I know that you can endure, but you must endure to the end to obtain salvation."

"The end?" Sara questioned. "Your seventy or eighty years is a blink of an eye. How much easier is it for you to endure? Had I been killed years ago the prize that you speak of would already be mine."

Gaspar knew from this conversation that everything he suspected about Sara was true. He believed that she was an ancient being. He believed that she was supernatural. He believed her words. These beliefs he did not share with Gonzalo, but he also knew that Sara understood the depth of his belief.

"Yes, it is all true, Friar," Gaspar thought he heard Sara say. *Did she really say that, or did I just think it?* he wondered.

Sara turned her attention to Gonzalo. "You spoke of a great task and of a need for my assistance. Please explain yourself."

During the next hour, Gonzalo and Gaspar told her everything. They laid it all out and spared no detail.

At the end, Gonzalo flatly told her. "You are not a prisoner, maiden. If it is your desire to pick up your things and leave us, know that I would not stop you. Also, know that an armada awaits our arrival at the Port of Malaga. Our quest is finished if you do not accompany us there of your own free will."

Sara got up and walked away for some time to think.

A new world across the great ocean! she marveled at it. *An unspoiled wilderness from which to begin my conquest, isolated and away from civilization.*

Maybe this is why I have survived through the ages, she thought. *Destiny has guided me to this point.*

Sara thought about Leon. *He and I could have done this together. They took him from me*, she grieved silently. *I need a man to be with me. One from which I can draw a continuous stream of strength. He needs to be one of the mightier ones, stronger even than Leon was. Someday he will come. It may be centuries from now, but I can wait. I have time.*

They eagerly waited as Sara returned. First, she approached Juana.

"Will you come with me?" she asked.

"To the new world?" Juana acted shocked. "I would like to see my parents before we leave, but yes, Mistress Sara, I will follow you."

"Mistress?" smiled Sara. "I like that."

With a more stern expression, Sara charged her, "It will be difficult at first, Juana, but your kindness to me will never be forgotten. I promise to return it to you many times over."

Sara went over to the men.

"I will play along," she told them. "After we reach this new world, I will

173

stay with you for a time, but it is my intention to leave. Also, understand that your emperor is hanging his hopes on a fantasy. There is no supernatural El Dorado. I would feel him. I feel no one. This grieves me greatly, for I fear that at this period of time there are not many of my kind."

After a few moments of silence she inquired, "What about the arrangements when we reach the others at Malaga?"

"You and Juana will remain isolated in the captain's quarters on the Nina," Gaspar explained. "The arrangements have already been made."

"Good," she sighed. "Gonzalo, Gaspar, there is one other thing."

They waited for her to speak.

"Don't ask me how I know, but don't deny it. Just accept it that I know both of you desperately yearn to have sexual relations with me. I'm inclined to grant this to you, because I also have yearnings. Beware though, if you do so, it is at your own peril. Consider yourselves warned."

Friar Gaspar ran away shouting a prayer and hid in the tent.

"What about you, Gonzalo?" she asked laughing.

"If this is what you want, maiden, it would not be possible for me to resist. I fear that if our eyes should meet, all walls between our worlds would crumble."

"Do you wish to do this thing now?" she teased.

Gonzalo's throat became dry, and he found it difficult to breathe.

"Soon, maiden," he responded. "I fear it will happen soon."

"Don't keep me waiting very long," she laughed again.

Gonzalo joined Gaspar in the tent. Gaspar looked at him and noticed how he trembled.

"You denied her?" he quizzed.

"No, Friar," Gonzalo gasped for air. "It is only postponed."

"Gonzalo, we've made a terrible mistake falling victim to our own pride. We can't handle her alone. It would be better to take our chances without her."

"It's way too late for that now, Gaspar. Can't you feel it? Our will is gone. Neither one of us could walk away from her now. Pray to God for us, Friar, for we are beaten."

"Your will power will return to you in a little while, Gonzalo. You just need to separate from her. I'm beginning to feel more in control now."

"How does she do it, Gaspar? Who is Sara? Do you know?"

"Yes, Gonzalo, forgive me for keeping it from you, but Father Rey confirmed it for me on the road to Grenada. I know exactly what she is."

As Gaspar explained the mystery of Sara, it opened Gonzalo's eyes. He was awestruck. That night, sleep eluded Gonzalo as he marveled at the wonder of it.

CHAPTER 17

Sharon was already in the fitness center using the stair climber when Elyria entered. She walked up to the treadmill next to Sharon. After fidgeting for some time at the controls, Sharon looked over and saw Elyria struggling with the device.

"Do you need help?" asked Sharon.

"You speak English?" replied Elyria. "Thank goodness, I thought maybe you were German. I can't speak a lick of German. Yes, actually I can't figure out how to make this thing work."

Sharon chuckled as she turned down the controls of the stair climber. "I'm afraid that English is all that I speak. Here, let me show you." Sharon turned on the power switch located at the back of the machine. It lit up and beeped at them. "See this knob in the middle? It regulates the speed. Those buttons on the side set the incline."

"Thank you," Elyria responded. "Sometimes these things are tricky."

Sharon eyed her and said, "Actually it surprises me that you don't know how to make it work."

"What do you mean?" Elyria asked defensively.

"Look at you! I would think that anyone with a hard body like yours works out on these things all of the time. You look to be in great shape."

"Thank you, again," Elyria smiled. "Actually I do a lot of running out of doors. I don't know my way around here real well, so I figured it would be safer to use the equipment."

"Did you just get here?" Sharon asked with curiosity. She restarted the stair climber and resumed her workout.

"Just passing through," Elyria answered her. "I'm a flight attendant for British Airways and am on a lay over for a few days."

"Really," squealed Sharon. "My boyfriend is a pilot for TransGlobal. I guess you could say that we are laying over for a few days too."

Elyria smiled, "We have two things in common. We both like to workout, and we are both stuck here in Frankfurt for a few days. My name is Elyria, but please call me Ellie."

"Pleased to meet you, Ellie, I'm Sharon McGee from Baltimore, Maryland. Say, that's a fancy name. Are you originally from England? I never heard a name like that before."

"It's Portuguese. I was born in Brazil. Actually, I still live there."

"Wow, that's exotic. How did you end up as a British Airways flight attendant?"

"The airline has landing rights in Sao Paulo. I'm based out of that city. They hired me, because I speak English and Portuguese."

Both of them continued with their workouts for about ten minutes. Elyria was mentally stalking Sharon, just as she would physically stalk a tapir in the jungle.

"Sharon, you said this pilot friend is your boyfriend. Do you have plans to tie the knot anytime soon?"

Sharon stopped the machine and started to towel herself down.

"I sure hope so, Ellie. We have a few things to work out, but I believe that everything is going to be just fine."

Sharon wandered over to a rowing machine and began to set it up. She laughed, "How about you, Ellie, do you have a man in every port?"

"No, there's just one," Elyria said. She was finally starting to breathe heavy from the exertion. "He doesn't know it yet, but the two of us are going to get really close very soon."

"That sounds like an interesting story."

"It's not that complicated. There's just one thing standing in my way, and soon that obstacle will be removed. Then, he's mine."

Sharon thought that this sounded a bit strange and didn't know how to respond.

Twenty minutes later Sharon stopped rowing. Elyria powered down her machine.

"Will you be back here tomorrow, Sharon? I'd enjoy the company if you were going to be back."

"Thanks, you're right. It is easier when there is someone to talk with during these fat-burning sessions. I don't know for sure, Ellie, but if I do workout, it will probably be around the same time tomorrow."

"Great," Elyria said as she walked over to her gym bag. She took out two plastic bottles of water. One had a yellow cap and the other a red cap. She walked back over to where Sharon was combing her hair and practically shoved the bottle with the yellow cap into Sharon's hand.

"Here you go, Sharon," she charged. "It's our lucky day. I put my money in the vending machine, and it dropped out two bottles. You can have this one."

Sharon accepted the gift. "Thanks, Ellie, I can sure use this."

They both unscrewed the caps.

"Here's to another successful workout," toasted Elyria.

Sharon raised the bottle. Before she could sip, the door to the fitness center opened, and Klaus Hall entered.

"Juan told me that I could find you here," he acted relieved.

"What's up, Klaus?" Sharon questioned.

"A detective friend of mine needs to go on duty in two hours. He doesn't have much time and needs to meet with us right now to talk about our plans for tomorrow."

Klaus stopped for a second after he noticed Elyria.

"You know," he continued, "our plans involving Herr Washington and Fraulein Sprague."

Sharon capped the bottle, placed it in her gym bag, and headed for the door with Klaus. She yelled back over her shoulder.

"Sorry, Ellie, I've got to go. Remember, it will be around the same time tomorrow if I get a chance to workout. It was nice meeting you."

Elyria was left alone in the fitness center. After a minute, she exploded with rage. Elyria threw her bottle with all of her might against the track on the treadmill. It burst and splashed throughout the room. She sat on the floor beside her gym bag.

Calm down, she thought to herself. *She still has the bottle. She will probably drink it soon. I may not be there to enjoy seeing her do it, but the results will be the same. Sharon McGee is going to die, and I will have accomplished my mission for the Mistress.*

As she gathered up her bag, Elyria thought about two other things. The first was that she used all of the rest of her stash of cobo in making the fatal dose for Sharon. The second was that she was still stuck for a while longer with that fool, Hank Kimball.

Sharon threw the gym bag in a corner of the room and jumped into the shower. She completely forgot about the bottled water given to her by Elyria. The yellow lid stuck out of the top of the bag begging for attention.

Twenty minutes later, she knocked on Juan's door. The two men were waiting for her. "Sorry for such short notice, but my detective friend is on a tight schedule," Klaus explained.

"I don't understand," Sharon began with a puzzled look. "Why does your detective friend need to see Juan and me?"

Klaus told her, "We have been talking and decided that this set up will be more successful if you and Juan were to play a part."

"How so?" asked Juan, now suddenly interested.

Klaus glanced at his watch. "I will explain it to you when we go to Derek. My friend, Dieter, will be waiting for us there."

Police Officer Dieter Horner was already talking with Derek when the three of them arrived. After Klaus introduced them all, Sharon took her seat beside Derek on the cot. Klaus assumed his now familiar position sitting backwards on the chair. Juan stood leaning against the cell door, his arms folded in front of him. Dieter stood at the table leafing through some notes. After they all settled down, he pulled a pack of cigarettes from his jacket pocket and lit up. Being polite, he held the pack out offering a smoke to each of them. They all declined.

After taking a few puffs, Dieter looked over at Sharon and Derek and began to reveal his intentions. "As you know, my friend here, Klaus Hall, has asked me to assist in a covert operation to persuade an individual, Joel Washington, to reveal information that may be pertinent to the defense of Herr Dunbar."

Germans, Derek thought to himself. *Why do they have to be so formal? Can't he just say that he is working with Klaus to set up Joel?*

Oblivious to Derek's thoughts, Officer Horner continued speaking. "We have already enlisted the assistance of one of your colleagues, Anne Sprague. Klaus spoke with her on the telephone yesterday, and she still resolves to participate in this operation." He stopped talking to take a drag on the butt.

Klaus took the opportunity to jump in. "During my conversations with Fraulein Sprague, she seemed a bit nervous about how she could broach this subject with Herr Washington. The last time he offered information, it was a spontaneous situation, and he had been drinking. Fraulein Sprague believes that it will be difficult to duplicate these conditions without raising the suspicion of Herr Washington."

As Klaus stopped, Officer Horner picked up on his train of thought. The two of them were an effective tag team.

"A further complication involves the law. In Germany, these covert operations are considered legal only if the subject being pursued is not forced into a corner. In other words, your Herr Washington must make the first move. It cannot seem as if he has been coerced into talking."

Officer Horner stopped to take another drag.

"That is correct," Klaus illustrated further. "Fraulein Sprague cannot simply wear a revealing outfit complete with recording device, walk up to Herr Washington, rub up against him and ask him to tell her all he knows about this situation. The courts would look upon this as coercion. Evidence obtained in this matter would be nullified. It is very important that he makes the first move by talking."

Derek began to look worried. "I understand what you are saying," he grumbled. "I don't get it how Juan and Sharon can help."

Officer Horner finished the cigarette and was in the process of stuffing it out in the ashtray. He looked up once again at Sharon and Derek.

"I've been doing this sort of thing for twelve years," he explained. "It is my specialty. The way to motivate a suspect to make that first move is to get inside of his mind. You are thinking about this only from your point of view, Herr Dunbar."

Klaus once again took over the conversation. "My friend, Dieter, and I have performed services like this for many of my clients. There is much wisdom in what he is telling you," he reassured Derek.

"So how do we get inside the mind of Joel Washington?" Derek repeated half joking.

"This is not so difficult given what we already know," stated Klaus. "You tell me. What is Joel Washington thinking right now?"

Derek closed his eyes as if concentrating and sighed. He looked at his watch. It was 3:30 p.m.

"Well, let's see. It's Saturday and right now it is 9:30 a.m. in Baltimore. He is probably out of bed and packing a bag for his flight to Frankfurt. Flight 38 leaves late in the afternoon for an arrival here early tomorrow morning. Later on he will go to the airport and do a walk around of *Adventurer*."

Officer Horner interrupted, "That is what he is doing, but what is he thinking? What is his state of mind?"

"I'll tell you his state of mind," blurted Derek. "He's happy as a pig in shit. He shafted me and screwed me and now he is the big man."

"Exactly!" applauded Dieter Horner. "He is puffed up with pride and totally self absorbed. He feels invincible. This man has trapped and defeated you in every possible way."

"Yeah, don't remind me," Derek groaned.

"Ah, but this is what we can use against him," cautioned Officer Horner. "His own arrogance will be his undoing. Think, Herr Dunbar, what would he relish that would further feed his elation over your condition?"

"I don't know," shrugged Derek. "I guess he would like to see me go to jail."

The officer lit another cigarette and continued. "Yes, this is true, however there is something more immediate that would have a greater impact."

In a dramatic fashion, Officer Horner paused and took in several long drags of smoke. Derek, Sharon, and Juan were all riveted in anticipation of the plan he was about to reveal.

Elyria felt alone and miserable. Sharon had left with the two men presumably to see Derek. She didn't know for sure and couldn't drive to the jail. She searched everywhere for Hank's keys but couldn't find them. Hank was still passed out on his bed.

"Did she drink the water?" Elyria asked herself. "Did she take it with her? If she didn't drink it, where is it?"

It really bothered her that she had used the last of the cobo. Elyria wasn't fond of the alternative, if for some reason Sharon would not drink the water. She was not squeamish about physical combat and getting bloody. Elyria was confident that she could easily overpower Sharon and slit her throat with a knife. She was less confident about being able to get away with it. Here in civilization, crimes could not easily be hidden. There were too many people. This is why she brought Blaze. He was supposed to do this deed for her by his own hands. If caught, she could throw Blaze away and flee back to the safety of the jungle and Casa Cobo. However, Blaze was dead and Elyria understood that she was stuck with completing this mission for the Mistress.

Elyria hid in a stairwell from where she could observe Sharon's door. Around 7:00 p.m., Elyria watched as Sharon and Juan returned. They both disappeared behind their respective doors.

"That bitch must have thrown out the water," she whispered to herself and returned to her room.

Elyria opened her door and found Hank Kimball sitting at the edge of his bed. He was naked and had his hands locked together behind his neck. He bent over with his head practically between his knees.

After she shut the door, he looked up.

"Geez," he groaned and coughed. "I have one hell of a headache. No way am I going to drink that brand of wine again. I can't believe I slept this long."

"I wore you out good, didn't I?" Elyria said passionlessly. "I watched Sharon today. She disappeared for some time, but now she is back. I couldn't follow her, because I could not find the damn car keys."

Hank wrinkled his forehead and thought about it.

"After I dropped you off today, you told me to call room service. You left me to go get that wine. I decided to let the valet park the car this time instead of parking it myself. The valet has the keys."

Hank rose and stood wobbling on his feet.

"I need to get some food in my stomach," he moaned. "After that I'm going back to bed." While smiling at her, Hank added, "to sleep."

From the time that Sharon arrived in Frankfurt, Derek's episodes with dreams and mental visions subsided. He had been resting comfortably the past few days. Now that the trap was being set for Joel Washington, Derek was beginning to become anxious once again.

What if something goes wrong? What if it doesn't work? those thoughts drifted around in his mind.

It was Saturday night. Klaus and Dieter explained the plan in detail to Derek, Sharon, and Juan. Everyone understood his or her role. Flight 38 would arrive Sunday morning. Anne Sprague would meet with Detective Dieter Horner and Klaus Hall to receive her final instructions. She would be wired for sound. Finally, it would be her turn to seduce Joel into spilling the details of what he had done to Derek.

There was little room for error. Joel and Anne would be returning to Baltimore Monday afternoon. Derek's hearing was set for Tuesday morning. If Anne failed, Derek's case would be severely diminished. His entire future would be determined by what happened in the next twenty-four hours.

Derek looked at the clock on the wall outside of his cell. It was almost midnight. He plopped himself down on the cot and pulled the thin prison issue blanket over him. Derek's mind was in a storm of doubt and fear as he drifted off into a troubled sleep. He began to dream.

"Is the knot straight?" he asked Sharon after quickly adjusting his necktie.

Sharon gave him a quick kiss. "It's perfect, Derek. You look great. They're going to love you. Just remember, don't bore them with a long speech."

The two of them walked out of the coat checkroom of the hotel and into the banquet hall. As they entered, everyone turned and smiled. The headwaiter led Derek and Sharon to their seats near the front of the hall. Juan Sanchez took his seat on the other side of Sharon. Joel Washington sat across from Derek.

All of the people that ever meant anything to Derek were in the room. His long dead parents, Kyle and Anita Dunbar sat in a far corner. Anne Sprague was sitting at the next table along with the rest of *Adventurer's* flight crew. Anne caught Derek's eye and winked. Derek watched as she stood up and approached Sharon. Anne whispered something into Sharon's ear and returned to her seat.

"What did she want?" he asked Sharon.

Sharon started laughing. "She told me that she has a secret."

He joined in the laughter, "What's the secret?"

Sharon's face turned serious. "I think you already know, you bastard."

He grabbed her by the arm. "Nothing ever happened between us."

Joel Washington stood and motioned the gathering to become silent.

"Ladies and Gentlemen, we are here to celebrate the promotion of our good friend to the position of Captain at TransGlobal Airlines. Let's have a warm round of applause for Derek Dunbar."

Everyone in the hall roared with approval and jumped to their feet. Joel pulled at Derek's arm and yelled, "You are their new king. It's time for your coronation speech."

Derek felt himself stand. The room grew silent. All of them were staring at Derek as he began to speak.

"First of all, I want to acknowledge that my promotion could not have been possible without the support of all of you, my friends."

He raised an arm toward Kyle and Anita sitting in the far corner. "Mom and Dad, thanks for raising me in a warm, positive environment and for instilling within me the drive and determination to succeed."

Anita's voice answered Derek's comment in a shrill tone. "We had nothing to do with it, you foundling fool."

The room erupted in laughter. Joel Washington motioned for silence.

Derek picked up where he left off.

"Next I want to thank the flight crew of *Adventurer*. A boss is only as good as the people serving under him, and you folks are the best."

Anne Sprague yelled to the room, "Yeah, he sure was good when I was under him."

Thunderous applause gushed from all of them. Anne curtseyed and took her seat. Derek looked at Sharon and shrugged his shoulders, not understanding. He was sweating. Joel handed him a napkin so that he could wipe his forehead. After the room quieted down, Derek started again.

"Finally, I want to thank Sharon, the kindest, most understanding, and most beautiful person in my world."

Derek looked down at her. Juan Sanchez had his arm around Sharon and she was holding a baby.

"Sharon, I don't understand. What is this? You, Juan, and this baby?"

This time Juan answered back.

"Stupid fool, did you really think that she would marry a freak like you?" He held up his hand and showed Derek a wedding ring. "She's mine now. This is our son."

"Wanna hold him?" Sharon giggled as she extended the baby toward him.

Derek backed away from the table. Joel Washington started a chant that everyone in the room soon picked up.

"Foundling freak, foundling freak, foundling freak, foundling freak."

The chant grew into a roar. It became mixed with the sound of *Adventurer's* jet engines at a full throttle. Derek covered his ears.

"I am not a freak," he screamed. "I am a man."

In quick succession, pictures flashed into his brain. First, it was the angel from his earlier dreams.

"A man, Derek? Maybe, but not one of them. Not yet."

"Who am I, then?" he howled. "Who am I?"

Sharon laughed hysterically. "Don't ask 'who am I,' Derek. Try asking 'what am I,' you foundling freak."

Derek found himself adrift in the waters again. It was the scene from his previous dream. The light beacon shown on him. A voice was carried on the wind, "Come to me."

He found himself back in the banquet hall. They were all laughing at him, and pointing.

Derek fell to the floor and hid his face. They continued to mock him.

"We will stop if you say the magic words," Sharon teased.

He felt the magic words pop into his head. Derek stood, climbed on top of the table, and confronted them all.

"Okay, you want to hear the magic words? Here they are."

They looked up at him in eager anticipation.

"What am I?" he asked. "The magic words form a question. What am I? Somebody, please, tell me so that I may be at peace."

The mocking stopped. As if some silent command ordered all of them, they took their seats. Finally, Sharon looked up at him.

She articulated slowly, talking to Derek as if he were a child. "She calls you. She has been calling you for a long time, but you've been ignoring her. Set me free, Derek, and go to her. She has your answer."

Derek awoke and sat trembling at the edge of his bed.

"What, what am I?" he stuttered. In his despair, Derek reached out with his mind. He searched.

Some time later, he felt a warm feeling enter into him. It was the same benevolent force that he previously resisted that day when he freaked out in his cell. It calmed him the same way that hugging Anne Sprague soothed him. This time he let it happen. The force flooded through him.

Derek lay back down on the cot and soon drifted off to sleep. He dreamed no more that night.

Werner Klopp's phone rang ten times before he realized what was happening. He was groggy with sleep as he picked up the phone.

"Yeah?" was all he could get out.

"Werner, it's Tabitha," the hollow voice sounded from the other end of the phone.

He gathered his senses and sat up in bed.

"Tabitha?" he mumbled. "So nice to hear from you again so soon, but it's three a.m. Is everything all right?"

"I don't know," the voice answered. "Have you found the American yet?"

"You want to talk about that now?"

"Have you found him yet?" the voice repeated.

"Tabitha, I've been really busy. I thought maybe next week I'd give it a try."

"Werner," the voice sounded disappointed. "You promised me."

"I know, I know. Look, I had to close this business deal. It's almost done now, and then I will try and find him."

"Werner," the voice grew stern. "I'm getting on the first flight tomorrow morning. Pick me up at the airport. We're going to see this thing through tomorrow."

"Ah, come on, Tabitha. Can't it wait until next week?"

"You know better than to argue with me, Werner. This man is desperately searching for answers. I took a terrible risk a little while ago."

Werner suddenly wasn't sleepy anymore. "Tabitha, you didn't try and touch him, did you?"

"I had to do something. He was virtually hemorrhaging psychic energy. Couldn't you feel it?"

"A little," he admitted. "As a woman you would be more sensitive to him. What happened when you touched him?"

"Nothing," she said. "He just stopped."

"I'm sorry, Tabitha. I didn't think that we needed to be in such a big hurry."

"Just pick me up at the airport."

"I'll be there."

Before he hung up, Werner added, "Tabitha, don't reserve such a quick return trip this time. I enjoyed your last visit, but it was too short."

"Absence makes the heart grow fonder. Good night, Werner."

CHAPTER 18

Friar Gaspar knocked on the cabin door.

"Sara, Juana, are you soon ready? The longboat is waiting, and Captain Pinzon is anxious to reclaim his cabin."

Juana unbolted the door and peeked outside.

"The Mistress is securing her robe. She doesn't want to cause undue stress among the men when she emerges."

"You're also a pretty one, Juana. After four months at sea, it might be a good idea for you to dress modestly."

"I always do, Friar," Juana told him while blushing. Actually, Juana dressed the same way as Sara so that the two of them would appear alike.

As they were lowered into the longboat, Juana thanked the captain for the use of the cabin. Sara never looked back. She concentrated on the exotic land in front of her eyes.

"Welcome to Lima," Gonzalo greeted the two ladies as he helped them out of the longboat and onto the shore. Gonzalo wisely decided to quarter himself on another boat in the armada for the journey. During the last few days, the fleet separated. All of the other vessels made port first, while the Nina lagged behind. This was purposeful. Gonzalo wanted to get the meeting with his brother out of the way before the arrival of Sara.

"Friar Gaspar," Gonzalo said enthusiastically as he helped him out of the boat. "I trust that you were a perfect gentleman with these pretty ladies."

Gaspar slapped him on the back in greeting.

"They were kind to me," he said. "We made a deal. I agreed not to bother them, and they agreed not to bother me."

The men around them laughed in delight, but Gonzalo understood what the friar meant.

Gaspar turned his attention to a tall, weather-worn man standing with Gonzalo.

Gonzalo performed the introduction.

"Gaspar, allow me to introduce you to the Governor of Quito, my brother,

Francisco Pizarro. Francisco, this is my friend and the soon to be appointed Archbishop of New Andalusia, Friar Gaspar de Carvajal."

Francisco greeted Gaspar and asked him, "Is it true what my little brother tells me? You took counsel with both the Pontiff and the Emperor?"

"Indeed it is true," Gaspar confirmed.

Before he could continue, the governor took notice of the ladies.

"Come, Gonzalo," he motioned. "You must show me to the one that you spoke of."

"Of course," Gonzalo smiled. "Ladies," he called out to them. "Come and meet my brother, Francisco."

As they approached, he pointed out to his brother, "Here is Juana, a sexton of the great cathedral in Grenada, and this other lovely maiden is Sara."

"I'm sure they are both lovely," teased Francisco. "It's too hot in this climate for those robes, and they hide your beauty. Lower those hoods and let me get a good look at you."

Sara laughed and told him quietly, "I fear it would be much hotter around here if I lowered my hood. Let's reserve the event for later, when we have a more private time."

"Remember what I told you, brother," Gonzalo warned. "It's best she remains hidden under there for now."

"Speaking of remaining hidden," Sara bumped Gonzalo with her hip. "That was sneaky of you traveling on another ship. Just remember, you can't stay hidden from me forever."

Gonzalo shuddered. He had longed for her every night of the journey.

"What you told me about Sara is just as unbelievable as that story about the Emperor and the Pope," mused Francisco. "I suppose the legend of Sara is also true, eh, Friar?"

"I can assure you from personal experience that every word of it is true," concurred Gaspar.

"And this business about gold?" Francisco asked quietly, making sure none of the men could overhear. "Charles is serious about such a quest?"

"The Empire depends on our success in finding it," Gaspar verified.

A few days later, after the party had rested from their long journey, Gonzalo called a meeting to plan a course of action. He invited his brother and Gaspar. He also requested the presence of Sanchez de Vargas. Since Sara supposedly was the key to this mission, he needed her to be there as well. Gonzalo decided to visit Sara and personally escort her to the meeting place. He wanted an opportunity to find out what she was thinking.

"Outside!" Sara exclaimed. "How wonderful, a meeting under the trees."

"Francisco conducts most of his business outside," smiled Gonzalo. He was happy to see Sara fully recovered from the abuse she had suffered in her prison. "My brother believes that staying close to nature keeps one's head clear when making important decisions."

He studied her for a little while. Sara sensed what worried him.

"Gonzalo, nothing has changed," she told him. "I fully intend to leave you after a time. Someday I will dominate all of you."

Sara lightened her tone. "Don't fret, Gonzalo," she continued. "I haven't forgotten my pledge. I will play along with your little game. Besides, this isn't the place. It took us months to sail around this continent. It is a vast land, maybe even bigger than all of Europe and Asia Minor. No, Gonzalo, my empire will begin in the interior of this continent, far away from here. We will journey together for a long time."

Gonzalo didn't push her further on this matter. He noticed that Sara was wearing new clothes. Juana had sewn garments for herself and Sara. They were three quarter length capes made from hemp that hung loosely on the women's bodies and tied in the front. A hood was also integrated into the garment.

"This is much more comfortable than those hot robes," she told Gonzalo with relief.

"They are suitable," he said with little emotion. "A little more revealing than those ugly robes, but I'm pleased that you are more comfortable now."

Francisco had a magnificent assembly hall carved out at the edge of the forest. Giant trees towered above them and the floor was maintained clean of weeds and vines. The canopy above filtered out the heat from the sun but allowed the light to penetrate. Breezes from the nearby ocean circulated the air and carried the exhilarating aroma of hundreds of species of wild flowers. Colorful birds serenaded them with an incessant background symphony.

"This is beyond words," sighed Sara. "Not even the tall cedars of Lebanon rival this majestic place."

"I come here as often as I can," Francisco told her. "I imagine that this is about as close to Eden as a man could ever hope to lay his eyes on."

After they had some time to drink in the scenery, Gonzalo called them together.

He summarized. "Gaspar and General de Vargas and I have been commissioned by the Emperor and the Pontiff to seek out El Dorado, defeat him, and return his treasure to Spain. Our lovely maiden, Sara, is to guide us on this quest. When we arrive at Guayaquil, my cousin, General Orellana, will provide provisions to our party for a journey into the interior."

General de Vargas thought about their options. "Our first decision is whether to reboard Pinzon's fleet and sail along the coast to Guayaquil, or whether we should go over land. It would save us several days, maybe even a week, if we went by the sea."

Sara quickly interjected. "No, General, it must be an over land route. There are three very good reasons. First, we will be along the coastline. This trip will help us all to get into better physical shape for the much more rigorous journey into the interior. Lounging on those ships for four months have made us all soft. The second reason is that we may find some of the indigenous peoples along the way. I want to hear from them about this El Dorado."

"Good thinking," encouraged Gonzalo. "Gentlemen, we have a brilliant tactician in our midst."

"Should I fear for my job?" General de Vargas joked with Francisco.

Gaspar looked at Sara and asked her, "What about the third good reason? Your first two reasons are very sound. The third must be brilliant."

"That's right," Sara told them with a smile hidden under her hood. "The third reason is that I'm not getting back on that ship. This land is gorgeous. I want to enjoy every moment of it."

The men burst into laughter.

"Well," General de Vargas resigned himself. "If the lovely maiden wants to go over land, so be it."

As the meeting broke up, Sara tugged at Gonzalo's sleeve.

"Can we speak here for a while, privately?"

"Wouldn't it be better if we sent for Juana first?" he asked her.

"Please, Gonzalo," she beseeched him.

He looked over at Gaspar. The friar nodded helplessly and walked away.

After the men left them, Gonzalo turned to her.

"Does something disturb you, Sara?"

"No," Sara started. She changed her mind.

"Actually, yes," she said coyly. "Look at this place, Gonzalo." She spun around in a dance, and lowered her hood.

"Now look at me," she requested.

"Sara, please," he expressed anxiously and started to back away.

"Gonzalo, this is probably the most beautiful spot on Earth. It refreshes my soul, especially after being locked away for so long. This place stirs my yearnings as a woman. I need you, Gonzalo. Please make love to me."

He closed his eyes and swallowed hard. "Are you forcing me?" he asked her.

"I could, you know," she told him in a vehement tone. Then she softened. "I would rather you do so because you want to."

Gonzalo's heart pounded within the walls of his chest.

"Oh, I want to," he told her as his resistance ebbed. "What will become of me?"

"The experience will be exquisite," she promised him. Sara untied her cape and allowed it to fall to the ground around her. She wore nothing underneath.

Gonzalo recalled the sight of her naked body in those few moments that she was exposed in the cathedral. He was just as stunned then as he was now.

"Come and hold me," she beckoned him.

He did just as she commanded. They kissed passionately. She held him with her eyes.

"Fill me," she entreated.

Gonzalo remembered very little of the next few minutes. They tangled together on the ground of the outdoor paradise. Every thrust sent fire into his brain until their simultaneous climax, an explosive seizure that ripped into his soul. In an instant of time, Sara tore Gonzalo's spirit outside of his body and absorbed some of his life force. She released him just in time to prevent his heart from stopping.

A few minutes later, Gonzalo regained consciousness. He found himself exhausted with his head lying on Sara's stomach. She was gently stroking his hair.

"Great God in heaven," was all Gonzalo managed to get out between gasps for air.

"Be still," Sara whispered to him. "You will recover soon."

She stole something from me, Gonzalo thought while feeling his head move up and down to her breathing. At first he resented it, feeling somehow less of a man. He rationalized that it was a small price to pay for such intense pleasure. Gonzalo immediately began to wonder when he could make love with her again.

Governor Pizarro inspected the deployment with a troubled look. "General de Vargas, it is unfortunate that I do not have enough horses to spare for all of your men. Are you sure that you don't wish to send some of them with Captain Pinzon? He is moving the armada to Guayaquil and will most certainly arrive there before your over land expedition."

The general looked over at Sara and Juana. They seemed to be enjoying themselves watching all of the excitement as the assembly made ready. Sara had a full basket of grass that she was using to feed the horses.

"Our guide, the maiden, has a point," de Vargas pointed out to the governor. "We're soft and need a journey to get us back into shape. Besides, most of my men share the lady's sentiments. They aren't interested in putting to sea either."

General de Vargas continued to talk with Governor Pizarro. "I have two hundred men. With the friar, your brother, the two ladies, and myself, our number is two hundred five. Your generosity in providing one hundred horses to us is more than adequate. We will be able to take turns riding. It will not be too much of a burden."

Friar Gaspar and Gonzalo joined up with them.

"How long do you figure it will take us to reach Guayaquil?" Gonzalo asked his brother.

"If you stick to the coast and do not tarry in any one place, you should be at your cousin's door in about two weeks," Francisco informed him.

Near the end of November, he thought. "I've asked Captain Pinzon to notify our cousin that we are on the way."

The governor laughed. "Orellana will no doubt have quite a reception waiting for you. Be sure to send my greetings."

Francisco made a motion with his head indicating to Gonzalo that he wished a private conversation with him. The two of them walked away from the deployment toward the water. They stared off into the dark horizon of the Pacific.

"I hate to see you go so soon, little brother," Francisco started. "You've barely just arrived. There is much that I would like to share with you about this strange, yet bounteous land."

Gonzalo smiled, "That's easy for you to say. All of Europe has heard of your great conquest. When they write the history books, my name, if mentioned at all, will be a mere footnote next to the chapter describing your colorful exploits. Don't you want your little brother to make a name for himself, too?"

Francisco bellowed with laughter. "Good luck, Gonzalo. Ten years ago, I conquered the mighty Incan Empire, plundered their great cities, and weighted the ships with so much gold that they dragged bottom in port. How are you going to top that?"

Gonzalo squinted at the horizon. It was difficult for him to not think about Sara. "Easy," he said with bravado. "I allow myself to be guided by a young woman barely an adult. We follow fairy tales told by superstitious heathens. We seek out an old man that exists only in legends. Finally when we find him, we steal his treasure, return to Spain, and save the Empire."

The two of them looked at each other and had a good laugh. A few moments later, they grew somber thinking about the folly of the situation.

"What are you going to do, Gonzalo?" his brother asked with concern.

"I really don't know," Gonzalo replied. "I have some time. It took us four months to get here. They must expect that it will take us at least a year and then another four months for the return trip. I figure that I have at least two years. A lot can happen in that time."

"Yes," Francisco interjected. "You could die."

Gonzalo laughed nervously and asked, "What do you mean, brother?"

Francisco started to slowly walk south along the shoreline. The waves were breaking near his feet. Gonzalo followed him and they continued their conversation.

"It wasn't easy, you know," Francisco preached. "The Incan Empire was strong. Many times, I came near to losing my life. In the end, it could have gone either way. God smiled on me this time."

"War is never easy," Gonzalo said with understanding. "Only a fool would think otherwise. Francisco, if you are worried about me, I promise that I will be careful. There are two hundred men riding with me. You already scattered the native peoples. They will flee from us."

"I suppose so," Francisco relented. "I have another worry. What will you do about the maiden? Will you flee from her?"

Gonzalo felt himself grow hot. "She is no concern of yours," he said angrily. "You can't have her. She stays with me."

"Gonzalo, I never expected her to remain behind," Francisco started to say.

"Sara will not remain behind," Gonzalo was now yelling. "I warn you. Do not get between us." Gonzalo put a hand on his sword.

Many in the nearby assembly heard Gonzalo shouting. They stopped what they were doing to observe the commotion. Sara dropped her basket of grass and began to run toward them.

"Her hold on you is strong, Gonzalo. It appears that she is the one that has already come between two brothers."

"What do you know of her hold on me?" Gonzalo scoffed.

"You slept with her, didn't you?" Francisco shouted, tired of his insolence.

"Don't speak of her that way," Gonzalo screamed in rage while drawing his sword.

"You would strike down your brother over a promiscuous harlot?" Francisco continued to push him.

"Naaaaa," screamed Gonzalo as he lunged toward his brother. Francisco drew his own sword and parried the assault. Gonzalo continued to lunge forward.

At that moment, Sara reached them. She grabbed Gonzalo from behind as he advanced on his brother. They stumbled together onto the sand. Gonzalo rolled out from under her. She jumped on his chest and laid herself out on top of him.

Pulling his face inside of her hooded head, she whispered to him, "Gonzalo, stop, look at me."

His eyes met hers. The sword fell out of his hand.

"Not now, my champion," she said in a soothing voice.

"This isn't the right time, is it?"

"They will take you away from me, understand?"

"You don't want to kill your own brother, do you?"

She successfully brought him back.

"Sara," he moaned. She felt him growing hard beneath her.

"Shhh," she scolded him. "Come to my tent tonight, after we are away from here."

Sara let him up. Francisco had his sword pointed at her.

"Get away from my brother," he hissed.

General de Vargas stood there not knowing what to do, and Friar Gaspar stared at them terrified.

"Mistress, are you all right," gasped Juana as she broke through the crowd.

This was a seminal moment, and Sara realized that she needed to act quickly. Everything could come crashing down during the next minute. Sara knew from many experiences that she possessed the power to influence events such as this, but these flirtations with death always frightened her. Sometimes when her emotions interfered with her concentration, it didn't work. She failed when Leon was killed and when they carried her away. This was Sara's first test since that disastrous night.

I can't fail now, Sara thought as she steeled herself.

Sara pulled the hood away from her head and shook out her hair. This definitely commanded the attention of all of the men. She made eye contact with Gaspar, then de Vargas, and finally with Francisco. They were frozen in place.

"This heat is enough to drive any of us mad, isn't it?" she asked them while flashing a beautiful smile.

"It was just an unfortunate misunderstanding, wasn't it?"

"Brothers sometimes get angry with one another, don't they?"

"It really is inconsequential, isn't it?"

"We should begin our journey now, shouldn't we?"

"Juana and I need to leave you men now, don't we?"

"You need to bid farewell to your friends, don't you?"

Sara abruptly pulled the hood from her cape back into place, grabbed Juana by the hand, and started back toward the horses.

After a few moments, the fog lifted. Gonzalo bowed his head in shame.

"Forgive me, Francisco. It must be this heat," Gonzalo offered timidly. "I'm not used to it, and must have gone temporarily mad."

Francisco hugged his brother and told him, "Don't worry, it was just an unfortunate misunderstanding."

Friar Gaspar separated the two and smiled. "Ever since the time of Cain and Abel, brothers sometimes get angry with one another."

"Cain and Abel!" Gonzalo shrieked. "Nothing like that would have happened. It was just something inconsequential."

"Ahem," the general interrupted, clearing his throat. "If you boys are done quarreling now," he winked. "We really should be beginning our journey now."

"Of course," Gonzalo agreed. "I believe the two ladies are ready to go. They seem to be done playing with the horses."

The four of them laughed.

"Farewell, friends," Francisco bid them as he hugged his brother again. "Gonzalo, tell that cousin of ours to come south and visit me."

"You can be sure that I will, brother," Gonzalo assured him.

The hundred horses and two hundred men presented the city of Lima with quite a spectacle as they rode away. Governor Francisco Pizarro visited his sanctuary under the trees near the spot where Gonzalo and Sara made love. He gazed up at the dappled sunshine as it warmed his face and sighed. Francisco realized that he would never see his brother again.

CHAPTER 19

On Sunday morning, Flight 38 landed on schedule. The flight crew made their customary trip to the Royale and settled in for the day. Anne presented all of the necessary signals to Joel. He picked up on them and asked her to have dinner Sunday night. The plan was going beautifully. That afternoon, Klaus Hall and Officer Dieter Horner led Anne through a coaching session filling her in on the final details.

Werner picked up Tabitha and they began searching for Derek.

Derek and Sharon spent the morning together as usual. This time Juan stayed behind in his room.

Elyria was fretting to herself about how, without cobo, she now had to murder Sharon through physical contact. It would be messy and dangerous. Hank Kimball was only aware of the fact that Derek's hearing was on Tuesday. Between now and then, Hank's only concern was how he could get more sack time with Elyria.

The day passed. That afternoon, Elyria went to the fitness center. Previously she stole a sharp steak knife. Elyria hid it in her gym bag. Sharon never showed up. With her new role in the sting that was about to unfold, Sharon was too nervous to workout.

At 7:00 p.m., Joel Washington knocked on Anne Sprague's door. She took a deep breath. *This is for you, Derek*, she thought.

After she opened the door, Anne watched as Joel's eyes opened in wonder. He was gazing at a pretty, young flight attendant dressed in a low cut, bright red cocktail dress. Her hemline was well above the knee.

"Damn," Joel said while staring at her. "Forget about dinner, you're good enough to eat right here." He started to push his way in. Another foot and he could have reached around and closed the door behind them.

Anne resisted and stopped Joel just short of his goal.

"Down boy," she scolded him. "Be good and maybe you'll get lucky enough to have me for dessert."

"Damn," he said it again.

Obnoxious asshole, she pondered. The way he was mentally undressing her made Anne's skin crawl.

At the restaurant, Anne encouraged Joel to have a few drinks before they ordered dinner. He started drinking vodka martinis. Anne had one and then switched to ginger ale. After two drinks, Joel was feeling no pain, but he was still in control of himself. Anne motioned the waitress to take their order.

"Joel, you are such a natural with *Adventurer*. It's as if you have a relationship with that plane. When I stand back and watch, I can tell how well you respond to her every movement."

"It's your movements that I'm interested in watching right now," he mused. "You move real nice, Anne."

"I'm serious," she continued. "You're a great pilot. I haven't known you that long, Joel. Were you a pilot on any other flights prior to *Adventurer*?"

"Not since the Air Force," he answered. "I was a damn good pilot there too."

"I'll bet you were," she confirmed. "You've logged a lot of hours for TransGlobal, haven't you? I mean, why do you suppose it took them so long to make a great pilot like you a captain? You certainly logged more flight time than Derek Dunbar, didn't you?"

Anne watched as Joel's expression changed. She suddenly feared that she was pushing him too hard.

"Dunbar," he said with revulsion. Joel grew strangely silent and ordered another martini.

Anne wanted to keep the conversation moving in this direction. She sensed that he was about to loosen up. She looked at him and smiled, "I guess TransGlobal management screwed up when they decided to make him a captain, didn't they?"

Joel's expression didn't change, but he startled Anne when he pounded his fist once on the table. It wasn't too loud, but it released some pent up frustration within him. "Management," he spewed the word as if vomiting. "You know what really gripes me about those assholes?"

Joel's fist was still pressed into the tabletop. Anne reached over with both hands and caressed the fist. She looked him in the eyes but said nothing, waiting for him to continue.

"I wouldn't be a captain, if it weren't for Dunbar screwing up. They didn't promote me, Anne. I inherited this job. It's not the same thing as a promotion. They still don't respect me."

"Shhh, it's all right," she said soothing him. "Your friends are the people that count. We respect you. To hell with management."

While Anne was talking, Sharon and Juan entered the restaurant. They sat at a table where Anne could see them, but Joel had his back turned to them. Juan looked over at her and nodded. It was a signal to Anne that they were ready.

The waitress arrived at Anne and Joel's table carrying a tray with three drinks, the one that Joel ordered, and two more.

"Compliments of the man sitting at the table behind you," she said. She set two vodka martinis in front of Joel and a ginger ale in front of Anne.

"It appears you have another fan," Anne said as she smiled.

Joel picked up one of the drinks and turned his chair around to determine the identity of the benefactors. When he saw them, he almost dropped the glass. Sharon was hanging all over Juan Sanchez. When Juan made eye contact with Joel, he raised his glass as if in a toast.

Joel looked at Anne. "How many of these have I drunk?" he said holding up the glass. "Am I dreaming, or is that Sanchez, the mechanic, over there with Dunbar's woman?"

Anne held her hand up to her chest. "It's them. Look, Joel, she is practically sitting in his lap. What do you suppose is going on?"

"I don't know, but you better believe that I'm going to check this out. Excuse me a minute."

Joel stood and approached the couple. "Sanchez? Sharon? Is that really you?"

Juan stood and shook his hand. "Señor Washington, fancy meeting you here."

Sharon squeezed Juan's arm with both of her hands. "Hi, Joel."

He stared at the two of them for a few moments and snickered. "It appears to me that you two have a story that needs telling. Would you like to join Anne and me for dinner?"

"Only if I get to sit beside Juanny," Sharon said with a fawning look.

The three of them returned to the table where Anne was waiting. Sharon and Juan sat opposite to Anne and Joel. Joel downed his drink and reached down resting his hand on the inside of Anne's thigh.

"Anne," he said, "Sharon and Sanchez have agreed to entertain us this evening while we have dinner together. You don't mind, do you?"

"Not at all," she responded. "It's good to see you again, Sharon. I believe the last time was at Derek's promotion party, wasn't it?"

"You mean 'the loser,'" Sharon snarled. "Don't say his name anymore in front of me. Whenever you talk about him, just call him, 'the loser.'"

Anne acted concerned. "Sharon, I'm sorry. What's wrong? What happened between you and Derek, I mean 'the loser?'"

"That bastard," she spat. "I flew here with Juanny. The loser's lawyer asked us to testify about our experiences with that Blaze character. I didn't want to believe that the loser was involved in anything so low as drugs. Can you believe that when Juan and I confronted him alone, and there was no one else with us, he lied to our face, Anne? The loser actually wanted us to believe with that mountain of evidence against him, that some conspiracy was being foisted on him."

Sharon's eyes started to mist over. "I thought he loved me, Anne. Instead, he almost got me killed and lied to my face." Sharon put her arm around Juan. "If it wasn't for this brave man, my Juanny, I'd be dead. He risked his life for me when that Blaze guy came after me."

As Sharon started to sniffle, Juan jumped in. "Dunbar really angered me. What man would expose his woman to such danger?" He hung his head. "I lost my wife some time ago to a disease. I couldn't fight for her." Juan raised his head and wore a defiant look. "I fought for Sharon. I'll be taking care of her now."

The two of them stared lovingly into each other's eyes.

Joel started on the drink that Juan bought for him. He started squeezing Anne's thigh. "Let me get this straight. You, Sanchez, and you, Sharon, are really together?"

Sharon batted her eyes at Juan and breathed, "Forever."

Juan gave her a quick kiss.

Joel Washington could hardly contain himself. His leg was bouncing up and down under the table, and he was squeezing Anne's thigh so hard that it started to hurt her. His face was beaming.

"That's rich," was all he could say. His lower jaw quivered. "That is so rich."

Anne looked somberly at Joel and asked, "You are his friend. Did you have any clue that anything like this was happening?"

Joel just smiled and shrugged his shoulders. During dinner, they talked about many things. From time to time, Anne would refer to Derek's situation, but she could not get Joel to crack. He was ready to burst; yet he remained silent. The four of them had after dinner drinks, and it soon became time for the gathering to break up.

Sharon started to cry.

Anne noticed the signal. "Joel, poor Sharon's been through a lot. I'm going to take her to the powder room for a minute. Is that all right with you?" she asked his permission.

"Sure, sure," he waved at her. "Sanchez and I will have another drink until you return."

Sharon was still wiping her eyes as they stood looking in the ladies' room mirror.

"Great job!" Anne exclaimed. "Tears and all."

"They're real," Sharon began to sob again. "Anne, I'm scared. It's not working. He hasn't revealed anything."

Anne put an arm around her. "It's going to work. He's had enough of those martinis to loosen up, and he's so full of himself. I'm going to take him up to my room. Don't worry, Sharon, he'll talk."

"Your room?" Sharon asked with a frightened expression. "Anne, no. You can't do that. Derek wouldn't permit you to do that."

"Sharon, your future with Derek is at stake here. If I have to do this thing for the two of you, it is of little consequence."

"No, Anne," Sharon pleaded. "Neither one of us could live with ourselves. We will find another way."

Now Anne started to cry. "I think we both know that this is our only chance. The hearing is Tuesday."

Anne paused to choke back some tears. "Sharon, you're a lucky woman. In my own way, I love Derek, but he loves only you. If this is what it takes to assure his happiness…"

She stopped talking, and they stood there. A certain understanding passed between the two of them.

Sharon hugged Anne and told her, "Please be careful."

Sharon remembered that they were being monitored.

"The wire," she said in alarm. "Anne, he's going to be all over you. Won't he discover the wire?"

"Not to worry," Anne reassured her as she held up the matching red purse. "It's built in here. I'll just set it on the night stand beside the bed."

On the way out of the ladies' room, Anne looked quizzically at Sharon and asked, "Juanny?" This broke the tension, and they both laughed.

Joel was so happy that he picked up the check for all four of them. They separated. Sharon and Juan broke for the surveillance van in the parking lot. Klaus and Dieter let them in.

"We can stop this now," Officer Horner told them. "This is going a lot further than we intended."

"No," said Sharon emphatically. "You heard Anne make her decision in front of us in the ladies' room. This is Anne's show for now. Just be ready to get up to her if she gets into trouble."

Joel Washington never felt more alive in his life. He was high on vodka martinis; he had destroyed his archenemy. Derek's losing Sharon sent Joel into euphoria. The icing on the cake was Anne. He was about to score with this delicious babe.

On the way up to her room, Anne continued probing. "Joel, when do you suppose Derek took those drugs? Was it before take off, or sometime during the flight?"

"Hell if I know," he said while laughing.

"Were you as scared as I was when he passed out?" she inquired while squeezing his hand.

"Are you kidding? I knew what was coming. I was ready to step in."

Anne's heart started beating faster. She was getting close.

"How could you know, Joel? Did you suspect something?"

Anne unlocked her door while waiting for his answer. As they entered the room, he told her, "I didn't suspect something. I knew something."

"What do you mean, Joel? Did you see him take the drugs?"

Joel closed the door, grabbed Anne, and started savagely kissing her on the mouth. Anne couldn't catch her breath. She managed to break away.

"I will not be much fun if you make me faint," she breathed heavily.

"Sorry, baby," he breathed back. "I've wanted to do that for a long time and got carried away. Don't worry, I want you to be awake and able to enjoy this." He pulled Anne down onto the bed and started groping under the red dress.

"Joel," Anne continued between shudders. "If you saw Derek take those drugs, why didn't you stop him right away?"

This caused Joel to stop dead. He eyed her suspiciously and asked, "Why all of this curiosity about Dunbar and me?"

She thought fast and acted with innocence. "We both know that you deserved to be pilot, and you said that management doesn't respect you. Stopping him would have changed their view of you, wouldn't it?"

Joel looked her in the eyes and asked her back, "Do you think Dunbar is a likable person?"

"Yeah, he was likable enough," she admitted. "But we both now know how much of a jerk he really is."

201

Joel smiled, "Do you believe that I am a likable person?"

"I've always been fond of you, Joel," she said as convincing as possible.

"How much do you like me, really?"

"You wouldn't be with me in my room if I didn't like you a whole lot," she smiled.

"Prove it to me," he demanded. "Stop talking about Dunbar, get out of that dress, and give me what I want."

Anne turned it around on him. "I don't let just any man make love to me. How do I know that you respect me, Joel?"

He tore off his shirt and unzipped his fly. Anne lay there waiting.

"After we're done, baby, maybe I'll let you in on a little secret."

Juan reached for the door of the van. "I can't let this happen," he stated sternly.

Sharon grabbed him around the waist. "No, Juan. She knows what she is doing."

"She's right," interjected Klaus. "Anne understands that all she needs to do is signal and we would be up there immediately. This woman is courageous. We must not allow this sacrifice of hers to be spoiled."

Juan put his hands over his ears. "I can't bear to listen to this anymore," he groaned.

Tears streamed down Anne's face as Joel worked away grunting on top of her. She maintained her composure by imagining that it was Derek.

In the van, Sharon was wiping her eyes. Juan still had his ears covered with his head looking down. Klaus Hall and Dieter Horner stared straight ahead. Neither one of them moved. They both felt horrible and wanted it to be over.

Joel rolled over and lay on his back looking at the ceiling. Anne tenderly placed her head on his chest. He started stroking her hair.

"My captain," Anne whispered and wiped her nose with the back of her hand.

She watched as several minutes clicked off the digital alarm clock. The wait was excruciating for Anne and for her friends in the van.

Finally, Joel took a deep breath. Anne thought that her head would roll off his chest. The vodka tonics still held him in a strong buzz. Joel was getting sleepy, but he did not intend to allow himself to fall asleep.

I'm good for another round, he thought. *I just have to wait another fifteen minutes or so.*

Joel looked down at Anne's head lying on his chest. "I didn't inherit the job," he told her. "I took it."

Anne stopped breathing. She didn't dare say anything. Anne began to massage Joel's stomach and waited for him to continue.

"Dunbar always thought he was such hot shit. I don't know how he did it, Anne. He must've found a way to kiss someone's ass in management. Everybody liked the guy. He projected that cutesy image, always so friendly hobnobbing with people like Sanchez and with the customers. That doesn't make him a good pilot, does it?"

Anne allowed him to ramble on.

"Yeah, he had some decent technical skills, but hell, I have a lot more experience than he does. If things really got hairy up there in the air, who would you rather have at the controls?

"I love you, Joel," Anne said with little expression. She was glad that she wasn't looking at his face.

"That's right," Joel went on apparently feeding off her statement. "They screwed me, Anne. *Adventurer* was supposed to be mine, and management knew it."

"*Adventurer* is yours now," mumbled Anne just loud enough for him to hear, "and so am I."

"There wasn't a damn thing I could do about it. I was frustrated, Anne. One day opportunity came a callin.'"

"Opportunity?" she inquired. Anne never moved her head from his chest. She never stopped massaging his stomach. This was working, and her heart was racing.

"That's right. It was a mysterious phone call from that woman with the accent. Apparently, good old Derek made some other enemies over the years. All I had to do was to plant the stuff in Derek's bag and spike his coffee. Her operative, that dumb shit, Blaze, was supposed to be her ace in the hole. I let him through security that morning with my badge. They didn't need him, though. I had it under control."

Anne felt faint. She was on the verge of emotional collapse but managed to maintain her poise. Anne couldn't be sure that this was enough. She wanted him to repeat it.

"So someone from the outside gave you the stuff, and you put it in Derek's bag and drugged his coffee?"

"Justice, isn't it?" he laughed. "You should have seen the look on his face in that hospital. I did it to him, and he never even knew what hit him."

"What about this woman with Blaze?" Anne asked. She began to feel the weight of the world lift from her.

"I never saw her," he squealed with delight. "Our only contact was by telephone and through that Blaze guy. She had a sexy voice though, and she went by the name of Elyria."

Back in the van, Sharon felt as if she was slammed by a freight train. "Elyria," she gasped. "Juan, I met a woman with that name. You don't suppose…"

Officer Dieter Horner interrupted by shouting, "That's all we need! Sharon, your Derek is home free. Let's go get that poor woman out of there."

The entire party burst out the back of the van and shot into the hotel.

Anne knew that her job was finished and finally allowed her emotions to break through. She stood up, pulled the top bed cover around herself, and sobbed.

"What's wrong, baby?" Joel asked shocked. He actually felt concern for her. "Did I hurt you? What's the matter?"

He got up and moved toward her. Anne backed to the door, reached a hand behind her, and opened it.

"Where are you going?" Joel was confused. "Let me hold you. I can make it better, baby."

Anne narrowed her eyes and growled, "Stay away from me."

He put his hands on her shoulders. She shook them off.

"Keep your fucking hands off of me," she screamed.

Juan Sanchez reached the door first. He pushed his way in and slammed into Joel, sending him backwards onto the floor. Joel lay there naked and stunned. Klaus and Dieter were a split second behind him.

"That's quite enough, Herr Sanchez," barked Officer Horner. Klaus pulled Juan away while Dieter handcuffed Joel. "You are under arrest," Dieter informed Joel Washington and began reading to Joel the German equivalent of America's Miranda rights.

Sharon embraced Anne. The two of them sat on the edge of the bed. Klaus and Dieter led Joel away. Juan waited by the door for Sharon, but she motioned him to leave them for a while. Juan understood and closed the door behind him.

"I need to take a shower," Anne said to Sharon. She was still crying. "Will you wait here for me? I need someone to talk to."

"Of course," Sharon answered. She tried to thank Anne, but couldn't find any words to even approach the gratitude that she felt. "Anne, there will be nothing that Derek or I can ever do to pay you for this."

"I don't want either of you to pay me anything," Anne said feeling somewhat insulted. "You just marry that man, and don't ever do anything to hurt him."

The hearing lasted about one hour. Derek was completely exonerated of all charges. Neither Derek nor Sharon had any idea of the media barrage waiting for them as they exited the courtroom. The flash of cameras startled them. Derek and Sharon found themselves surrounded by reporters.

"Did you know that this whole incident has been big news in America?" one of them asked. "What is your reaction to co-worker, Joel Washington? Can you give us some insight as to why he would do something like this?"

Klaus Hall jumped to their rescue.

"My client, Mr. Dunbar, has been through a terrible ordeal. He would appreciate some privacy for a while. I'm sure you can understand. I promise all of you that we will be providing a full statement covering all of the details within the next 24 hours."

Klaus led Derek and Sharon to his car. He drove them back to Sharon's room at the Royale.

Werner and Tabitha watched from Werner's parked BMW. "That's him," she told Werner.

"Good God," he moaned. "Can it get any worse? This guy is going to have his picture plastered in every newspaper in the free world. What are we going to do?"

"I don't know," she replied. "His destiny lies in his own hands. Follow him, Werner. We must figure out a way to make contact."

"Are we ready?" Derek asked Sharon. "Our guests will be arriving any minute."

"It's as good as it can be for a hotel room," she smiled and kissed him. It was Derek's victory party, and they invited their friends to join them.

"Oops, just one last thing," Sharon said as she picked up her gym bag and threw it in the closet. She noticed the bright yellow cap on the bottled water and removed it from the bag.

That's right, she thought. *I never opened this one, did I?* She placed it in the tub of ice along with the rest of the drinks they bought for their guests.

They heard a knock on the door.

"Come in," Sharon yelled.

Juan Sanchez entered. Derek hugged him. "Thank you for everything, friend. I'll never forget this."

"That goes for me, too," confirmed Sharon. She put her arms around Juan and gave him a long kiss on the mouth."

Juan blushed. "Consider our debt paid, Derek."

Klaus and Dieter entered next.

"Hide the checkbook, Sharon," Derek joked.

"You had better make it cash, Herr Dunbar," Klaus fired back at him. "You'll be skipping town soon, and I'm not so sure I can trust your check."

Finally, Anne Sprague walked in. She had taken some personal time and did not return to Baltimore. The room fell silent. Derek took both of her hands in his.

"Annie," he whispered. "You shouldn't have. I would have rather rotted in jail for the rest of my life."

She moved her head forward and kissed him while still holding on to his hands.

"Not now, Derek. Maybe you and I can talk about it alone at a later time, but now is not the time."

Sharon popped the top of a beer and handed it to Juan.

"Hey everybody, drink up. There's plenty of beer, soda for mixers, and water in the tub over there."

Tabitha and Werner stood outside of Sharon's hotel room door.

"Do you really think this is a good idea?" Werner whined. "There are other people in there. Shouldn't we try and approach him when he is alone?"

"Werner, we aren't going to reveal the mysteries of the universe to him right now. I just want to make sure that he doesn't slip away back to America without some kind of contact."

"What if he doesn't take this well?" he continued to groan.

"You forget I'm a woman. I can calm him."

Werner looked at her. "There's no way that I could ever forget that you are a woman, Tabitha. Anyway, I thought he scared you."

"He does. This is going to be my one and only meeting with him. After tonight, he's all yours."

"Gee thanks," Werner moaned and rolled his eyes. "Me, a teacher, what next?"

"You'll do just fine," she reassured him. They heard laughter coming from behind the door and the banter of close friends sharing a good time together.

Werner raised his hand to knock on the door. Tabitha stopped him.

"You will not need to do that," she told him.

"Tabitha, remember what he is," he reminded her. "You're playing with fire."

She blinked her eyes. "It's already done, relax," she chided Werner.

In the middle of a conversation with Dieter, Derek stopped short. He turned white.

"Herr Dunbar. Are you all right?"

"Excuse me, Officer Horner," Derek said as if in a trance. "I'll be right back."

Derek looked at the door. Everything rushed in on him, the ordeal of the last few days, the dreams, the visions, and the feelings. Behind that door was something terrible. He could run into the bathroom and hide for now, or he could confront it. If he hid, Derek knew that it was only postponing the inevitable. If he opened the door, he knew that the Derek Dunbar existing in his present skin would be forever changed. It would be a death and a rebirth. He shuffled across the room and turned the doorknob.

Anne Sprague noticed a change in him.

"Derek?" she asked as the door clicked and opened.

The three of them stared at each other. No words needed to be spoken. In that instant, Derek knew that he was no longer alone in the world. Here were two others. They were strangers, just like him.

Tabitha reached up and touched him on the cheek.

"You've been waiting a long time, Derek Dunbar," she said. "Don't be afraid. We are here to help you."

He was mesmerized. "Forgive me for being so forward," he said. "You are perhaps the most beautiful woman that I've ever laid eyes on." Derek couldn't help himself. He put both hands around her neck and pulled Tabitha toward him.

"Whoa, not so fast, American cowboy," Werner stepped between them. "Yeah, they have that effect on men. You're going to learn about that."

This broke the spell, but Derek realized something that he needed to confirm. He gazed at Tabitha and asked, "You are the one that soothed my soul on Saturday night, aren't you?"

"It was me, Derek," she affirmed. "I'm the one that touched you."

"Who is the one that wants me to come to her? That's not you, is it?"

Tabitha looked down for a moment and glanced over at Werner. "Derek, you need to learn about that one. It's not my doing."

"You're an angel, aren't you?" Derek was getting his dreams confused.

"Please, Derek, you are going to have many questions. Werner is going to answer them for you. We wanted to introduce ourselves. Now, you and Werner need to set a time to meet."

"What about you? When will I see you again?" Derek begged.

"I don't know, Derek. There is a danger, my being with you. It has to be Werner. He will explain it to you."

"At the very least you should come in and meet my friends."

"Not a good idea," Werner chimed in. "How would you explain us?"

"You are friends that I made during my many trips to Frankfurt."

"I don't think so," Werner protested.

It was too late. Anne had become concerned about Derek's change in behavior and opened the door wide.

"It's okay, Annie," Derek said. "Some good friends of mine have stopped by."

Tabitha pulled at Werner's shirt cuff. "Come on, just for a short time. You might even have some fun."

Derek introduced everyone. He was completely at ease with Tabitha and Werner and wanted to share these new friends with his old ones. Derek's instincts told him that these two sets of friends represented a bridge between his current and future life.

"I'm Sharon," she said while shaking Tabitha's hand. "Help yourself to drinks over there in that tub."

"Uh, no thanks," said Werner. "I'm fine for now."

"Don't mind if I do," Tabitha announced. "I could use some water." She walked over and was attracted to the bottle with the yellow cap. "Good, it's nice and cold."

"You look nervous, Elyria," Hank noticed. "Come on, we owe it to them." Hank Kimball insisted on revealing himself to Sharon again. It was also a courtesy. He wanted to let Derek know that given what happened in the hearing, the Bureau had no further interest in pursuing him. The investigation now centered on Joel Washington.

Elyria reluctantly agreed with him. She made it clear to Hank that her secret agency was also no longer interested in pursuing Derek. Of course, this was a ruse. She still had a job to do. She needed to murder Sharon

McGee, and time was running out. Elyria felt for the steak knife on the top of her purse. "Okay, let's go," she told him.

Sharon heard a knock on the door.

"Derek, how many more friends do you have?" she jested and walked to the door.

Sharon was stunned.

"Hank Kimball? Is that really you? What are you doing here, Ellie?"

"Geez, Sharon," he said. "Let us in. We have some explaining to do."

They entered. Juan perked up, "Hey, don't I know you?"

"It's Hank Kimball, Juan. Remember, I'm 21C on Flight 38. Elyria and I have come to set the record straight. We want to put Derek's mind at ease about his status back in the States. He's in the clear."

Sharon held her head and walked to the back of the bathroom. *Hank and Ellie*, she pondered. *Hank just said her name is Elyria.* Sharon made the connection and turned around eyes wide with terror.

At the same time, Officer Dieter Horner remembered something from the taping of Joel Washington. "Did you say, this lady's name is Elyria?" he asked.

"The coffee," Sharon shrieked. "They drugged Derek's coffee. Joel Washington said that a woman named Elyria was the mastermind." Suddenly it became clear to Sharon. She burst from the bathroom and ran over to the tub.

"Where's that water?" she screamed.

Everyone in the room had their eyes riveted on Elyria. Sharon ran up to her face screaming, "Why are you doing this? Why?"

Elyria felt like a trapped animal. Her jungle instincts took over. She kneed Sharon in the stomach. Sharon doubled over. Before anyone could react, Elyria pulled the steak knife from her purse and grabbed Sharon around the neck. Holding the knife against Sharon's right eye, Elyria made her move.

"This woman and I are going to walk out of here. The slightest interference from any one of you and this goes through her eye and into her brain."

"You're not taking her anywhere," Derek hollered.

"Elyria?" muttered a stunned Hank Kimball.

"This is your doing, Derek Dunbar," Elyria cried as she started dragging Sharon toward the door. "The Mistress wants you to come to her. She thinks that this is the only way."

Werner poked Tabitha in the side. "Did you hear what she said? I believe that this one is working for Sara." He looked and saw Tabitha folded over the arm at the end of the sofa.

"Tabitha?" Werner shook her. "Tabitha?" he screamed.

The scream momentarily distracted Elyria. She relaxed the pressure against Sharon's eye. Sharon yanked her head away and elbowed Elyria in the side. Elyria still had one arm around Sharon's throat as they both tumbled to the ground. Elyria was stronger and quickly got the mastery over Sharon. She raised her arm to make a fatal stab to Sharon's throat. Derek grabbed Elyria's arm from behind. He pulled her off Sharon and punched her square in the jaw. Elyria fell over backwards. She was unconscious before she hit the floor.

Werner held Tabitha's face between his hands. Their eyes locked.

"So tired, Werner," she whispered to him. "It's time for me to depart."

Tabitha reached up with the last of her remaining strength and touched Werner on the cheek. She smiled. "Too much damage," she whispered. "I can feel my nervous system shutting down."

"No," he screamed in protest. "Don't leave us, I need you, Tabitha."

Tabitha's eyes began to fade. She squeezed Werner's wrist and smiled.

"Look, Werner!" she exclaimed in a whisper. "She's smiling at me. The prize, Werner, I've won the prize." The light went out of Tabitha's eyes and her soul departed. Werner buried his head in her chest and wept.

Derek slumped down to the floor in a sitting position. His face was twisted. "Now who will pull me from the darkness," he lamented.

Hank Kimball was trying to make sense of things. "Geez, can someone tell me what is happening here?"

Klaus and Dieter bent over while tending to Elyria.

Anne Sprague sat beside Derek and put an arm around him.

Sharon sat on the other side of Derek. She knew that something about him had changed, but her mind did not yet have everything clearly in focus. "Derek?" she asked. He turned and looked at her. "Derek, now I understand why I haven't been able to commit to marriage. We've spent years together, but I feel like I still really don't know you? Derek, who are you?"

He hung his head.

"That's the wrong question, Sharon," he corrected her. Derek looked over at Werner. "What am I?"

CHAPTER 20

Guayaquil, New Andalusia — November 1540

Uanica arrived red faced and out of breath at the bivouac where his captain slept.

"Captain Pinzon, are you here?" gasped the young man as he entered the tent. "It's General de Vargas and his party. They are near."

Most of the younger sailors in the armada continued to sleep through this intrusion. The heat and humidity were stifling. The sailors preferred camping on the beach where the nighttime sea breeze kept the mosquitoes at bay.

Captain Vicente Yanez Pinzon moped out of the tent, still half asleep, and started coughing. It took some time for him to clear his aging lungs.

"You sure?" his voice rasped while he began to look around for the rum bottle to clear his throat.

"Yes, Captain," Uanica responded, still breathing heavily. "During my scouting mission, I stumbled onto some friendly Irimaris. They told me that a party of white-skinned people were half a day behind them. I got close enough to see their campfires at dusk, then I turned around and ran all night to get back."

Pinzon's eyes widened as he spotted what he was looking for. He uncorked the jug and guzzled a full measure of the liquid. Uanica noticed as some color began to appear in the captain's face. Pinzon coughed again and spat onto the ground.

"Ran all night, eh?" he looked admiringly at Uanica. He offered the bottle. Uanica politely declined.

"You sure it was their campfire and not just another party of Indians?"

"The fires were scattered and large," answered Uanica. "It was a large party of travelers. Indians keep their fires low and barely noticeable. It has to be them."

"Good work, mate," the captain congratulated his subordinate. "Clean yourself up, I want you to come along with me to see General Orellana. He has a big party planned for their arrival."

The two of them walked down the main boulevard in the settlement of Guayaquil toward the mansion situated at its terminus. The place was teeming with activity as the merchants and Indian traders began to prepare for market. Unlike Lima, which was a clean and tidy military establishment, Guayaquil had become a true center of commerce, gritty and alive.

"Reminds me of Malaga," Uanica spoke to his captain.

"Ah, Malaga," Pinzon uttered. "The voyage from this place back to our home in Spain will be my last, Uanica. I'm getting too old for these adventures. Fools chasing after legends of gold are the stuff of younger men, like you. Men who can run all night."

"Well, maybe not all night," Uanica admitted.

They climbed the staircase leading up to the balcony. From here, the entire city could be observed. One of the servants noted their approach and ran inside to alert his master.

As Pinzon and Uanica approached the doorway to the main house, a large well-dressed man emerged to greet them.

"Captain Pinzon!" the man exclaimed. "Just in time for breakfast. You sailors have a nose for a free meal, don't you?"

Pinzon smiled. "We sailors have large stomachs, too. General Orellana, this is one of my mates, Uanica, a fine young man. He was scouting along the shore for me last night and spotted your cousin's group."

"Finally," Orellana expressed enthusiastically. "How far out do you make them?"

Pinzon turned and looked at Uanica.

"They should be here late this afternoon, sir," Uanica reported. "At the very latest, this evening."

Orellana took a long, deep breath.

"Gentlemen, you know what this means, don't you?" he asked with a smile.

Pinzon and Uanica looked at each other not knowing what to say.

Orellana waited a moment and blurted it out.

"It's time for a celebration! You sailors know about celebrations, don't you?"

"Aye, sir," shouted Uanica with glee.

"You can't be serious," Gonzalo expressed with shock at what Sara just told him.

"I'm quite serious, Gonzalo," she stated. "When we reach Guayaquil, I want you to move out of my tent."

He sank to his knees and embraced her thighs.

"Have I displeased you in some way, Sara? Can't you understand that I need to be with you? I'll do anything for you. All you need to do is ask. What is it that you need?"

Sara put his head between her hands and pulled Gonzalo up. It took his breath away as his face passed by her breasts.

"Look at me, Gonzalo," she ordered him.

Whipped and broken, he stared into her eyes.

"I need you to become a man again, understand. Pull yourself together. You are a ruler soon to ride into his realm. I want you to conduct yourself accordingly. Be a man for me, Gonzalo. That is what I want."

After she released him, Gonzalo stood there looking like a little boy. Suddenly he leered at her.

"A man takes what he wants," he jeered. Grabbing Sara by the arm he threatened, "I'm taking you, and I'm taking you now."

Sara slapped him hard. He stepped back holding his cheek. Juana, who had been sewing quietly in the corner, winced.

"That's better," she affirmed. "Get some fire back into those eyes. Now go."

Sara pointed to the entrance of the tent.

Gonzalo slinked away. His mind was tortured with his need for her. Before walking out, Gonzalo stopped. He didn't turn around to look at her, but uttered what was on his mind.

"For how long, Sara?"

"Not until we leave civilization again, Gonzalo. Keep things moving. Don't allow us to dilly dally anywhere. Do you hear me? You may have me again, but not until we are well on our way."

Gonzalo nodded his head in acknowledgment but didn't say anything. His face twisted as he emerged into the brilliant morning sun.

The two women said nothing to each other for some time. Sara anticipated Juana's concern. "I've ravaged him badly, Juana. He needs to get away to heal. Also, his desire for me will motivate him to get us to the end of our journey sooner."

Juana continued working on the garments that she was sewing.

"What eventually happens to them, Mistress Sara?" Juana asked. "What happens if they continue to sleep with you?"

"They die," Sara told her flatly.

As the over land travelers descended from the Cordillera Mountains toward Guayaquil, the first hint that they were expected was the incessant ringing of the church bells. These could be heard many kilometers distant. At the outskirts of the city, an emissary met them.

"General Orellana asks that you follow me," the young man told them. "I will lead you along the processional route to his estate."

He took them the long way around so that they could enter the main street from the direction of the sea. That way they could travel the entire road all the way up to the estate perched on the overlook. Throngs of settlers and Indians lined the thoroughfare to witness the event. Two hundred soldiers from Lima, half of them on horseback, was an exciting spectacle. General de Vargas led his men. Gonzalo, Friar Gaspar, and the two ladies on horseback brought up the rear.

At the estate, Pinzon's sailors lined the stairs leading up to the house. Orellana and Captain Pinzon stood at the top.

General de Vargas dismounted at the bottom of the staircase and handed the reins of his steed to one of the stable attendants. Despite the heat of the evening, he briskly ascended the staircase and grabbed onto the hand of his host.

"General Francisco de Orellana, it has been too long since we've had the pleasure to share some time together," de Vargas beamed.

"Too long indeed," Orellana acknowledged. "It is my pleasure to have you here. I look forward to tales about our homeland."

Looking down the long line of soldiers, Orellana was unable to pick out Gonzalo. "Where is that cousin of mine?" he asked de Vargas.

"At the rear, with our special guests," de Vargas responded.

"Captain Pinzon filled me in about the friar and two mysterious ladies," Orellana said while scanning the crowd for them. "I can't wait to meet these beauties."

General de Vargas scowled, "I suppose he also warned you about them?"

Orellana laughed, "Yes, I've been warned. This makes me want to meet them all the more."

"Do not underestimate what you have been told," de Vargas rebuked him mildly. "I've seen what she can do. I fear that your cousin has fallen under her spell."

"You two go first," Sara giggled nervously at the bottom of the staircase. Friar Gaspar shrugged his shoulders at Gonzalo and the two of them began

214

their ascent. Juana and Sara followed them a few steps behind. The hemp fabric of the capes the ladies wore was porous and cool. They really didn't mind the heat all that much despite being covered from their heads to their knees.

From his place beside Captain Pinzon, Uanica gasped when he spotted Gonzalo and tugged on the arm of the captain.

"Yes, I see, Uanica," the captain told him. Before Gonzalo could get to the topmost steps where Orellana waited for him, the captain stopped him and looked him over.

"Gonzalo, this journey has been difficult for you. Are you ill?"

Gonzalo just shook his head and continued onward toward his host.

When Orellana finally shook the hand of his cousin, he also noticed Gonzalo's condition. Before him stood a man, gaunt and pale with lifeless eyes.

"It pleases me to see you once again, Gonzalo," Orellana told him. "It has been many years since we played together as children in our beloved Trujillo."

"Life was simple then, wasn't it, cousin," Gonzalo responded with a far away look. "Now that we are burdened with the fate of our entire civilization, things are less clear now, aren't they?"

Orellana turned serious. "This weighs too heavily on you, Gonzalo. Take heart, for you are not alone in this quest."

Friar Gaspar introduced himself and the two ladies to Orellana. Sara kept her eyes cast down, but Juana found this man quite attractive and couldn't help staring at him. Orellana noticed and kissed the back of her hand.

"This land is fortunate to count as one of its visitors a beauty such as you," he told her.

Juana curtsied and told him, "I fear that you have been away from European women for too long, sir."

"Maybe so," Orellana told her. "Still, I would be honored if you were to sit by me for our evening meal."

Sara giggled under her cape and poked Juana. "Go ahead," she whispered to her companion. "Have some fun."

"Ah, our bashful one speaks," Orellana said as he turned to look at Sara. "You must be the one that all of the men constantly murmur about."

Sara giggled once again beneath her cape but said nothing. She felt happy for Juana and didn't want to steal this moment from her.

General de Vargas and all of his men and Captain Pinzon and all of his sailors were too many to fit into Orellana's estate. As a result, a great outdoor banquet was prepared for them. Orellana sat at the head table with Juana. Also seated here were Gonzalo with Sara, Captain Pinzon with Uanica, and General de Vargas with Friar Gaspar. They ate greedily, told many stories, and drank rum far into the night.

Captain Pinzon made an inquiry to Gonzalo about native peoples that they met along the way from Lima.

"They all fled from us," Gonzalo responded. "Evidently news of my brother's conquest of the Incas has spread terror."

Friar Gaspar agreed, "This is most unfortunate. One of the purposes of this over land trip was to gain news of the man, El Dorado. Now we need to rely solely on our own sources," the friar said as he looked over at Sara.

General de Vargas added. "True, but my men are now in decent enough physical shape to tackle them," he said pointing at the mountains and the jungle beyond.

"You should have come with me on the Nina," Captain Pinzon said quietly to Gonzalo.

The next morning, a beam of sunlight crossing Sara's eyes woke her when Juana lifted the tent flap and entered. She was returning after a night with General Orellana. Amused, Sara sat up on her bed roll and invited Juana to speak with a look that indicated, "Tell me all about it!"

Juana sat across from Sara.

"He's a very good man, Sara," she began. "We talked about this wonderful land and then he confided in me about how much he misses home. He has a yearning to see Spain again."

"Juana, you represent home to him. That is one reason why he is so attracted to you," Sara told her.

"Really?" Juana asked.

"Trust me," Sara said while smiling. "I have lots of experience with men. It only takes me a few seconds of time to determine exactly what motivates each of them."

Juana's head fell as she sighed, "Gonzalo is pressing Orellana. He wants to move on quickly."

For the first time in centuries, Sara felt some guilt.

"That's my doing, you know," she said. "I'm sorry."

"I think Orellana is resisting because he wants to see me some more."

Sara reached over and took Juana's hand.

"Do you want to stay, Juana?"

Juana looked up, and Sara noticed a hesitation in her eyes. She knew that Juana wanted to remain with Orellana, but she also realized that Juana was frightened of her possible reaction to this.

"I pledged to travel with you, Mistress Sara," Juana reminded her.

Sara was overcome. The repressed desire to do good gained temporary mastery over her. *How fragile they are*, Sara thought to herself. *Their years are filled with struggle and grief, and then they die.*

She leaned over and hugged Juana.

"I remember your pledge, Juana," Sara told her. "I also remember telling you that you are a sister to me. You have been a source of much comfort, sister. This pledge of yours is not meant to run your entire life. If it is in your heart that you should stay with this man, then I release you."

Sara immediately felt Juana's body relax. She let go of her.

"You never told me," Juana said. "Where does this end for you? What is the final destination of your heart?"

Sara stood and walked to the flap of the tent. She lifted it and looked outside. Already the morning was growing hot.

"I don't know for sure yet," she told Juana. "I am leading these men far away from here. When I find a place that is suitable to begin a new life, I will leave them."

"What about all this gold and of this man, El Dorado, that you are supposed to find for them?"

"I told all of you before back in Spain. There is no El Dorado. Who knows, at one time he could have existed. He may have been like me, but he is no more. These men seem to be blind to that. This is to my advantage. Let them escort me safely beyond the mountains to the place that I seek."

Juana walked over and looked out of the tent with Sara.

"I would like to see you to your destination, Sara. It would bring me joy to see you finally happy. If only I knew that I could find my way back here again."

Sara was torn. Emotionally, she needed Juana to stay. The little humanity remaining in her wanted to make Juana remain behind with her new man. Dwelling on this, Sara derived a scheme.

"I can fix this for you, Juana," Sara assured her. She noticed a hope spring into Juana's face. Sara smiled back at her and said, "Don't ever be afraid of me, Juana. I promised you a great reward, and I will deliver it to you."

Orellana could hardly believe what she asked him.

"In your bashfulness, you spoke not a word to me when we met," he told Sara. "Now, how is it that you have become so bold?"

"She's a sister to me, and I'm looking out for her feelings. This is what emboldens me, General," Sara answered him. "Therefore, I ask you again. Are you in love with Juana?"

He honestly answered, "We've only just met, but yes, I love her. She is so beautiful and so innocent."

He took a deep breath and glanced up at the ceiling of his estate. "Alas," he moaned. "A madness has gripped my cousin, and he wants to move immediately to the city that Charles promised to him. All of you are leaving for Quito tomorrow morning."

"Can I trust you well enough to release Juana to you?" she asked him.

He wheeled around and looked at her.

"I would protect her with my life. She would rule this land by my side. She would become…"

"A queen?" Sara asked as she finished the sentence for him.

"I am no king," he corrected Sara, "but she would be a queen to me."

Sara considered his words and used her instincts to determine what was in his heart.

"Juana judges well," she told him. "I believe you to be an honorable man. I am comfortable that the two of you could live a happy life together."

"You will allow her to stay here with me?" Orellana asked hopefully.

"Not exactly," Sara smiled. "I need your help. Would you do something for me in return for Juana?"

They talked for some time and then Orellana walked with Sara to visit Gonzalo. They found him barking orders to General de Vargas's men in preparation for their trip to Quito. Friar Gaspar was out purchasing some swine to butcher.

"I'm coming with you, cousin," Orellana said as he confronted Gonzalo.

Gonzalo narrowed his eyes and spat.

"Emperor Charles has given Quito to me. I am the governor there. You have your place, and I have mine." He grabbed Sara by the arm and tugged at her. The force made her stumble and fall to the ground. "You've been spending time with Sara. She's mine. Stay away from her." Gonzalo put a hand on his sword.

"I knew your mother and father well," Orellana raised his voice to Gonzalo. "I know that they taught you proper manners. How dare you dishonor them by rough handling this maiden."

"Stop it!" Sara yelled before the situation became more serious. "Orellana, I'm okay. Gonzalo, hear him out. Your cousin intends no threat to either your authority over Quito or to your claim to me."

The general took Sara's hand and gently helped her to her feet. Sara had been very careful about keeping herself from Orellana. She always remained fully covered inside her cape and never looked him in the eye. Now he was holding onto her hand. Sara's warmth and her power were hypnotic. He didn't want to let go of her.

Dreaded curse, Sara thought to herself. *I was afraid of this.*

Sara gambled and made eye contact.

"Think of Juana," she spoke softly to him. "Juana is the one that you desire." Sara looked down and withdrew her hand from his. This broke the spell.

"Juana," repeated Orellana.

"Gonzalo," he said a little less forcefully this time. "This maiden is correct. I am no threat. You misunderstand. Let's talk like reasonable men."

"What is it you want?" Gonzalo asked, still suspicious of his motives.

"There is a vast wilderness beyond those mountains, cousin. Sara suspects that El Dorado is far, far away. You will need many provisions and many beasts to bear those provisions."

"What of it?" Gonzalo asked seeking clarity.

"Go to Quito," Orellana continued. "Set up your administration and prepare for your journey to the interior. I will have my men conscript a large party of Indians along with their llamas. Wait for me, and I will bring them to you. Together we will complete your quest into the interior."

"I already have de Vargas and his men," sniffled Gonzalo.

"I have no intentions of bringing an army with me," stated Orellana. "I wish only to provide my personal services, a few of my body guards, and supplies enough for all of us."

Gonzalo looked at him and blurted out, "Do as you wish, but Sara stays with me."

"Sara goes where she wills," she corrected him with a stern voice.

Gonzalo walked away.

"He's changed, Sara," Orellana said with disgust.

"I know," she responded. "Don't worry, I can handle him. How far behind us will you be?"

"Two, maybe three weeks should be all the time I need to gather enough supplies for the young fool," he answered her.

"Take care of Juana for me," she charged him. "I will greatly miss her during these weeks. If the two of you still feel the same way when we meet again in Quito, I will ask Friar Gaspar to marry you."

Orellana couldn't help but to laugh.

"So now the lowly maiden orders around the mighty general? Where does this boldness come from?"

Sara laughed with him. She was happy to arrange for this trial relationship between Juana and Orellana. In her heart, she suspected that after these few weeks together, the general would be begging Gaspar to marry the two of them.

CHAPTER 21

"I hate this," Sharon complained. "I didn't even know this woman, and you barely knew her. Why do we have to go?"

Derek tried to be patient with her. "Sharon, she died in our room. I know that we were not responsible, but still it seems the right thing to do. Don't you think we owe it to Tabitha to pay our last respects?"

"No," she told him forcefully. "I'm tired of thinking about the interests of others. When are we going to think about our interests, Derek? I've had enough of this place and all of the people involved in this mess."

Sharon moaned and lifted both of her forearms against the sides of her head, locking fingers behind her ears. Closing her eyes, Sharon whimpered to him, "Derek, all of this is closing in on me. I just want to get out of here. I want to go home."

Derek hugged Sharon and kissed her on the forehead. "I know this hasn't been easy on you," he consoled her. "It will get better soon, I promise." After he let go, Derek walked over to the window and lifted one of the slats of the blinds. Peering out onto the parking lot of the Royale, he allowed his thoughts to wander for a short period. Derek knew that this chapter in his life had not concluded. On the contrary, it was far from over, but he didn't know yet where it was all going to end. He was torn. Derek didn't want Sharon to suffer through any more of it, but he also wanted her to stay. He needed her to be with him. Derek was scared. He understood that all of these events centered on him, but he didn't have all of the answers yet.

"Another day yet, Sharon," he told her. "Come with me to Tabitha's funeral this afternoon. I need to have a long talk with her friend, Werner. Tomorrow we can get the hell out of here."

Sharon understood more about the events than Derek suspected. She also realized that Derek was the center of the malevolence. Sharon was scared, too. The difference between them was that Derek wanted to confront the mystery. Sharon wanted to run away from it.

During times that she was under stress, Sharon would go to the gym and soothe herself with a vigorous workout. Thinking about the fitness center at the Royale and what happened with Elyria made her skin crawl. She didn't want to go back there.

Well, if I can't work out, I might as well eat, she thought to herself. Opening the door of the room's mini-fridge, Sharon found nothing but bottled water. Memories of the yellow-capped water bottle lying beside Tabitha's lifeless body flooded back into her mind. Sharon threw her arms up beside her head again and closed her eyes.

"I'm freaking out, Derek," she moaned. "Can we go for a walk, or something?"

"It's raining pretty hard outside," he told her. "How about if I take you shopping instead? We can drive to the Kaufhaus."

Sharon disappeared into the bedroom to grab a coat. Derek heard her voice as it drifted out to him from around the corner. "Sure, anything, I just need to get out of here for a while."

The prison that Elyria found herself in was nowhere near as accommodating as Derek's former cell. The three-meter by three-meter cube contained a small cot, a toilet and sink, and one open shelf for storage. Elyria was depressed. She had failed her mission, and she had failed her Mistress. There was no way to get word back to Casa Cobo. She was alone and frightened.

Elyria fidgeted as the matron approached and opened the door to her cell. "Now what do they want?" she despaired.

"You have a visitor. Come with me," the matron beckoned in German.

Elyria didn't understand but got the gist of it. She obediently followed the surly woman who led her to a conference room.

Another interrogation, she thought.

"Sit," the woman told her and abruptly left her alone in the room.

Elyria laughed and thought to herself, *These fools don't even handcuff me. What prevents me from walking out that door and causing trouble?*

Before she had time to finish her thought, the door opened and in walked Hank Kimball. Elyria never expected to see this man again. Although she didn't particularly like him, it made her feel good to see a familiar face.

"Hank," she squealed with a smile and walked over to give him a hug.

He resisted her and pointed to the corner of the ceiling. Elyria glanced up and saw the camera.

"I don't care," she said defiantly and tried to hug him again.

"Stop it," Hank complained.

"What do you mean, stop it?" she shot back. "You didn't want me to stop the other day, did you? Why the change in attitude all of a sudden?"

"This is an official visit, that's why." Hank pulled a chair for Elyria and motioned her to sit. She felt too dejected to fight on and complied. Hank sat beside her.

He looked at her and shook his head. "Your passport indicates that you are a Brazilian national. Other than that, you are a blank, a nothing. You show up in nobody's computers."

Hank folded his hands on the table in front of him and looked up at the ceiling. Elyria stared down at her own hands folded on her lap.

"Geez, Elyria, who are you? What's this all about?"

She groaned and rolled her eyes. "What does it matter?" she retorted.

Hank stood and walked around the table taking a seat on the other side directly opposite.

"It matters," he said. "It matters, because I am an FBI agent. I was sent here to investigate the relationship of drugs on board an international flight with murders in Baltimore."

Hank glanced up at the ceiling again. "It matters, because you tried to kill Sharon McGee and you poisoned Tabitha Carr."

Hank looked down and straight at Elyria. She still held her head down looking at her hands. He began to whisper. "Furthermore, it matters because we slept together. Geez, Elyria, this isn't only an official visit, it's personal, too. Let me try and help you."

Elyria lifted her head and looked at him. "Help me?" she squeaked. "How? I'm done for, Hank. Don't you get it? I poisoned a woman to death. I'm going to spend the rest of my life here."

He paused before answering then admitted, "I really don't know how I can help you, but I want to try. Maybe we can begin by you telling me the truth."

Elyria laughed, "The truth? The wildest story I could fabricate would be more believable than the truth."

Hank slammed his fist down on the table. Elyria jerked.

"Come on, Elyria," he said forcefully without yelling. "I'm the only friend you have, and you know it."

She laughed again, "All right, Hank. You want the truth. Try this. I am a soldier on a mission. My orders were to kill Sharon McGee and to persuade Derek Dunbar to travel to Brazil to meet my queen who wants to have sex with him. She has a plan to take over the world. Oh, yeah, and by the way, she's two thousand years old."

After an uncomfortably long pause, Elyria was surprised to find that this did not provoke the reaction that she imagined. Hank sat there staring at her.

"Did you hear me, Hank? Do you want me to repeat any of that?"

"I heard you," he replied. After some time Hank responded, "You're telling me the truth, aren't you?"

This time Elyria did the staring. "Yeah, right," she groused.

"Did you know Werner Klopp?" he asked her.

"I never heard of him before the other night. The same goes for that Tabitha woman," she said wondering how this all mattered.

"A funny thing about Werner Klopp," he related to her. "After they took you away, I gave him a shot of rum to calm his nerves."

"So what?" Elyria shrugged.

"We had a short conversation," Hank went on. "He mumbled something to me about some ancient woman in South America, and how she was seeking out Derek Dunbar so that she could take over the world. It's funny what people sometimes say when they are traumatized with grief."

Hank Kimball stood and returned to his original seat beside Elyria. After sitting, he reached down and caressed one of her hands that remained in her lap.

Looking her in the eye he inquired, "Why do you suppose that what Werner Klopp said in his grief sounds so much like the story you just told to me?"

Elyria said nothing. She honestly didn't know.

"Drugs, Elyria, that's how I can help you. That's the key to me maybe getting you out of here. Tell me everything that you know about this cobo stuff."

Juan Sanchez dialed the number for Anne Sprague's room. His palms were sweating. The phone rang three times, and he was just about to hang up when she answered.

"Hello?" he heard the voice ask at the other end of the phone.

"Annie?" Juan responded. "Uh, this is Juan."

"Hi, Juan," she said back to him in a friendly voice. "I didn't know you were still here. I thought that maybe you returned to Baltimore on this morning's flight."

"I thought about it," he confessed. "I decided to hang around and go home with Sharon and Derek. They're leaving tomorrow."

Anne started twisting the phone cord around her left index finger while she continued the conversation. "I decided the same thing," she told him.

After she said that, a long pause followed. Anne started twisting the cord around in the other direction. Juan began rocking back and forth on his feet.

"After all the excitement of the past few days, these last few hours are going to be boring, aren't they?" she asked him breaking the silence.

He chuckled nervously and responded, "I sure hope so." Juan took a deep breath and continued, "You going to the funeral?"

Unconsciously, Anne changed direction again in twisting the cord. "I don't know, Juan. I thought about it, but it seems like I would be intruding. I mean, Sharon and Derek will be together, and I will be tagging along like unwanted dead weight."

"Yeah," Juan spoke up. "That's exactly the way I feel about my going, too."

Juan stopped rocking back and forth and moved the receiver to his other hand and ear. "Somehow, though, I think I should go. That poor woman, we were all with her at the end. It might easily have been one of us. It just seems proper that we should be there for her."

"Uh huh," Anne said as she thought back to that dreadful night.

Juan took another deep breath. "Annie, you want to go there with me? If we go together, it wouldn't seem like we were intruding on Sharon and Derek's space. Afterwards, well maybe I could buy you dinner."

Anne giggled, "Your asking me out on a date, aren't you? Wow, you want to take me to a funeral for our first date!"

Juan was glad that he decided to telephone Anne instead of asking her in person. That way she couldn't see just how much of a jackass this made him feel.

This was a mistake, he thought. *I'm an airplane mechanic, a grease monkey, and she's a glamorous flight attendant, pretty enough to be a cover girl.*

"I wish you wouldn't put it that way," he struggled to get the words out. "I just thought…"

Anne sensed his discomfort and bailed him out. "Juan, I'm just teasing. Thank you for asking. I think it's a wonderful idea."

"Thank you, Annie," he said with relief.

Anne began twisting the phone cord again.

"You were the first one to my room the other night," she spoke into the receiver.

"Huh?" Juan asked. It took him a moment to catch up with the change of subject.

"You busted through my door and knocked that bastard away from me," she reminded him.

"That's right," Juan acknowledged, suddenly realizing what she was talking about. "It seems I've been doing a lot of that sort of thing lately," he continued. Juan thought about his part in the incident with Blaze and Sharon at the Best Western in Baltimore.

By now, Anne had the phone cord twisted so tight that it was cutting off the circulation in her finger. She unwound the cord and began to shake her hand to get the blood flowing again. "I will not forget it that you were the first one there," she told him.

Juan started to feel his blood pressure rise as he recalled the incident. "I'll never forgive myself for allowing it to happen, Annie. What kind of a man am I for sitting idly by?"

"A brave one," she answered him. "It had to be done, otherwise Derek would still be in jail."

Yeah, well, I still don't have to like it, Juan thought to himself. *That poor woman, Tabitha, might still be alive.*

"Juan, I don't want to eat at the restaurant here at the Royale," she told him. "As a matter of fact I may never eat here again."

"You'll get no argument about that from me, Annie. I'll take you anywhere you want to go."

Klaus Hall leaned back on the chair in his office with his hands locked behind his head as Hank Kimball explained the situation to him.

"It's not unprecedented," Hank pleaded, trying to convince him. "I can think of a dozen examples of our two governments cooperating in shared custody of a prisoner during a narcotics investigation."

"True," Klaus observed. "Yet none of those cases involved shared custody of a murderer. Be realistic, Herr Kimball. You are asking my government to release a killer to you, so that you can take her to Brazil of all places, a country that has no formal extradition agreement with either of our nations."

"I've done some checking," Hank said while tapping the end of his pen on Klaus's desk. "You're a great lawyer, Herr Hall. That's why our State Department hires you to represent our citizens. You performed a great service for Derek Dunbar. I know you can help me."

Klaus rocked forward on his chair and rested his hands on the desk. He glared at Hank Kimball. "I've done some checking too, Herr Kimball. You and Elyria were sharing a hotel room. You care to comment on that?"

Hank thought about all the things he could say. Most of them wouldn't wash. He began to admire this man. *Very observant, just like me*, he pondered.

"That's a fair enough question for you to ask," Hank conceded. "Elyria was good, a shrewd one. She had me convinced that she was an agent, one of us. Yeah, we shared a room. It made it easier for us to work together. It's not all that unreasonable, is it?"

"You tell me," Klaus responded.

"Geez, I know how it looks," Hank admitted. "What do you want me to say? You think I'm here to free my girlfriend?"

"You tell me," Klaus echoed.

This guy really is a good lawyer, Hank thought. *He hardly says a word, yet has me backed into a tight corner.*

Hank recoiled, "Yeah, I'll tell you. The answer is no. This is strictly business."

Klaus swiveled around in his chair and gazed out the window behind him. He said nothing.

Hank grew impatient at the silence and asked him, "Well, what do you think?"

Klaus swiveled around to face him. He wore a stern expression.

"I think you secret agent types have huge egos. I think that this has nothing to do with drugs. It's very personal. This woman completely out maneuvered you and made you look like a fool. You can't handle it. Regaining control over Elyria is nothing more than a way to soothe your bruised ego, isn't it?"

"Sure that has a lot to do with it," Hank admitted. "There's also the bigger picture. Elyria is part of a very dangerous organization and represents a real opportunity for us to crush it." This time Hank walked over to gaze out the window. He bluntly addressed Klaus, "Do you think you can help me, or not?"

"I don't know yet," Klaus shot back. "It will not be easy. I need to consult with my friend, Officer Horner. In the meantime, go back to your hotel room. I'll call you."

"Geez, Herr Hall, thank you," Hank said as he left the office.

"I also think that you are trying to free your girlfriend," Klaus Hall said, talking to himself.

CHAPTER 22

Sara allowed Gonzalo to move back into her tent after they left Guayaquil. They made love during the first night of their trip to Quito. His addiction to her grew stronger. Gonzalo semi-slept during the afterglow with his head snuggled tightly against her breasts.

"Don't keep yourself from me again, Sara," he whispered. "I almost died."

"No, Gonzalo," she warned him. "Stay away from me and live. A few more times lying with me and you will die."

"Impossible," he murmured. "You are my reason for living. You give me strength."

"I rob you of your strength," she corrected him. "Your life force is draining."

He listened to her heart beating. It was a forceful and strong thumping. Gonzalo was soothed and fell asleep.

Sara knew that she had to ration Gonzalo, so to speak, or he would die too soon for her purposes. She would allow him to make love to her once again after they left Quito for the interior. At the journey's end, she would lie with him one final time, one final resplendent moment for Gonzalo, a happy death. All of his life's energy spent through his addiction.

Sara dwelled again on what happened to her during the past two hundred years. She deadened her feelings about Gonzalo's doom. "The first of many to come," she considered.

The next morning, after Sara told Gonzalo once again to get out of her tent, he became enraged.

"What games are you playing with me, Sara?" he screamed.

"It's no game, you fool. Be happy that I am casting you out. Maybe you'll live long enough to find El Dorado's gold for your precious Spain."

Catching Sara off guard, Gonzalo grabbed her around the throat and forced her down onto the bedroll. She clutched for the dagger beneath her cape. This caused Gonzalo to tighten the grip around her throat.

"Don't even try," he leered at her. "I'll choke the life out of you right

228

here, right now."

He lifted Sara's cape up around her chest with his free hand and began to undo his trousers.

"I'm through allowing you to emasculate me," he yelled. "From this moment, I will decide when and where we can be together."

She resisted as he attempted to force her legs apart. Unable to force her with his one free hand, he punched her hard in the stomach. Sara felt herself lose consciousness from the pain of the blow and from her inability to breathe as he cut off her air flow. Black dots swam in the back of her eyes. The dots grew steadily larger until they blocked out all of the light. Sara went limp.

Gonzalo released his grip and he felt her chest heave up and down as unconscious Sara's nervous system ordered her to breathe. Gonzalo tore Sara's cape away and violated her many times over like a wild animal in heat. He suffered no ill effects, because she was unaware and unconscious.

Sara felt the shock of cold water splatter on her face. As she regained consciousness, she began to cough and curled up from the pain in her stomach. Her throat was bruised and swollen.

"Common bitch," he hissed at her. "You'll never deny me again." Gonzalo looked down at her in defiance. He strutted from her tent feeling like a man once again.

Sara panicked. *The situation is out of control,* she thought. *I can't kill him yet. He is the one with the authority to lead this mission. I still need Gonzalo for a little while longer.* She slowly dressed herself. Her body was racked with pain, and she could barely stand. Sara dragged herself to the entrance of her tent and stopped one of the soldiers passing by.

"Help me," she pleaded hoarsely.

The young soldier helped her down into a sitting position.

"You're hurt," he shrieked. "Allow me to get you some water."

"No," Sara coughed. "Go get General de Vargas. Tell him that I need him."

Sara coughed some more. "Hurry," she begged.

Gonzalo returned to tear down the tent to make it ready for the day's trip. He found de Vargas waiting for him with a dozen men.

"General de Vargas," Gonzalo greeted him. "Are we ready to ride?"

The general gave him a cold look.

"The Emperor provided you with the charter for this quest," de Vargas told him. "Out of respect for Charles I do not kill you where you stand. Pay attention to my words. I am the leader of the military escort. They obey me.

The maiden will now be staying under my protection. Friar Gaspar will see to her needs."

The general drew his sword and held it under Gonzalo's chin.

"Touch her again, and you will die. Go near her again without my permission, and you will die. Try to speak with her without my being present, and you will die. Do you understand this?"

"You have no right," chided Gonzalo. "I am soon to be the Governor of Quito and in command of all of the Emperor's soldiers."

"You can command all that you want to," growled de Vargas. "They are loyal only to me."

"I'll send word to Francisco," Gonzalo threatened. "My cousin, Orellana, will be here in a few weeks. You and your men will be crushed."

"I sincerely doubt that, Governor," de Vargas mocked him. "Now get ready. We ride on to Quito."

All of them left him standing there with the exception of Friar Gaspar.

"I suppose that you feel the same contempt for me that they do?" he asked the friar.

"No, Gonzalo," he replied. "You and I both know that Sara is hardly the helpless maiden that she portrays herself to be. Just the same, you beat her, and then you raped her. How could you?" He asked this with incredulity.

"You don't understand," Gonzalo said as he lowered his head. "None of you do. She stole my manliness and my will. Look at me. I am a shadow of my former self. This thing that I did to her, it allowed me to take back some of what she stole from me."

"He meant it, you know," Gaspar said referring to General de Vargas. "He will kill you if you try anything like that again."

"Not if she returns to me of her own free will," Gonzalo retorted. "She'll be back."

Friar Gaspar rode on a horse beside Sara. She was uncomfortable and slightly hunched over.

"Should I ask them to stop for a while?" he asked her.

"You're very kind, Friar," she answered him. Sara's voice was still raspy. "My pain will pass. It's more important to continue with the quest. Quito is only a three-day journey from Guayaquil. I can hold out until tomorrow night."

After some time, Sara felt the need to set the record straight with the friar.

"Gaspar, until Juana returns to me from Guayaquil, I have nobody to talk with. Will you converse with me for a while?"

"Of course," he said happy to have her confide in him.

"You know what I am, don't you? I'm no monster. This thing with men, it doesn't please me. It's a curse. Can you imagine what it is like as a woman not being able to just look a man in the eyes or to feel a man's hug without driving him mad?"

"Not everything about you is cursed," the friar answered her. "I understand that you experienced ancient Rome. Is it possible that you could have met one of Christ's disciples in your time? What a wonderful experience that could have been."

"Sorry, Friar," she admitted. "I met many early Christians, but none of the famous ones from the scriptures. Those people were all just slightly before my time."

Talk of this took her memory back to those days. Sara shuddered as she recalled the games that Nicanor took her to see. She remembered how the friar's predecessors died in the arena.

"You wouldn't have liked it, living back then," she told him. "It was brutal, even more so than present times."

"He was brutal to you, Sara. I feel for you. Are you afraid of Gonzalo?" Gaspar questioned her.

"No, Friar. He was no more brutal to me than I have been to him. I am going to heal. He will not. This may be hard for you to understand, but by going to De Vargas, I am protecting Gonzalo. If I allow him to continue to sleep with me, he will die."

"I don't want to hear about the two of you like that," Gaspar said as he covered his ears.

"I know," Sara understood. "Fornication is wrong in your eyes. Friar, I tell you these things so that you may be aware. Don't you understand, I don't want further harm to come to Gonzalo."

"No, it's you that does not understand," the friar said with his voice shaking. "It's not about the fornication. It's about me. I don't want to hear about this, because I want it to be me. I want to be the one sleeping with you. God help me."

Friar Gaspar kicked his horse and rode away from Sara.

"I know, Friar," she said talking to herself. "I'm sorry. It's a curse after all, isn't it?"

The travelers arrived in Quito late in the evening of December 1, 1540. No fanfare greeted them. This was a primitive mountain town at the base of the Cordillera Range. Most of the area was settled by the indigenous Huaorani people, friendly to the Spaniards. As the weeks passed, Gonzalo and de Vargas set aside their differences and began to plan for the journey over the mountains and into the jungle. They waited for the arrival of Orellana.

Sara kept her distance from Gonzalo. Things had been peaceful between them, and she did not want to risk further confrontation between Gonzalo and de Vargas.

All of December passed, then January, then most of February. There was no sign of Orellana. Sara grew concerned. She was worried about Juana.

Gonzalo arranged for a meeting with General de Vargas. He asked the general to bring Sara.

"The Empire cannot wait forever," he reminded them. "Sanchez, you heard the Emperor. Time is of the essence. It's time for us to once again set out on our quest."

"What about your cousin?" Sara reminded him.

"It is on account of Orellana that we have waited this long. We should not tarry in this place any longer."

"Gonzalo is right," de Vargas agreed. "Sara, one of my men just returned from Guayaquil. General Orellana has miscalculated the amount of time in gathering the stores for our journey. It may be another two weeks until he is ready to move."

"Two weeks is just a guess," interrupted Gonzalo. "It could be four, six, or eight weeks for all we know."

"What is your plan?" Sara asked him.

"Tomorrow I am going to formally take office as Governor of Quito. This will provide me with the authority to sanction our trip. I've already enlisted the aid of the Huaorani. Four hundred of them have been conscripted to pack food and supplies. We leave in four days."

Gonzalo stopped talking and looked at Sara.

"What is it that you wish from me, Gonzalo?" she asked him.

"El Dorado, Sara. This is the reason you have been delivered here, remember? Now it is your time. Where do we go?"

"Gonzalo," she started. "Remember what I told you back in Spain, before we started this journey? You know about El Dorado."

Gonzalo said nothing.

"General de Vargas, can I have a few moments alone with Gonzalo?" Sara requested.

The general glared at Gonzalo.

"You need not be concerned, Sanchez," Gonzalo assured him.

"I'll be within range of your shout," he directed to Sara.

The two of them were alone for the first time in almost three months.

"I haven't forgotten," Gonzalo said to her. "There is no El Dorado. Just the same, where we go needs to appear to come from your mouth. The Huaorani speak of a strange land over the Cordilleras and slightly southeast. I suggest you lead us in this direction. I don't know what we will find, but at least we can try. It will lend some legitimacy to my governorship."

"I did it to save your life," Sara told him unexpectedly. "You know who I am. I told you a long time ago that it is at your own peril to desire me."

"The way I remember it, I had little choice," he fired back at her. "You threw yourself at me back in Lima. You knew that I wouldn't have the will to resist such an assault."

"I could read you," she said defensively. "You wanted me ever since that night you carried me out of Grenada Cathedral. If it wouldn't have happened in Lima, it would have happened somewhere else along the way."

"Sara, every man wants you. You chose me."

"All of them have a little more self control, Gonzalo."

"Control!" he argued. "Strip naked in front of Friar Gaspar and implore him with your gaze. Do you believe that even the good friar has enough control to fight that off?"

"He has enough control to run away and not to beat and rape me like you did."

"That's not fair, Sara. You held a power over me, and you toyed with me."

"I'm sorry, Gonzalo," she finally relented. "It was necessary to keep you moving toward my destination."

"You now have your wish, Sara. Tell us where you want to go. You command an entire army of men to do your bidding. We will keep you safe and sound until you flee from us."

"That day will soon come," she told him.

"Please, Sara, I didn't mean it. Don't leave me. I still need you."

"Gonzalo, you have tasted me. This means that you will have a yearning for me for the rest of your life. One of two things will happen. If we separate, you will eventually grow stronger, never to the level that you once were, but stronger nonetheless. Look at you. In these three months, you have healed considerably."

"I still burn in my heart for you, Sara."

"Once we get closer to where I want to go, if it is your desire, I will allow you to have me again. You have free will, and I will not deny you. Beware, Gonzalo, on that day you will die."

Gonzalo smirked, "So my choice is either to live the rest of my life in pain yearning for you, or to die?"

"It's that simple," she said.

Gonzalo stared at Sara. He mentally visualized the curves from her smooth olive skin underneath the cape. He studied Sara's dark flowing hair as it was gently tossed in the mountain breeze. He dared to catch a glimpse of her clear hazel eyes. Finally, he decided.

"I choose death."

"So be it," Sara said with no emotion. She motioned General de Vargas to rejoin them.

The general had been thinking during the time that Sara and Gonzalo had their conversation. He was anxious to ask Gonzalo something. As he approached them, de Vargas let it out.

"These conscripted Huaorani haven't been told anything about gold, have they?" the general asked with concern.

"No, Sanchez," Gonzalo confirmed. "They believe that it is cinnamon that we are seeking. I've convinced them that they will be paid after they carry it all back to the port of Guayaquil and Captain Pinzon's awaiting fleet."

"Aha," de Vargas shrugged with relief. "One more thing," he continued. "Eventually Orellana will arrive, and he will want to follow us. How will he do so?"

"We will mark a clear trail," Gonzalo said. He had already thought this through. "I'm also going to leave Friar Gaspar behind to explain things to my cousin."

"Wonderful idea," Sara said with a smile. "I need to talk with Gaspar before we depart. He may have a wedding to plan."

Gaspar watched as the large sea of humanity was finally swallowed up by the forest covering the base of the mountain. The two hundred soldiers along with four hundred Huaorani and assorted livestock made up the party.

"Please hurry, General Orellana," he said to himself. "God save me, but I feel the need to once again be in her presence."

Orellana finally did arrive in Quito. It was at the end of March, and Gonzalo's party had been gone for one month.

"Where are all of the provisions that you were gathering?" Gaspar asked as he witnessed Orellana's men enter Quito.

"I've had terrible problems, Friar. The Irimaris revolted, and I had to quell rioting in my own city. We were lucky to be able to come at all. Captain Pinzon's men lent their assistance to me. These domestic problems delayed me."

"What do you bring?" Friar Gaspar continued to inquire.

"Other than myself, I have twenty-one seasoned men, and a herd of llamas bearing food and supplies."

"Don't forget to mention me, Francisco," Juana yelled. She was happy to see the friar again. Once Sara had left, Juana abandoned her cape and dressed in a more traditional riding outfit.

Friar Gaspar raced over and helped Juana from her horse.

"My heart rejoices to see you looking so well," he told her. "How do you fare?"

Orellana walked over and put his arm around her.

"I cannot imagine being happier," she said beaming. "Last year, I would have considered you a madman had you told me a tale of emigration to a new and pristine world where I would meet the man of my dreams. I wake up every day realizing that the dream is wonderfully true."

Orellana leaned over and kissed her.

"Sara will be so happy for you," Gaspar said to Juana.

"Mistress Sara?" Juana asked. "I miss her. How was she when you saw her last?"

"Happy to be on her way, but missing you as well."

This time Orellana spoke. "Friar Gaspar, we will rest here a few days and proceed with haste to catch up with Gonzalo. He may be depending on these provisions."

"I'm going with you," the friar informed him. "I have a need to see this through. When we return successful from our quest, it will finally be the appointed time to assume my role as Archbishop of this great land."

"Friar Gaspar," Orellana spoke again. "There is one more order of business." Both he and Juana stared into each other's eyes. "The maiden was wise in arranging for Juana to remain with me for a while. We now know that the love between us is real. Our bold little Sara ordered me to marry Juana after we arrived here."

"So I have also been informed," Gaspar said laughing.

"Far be it from us to disobey the Mistress," Juana added.

The next day Friar Gaspar presided over the wedding of Juana and General

Francisco de Orellana. Three days later, they set out in pursuit of Gonzalo.

Gonzalo and General de Vargas both underestimated the terrain. It was tortuous. One mountain after another loomed in front of them. In many cases, the only way to go on was nearly straight up. The vegetation was so thick that every inch of the way had to be hacked out by hand. The heat and humidity sapped their strength. Soon they traveled only during the first few hours of dawn and again during the last hour or so of evening light.

Near the end of the month of March, Gonzalo sat under the shade of a large tree with Sara and General de Vargas.

"How are your men?" Gonzalo asked the general.

"I've buried seven of them so far," he moaned. "Tens more are dehydrated and morale is low. It's hell, a green hell."

Sara rested with her back to a neighboring tree. Her cape was soaked through with perspiration. It clung to her body revealing the supple curves of her breasts. Both men noticed but were too weary to even consider anything. She no longer wore her hood. Instead, Sara wrapped her hair in a linen headband. When the men passed her by, she always kept her gaze to the ground.

The general looked over at her. "Are you sure, Sara?"

She watched a bead of sweat run off the end of her nose and disintegrate into tiny droplets as it bounced off the ground.

"El Dorado," she panted and pointed to the east. "I know these mountains are impenetrable. That is probably why he picked this place. We need to persevere. I'm sure it will eventually lead us to a hidden valley."

"I pray that you are correct, maiden," de Vargas told her. "I don't like burying my men."

"What about the Huaorani?" Gonzalo asked the general.

"Maybe two or three dozen remain out of the four hundred," de Vargas informed him. "The savages sneak off at night taking the pack animals with them."

"This is unacceptable. We need these beasts after we find the gold, I mean cinnamon," Gonzalo burst out and glanced around nervously. "Assign some of your men to keep watch over the remaining savages. Cut them down if they attempt to leave."

"Who will keep watch over my men?" de Vargas wondered aloud. "They will soon be just as inclined to leave as the Huaorani."

"They wouldn't dare," Gonzalo speculated.

Sara stood up. The eyes of the two men were instinctively drawn to her.

The general begged her pardon. "All this talk about the men and we forget about you, maiden. Can we make you comfortable in any way?"

"I suffer the same as you," she admitted. "If either one of you stumbles onto a stream, call for me at once. I need to jump in."

The general thought, *I wouldn't mind seeing that.*

"Sara, we are soon at the point of no return," Gonzalo pointed out to her. "Right now we have enough food to make a retreat back to Quito. Soon we will have no choice but to go on."

"I know, Gonzalo," she sighed. "Don't worry."

Sara drank some water and yawned.

"Gonzalo, will you watch over me while I take a nap?"

"I would be honored to do so," he replied.

She noticed the look in the general's eye.

"Don't concern yourself, General," she managed to laugh. "I don't believe any of you would be interested in me during the heat of the afternoon. It's too damn hot to move, and I smell like a llama."

Sara looked peaceful as she stretched out in the shade. The movement of her chest hypnotized Gonzalo as it slowly pulsated up and down as she slept. He took note of her perfect legs and how the bugs bit them up.

Actually, she wasn't sleeping. Sara was deep in thought about their predicament. *It couldn't be better*, she thought to herself. *A savagely beautiful, remote land hidden from the eyes of the world. There could be no better place to build my empire. This is not the spot, not yet. There is always another side to a mountain range. That is where I will maybe find a river flowing through a lush paradise. I just need to survive and to keep these men together to protect me.*

The reports of dying men and deserting Huaorani disturbed Sara.

I need to keep them together no matter what the obstacle, she thought. *So many of them. Am I strong enough?*

General de Vargas returned to Gonzalo after checking on his men. He slumped down against a tree beside Gonzalo. Now the two of them were staring at Sara. It was one of those rare times that they could admire and study the exotic features of her face. With her eyes closed, Sara was less threatening to them.

"She seems so fragile and vulnerable," the general whispered to Gonzalo. "What is it like to be under her spell?"

"It is both ecstasy and torment," Gonzalo answered him. "That is the best way to describe it to you, but even that does not adequately explain it."

"Is it worth it?" de Vargas pressed him further. "You seem to me to be in perpetual torment over her."

"I am in perpetual torment," Gonzalo agreed. "The ecstasy makes it worth it. Ah, the ecstasy that is Sara!"

"Are you in love with her, Gonzalo?"

"Love?" Gonzalo pondered. "Again, I don't know if that is the right word for it. Does a man love the air that fills his lungs? Does he love the cool water that quenches his thirst? Does he love the warmth that the sun provides for him? These are all things that a man needs to live."

"You feel that way about her?" de Vargas asked Gonzalo.

"I can't imagine living without her," Gonzalo replied.

The general smiled and whispered, "Love is the right word for it." He put a hand on Gonzalo's shoulder, stood, and walked away.

Take pity on me, General, Gonzalo pondered to himself. *I am a walking dead man. Leave her and I will die inside. Love her and I will lose my life. Torment and ecstasy, that is the enigma of Sara.*

CHAPTER 23

"This must be the place," Derek realized as they drove up the driveway of the stately-looking mansion. "Funeral homes here look the same as they do in the States."

"Creepy," Sharon seconded as she stepped out of the car. "There are very few vehicles here," she observed. "You don't suppose that we are early?"

"They told me five o'clock," Derek said as he glanced at his watch.

A somber-looking man in a black suit met them at the door. Sharon guessed that he was the funeral director.

"Tabitha Carr," Derek spoke.

The man pointed a long spindly finger toward a set of double doors on his right. When Sharon and Derek entered the room, Anne and Juan greeted them.

"Annie and Juan," Sharon whispered with delight. "I didn't know you were coming. It's good to see some familiar faces."

"It was Juan's idea," Anne told her as she grabbed hold of his arm. "We feel so bad about this entire mess."

"Tell me about it," Sharon quipped.

The only other person in the room was Werner Klopp. He sat at the head of Tabitha's casket with one arm resting on the side. The man was glaring at the rest of them as if keeping a protective vigil over the body.

"Tabitha's bane," Werner spoke for the first time. He directed his comments at Derek. "Her kindness was her downfall. She wanted to help you, American. Come here and look where it got her."

Derek answered the summons feeling like a puppet on a string as he slowly approached the casket. Tabitha lay in front of him dressed in a tight, low-cut, white gown. Her folded hands resting on her chest clutched a single red rose.

"Even in death, she is radiant," Derek whispered subconsciously. Werner heard this and wiped away a tear. Despite Tabitha's beauty, Derek felt that her power was gone. He began to feel guilty. Derek longed to feel her mental presence and to hear her sweet voice.

"I only had a few short moments with her," Derek lamented to Werner. "She was an angel." In a confused state of grief and guilt, Derek tried to reach out to her.

Werner felt the wave and began to laugh. "Stupid American," he gasped for air between chortles. "It's too late for that now."

Suddenly he felt Sharon step between them. Taking Derek's hand, she glowered at Werner. "His name is Derek," she growled. "Stop treating him with such disrespect."

Werner paused for a moment and began to laugh again. Slowly the laughter gave way to sobs.

"Disrespect," he sneered. "Let me tell you about disrespect. Disrespect is when a woman cares for children orphaned by the French Revolution, only to be imprisoned as a criminal due to her royalty. She almost lost her head," Werner told them as he stared down at the body.

He went on. "Disrespect is when a friend to poor slaves in your own country organizes an escape route, only to be jailed as a northern sympathizer. Disrespect is being beaten senseless by Italian Fascists for daring to question their authority."

Werner stopped to blow his nose.

"Then the final insult," Werner continued. "After doing so many things for so many people, to fall victim to some insignificant chemical compound in a meaningless bottle of water. How is that for disrespect?"

Derek said nothing.

Anne poked Juan and pulled her lips up close to his ear. "He can't possibly be talking about Tabitha, can he?" she asked in a whisper.

"Never mind him, Annie. He's full of despair," Juan concluded.

Sharon took hold of Derek's arm and looked at his watch.

"Shouldn't a minister or priest or someone be here by now?" she muttered nervously.

"Priest! We are not worthy of a priest, are we, Derek?" Werner laughed at him.

Derek looked at Sharon and shrugged.

"No friends, this is it," Werner said as he waved his arm out at the nearly empty room. "We live in the shadows, and we die in ignominy. Tabitha foolishly believed that she could change that."

Werner looked down at Tabitha's face. "If there was a way, I'd trade places with you," he spoke to her tenderly. "I could have been a better friend. I know how you suffered in your solitude. Why couldn't I have taken better care of you?" He broke down.

"How sad," Anne sniffled just loud enough for Juan to hear.

Derek asked Sharon to join the others. "Let me talk to him now," he pleaded. Derek was troubled. He desperately needed to get the answers from Werner but didn't know how to begin. Derek put a hand on Werner's shoulder and asked him quietly, "Was there anything I could have done?"

Werner ignored him.

Derek tightened the grip on Werner's shoulder and tried again, "The two of you visited to tell me something. I know that I'm connected to all of this. How?"

Werner looked up at him and moved his eyes to Derek's hand as it rested on his shoulder. Derek got the message and removed his grip.

Werner spoke to Derek in a low and defiant voice. "Let me start by saying that I don't like you, American. Your presence here reminds me of my own guilt in not dealing with you sooner. Tabitha would still be alive if I would have acted."

"What do you mean by 'dealing with me'?" Derek felt himself grow defensive.

"Tabitha assigned a responsibility to me, one that I am not well suited for. Understand that unlike her, I am not a giving person. My way of life is self serving and exploitative of their kind," Werner explained to Derek as he nodded in the direction of those seated in the room. "I don't plan to change who I am."

Werner looked at Derek with scorn and spoke again. "Don't expect to be my protégé. I have little time for you, American. In honor of Tabitha's wish, I'm going to explain a few things to you. After we leave this place, I never want to see you again. Anything else you want to know, you will have to find elsewhere."

Derek nodded his head in agreement.

"Get them out of here," he ordered Derek as he pointed to the others. "What I have to say is for your ears only."

"Can all of you wait for me in the lobby?" Derek asked them. "I need to be alone with Werner and Tabitha for a little while."

"Bullshit, Derek, I'm not going anywhere," Sharon argued.

"Please, Sharon," Derek said as he tried to reason with her.

"Look, Derek, we've been together for a long time. Whatever this is, has been affecting me, too. We've worked through many problems together, and a few big ones remain. I have a right to hear what this man has to say to you."

"It's best you leave," Werner said forcefully. "You will not be able to grasp this."

Sharon was vehement and shot back at Werner. "In case you haven't noticed, I am an adult. Stop treating me like a child."

"You are no child," Werner agreed. "There is a danger to Derek and I that requires absolute secrecy. You can't be a part of this."

Sharon folded her arms in front of her chest and announced, "I am not leaving."

Werner gave Sharon a menacing stare and told her, "You are a spoiled American fool."

"That's enough," Derek chimed in. "If she feels this strongly about it, she stays."

Sharon gave Werner a mocking smile.

"She is your responsibility," Werner chided Derek. "You'll need to ensure her silence."

Sharon sat, and Derek walked around behind her. He placed a hand on each of Sharon's shoulders. "Sharon will do just fine," he told Werner. "Now get on with it."

Werner looked back and forth between the two determined faces of Derek and Sharon and laughed nervously. "As you wish," he told them. Werner walked over and picked up a Bible that lay on the dais in front of the casket.

"American," he began. "How familiar are you with antediluvian history?"

"Not very," Derek acknowledged.

"What?" Sharon asked with a confused look.

Werner opened the book to a passage in Genesis. He handed the volume to Derek and pointed to Chapter 6. "Don't worry," he mentioned to Derek. "This Bible is written in English. Read it."

Derek spent several minutes absorbing the passage. Sharon noticed his face light up. Later she saw Derek's forehead wrinkle with doubt.

"Do you begin to understand, American?" Werner smiled.

"This can't be!" Derek gasped.

"Give it," Sharon demanded and pulled the Bible from Derek's grasp. She looked for Chapter 6 and began to read.

"When humankind began to populate the world, and girls were being born, some of the spirit creatures noticed that these daughters of men were beautiful, so they materialized in human form and had sexual relations with them…In those days, and even later, mighty ones existed on the earth, the descendants of human women and the spirit creatures. They were the great ones — men of renown."

Sharon looked up at Derek. He was trembling. "What does it mean?" she asked him.

Derek didn't hear her question. He was trying to fit together the pieces of the puzzle that made up his own life. *My mother*, he thought. *She died when I was born. I never knew my real father. I'm outstanding physically. I've never been sick. I can't get sick. I don't age like my friends.* Derek's mind was racing. He stared at Werner and saw the same type of being reflected back. Just like himself, Werner was a large, strong, handsome man.

His mouth moved and his voice spoke, but Derek could not believe the words as they past his lips. As he said them, his eyes pleaded with Werner for some sort of confirmation. Werner's smile revealed the truth.

"Our fathers were angels," Derek droned, "fallen angels."

"Huh?" Sharon uttered as she gaped first at Derek then at Werner.

"It's really a question of free will," Werner explained to Sharon. "You may choose to live or die. Heaven or hell, if you prefer to think of it in that way. Humans are not the only creatures with this option. Just after Creation, a host of angels grew jealous of men. Human beings were God's special children."

Werner made imaginary quotation marks in the air with his fingers when he spoke the words, "special children."

He continued to reveal it to them. "They lusted after the daughters of men. These angels started a great rebellion in the heavens." Werner walked over to Tabitha and looked down at her. "They fell by the thousands," he said with authority. "Their choice; they wanted to materialize in human form and have sexual relations with the daughters of men. Of course, there were consequences. Their punishment was banishment beyond either heaven or earth."

"You're out of your mind," Sharon blurted out.

"Shut up, or get out," Werner shouted at her and gestured toward the door.

Derek interceded. "Sharon, honey, let the man finish, please."

She walked back a few rows, sat, and pouted while listening to the rest of it.

"Tell me about the offspring," Derek begged him to continue.

"Look in the mirror, American," he chuckled. "What do you see? Are you human, or are you a man of renown, a giant?"

Derek grew silent and introspective.

"American, as you have discovered, we possess many physical and mental gifts, thanks to our fathers. As men, we are alluring to women, aren't we? How many have you slept with?" Werner asked sarcastically.

Sharon rolled her eyes in disdain.

"Because of our fathers, our physical makeup is exceptional. We have perfect DNA. We are immune to everything. The aging process stops when we reach maturity."

"You mean we can't die?" Derek inquired.

"Fool," Werner barked and pointed to Tabitha. "Look at her. She's dead, isn't she? We live on until killed by trauma. Even our perfect bodies can't recover quickly enough from a mortal wound."

"Tabitha," Derek recalled. "She was somehow different from the two of us."

"Of course," Werner said matter-of-factly. "She was a girl child. They have a different kind of mental gift."

"How so?" Derek asked with genuine interest.

"Boy children are born with an infinite supply of psychic energy, but our ability to use that energy is limited. Girl children are like rechargeable batteries. They need to occasionally renew, but oh, their power! You felt it when you gazed into Tabitha's eyes. Wasn't it wondrous? When they choose to turn it on, every pore of their bodies oozes with a kind of psychic pheromone intoxicating to men. It affects us as well as human men."

Werner paced over to Sharon and deliberately addressed his next comment at her.

"Have sex with one of our kind, American, and you will never again dip into one of these."

"Fuck you, asshole," Sharon snarled at him.

"Stop it, Werner," Derek warned. "Tell me more. When do these powers develop?"

"Our mental powers ripen the same time as our bodies do," he explained. "It starts at puberty."

Derek probed further. "You said that females of our kind have to renew. What happens to them if they don't?"

Werner answered him. "They don't die, if that's what you mean. Their spirit grows tired. They lose a zest for life, but they go on."

"So how do they renew?" Derek asked the logical next question.

A smile crossed Werner's face. "The pleasure of it is indescribable, American. During intercourse, they lock minds with their male partners. Are you aware that orgasms are nothing more than pure, unfiltered mental energy? They allow us to climax at the exact same moment as they do. It's a literal out of body experience. We lose consciousness, and at that moment they hold us out there while absorbing all of that pure energy into themselves."

Werner had to catch his breath just thinking about it.

"Now here's the good part, American. Remember how I told you that we have an infinite supply of that energy? That means that they can take from us all that they need. Then we can do it again and again and again."

Werner returned to Tabitha's casket, put both hands on the head end, and despaired, "Who will grant me that kind of pleasure now, Tabby? Why did you have to leave me?"

Derek left Werner alone in his grief for a short time but soon pressed him some more.

"What about plain human men and them?" he asked while motioning with his head toward the body.

"Our women must take great care," Werner responded. "When held out there for too long, the human man's heart can stop. Also, he can die if too much energy is absorbed all at once. Anyway, after a few love making sessions, they get used up and die."

"We don't have the same effect on human women?" Derek asked wanting to make sure that he understood.

"No," Werner answered coldly. "I already told you that we don't have that kind of power."

Werner lit up as if remembering something. "Of course, there is the one exception."

"What's that?" Derek asked with fear, thinking about Sharon. He didn't want to hurt her in this way.

"Our birth," remarked Werner. "Both boy and girl children completely absorb all of their mother's energy at the moment of birth. This is what ignites the gift implanted within us from our fathers. Of course, all of our mothers die immediately."

"We kill our mothers?" Derek asked for clarity.

"Yes, American. That is why it is said that we are born of evil. All of us are orphaned at birth."

Derek thought of something and changed the subject. "If our bodies are so perfect, why can't we have children?"

Werner moaned, "Do I have to explain everything to you? Think, can a mule give birth to other mules? Being an offspring of a horse with a donkey, they are sterile. The same goes for us, American. We are hybrids."

This led Derek to the big question. "Werner, what happens to us when we die?"

Werner laughed. "This is where Tabitha deluded herself. She maintained that since we are half human, there exists some chance for our salvation. If you believe the holy writings, it indicates that we are considered 'unauthorized' life forms and ineligible for the same consideration as our human counterparts.

"Read the rest of Chapter 6," he explained further. "It states clearly that our kind was considered evil. The flood wiped those living at that time from the face of the earth. We are born of evil, and we practice evil. Tabitha spent most of her life struggling to accomplish good things. Now look at her."

"How can you judge where her soul rests?" Derek fired back.

"What do you think, American?"

Derek recalled it in his mind, "I remember her last words. She claimed that she won the prize."

"Delirious words of a dying woman," Werner responded, dismissing it.

"I wonder?" pondered Derek.

After reflecting on the things that Werner revealed to him, Derek had a few more questions.

"I sense that there are not many of us and that we are scattered," Derek assumed.

Werner commented, "Most of the angels that were so inclined abandoned their heavenly station during that great rebellion. Now, only occasionally does one of them make the willful choice of taking a human woman. Think of it, American. Can you imagine exchanging eternal life as a spirit creature for one moment of ecstasy? You're correct, it doesn't happen often, and as a result there are only a few of us."

"Excuse me," they heard Sharon yell. She was waving her hand in the air like a school child. "What about the little girl angels? Do they materialize to seduce studly men?" Sharon giggled and mocked Werner.

"Angels are sexless, your ignorance," Werner said and bowed down to Sharon as if she was a queen. "They choose to materialize in a man's body due to its obvious superiority."

"Ah ha," Sharon laughed. "If your body is so superior, why do you keep ogling mine?"

Derek ignored this exchange and brought Werner back on track with his next question. "Why don't we gather ourselves together like you and Tabitha sometimes did?"

"Each of us needs to be free to pursue our own destiny. We can pair off with the opposite sex, like Tabitha and I did on occasion, but the same sex of our kind cannot dwell together," Werner explained.

"Why not?" Derek wondered.

"It is in our nature to compete," Werner told him. He was starting to lose patience. "How long do you think you and I could remain together before we started to tear each other to pieces?"

"Okay, I get your point," Derek acknowledged.

Derek walked over to the casket and gazed one final time at the body of Tabitha Carr. He reached down and gently brushed her cheek. It was cold.

"Thank you for coming to me, Tabitha," he whispered. "I'll remember you always."

Next Derek walked right up to Werner's face and studied him for a moment.

"I know what you are thinking, American. I can assure you that it's all true."

"I believe you," Derek said softly so that Sharon could not hear. He added in a normal tone of voice, "What should I do now?"

"We all deal with this in our own way," Werner laughed, "but we both know that there is something that you soon must do."

Without thinking, Derek faced a southwest direction and wore a worried look.

"Ah, yes," Werner acknowledged. "Her name is Sara, and she is waiting for you."

Derek felt afraid, but he couldn't explain it.

Werner laughed again, "We all fear her. Sara is legendary and very powerful." He stopped laughing and grew serious. "Derek Dunbar, we fear you as well."

"What makes her special?" Derek wondered.

"It's the two of you together that would be special," Werner admitted with a sullen expression. "Can't you feel it?"

"Yes," confessed Derek. "It feels like you and the others of our kind are somehow lesser beings."

"That's very perceptive of you," Werner corroborated. At this point, he changed to a more friendly tone. He was frightened.

"Derek Dunbar, unlike humans who are all equal, there are different kinds of angels. Some are lesser and some are greater. Both you and Sara were fathered by a type known as Seraphim, among the most powerful of the spirit creatures."

"What does she want from me, Werner?"

"Derek Dunbar, if Sara were able to draw on your immense strength, she could reach out to our kind all around the world and seduce them into doing her bidding. Think, just a few of us in the right positions of power. She could rule the world."

"So, she wants to sleep with me?" Derek asked, feeling a bit giddy.

"Don't flatter yourself into thinking that you would be able to resist," Werner warned. "Remember, she is ancient and an expert on human nature. She could read your weaknesses within seconds and exploit them."

"What if I ignore her?" Derek considered.

Werner counseled him, "Look at the trouble that she has already caused you. She will torment your mind until you capitulate and go to her."

A few minutes of silence passed between them. Sharon flipped her hair around behind her head. She was just about at the breaking point.

"Derek Dunbar," Werner continued. "Go to her. If she can be reasoned with, tell her about the modern world. Explain how technology has changed within the last hundred years. Our kind can no longer just disappear from one country and reappear in another. If she causes undue attention, the humans will find out and track us down. God only knows what unspeakable things they would do to us."

Derek shook his head affirmatively, patted Werner's arm and worked his way back toward Sharon. He reached down and helped her up.

"Let's go," he told her.

"Yeah," she said giving Werner a hard look. "What a crock of shit."

As they neared the door, Werner yelled after them. "American, if that murderess, Elyria, doesn't tell you what you need to know, there is a man in Manaus named Stamos. He is a professor of anthropology at the university there. Tabitha and I read some of his work a few years ago about a mysterious group of women. It could have been Sara and her minions. He may be able to point you in the right direction."

Sharon walked out in front of Derek. He turned and faced Werner one final time.

"Thank you," he said with sincerity. "For everything," he added.

Werner Klopp ambled over to the casket and returned to his vigil over Tabitha's corpse.

"We heard yelling from in there. Is everything okay?" Anne asked with concern.

"That Werner guy is a real buffoon," Sharon told them. "Wait until I tell you all about his bombast."

Derek grabbed Sharon by the arm. "Tell them nothing," he warned. "I want a chance to talk with you about all of this first."

"You don't believe him, do you?" Sharon cried out in shock.

The four of them started walking toward the door of the funeral home as they continued their conversation.

"Sharon, think about it. Have you ever known me to be sick?"

She gave him a sidelong glance.

"Do I look like I'm thirty-three years old?" he whispered. "More like twenty-three, wouldn't you say?"

"Stop it, Derek, you're scaring me. You act like you really do believe him."

Juan opened the door and they were momentarily blinded by the sunlight streaming in.

"It's true, Sharon," he tried to convince her. "It does explain all of the problems we've been having."

"It can't be," Sharon shook her head.

The four of them realized that it wasn't actually the sun streaming in. It was the popping of flash bulbs. A dozen reporters and photographers were waiting for them to emerge.

"There they are," one of the reporters screamed. The rest of them gathered around like a pack of wild dogs.

A female reporter from a cable news network shoved a microphone into the bewildered face of Juan Sanchez.

"Mr. Sanchez, what is your reaction to TransGlobal's decision? After all you have been through, do you think it's reasonable?"

"What?" was all that Juan could muster.

Derek parted his way between Juan and Anne. He bellowed out to all of the reporters and photographers gathered there. "What is this? What do you people want?"

The female reporter spoke for all of them.

"Are you Derek Dunbar?" she asked.

"Yes," he quipped. A dozen flash bulbs fired to capture his expression on film.

"I have a press release from TransGlobal Airlines. It says in part and I quote, 'During the past week, controversy has surrounded four of our employees, Derek Dunbar, Joel Washington, Juan Sanchez, and Anne Sprague. Significant negative attention has been directed toward TransGlobal because of their alleged involvement in drug allegations and murder. With the mysterious death of another woman at a gathering in which three of these four were in attendance, the corporation immediately terminates their employment and assumes no responsibility for acts while they were associated with TransGlobal.'"

"Wait a minute, we had nothing to do with any of that," Anne shrieked.

"Were all of you there when Tabitha Carr was murdered?" another reporter shouted from the back of the pack.

"Yes, we were there," Anne answered him, "but it wasn't our fault. This is so unfair."

Derek stopped her. "Don't tell them anything else, Annie. Come on, let's get into our cars and go."

With Derek in the lead, the four of them muscled their way through and got into their respective vehicles.

Anne looked over at Juan with pleading eyes. "Will you take me back to the Royale? I don't feel like dinner anymore."

"Sure, Annie," Juan assured her. "Whatever you want, I'll do for you."

In the other car, Sharon was excoriating Derek.

"Great," she gasped for air. "This is just great. A madman fills your head with delusions, and now your career is in the tank. Derek, with Lisa Dane out of commission, I don't think I have a job to go home to either. What are we going to do?"

"Don't worry, Sharon," he tried to console her. "We'll get through this. I love you."

"Will we?" she spouted. "Derek, it keeps getting worse and worse. When will this nightmare end?"

Sharon was still seething when they returned to the Royale. Derek pulled into a parking space beside Juan. They all got out together. Anne noticed that Sharon was distressed and tried to talk with her.

"The four of us will work this out," Anne said trying to comfort her.

"Anne, you don't know the half of it," Sharon choked. "Derek and I have some real problems." Sharon faced Derek and spoke with great intensity. "I can't take any more of this, Derek," she told him. "I don't think I love you anymore." She ran away from them into the hotel.

"She's just terribly upset, Derek," he heard Juan's voice tell him. "She didn't mean that."

Next, he felt Anne's warm embrace as her arms reached around his waist and her head rested on his chest. "Juan's right," Anne said. "This isn't the Sharon that I know. Still, I wish she were a little more supportive of you."

Derek swooned. Everything was sinking in. It was he who had changed and not Sharon. The old Derek Dunbar ceased to exist, and all of the things that were important to him no longer mattered. Derek felt reborn. He was a demigod with all new concerns and responsibilities. It had happened too fast, and he finally reached his saturation point. Derek fainted in Anne's arms.

CHAPTER 24

General Orellana and his party had an easier time with the journey. The trail was already blazed from the passage of Gonzalo's party. They managed to cover three to four times as much territory each day and were catching up. The heat was intolerable. Orellana wisely ordered his men to rest during the heat of the mid-day and to travel only in the morning and evenings.

It was a few hours before sundown, and Juana stirred from her sleep. Gently she removed her sleeping husband's arm from around her midsection and stood up. She felt woozy.

Not again, she thought to herself and walked quickly into the forest. Juana felt overcome with the heat and knelt down in the undergrowth. The waves of nausea were too much, and she vomited. Perspiration ran down her face. After a few minutes, she felt better and returned to the spot where her husband slept.

Friar Gaspar stood nearby and walked over to check on her.

"Juana, I noticed you bolt away from here. Are you feeling poorly?"

"No, Friar," she responded in a whisper. "I am not ill. I believe that I am with child."

He motioned Juana to follow him and led her some distance away from the main group.

"Are you sure?" he asked her.

She turned red and looked down in embarrassment.

"Friar Gaspar, Orellana and I have stayed together as man and wife since the time you and Sara left us in Guayaquil. I fear we have sinned. I suspected my condition around the time you married us."

The friar smiled at her.

"Be at peace, Juana. Your marriage has made things right in God's eyes. The child will be born in wedlock. It is a blessing."

"I'm afraid, Friar Gaspar," she fretted. "When Orellana finds out, he will want to turn back and return me to Guayaquil. Our attempt to overtake Gonzalo and my Mistress Sara will be ruined on my account. I don't want him to find out about this yet."

"Juana, Orellana is responsible for everyone in this party, and he is your husband. The general must be told. If I were your husband, nothing would prevent me from seeing to your safety and to the safety of your child. This unbearable heat cannot be healthy for a woman in your condition."

"Please, Friar Gaspar," Juana begged. "I am only in my second month and am strong. The Huaorani that we encountered on the trail this morning told us that we are now only three days behind. Please, don't reveal our secret until we reach Gonzalo's party. It is possible that they are in desperate need of our supplies. Besides, I need to see Mistress Sara again to tell her the news. I need final release from an oath that I swore to stay with her. If she grants this to me, I will gladly return."

"Your loyalty now lies first with your husband and not with Sara," Gaspar chastised her. After making this point, he softened his tone. "You do make a convincing argument. If the Huaorani are to be trusted, we are close to catching up with Gonzalo. He may well need our supplies and the reinforcement of Orellana and his men."

Juana observed while the friar seemed to meditate on the matter. He seemed to reach a decision.

"I will give us one week, Juana. If we do not overtake Gonzalo in that amount of time, it will be your duty to inform your husband. If your condition worsens in any way, you will need to tell him sooner."

Juana felt relieved. Gaspar smiled as he watched the color return to her face.

"Thank you, Friar," she said. "I will be just fine."

A few days later Gonzalo awoke startled in the middle of the night. He heard a loud noise and felt the earth vibrate.

"Was that thunder?" he spoke out to nobody in particular.

One of the soldiers answered back. "Yes, Governor, a storm has been forming for some time, and it is getting closer. I think it's going to be a big one."

Rain during the day was nothing new to the travelers. It rained often for brief periods. This time it was different. Gonzalo could feel an ominous energy in the air as the squall approached.

All of the men camped in the open, but they carried a small tent covering that Sara could use at night. Gonzalo jumped up and walked over to check on her.

"Sara," he whispered at the entrance to the covering. "We are in for a storm. Is this tent secure enough for you?"

Gonzalo heard a rustling from inside. Sara crawled out pulling the cape around her body.

"I felt the thunder too, Gonzalo. Rain, isn't it wonderful?"

"You're on a high point, Sara. You should be able to stay dry in there."

"Are you joking?" she said with astonishment. "I have no intention of staying dry. I'm going to revel in it, Gonzalo. Let it come and wash me clean. I want to feel the drops bounce off my face as I stare into the sky. After all of this heat, it will be welcome refreshment."

"I will stay here with you, in case you need me for anything."

They heard another rumble of thunder. It was very close.

"Gonzalo, you do not need to be my champion all of the time. You must stop being so protective of me," Sara sternly told him.

"I'm concerned about you," he protested. "I constantly fear for your safety."

"Stop it," Sara said and turned her back to him.

He walked over and spun Sara around. They faced each other in the darkness of the night.

"Sara, despite all we've been through, and despite all that you are, I love you."

"No, Gonzalo," she corrected him. "You confuse love with desire."

"I used to think that, too, until a conversation I had with de Vargas a few days ago. It was a revelation to me. I love you, Sara," he insisted.

Lightning streaked across the sky and the two of them felt the first drops of rain.

"That cannot work for us, Gonzalo. You know that."

"Do you think I wanted this?" he asked her. "How can I gain a mastery over the feelings that I have for you? My feelings are what they are, Sara. I love you."

Sara laid her hand on Gonzalo's shoulder for a brief moment.

"Drive it from yourself," she told him.

Gonzalo closed his eyes and soaked up the warm energy from her touch.

"How can I?" he asked her frantically.

"Let me go, sweet Gonzalo," she whispered to him. She repeated, "Let me go."

The heavens burst open and a soaking rain flooded over them. Gonzalo caught a glimpse of Sara's lovely form as lightning flashed across the sky.

He turned away and walked dejectedly back to his place with the rest of the men.

Sara was grateful that Gonzalo could not see the tears as they mingled in among the raindrops on her face.

The storm washed over the travelers for the rest of the night and the entire next day. Close to dusk, the skies cleared revealing brilliant, orange-colored clouds in the western sky. Gonzalo was deep in thought while contemplating the cottony shapes when General de Vargas interrupted him.

"We lost a lot of time waiting out that storm," he observed. "Maybe we should cover some ground yet this evening."

"How far away do you think they are?" Gonzalo asked him pointing at the clouds.

The general studied the shapes and answered, "I don't know for sure, maybe one hundred kilometers."

"How far do think we've traveled since leaving Quito?" he probed again.

"Not far enough, Gonzalo, maybe one hundred fifty kilometers. This cursed vegetation and the steepness of the terrain impedes our every step."

"Only one hundred fifty kilometers in two months," Gonzalo moaned. "What are we doing, Sanchez? At this rate it will be years until we return to Spain."

"Home," sighed de Vargas. "I miss it as well." The general sensed that something more was on Gonzalo's mind. This was more than just small talk. He thought about it some and floated a question.

"Do you still have faith that the maiden can find El Dorado?"

Gonzalo stared blankly at the general and replied, "Do you believe he exists?"

This time the general turned his face toward the orange apparitions floating in the distance.

"I don't know, Gonzalo, maybe it doesn't matter. We are forging into a land that has never been explored. Maybe Sara cannot find our mythical man, but we may find something even more wondrous than gold."

"Sometime soon Sara is going to leave us, Sanchez," Gonzalo said bringing to the surface his deeper thoughts.

"Look, Gonzalo," de Vargas counseled him. "Every man here realizes that Sara is a precious being, above us all. In many ways, she is a stranger to us. Her destiny may be even greater than ours. When the day comes that she leaves, rejoice for her, Gonzalo. It means that she will be one step closer to greatness."

"I fear to let her go, Sanchez. She could die out here and never achieve that greatness you speak of."

"That means her destiny lies beyond this world," de Vargas said trying to provide Gonzalo with some closure. He changed the subject. "If we break camp now, we could make it to the summit of this range by nightfall."

They trudged on. It was well after dark until they reached the top. By this time, the remnants of the storm clouds had completely vanished and the night sky was clear. At sunrise, an excited de Vargas awakened Gonzalo.

"Come, Gonzalo, and behold God's new Eden!"

The morning sun blinded him as Gonzalo stared out over the horizon. What the travelers didn't realize was that they had arrived at the final pinnacle of the mountain range. Laying before them as far as they could see out over the horizon was a carpet of green.

"It is as vast as the ocean," reported the general.

Sara joined them and drank in the sight. Under the hood of her cape, she beamed with an exquisite smile. Noticing a far away ribbon slicing through the green, Sara pointed and announced, "We need to follow yonder river. It leads the way to your El Dorado."

The day was torrid, but it seemed much less humid than previous days. The storm had washed the air clean. Instead of taking their customary mid-day rest, the party forged ahead all day, closing in on the river.

Late in the afternoon, they arrived at the river's edge beneath a precipice. A mighty cataract plunged from above into a deep shimmering pool. Exotic fruit trees surrounded the oasis. A startled herd of wild peccaries scattered from beneath their feet. For several minutes, the entire party was speechless while soaking up the visual beauty of this paradise.

Gonzalo was just about to say something to de Vargas when he heard a giant splash. This was quickly followed by another and then another. Soon the surface of the water was boiling with the sound of professional soldiers and Huaorani Indians as they stripped down and plunged into the inviting pool. They were all laughing and squealing like naughty little boys.

General de Vargas looked at Gonzalo and shrugged his shoulders. In a flash, he was out of his clothes and in the drink with his men. Soon the only ones left standing on the bank were Gonzalo and Sara.

"What are you waiting for?" Sara scolded him. "Get in there. I'll guard your clothes. When all of you men are done, I want that whole pool to myself. You'll stand watch for me, right?"

She scarcely got the words out before Gonzalo lunged into the water.

Sara cherished the sight of all those men together in the water. *How alike all of them are*, she marveled to herself. *Generals, holy men, soldiers, and Indians indistinguishable in their nakedness. Floating and bobbing children are moved along by the random whim of a gentle current.*

A bright first quarter moon lit up the night before they relinquished the pool to Sara. Gonzalo and de Vargas stood near the water's edge with their backs turned while Sara bathed. She took the opportunity to wash her cape. Gonzalo set a linen sheet on the bank that Sara wrapped around herself after emerging.

"Take some more time for yourself, Sara," General de Vargas suggested. "Gonzalo and I will stay here for as long as you like."

"Thank you both," she said. "I needed to get out. I was being watched."

"Who dared," Gonzalo growled. "One of our men must have sneaked over to the other side of the pool. Did you see who it was?"

"Not one of ours, Gonzalo. An Indian, but not one of the Huaorani."

"Are you sure, Sara?" de Vargas asked her to confirm.

"Men have been sneaking around to watch me bathe my entire long life. I know what it feels like, General. I could feel his eyes. I caught only a glimpse before he slipped away. He was like a cat, very slick movements."

The general assigned soldiers in shifts to guard the camp during the night. Gonzalo's sleep was fitful.

The next morning General de Vargas met with Gonzalo to discuss a plan.

"This river is not too narrow here near its source. I believe that it could be navigable."

"What is it that you are thinking, Sanchez?" Gonzalo asked him.

The general explained further, "As we go downstream, the river will become wider and deeper. This spot where we camp is a place of great abundance. We could stay here for a number of days, maybe a week or two for the purpose of building some vessels that we could use to float downstream. It would be much easier than hacking our way through the jungle at the water's edge. We could build up a great store of food from here to take with us. It would also be a morale boost for my men. It will give them something else to work on to take their minds off of the drudgery of our trip."

Gonzalo liked the idea. "How many vessels do you think we would need to carry all of our men and supplies?"

"They can't be too large," the general considered. "We will have to engineer their displacement to remain shallow. A half dozen or so flat bottom

257

brigantines should work."

Lupo struggled back to the village. He arrived exhausted and collapsed outside of the chieftain's house. One of the children ran inside and dragged the elder out by the hand. He found the runner on his knees gasping for air.

"Lupo, you are not due back for two days. What alarm brings you back so soon from wide area patrol?"

The runner motioned with his hand for the child to fetch him a ladle of water. After slurping it down, he wiped his mouth with a grimy arm. Remaining on his knees, the runner gaped up at the elder wide eyed.

"They are coming, Goma," he said still breathing heavily. "They are the children of the sun."

Word spread quickly among the villages of the discovery made by Lupo. That very night, the elders of the seven Shuhar tribes gathered in their central city of Napo to listen to the details of the strange story.

"One great queen in a full mantle complete with head covering stood watch as she ordered her tribe of men to bathe in the great pool near the mountain," Lupo explained to them.

"How many of them were with the queen?" Elder Goma asked with concern.

"A few darker-skinned men, like us, probably their slaves," Lupo clarified. "A vast number of white-skinned men, hundreds of them, mingled with them. I have never seen men such as this."

A murmuring started among those gathered and Goma raised a hand in an order of silence.

"Tell us about their queen," he requested.

"A goddess come to Earth," Lupo began to say. His eyes looked straight ahead and his nostrils flared as he summoned up a recollection of the incident.

"She waited until her children finished bathing. Two of them guarded the queen, but they dared not look directly at her. By the light of the moon, I watched as she let the garment slip down around her feet. Her skin reflected the brilliance of the moon. It was dazzling. I understood why these men, her children, could not bear to gaze directly at her body. In the full light of the sun it would blind them."

More murmuring broke out among the elders.

"Go on, go on," Goma instructed impatiently.

"She witched me. My eyes could not break away while she bathed. I felt myself grow hard as I was drawn toward her. I must have made a noise, because she sensed my presence, and jerked her face around. Our eyes met."

Lupo paused and his face grew pained.

"Her eyes," he repeated. "Their allure reminded me of great jewels. The brightness of the sun shown from within her. A great fear overcame my desire for her, and I ran away."

"How do you know they are coming?" one of the others in the back shouted out.

"The great queen told me with her eyes. They are coming. Their numbers are greater than our combined tribes. We should flee from them."

Goma fingered the many shrunken heads attached to his spear. "The Shuhar peoples flee from no men," he affirmed.

"Have you not heard what I told you?" Lupo complained in desperation. "The mighty white queen surely is the daughter of the sun, and the men are her children. Who will be able to stand against her? I grew hard with desire for her. I, Lupo, a mighty warrior, killer of many of our enemies, one glance from her and I was frozen with fear like a cornered tapir about to be slaughtered."

A heated debate raged among them as to whether they should confront these men or flee. Some chose to believe that Lupo was lying. Finally the great elder and chief, Goma, had heard enough. He stood and the room grew silent.

"I have never known Lupo to speak falsely," Goma said as he addressed them. "He is a seasoned warrior and unafraid. I believe his story."

"Do we fight or flee from these strange peoples?" another one of the elders asked.

"Neither," Goma answered with a clear and determined tone. "If it is true that men cannot stand against this great queen, the men will remain in their villages. Our women are also great warriors. They will not grow hard with desire for this queen. We will send my daughter, the war chieftain, Lani, as our ambassador. Twenty of her best women warriors will accompany her. Lani will seek out and confront the great queen to learn her intentions and those of her children."

CHAPTER 25

In Derek's dream, it wasn't Anne. It was the lovely angel into whose arms Derek had fainted. She was tall, and Derek felt himself slip down through her arms until he was standing at her feet. Looking up into her face, he noticed that he was only tall enough so that his head was level with her knees. The angel smiled down at him.

Derek spoke, but he remembered his voice sounded like that of a little baby.

"Are you a seraph?" he heard himself ask.

The angel's face turned to a frown as she scolded him. "That is unimportant. Don't speak of such things."

She lifted him high into the air and placed him in the driver's seat of the circus wagon. He shook the reins and the horses began to bob up and down as they moved around in a circle on the carousel. Always moving around and around forever, never going anywhere, the angel sat beside him and began to sing along with the circus music.

When the song was over, Derek felt her kiss him on the cheek. She asked him, "Derek, when you were older I once asked you a question. Do you remember what it was?"

He thought about it and replied, "You asked me whether my will is strong enough."

The angel clapped her hands and laughed with glee. "Very good, little Derek. I knew you would remember. Now that you are a baby, do you have a different answer for me?"

Derek felt more unsure of himself than before and began to cry little baby tears. "I don't know if I can do it by myself," he heard himself pout.

The angel stroked his hair and told him, "You will not be alone. She will help you."

"Who?" he wondered. "Sharon, Annie, Elyria?"

The angel winked at him and said, "That's all for now, little Derek. Remember, if her death does not occur at your hands, someday you may become like them."

The angel began to fade away.

"Wait," Derek screamed. "What am I supposed to do?"

"Why, the prize of course," she spoke softly and from far away. "Reach for the prize, Derek. It's the gold ring, but you need to reach way, way out for it." She spoke no more.

As the carousel rotated on its great center pole, Derek spotted the ring. He worked his way over to the inside edge of the wagon's driver's seat.

Whoosh, it passed by.

He wasn't reaching out far enough. Derek slid farther out so that he was now sitting half on the seat and half off. It was almost in reach. He stretched his baby arm out as far as it could extend.

Whoosh, it passed by again.

More determined than ever, Derek got up off the seat and held onto the edge of the wagon with one hand while reaching out with the other. This was dangerous. If he let go, the tumble would leave him at the mercy of the horses. Their pointed hooves went trampling and gouging as they were pulled up and down repeatedly on the poles of the carousel. Derek wanted the prize and reached way out.

"Come to me, Derek. I'm waiting for you," the ring seemed to beckon to him.

Whoosh, it passed by, but this time Derek's fingertips brushed it. He was so close.

A voice boomed over the loudspeaker of the carousel, "This ride never stops."

Another voice echoed, "Not all things are as they appear."

The carousel made it around again and Derek was ready. The ring, his prize, was almost there. "Reach, Derek, reach," he shouted to himself. As the ring came into his view, it suddenly transformed into the image of Sharon's face. Her countenance was wrinkled with age and haggard.

"Foundling freak," it screeched in an old woman's voice.

It startled him. Letting go of the wagon, Derek covered both ears with his hands and felt himself fall. He bounced off the deck of the carousel and started to roll toward the horses.

Up and down, they bobbed menacingly. Their sharp, pointed hooves were dressed up with enamel paint, shiny and black.

Up and down, they bobbed inches from his head. Their white enamel teeth under the silently snarling yellow lips chomped down onto their wooden bits. Hateful eyes painted red bore into him.

They always went bobbing up and down and never stopping. Derek felt their hatred. Round and round and up and down, they were coming for him!

He woke to a pungent smell. Anne sat on the pavement of the parking lot with Derek's head in her lap. She was waving a bottle of perfume under his nose. Derek noticed the look of concern on her face evaporate into a smile as consciousness returned to his eyes.

"Sorry, Derek," she said while holding the perfume up for him to see. "It's the only thing I could find to bring you out of it."

"Señor Dunbar, my friend, are you all right?" Juan inquired.

Derek gathered himself and tried to sit. Anne resisted letting him up.

"Take it slow, Derek," she suggested and continued to caress his face.

"It's okay, Annie. Once again I owe you my thanks."

Anne helped him to his feet. As he looked into her lovely green eyes, Derek thought that he read something in her face.

"I know," he told her and smiled.

"You look like you could use a drink," Juan reminded him.

Derek shook his head. "I believe we all could," he said with a deeper voice. He was beginning to regain control of himself. "Come with me to my room," he summoned. "The four of us need to think this through and make some decisions."

"Now?" Juan asked, thinking that it might not be a good time given Sharon's state of mind.

"Now," Derek answered him forcefully.

Sharon heard the key turn in the lock of the door and looked up as the three of them walked in. They found a suitcase on the bed. Clothes were strewn about. Before they could say anything, she made her point.

"I'm packing," Sharon told them. "There's a flight leaving for Baltimore tomorrow, and I'm going to be on it."

She turned toward Derek, looked him straight in the eye and finished the thought, "With or without you."

"Sharon, aren't you being a little hard on him right now?" Anne asked, trying to reason with her.

Sharon threw a pair of shoes into her suitcase and snickered, "Tell you what, Anne, go through what I have during this past week and then ask me that question."

"Hey wait a minute," Anne grew hostile. "Nothing you've experienced compares to what I've endured with that bastard, Joel Washington."

"Give me a break," Sharon snarled. "Don't tell me about how magnanimous you were for Derek's sake. You did that thing so that Derek would develop feelings for you, didn't you?"

Anne felt herself grow hot with anger. It was true. She would give just about anything to be in Sharon's place, but she was also embarrassed by how easily Sharon nailed her on it.

She blurted out, "How dare you try and cheapen what I've given up for you and Derek. I wouldn't do a thing like that for just anyone, you know."

Sharon marched over and stuck her face close to Anne. "That's exactly my point," she said with a lowered voice.

"Stop it," Juan growled as he stepped between them. "Both of you are acting like school girls."

"Thanks, Juan," seconded Derek. "I couldn't have said it any better. Look, I have a plan about how to get to the bottom of this. Hear me out."

Sharon put her hands on her hips and interrupted him. "Another plan?" she asked. "Does this plan of yours include coming home with me tomorrow?"

Derek felt hollow, but he understood that there was no turning back. "We need at least another day, maybe two here in Germany. Then we may have to make another trip."

"Yeah, that's what I thought," Sharon interrupted him again. "Forget it, Derek. Count me out of this plan of yours." She clicked shut the clasps of her suitcase and jerked it off the bed. "If you aren't sitting with me on that plane tomorrow, you can count me out of your life, too." With that statement, she stormed out of the room.

"Wait," Juan beseeched her. "Sharon, where are you going?"

"Don't worry, Juan," she yelled back to him over her shoulder. "I'm just going down to the front desk to book another room. I'll call you later."

"Sorry, Derek," Juan addressed him sheepishly. "I don't know what to say."

"Derek?" Anne spoke and walked over to his side.

He blinked his eyes and took a deep breath. "Maybe it's better this way," Derek told them. "Now I will not have to worry. She'll be safer at home. It's going to get a lot more dangerous before this is over."

"Tell us about your plan?" Juan asked him.

"Elyria is our key to the mystery," Derek confided. "We now know that Blaze, and Joel Washington, and Elyria are tied together. What the two of you don't know is that there is another person, their ringleader. We need to confront that one to get to the truth."

"You think that Elyria would willingly give him up?" Juan asked with skepticism.

"I believe so. The thing is, this person, she wants me to find her," Derek revealed to them.

"She?" Anne wondered and put her hand to her face.

"That's right, Annie. It's a woman. I know a couple of other things about her, too. She goes by the name of Sara, and she lives somewhere in Brazil."

"My God," Anne gasped. "What have we done that would cause her to do these hateful things to us? I don't even know anybody in South America."

"Neither do I," Juan added. "I've done nothing to anybody to cause them to seek such vengeance."

Derek waved his hand at them. "Thank you both for being such good friends and trying to transfer this onto yourselves. It's not about you. I'm the one that she wants."

"Why?" Anne pressed him. "I don't understand."

"I can't explain that yet. I need you to trust me for now. I must talk with Elyria, find out where Sara is, and go to her."

"To Brazil?" Juan asked in disbelief.

"Yes, my friend. See now why poor Sharon is so distraught?"

"It's not such a big thing," Anne said with a smile. "I'll go with you, Derek."

"No way," Derek waved her off. "It's way too dangerous."

"See here, Señor Dunbar," Juan said as he shook a finger at him. "Like it or not Annie and I have also been ruined by this woman. I want to have a little chat with her. We are going with you. Besides, you're going to need a translator and someone to watch your back."

"Okay, friends," Derek acquiesced. "Let's take it one step at a time. Tomorrow we pay a visit to Elyria. Now go get some sleep. We'll start early."

"Good night, Señor Dunbar," Juan smiled as he left. "I'll call as soon as Sharon tells me what her new room number is."

"Thanks, Juan. Make sure she is all right."

"Count on it," Juan assured him.

"Walk you to your room?" Derek offered to Anne.

"Are you sure you're going to be okay?" Anne asked.

"I'm fine," Derek smiled and playfully pinched her nose.

"Are you sure, Derek? You've been under a lot of stress, and the way Sharon just treated you, it's not right. Are you sure you don't want me to stay for a while, to talk?"

"We better not, Annie."

"Derek?"

"Yes, Annie?"

"I'm asking to stay. Please, let me stay."

Derek embraced her. "I can't abandon Sharon."

"She's the one that left. She told you that she doesn't love you," Anne protested.

"Neither one of us believes that, do we?" he asked.

"I don't know, Derek. All I know for sure is that I love you. I would never be hateful like that to you."

"She's just confused, Annie. Her mind was blown tonight. It's going to take her some time to get over her denial."

"What are you talking about?" Anne asked looking him in the eye.

Derek placed a finger to her lips. "Shhh," he told her and unlocked the embrace. "Trust me for now, Annie."

"That's it then?" she shrugged. "It will never happen between us?"

Derek looked down and shuffled his feet. "I, I don't know," he stammered. "I have deep feelings for you, Annie, but I also love Sharon. Maybe I'm confused, too."

Anne's green eyes twinkled, and she smiled.

"Thanks for keeping my hope alive, Derek." She gave him a flirtatious goodbye wave and walked out of the room. Later, as she lay in her bed staring at the ceiling, Anne thought about it.

"I'm so pathetic, and Sharon is such an idiot," she said talking to herself. "I need to fix this, before it's too late."

Klaus Hall picked up the phone in his office. It was just after eight in the morning, and he hadn't had a chance to finish his second cup of coffee.

"Herr Dunbar, I thought you would be on your way home by now."

Derek wore a frown as he spoke into the mouthpiece of the phone. "Believe me, Klaus, there is nothing that I would like better than to get out of here."

"So what's keeping you?" Klaus asked with curiosity.

"I wanted to go to Tabitha's funeral," Derek said in a respectful tone.

Klaus felt a pang of guilt as he spoke to Derek. "I also had thoughts about going, but I got caught up in a new case. She was extraordinarily beautiful, wasn't she, Herr Dunbar? There was something different about her. It's such a terrible waste."

"It is a shame," Derek agreed with him. "You wouldn't have believed the media circus afterwards."

"What do you mean?" Klaus inquired.

Derek related the situation to him, and how they had all lost their jobs.

Klaus rested his head in his hand before continuing. "I'm so sorry to hear about that, Herr Dunbar. Is there anything I can do?"

"Actually, yes," Derek began.

Klaus immediately regretted the offer. *If this is going to be about money,* he thought. *I already deposited Dunbar's payment to me.*

"It's about that woman, Elyria," Derek continued. "Do you know where they are holding her?"

"Elyria?" Klaus repeated. He grew suspicious. "What is it that you want from her?"

"The consensus is that she is working for someone else. That person is at the root of everything that's happened to me. I need to find out why, and Elyria is the only one that may be able to help me. So, do you know where she is?"

Klaus considered his response before answering. "Actually, Herr Dunbar, I do know where she is. Dieter Horner told me. I'm going to visit her today."

Derek was surprised. "You, Klaus? What do you want to see her for?" Derek thought it through while asking the question and concluded the improbable. "Good God, Klaus, you aren't representing her, are you? How could you? You were there."

Klaus closed his eyes with his head still resting in his hand. He wished he had finished his coffee before taking Derek's call.

"Relax, Herr Dunbar, Elyria is not my client. At least not directly."

"So why do you want to see her?" Derek asked to clear his confusion.

"Hank Kimball has retained me on behalf of the U.S. Government. He wants Elyria released into his custody."

"Kimball?" Derek asked more confused than ever. "What's going on?"

"Sorry, Herr Dunbar, I can't comment on the specifics. I'm going to visit with Elyria at nine. I know it's a short notice, but if you want to meet, and if you get over here by 8:30, I'll take you to see her."

"Thanks, Klaus," Derek said with relief.

Derek heard a knock on the door to his room. Looking out through the window, he saw it was Juan and Anne. He didn't like the look on Juan's face.

"I gotta go, Klaus. See you there."

Derek hung up the phone with his right hand while opening the door with his left.

"What's wrong, Juan?" Derek wanted to know.

"Sharon called me from the front desk. She told me that she was getting into a taxi and heading for the airport. She wanted me to give you that message."

"Shit," Derek uttered. "Why couldn't she give me a chance to talk to her first?"

"The flight to Baltimore doesn't leave until this afternoon," Anne reminded him. "There's still plenty of time."

"I just got off the phone with Klaus Hall," Derek informed them. "I have to hot foot it over to his office. He's going to escort me to visit with Elyria."

"Derek, the timing couldn't be worse. You need to go to Sharon," Anne told him with a sense of urgency.

Derek considered his options. "You're right, Annie. I'll try to find her, but as you said, I have until this afternoon. This could be my only opportunity to get to Elyria. I have to leave now."

"Can I come along, Señor Dunbar?" Juan asked with enthusiasm.

"Only if you stop with the Señor Dunbar thing and start calling me Derek. How about you, Anne?"

She stood there kicking at a bump in the carpet. "I don't think so, guys," she told them. "I'll just hang around here, but I expect you to come and get me the instant you get back."

"I'll come for you, Annie," Juan promised.

She acknowledged Juan with a warm smile.

Elyria backed up tight against the interrogation room wall when the four men walked in. She was scared. All of them had been there that night, Derek, Juan, Klaus, and Dieter. She assumed this was a vendetta and that they had come to kill her.

"What do you want with me?" she squealed like a cornered animal.

Derek sensed her fear and decided to take quick advantage. He walked up to within inches of her face and glowered, "Do you have any idea who I am?"

"Halt, Herr Dunbar," Officer Horner warned him as he wedged himself between Elyria and Derek. "Have a seat and behave. You wouldn't want to embarrass Klaus Hall, would you? He vouched for you to get in here."

With reluctance, Derek sat quietly beside Juan and waited. The two Germans asked her many questions about where she had come from and the source of the cobo. Klaus Hall was especially interested in her relationship with Hank Kimball.

"I just used Kimball to get close to him," Elyria told them as she nodded her head in the direction of Derek.

"Why did you want to harm Herr Dunbar?" Klaus pressed.

Elyria looked up at the ceiling and didn't answer. Klaus repeated the question.

"Maybe I wasn't trying to poison him," Elyria said evasively.

Officer Horner lit a cigarette and began puffing. "Tell me again about Kimball," he asked her. "Exactly how far did you go with him to get what you wanted?"

"I don't have to tell you that," she snarled.

Klaus Hall saw the real answer in her eyes and told her, "He wants us to release you into his custody."

Elyria smiled and confirmed, "I'm the one that suggested that to him. I will deal only with him. If any of you want to know more about the drugs, you will need to free me."

Officer Horner puffed and looked over at Klaus who nodded at him. He smothered the butt in the bottom of the ashtray and spoke to Elyria. "I'm afraid you are confused, young lady. If you want any chance at freedom, you are going to have to first tell us everything we need to know about the drugs and the reason behind the poisoning."

Klaus touched Derek's forearm. "Now, is there anything you would like to ask the lady?"

Derek directed a stare at her.

"You've made a big mistake," he told her.

"Obviously," she laughed and held up her handcuffed wrists.

"The person you work for is going to be angry with you," he continued.

"You don't know a thing about her," she mocked him.

"Her name is Sara," Derek said dryly. Elyria sat up straight and grew serious but said nothing.

"She's a very special woman, isn't she, very powerful and very…" Derek paused for effect, "old."

Both Klaus and Dieter took notice to the uncertainty in Elyria's eyes. He had definitely pressed a hot button, and they fixed their gaze on him.

"What could you possibly know?" she asked aloud, but the question was really to herself in wondering about Derek.

"Look at me, Elyria," Derek ordered. She gave him a defiant stare. "I know, because I am just like her."

Elyria's mind was racing. *Could this be?* she thought. *The Mistress wants him, because they are the same?* Her eyes grew wide.

Klaus and Dieter were amazed. In a few short minutes, Derek Dunbar had gotten inside her head. He was very close to a breakthrough.

"If what you say is true, why is it that she wants you to come to her?" Elyria asked, trying to seek some clarity.

"Let me whisper the answer to that question into your ear. If it satisfies you, will you tell me how to find her?"

"Herr Dunbar, I don't think so," Officer Horner apprised him. "I don't want you within arms' reach of her."

"No, it's okay," Elyria jumped in. "I want to hear what he has to say."

Dieter Horner gave Derek the evil eye. "Don't do anything stupid, Herr Dunbar. You wouldn't want to end up back in prison."

Derek walked over and got down on his knees so that he was level with Elyria's head. He cupped his hands around his mouth. Elyria leaned her head into his hands.

"She wants me, since I am like her. I will not get used up."

Elyria's eyes grew even wider. *Of course*, she thought. *How plausible. It all makes sense now.*

Klaus and Dieter were almost jumping out of their skins wanting to know how Derek was able to have such an impact on her. Even Juan was paying rapt attention.

Derek started to walk back to his seat, but Elyria stopped him. "Wait," she urged. "Now I have something to whisper to you."

He returned to his knees by her side. Elyria leaned over and whispered, "If I let you sleep with me, will I get used up the same as when men lie with her?"

Derek stood again. He couldn't help smiling. After Derek took his seat, he answered her, "Only women have that power. It doesn't work the same in reverse." Derek was still amused at her question, and added a teaser at the end. "You would really like it, Elyria."

For the first time since the night she was arrested, the four men saw Elyria crack a smile. Klaus and Dieter looked at each other and shook their heads.

"Where can I find her?" Derek asked again in a more serious tone.

Elyria looked at him with softer eyes, less defiant. "Find a way to get me out of here, and I will take you to her. I promise."

"I believe you," he told her. "Unfortunately, that is not my call. It's up to them," he nodded at Dieter and Klaus.

"You'll never find her without me," she stressed in desperation.

"You're not my only lead," Derek bragged. He was fishing for a reaction. "There is a man in Manaus who knows her."

"Manaus!" she scoffed. "You couldn't be colder, and no man who gets to know the Mistress lives long enough to talk about it."

"Let's go," Derek motioned to Juan.

"Well, what about it?" Elyria begged Officer Horner. "Do I get out of here?"

"In the end, it all depends how persuasive your boyfriend, Herr Kimball, can be," Klaus mused. "We will see."

As they left the room, Derek turned and spoke once more. "It wasn't necessary to come after Sharon, or to do any of these terrible things," he said, wanting Elyria to know the truth. "I would have willingly gone to your Mistress."

"Derek," Elyria shouted after him. "Brazil is a very large country. Whatever you think you have in Manaus, forget about it. It is a dead end."

Officer Horner eyed Derek with misgiving. "Maybe we should be interrogating you, Herr Dunbar. You seem to know a great deal about all of this."

"I was just toying with her," Derek lied. "It didn't lead anywhere." He addressed Klaus, "Do you think Kimball has enough influence to spring her?"

Klaus Hall shrugged. "Who knows?" he speculated. "Stranger things have happened."

CHAPTER 26

General Orellana spied the men working on the brigantines near the water. He smiled and waved the rest of his party off from approaching. Slowly, he sneaked around behind the tree where their supervisor sat resting.

"What's an old foot soldier like you doing trying to build a boat?" Orellana boomed in his sternest voice.

General de Vargas sprang to his feet and wheeled around ready to do battle. When he saw who it was, he shouted in glee, "Francisco de Orellana, you found us!"

"A blind child could have followed that trail you blazed," Orellana beamed. "I swear you must have cleared half the jungle."

All work stopped as the soldiers, now shipbuilders, noticed the rest of Orellana's group stream in to the camp. It became a passionate reunion among many old friends.

"Friar Gaspar!" Gonzalo yelled in delight and embraced his old friend.

"You are looking so much better than when you left us," the friar observed. "This journey has proven to be good to your soul."

"No, Gaspar, my body may be healing, but my soul remains in turmoil."

The two of them walked together toward the pool under the tumbling cataract.

"Does she remain yet with you men?" Gaspar inquired.

"Sara is here," Gonzalo confirmed. "I fear that my time with her is soon over. It weighs heavy on me."

Friar Gaspar wiped perspiration from his brow.

"I also remain deeply affected by the maiden," he admitted. "I would like to speak with her again sometime soon, if you suspect that her departure is imminent."

The two old friends spent an hour together as Gonzalo confessed his love for Sara and of his frustration at the impossibility of their relationship.

Sara and a few other soldiers were picking fruit when they heard the news. She dropped her container and ran like a deer while making her way

271

back through the woods to the river. The men accompanying her could hardly keep up. Sara found them all laughing and partying together. She noticed Orellana and de Vargas drinking some wine and ran up to them.

"Ah, maiden," General Orellana gasped. "If only I could embrace the one that is more beautiful than this wondrous land. If only I could gaze deeply into those eyes."

"You can do so, mighty general," Sara flirted with him. "As you well know that would be a risky business indeed. I would also like to feel the embrace of those strong arms."

"Risks are not allowed anymore, young lady," he flirted back at her. "Now that I am a married man."

"Married!" Sara exclaimed. "You and Juana?" She could hardly contain herself.

Sara felt a gentle tap on her shoulder. She turned around.

"Greetings, Mistress Sara," Juana expressed warmly. "My husband may be in a peril of your embrace, but I can squeeze you hard enough for the both of us."

The two ladies hugged. Jumping up and down, they squealed with delight, ran off and jumped into the pool. Splashing at each other, the two of them played until they were exhausted. Sara dragged herself to shore and took her place on the blanket beside Juana.

"Thank you so much for coming, sister," Sara expressed with much sincerity. "After all these many months with only men to deal with, it eases my burden greatly having you here."

Overcome with emotion, Sara felt the tears begin to flow.

"Juana, I reflect often on the kindness you showed to me from the time we first met in Grenada. I still cannot thank you enough." Sara wiped her eyes.

Juana reached an arm around Sara's neck.

"These are happier times now, Mistress Sara. We never have to think about that again."

"You've remained a loyal sister to me throughout," Sara reaffirmed. "I know there have been times that I frightened you. I never meant to do that, not to you, Juana."

"I know," Juana said as she tried to soothe her. "You endured such things that no one should have to. It made your soul sick. What sister would I have been, had I walked away from you while you were hurting. I only wish that your healing will someday soon be completed."

As Sara began to return from her self-indulgent spasm, she began to sense something different about Juana. Her face lit up.

"Juana, are you pregnant?" Sara asked her.

"Shhh," Juana scolded her and looked around nervously. "My husband doesn't know yet. I withheld this from him for fear that he would not allow me to come."

"And he would have been righteous in preventing you," Sara reproved her. "How far along are you?"

"By now, close to three months," Juana answered.

"You're going to have to tell him soon," Sara warned her.

"I will tell him tonight," Juana decided. "Now that we are together again, I can ask you for my release. If you grant it to me, I will return when he orders me."

Sara was stunned.

"Release?" Sara stared at Juana with disbelief. "You are no longer bound to me. When you consented to marry Francisco, he became your master. Just as a sister leaves her siblings to live with the man she loves, so you have left me."

This time Juana broke down in tears.

"Distance may separate us, but you will always be here," Juana said as she patted her chest.

"Come on," Sara ordered as she grabbed Juana by the hand. The two of them plunged once again laughing into the coolness of the great pool.

Several days passed as all of them worked to construct the vessels and gather food and other stores for the journey downstream. Orellana was joyous over the news of Juana's baby, but he also knew that this changed things. General de Vargas understood that new plans would have to be made, but he waited on Orellana to come to him after he had an opportunity to consider the options.

That day came after the combined parties successfully floated their first brigantine.

During the celebration, Orellana walked over and offered de Vargas a drink.

"It bothers me more than you could know, Sanchez, but I'm going to have to return to Guayaquil with my Juana," Orellana told him sullenly.

"Once an explorer, always an explorer, eh, Francisco," his friend joked with him and raised his cup.

"There is no other way," Orellana admitted. "I'll also need a contingent of men to serve as an escort. Who knows how many savages know of our incursion."

"Many of these men will be more than happy to return to the comfort of their homes. You'll have no problem soliciting volunteers," de Vargas pointed out.

"Where do you suppose it goes?" Orellana asked as he nodded his head toward the river.

"Sara is sure that it leads to El Dorado," de Vargas contemplated. "After that, who knows? Old Captain Pinzon tells tales of a mighty river that empties into the Atlantic. Maybe this stream is a tributary of that river."

The two of them gazed down the silvery ribbon of the river as it twisted and turned from view.

"When are you leaving?" de Vargas asked of Orellana.

"In a few days," he responded. "My men will help you launch that second brigantine. Then we will need to go."

Lani and her band of female warriors remained hidden for two days on the far shore of the great pool near the mountain. From their location opposite Gonzalo and his expedition, they were in perfect position to observe the activities of these unfamiliar people. As was the custom among the Shuhar, the women were bare chested and wore only a waist belt around which hung strips of animal skin and hemp.

"It is just as Goma described," one of Lani's lieutenants named Cora whispered. "These pale men are the children of the sun. They must have come here from the heavens on that mighty vessel that floats in the great pool."

"These men work like ants building more vessels," expressed Lani. "Maybe they are making ready to return to the skies and will not come to bother us."

"What do you make of their chain of command?" asked a fascinated Cora. "It appears like the darker-skinned ones that look like us are slaves. See how they do the menial tasks like preparing food and bearing burdens for the pale skins?"

"Yes," Lani confirmed. "The pale ones in turn do obeisance to their mother, the great queen. These darker ones may be from the Irimaris nation, but their garments are strange."

"The other woman that stays close by the queen must be a maidservant,"

Cora continued with her observation.

"Possibly," Lani said although she wasn't so sure. "The way they play together does not convey the proper respect of a subservient maid to her mistress. It is more like she is a close friend or maybe a sister."

"Why do you suppose there are no other women?" Cora asked. "Does this daughter of the sun bear only male children?"

"I do not know," Lani admitted, "but we are going to find out."

"With you there are only twenty-one of us," Cora reminded Lani. "Do we risk contacting these men?"

"No," Lani told her. "I will speak only with the queen, the sun's daughter. This afternoon when she bathes, I will be waiting. Her sons guard the queen at all times except when she bathes. Then they turn their backs out of respect."

"What if she cries out?" Cora asked.

"If that happens, I want all of you to spring from hiding with arrows nocked and cover my escape back to this place," Lani instructed her and slowly moved into position near the water's edge.

Sara and Juana entered the pool during the hottest part of the afternoon. At first Lani was reluctant to approach since Juana had come along with Sara. Then she reasoned that the added risk was minimal and slid into the water. Lani breathed through a reed as she stealthily maneuvered her way underwater in the direction of the two women. As Lani approached, Sara sensed something unusual and stopped splashing. Juana noticed a change in Sara's expression.

"Mistress Sara, why are you looking around so? I don't see any of the men spying on us."

"Hush, Juana," Sara said in a low voice. "Listen to me. I need you to be brave. Do not scream unless I do. Remain very still."

"What do you mean?" Juana began to ask.

Out of the corner of her eye, Juana saw a form like a giant fish pass between them. Lani used this tactic to draw the attention of Sara and Juana away from the opposite bank so that their backs would be turned to her warriors. The water broke into tiny ripples as Lani surfaced.

In reaction to Sara's request, Juana slapped both hands to cover her mouth in order to stifle her desire to yell out.

Sara quietly stared into Lani's eyes. *A woman*, she thought to herself. *This is always more difficult than dealing with a man, but I can still master her.*

Lani felt the warmth of Sara's gaze. *She welcomes me and is unafraid!*

Lani pondered in wonder. She felt an immediate affection toward Sara. It made her feel like she was in the presence of her own mother.

This cannot be, Lani reflected. *My mother was taken from me when I was just a child. This one must be the mother of us all. She is the daughter of the sun.* Instinctively, Lani raised both hands out of the water and held them in front of her as a display of submissiveness. Sara reached out and took her hands. They stood there together looking at each other.

"Juana, are you all right?" Sara inquired.

"Yes, Mistress Sara," she answered meekly. "Who is she?"

Without breaking eye contact with Lani, Sara gave Juana her instructions. "Go get one of the Huaorani men that understands our language. We need an interpreter. Make sure he wears a blindfold, since I am uncovered. Warn all of the rest of our party to stay away. If anyone asks, say that we need one of the Huaorani men to run an errand for us. Come back quickly."

Sara felt Lani gently tug at her hands as Juana left them, but Sara didn't let go. "Don't be afraid," Sara spoke soothingly. She started to relate to Lani the story of their journey. Although Lani could not understand the words, Sara spoke them as a means to keep her engaged and comfortable until Juana returned.

Some time later, Juana returned with one of the men. She was leading him blindfolded by the hand toward Sara. Lani grew uncomfortable but understood when she saw the blindfold that this one man would not be a threat to her.

"What do you wish of me?" the man asked somewhat frightened.

"What is your name?" Sara asked.

"I am Terro," he responded.

Sara explained the situation. "Terro, thank you for coming to our assistance. Please excuse the blindfold, but I am naked and holding on to an Indian woman. I would like you to try and communicate with her."

Terro spoke out a greeting in a number of native languages. Although they could not completely understand one another, there was enough in common between their tongues that Terro and Lani could converse in a meaningful way.

"Her name is Lani," Terro informed them.

Sara smiled. "Please tell her that my name is Sara."

"Sara," Lani repeated.

"Tell Lani that we need to continue this conversation on land and that she is in no danger."

Sara heard Terro and Lani talk back and forth, and she heard Terro snicker.

"She is afraid," he explained. "She thinks that you are the daughter of the sun and that your children will kill her."

"Play along, Terro," Sara ordered. "Don't exasperate her, tell her that I am the daughter of the sun and that my children obey my commands. Tell her that they will not harm her."

Sara let go of Lani's hands and motioned her to follow. When they got to shore, Sara put on her cape and told Terro to take off his blindfold.

"Juana, you keep watch for us," Sara directed. "I don't want to be interrupted. It would scare Lani. Tell the men that I need some private time here and to stay away."

"Yes, Mistress," Juana acknowledged and obediently ran off a short distance up the trail.

While Terro translated, Sara and Lani talked. Lani explained that the man Sara caught looking at her had warned the Shuhar tribes of their presence and that the rest of the men were afraid of her power. She went on to tell her about the party of women warriors waiting on the opposite shore.

"Is it customary among your people for women to fight?" Sara asked her.

"We are more fierce than our men," Lani explained. "They may be physically stronger, but we are more cunning and less fearful. That is why I have come and the men remain behind."

"How many women among your people are soldiers?" Sara asked.

"There are twenty with me and about the same number remain behind," responded Lani. She told Sara many things about her people and their history.

Forty fierce women warriors among this region's most feared Indians, Sara thought to herself. The seeds of a plan began to take place in her mind.

Lani began to inquire about the intentions of Sara and her children.

"Have you come to enslave our peoples?" she asked.

Sara began her plan with this answer. "I have come to build a great empire out of your tribe. My father, the sun, has become displeased with your men. They dishonor him with their cowardice. He has sent me to organize your warriors to usurp these men and to take your rightful place as rulers of the Shuhar people. Your men will become your slaves."

Under Sara's influence, Lani became enthusiastic over this plan. *Why not?* she thought to herself. *This queen speaks true. We women gain victory for our people on the field of battle. Why shouldn't we rule?*

Lani waited for more information, but Sara sat quietly studying her reaction. "Mistress Sara, what about your sons? Surely they will fight on the side of our men, right?"

"They will do as I bid them," Sara stated coldly. "They are on a different mission and will soon part from us. The great ships they build will carry them downstream in search of an old man. It is said that he has a great store of yellow metal in his possession. Do your people know of this man?"

Lani shook her head "No," but Sara sensed that she was holding something back. She embellished the story about El Dorado.

"This man stole the yellow metal from my father, the sun," Sara went on to say. "It is the same color as his glowing radiance that you see in the daytime sky. It is part of my father's body. He is hot with anger at this man and is sending my sons to find the metal and to punish the man. Lani, it would go well with you if you tell me now if you know where to find him."

Lani looked at the great pool and pointed down the river. "A very old story says that a man like you describe lives beyond the reaches of this stream. He dwells up another hidden stream that also flows into the great river that divides the land. Mistress Sara, I don't know if the story is true, but if this man lives, he is far from here."

"I speak the language of the gods," Sara explained to Lani. "I do not yet understand your lowly tongue. I want you to teach me. Tonight when the moon rises, I will cross this pool and join with you and your warriors. Watch for me. We will fulfill your destiny, Lani. You shall become queen of your people. I go now to say goodbye to my sons."

An enthralled Lani bowed to Sara and swiftly departed.

Terro and Sara watched as Lani swam across the pool. They witnessed the woods come to life with the forms of other women as they surrounded Lani and checked her over. All of the women warriors disappeared into the trees.

"Why would you have this woman believe such things about us?" Terro demanded in disbelief over what had transpired.

Sara lowered her hood and ordered Terro, "Look at me."

He stared into her eyes.

"The Indian woman is of little concern to us, isn't she?" Sara programmed him.

"Maybe she was never even here at all. You could have dreamed it, couldn't you?"

"Even if she was here, this whole matter is unimportant, isn't it?"

Sara raised her hood and broke eye contact with him. "What were you asking, Terro?"

Terro thought for a moment and responded, "Never mind, it wasn't important." He walked away.

Sara started up the path to her tent when she met up with the eagerly waiting Juana. This next meeting was not going to be easy for them.

"Juana, could you please fetch Friar Gaspar for me and meet me at my camp?"

"Of course, Mistress Sara," Juana grinned. "Are you going to tell me about that strange Indian woman?"

"Certainly," Sara responded. "I'll tell both you and the friar everything."

As they wandered toward Sara's tent, Juana explained about the meeting with the Indian woman to Friar Gaspar. He understood the significance of this encounter and what was about to happen in their meeting with Sara. Juana also understood but remained in a state of denial.

"She wanted only me and not Gonzalo also?" he asked of Juana.

"Mistress Sara asked only to see the two of us," Juana confirmed.

There was barely enough room for the three of them to squeeze into Sara's makeshift tent, but they required privacy.

After they sat on the ground, Sara began the conversation.

"There are three people in this world that I love dearly. The two of you, along with dear Gonzalo, liberated me from a purgatory so evil that the very notion of it I hope you will never be able to grasp. You've enabled me to journey to this new and wonderful world and remained close friends despite my behavior. It is important to me that you know that I will always remember your kindness forever."

With a heavy heart, Friar Gaspar drove right to the point. "When are you leaving?"

"Tonight, Friar. I would like it if the two of you accompanied me to the pool to see me off."

"What of Gonzalo?" he asked her.

"If he were to find out before I am gone, it would tear him to pieces. His healing is well advanced, Friar, but he remains vulnerable for a long time."

Sara looked at Juana and noticed that she had buried her face in her hands. Her chest heaved with quiet sobs.

"Juana," Sara started, but Juana, unable to bear what was happening, ran out.

"She will not tell him," Gaspar said.

"I know that," Sara replied. "Friar Gaspar, after a long time, after you know that Gonzalo is steadier, I want you to tell him something for me."

Gaspar waited in silence for Sara to continue.

"Tell him that it had to be this way. Tell him that a final meeting would've torn me to pieces, too. Although I dared not reveal it to him at the time, tell him that I returned his love."

Friar Gaspar nodded.

"There is another purgatory, Friar Gaspar," she conveyed to him. "It is the purgatory of a love that is hopeless to pursue."

"I understand," he muttered.

"One more thing," she remembered. "Follow the river and talk to the Indians that you meet along the way. They will lead you to El Dorado, if he exists."

Sara had very little in the way of material possessions. There was her cape that Juana made and her dagger that always remained in the folds of Sara's garments. Friar Gaspar met her after dark and they journeyed together for the last time. Soon they were standing on the shore of the great pool.

"I had hoped that Juana would be strong enough to come," Sara expressed with sorrow. "A woman could ask for no greater sister."

"Good bye, Sara," Friar Gaspar told her tenderly. "I will pray for you every day until I die."

"Thank you, Friar, but don't waste your prayers. I have no soul to save," Sara said dejectedly.

"I no longer believe that to be true," he said with a certainty. "You have demonstrated otherwise to me over and over again."

Sara took his hand. She felt the friar spasm as if rejecting the pleasant feeling.

"Friar Gaspar," she shook his arm. "I have something for you to remember me by." Sara lowered her hood. The rising full moon bathed her lovely face in ethereal white. "Don't be afraid. Look at me."

After his eyes met hers, they embraced, and she squeezed him.

"No guilt, Friar Gaspar," she whispered while holding his gaze. "No guilt."

Standing on tiptoes, Sara planted her lips firmly against his. The kiss was long, slow, and passionate. Gaspar felt himself grow hard, but he allowed it to happen. Unencumbered by the yoke of shame that Sara suspended from his mind, Gaspar experienced the searing wave of ecstasy float through him.

After they separated, Sara whispered into his ear, "Remember this moment, Friar Gaspar, and remember me."

"I remember," he repeated.

They were startled by the approaching sound of running footfalls. It was

Juana.

"Forgive me, Mistress Sara," she said breathing heavily from the run. "I wasn't going to come. It hurts too much to see you leave, but I need to ask your permission for something."

Sara responded, "Juana, you are your own woman now. You need no permission from me to do anything. Just make that husband of yours very happy."

Juana ignored her and continued, "Sister, if it is a girl child, can I name her after you?"

Sara smiled and nodded affirmatively. Keeping her emotions in check, she turned her back, entered the pool, and began to cross.

"Good bye, Juana," she choked. "Good bye, Gaspar. Take care of Gonzalo for me."

Juana and Friar Gaspar held onto each other for support. The full moon lit the way for Sara. They watched as she ascended from the pool on the far shore. There was a rustling of branches. Sara seemed to be surrounded by a few indistinguishable bodies. In an instant, she was gone.

Sara anticipated what would happen.

"Some of the children will miss their mother and try to follow," she conveyed to Lani. "We cannot allow this to happen. They have a duty to find and return the yellow metal to the sun and cannot mourn for me."

"How is it that we may help?" Lani asked.

"Have several of your warriors set a false trail. While you take me away in one direction, my children will pursue in another. Set an ambush for my children."

"You do not want us to kill them, do you?" Lani pleaded in horror. "The great sun would be angry."

"Of course not," Sara calmed her. "Have them hide in the trees. Shoot them in the legs with your arrows. This will stop them, but it will not kill them."

Lani arranged for Cora to take sixteen of the women to set up the trap. Lani and five others would run away with Sara. They would wait for the ambush party to return at a prearranged meeting place.

CHAPTER 27

Sharon sat at Gate C4 trying to make sense out of the foreign words in the *Frankfurter Allgemeine Zeitung*. Although German was unintelligible to her, Sharon studied the pictures. It was four hours until departure, and this newspaper provided a diversion from what was bothering her. During the past week, she found a new strength as she worked her way through crisis after crisis. Just as Sharon was building her confidence and self esteem, the truth about Derek stung her heart. Of course, she believed what Werner had revealed to them. As wild as it sounded, it was so logical. Sharon knew that she would not be able to bear the inevitable outcome. She needed to escape. She wanted to go home.

As Sharon sat there looking down at the newspaper, a person entered her periphery and stopped. She lowered the newspaper and found herself staring at a pair of shapely legs in black pumps. Glancing up to see this person's face, Sharon noticed that it was Anne.

She moaned and lowered her eyes, pretending to be looking at the newspaper. "Did Derek send you?" Sharon asked with little emotion.

Anne took a seat directly across from Sharon and answered her. "He doesn't know that I am here." She crossed her legs and leaned back into the black vinyl seat studying Sharon's demeanor. After it became obvious that Sharon wasn't going to say anything else, Anne took the initiative.

"You were right, you know," she began. "I secretly hoped that Derek would return some affection to me for what I had done. I have a serious crush on him. Actually, I think I fell in love the first time I laid eyes on him."

Sharon peered out at Anne over the top of the newspaper with narrow eyes. "Get in line," was her catty response. "Every other woman that meets him feels the same way."

Sharon turned the page for no reason other than to make Anne believe that she was actively absorbed in reading an article. In reality, Sharon was hurting. She always trusted Derek, but after the past week, and given all of the stress everyone endured, she began to have doubts. Finally, Sharon's feelings overcame her desire to act aloof. She put the paper down and looked straight at Anne.

"Did he?" Sharon wanted to know.

Anne smiled. This was the reaction that she hoped to get from Sharon. Now there was no doubt in her mind that this woman was still in love with Derek. Anne understood that the complete sentence Sharon meant to ask was, "Did Derek fall victim to your seduction and return the affection that you so eagerly desired of him?"

"God knows I tried," Anne responded candidly. "Every move I put on him was spurned with words like, 'I can't betray Sharon,' or 'I still love Sharon.'"

Sharon subconsciously began to arrange all of the sections of the newspaper in order and neatly folded them while Anne spoke to her. She couldn't understand why Anne was here and why she was torturing her with this talk of Derek. After some time listening, Sharon had enough.

"You bitch," she snarled. "Why would you do something like that and then have the gall to brag to me about it?"

"Why should you care?" Anne shot back. "Didn't I hear you tell Derek that you don't love him anymore? Aren't you here by yourself? Look, Sharon, you're the one that walked out on him."

"I'll bet it wasn't five minutes after I left that you were throwing yourself at him," Sharon snapped.

Anne responded, "Why not? You're not married to him, are you?"

"Damn it, Anne, Derek and I have been together for seven years. That's longer than most marriages. Don't you realize that I still have feelings for Derek? I still..." Sharon stopped in mid-sentence.

"Go ahead, Sharon, say it. Admit it," Anne goaded her.

"All right, damn you. I love him. What kind of sick game are you playing with me? I hope you enjoy gloating over my misery."

Anne uncrossed her legs and removed the folded newspaper that was on the seat beside Sharon. She moved into that seat. Sharon looked the other way.

"It took me an hour to find you," Anne said in a softer tone. "I didn't suspect you would actually go to the gate this early. I was worried that I wouldn't be able to track you down in time." She paused for a moment and continued. "Sharon, what's wrong with you? I don't get it. You two were made for each other. Derek is completely devoted to you."

As Anne spoke, Sharon's began to realize that it had all been a ruse. Anne had tricked her into admitting her feelings for Derek.

Sharon shook her head and told Anne, "You don't understand the circumstances. It can't work."

Anne was bewildered. "What is there not to understand? I'm an expert at this. My life is littered with the debris of relationships that didn't work. Don't you know how special Derek is?"

Sharon couldn't help but to laugh at that statement. "You have no idea how special he is."

"Come back to the Royale with me," Anne urged. "Derek needs you."

Sharon reached into her purse and removed a small makeup mirror. She stared at the image of her own face as it was reflected back at her.

"Look at me, Anne," she charged. "I'm twenty-nine going on thirty. Derek is thirty-three going on twenty-five."

"Yeah, he is in great shape," Anne confirmed for Sharon.

Sharon speculated while gazing into the mirror. "Do you know why a sixty-year-old woman isn't attractive to a thirty-year-old man?"

Anne had no idea what Sharon was getting at but played along. "Probably because the sixty-year-old woman is his mother," she joked.

"Nope, that's not it," Sharon corrected her. "It's because there will always be someone younger and prettier, like you, waiting to take the thirty-year-old man away."

Anne reached over and broke the spell by gently pushing the mirror down away from Sharon's face.

"Sharon, I'm the same age as you, and nobody is going to take your Derek away. You are the only person that can mess this up for yourself. Forget all of this nonsense about being sixty years old. So what if things change? Can't you just be happy right now?"

"Maybe you're right," Sharon admitted looking down. She reconsidered, "As difficult as it is now, I don't think I could have the strength to deal with it later."

Anne tried another angle. "You're thinking only of yourself, Sharon. Derek is desperately seeking the cause of all of the evil that has been happening. It's taking a lot of his strength to do that, and he needs you. Whatever it is that has you freaked out, can't you set it aside at least until this is over and until we can all think more clearly?"

Sharon thought it through to herself. *Anne is right. This terror has to end soon. So what if we have to go home by way of South America? Maybe I am being unreasonable. What if it takes a whole year? It will not, but even if it did, it's only one more year. I can be there for Derek. It's the least I can do for him given the seven wonderful years that he has given me.*

She became more at peace with herself and was grateful that Anne had turned out once again to be such a good friend.

"Well, what are we waiting for?" Sharon stood and smiled.

They walked together back through the terminal toward the parking lot. Sharon recalled Anne's confession about the relationships that didn't work for her. She speculated about Anne's current situation.

"So why is it that someone as pretty as you doesn't have a man?" Sharon asked her again.

Anne snickered, "I'm one of those unfortunate souls that seems to pick losers."

"Did you ever hear the expression, 'You can't see the forest for the trees?'" Sharon asked her.

"Of course," Anne told her.

"Sometimes we are so close to a situation that we don't realize a good opportunity when it presents itself," Sharon counseled.

Anne didn't get it. "What do you mean, Sharon?"

They walked a few paces in silence. Sharon didn't quite know how to say what needed to be said. Finally, she just let it out.

"Juan was a good husband to his wife until cancer took her. She's been gone for a while, and now he cares a great deal for you, Anne. I've spent a lot of time with him, so I know that he is a decent guy who would never let you down. That night when you were with Joel, it killed Juan to passively sit there and let it happen."

A few more paces passed in silence as Anne considered what Sharon said. There was chemistry with Juan. She liked him. He was stable and loyal to his friends. Sharon was right. Here was a guy with some character.

"Juan is a good man, isn't he?" Anne directed at Sharon while grinning.

Derek found Sharon waiting for him in their room after his return from visiting Elyria. He was elated to see her but concerned about the impending risk. As they lay together underneath the covers, Derek thought of a way to express these feelings to her.

While stroking Sharon's hair, he whispered into her ear, "Despite everything that's happened to us during the past week, I'm the happiest man alive when I am with you."

Sharon rolled around on top of Derek and kissed him. "I love you," she assured him. "Forgive me for acting the way I did. I couldn't handle it. I'm still having a difficult time adapting, but I trust you. You're the same Derek Dunbar as you've been for the past seven years. I know that you will not hurt me."

After she told him this, Sharon could feel Derek tense up as she lay on top of him.

"What's wrong, Derek? Am I too heavy?"

"You're as light as a ray of sunshine," Derek said as he returned her kiss, "and just as warm. I'm anxious about what happens next and about your safety."

Sharon remained on top but slid down a few inches using Derek's chest as a pillow.

"You're going to confront this woman, Sara, right?" she asked.

Derek began to lightly stroke her back between the shoulders and replied, "I must. She will keep coming after us until I go to her. I'm worried that I will not be able to protect you when we enter her domain. She's a formidable foe."

Sharon locked her hands together on top of his chest and rested her chin on the back of her hands. Looking up into Derek's eyes, she spoke softly, "I'm the one that's worried. You think that I'm going to allow you to visit some super bitch by yourself? How did Werner put it? 'Every pore of her body oozes with psychic pheromones.' Hell no, Derek, you're the one that needs protecting."

He chuckled at that. Sharon liked the way the vibrations from it caused her to bounce around on his chest. Derek rubbed his eyes with one hand while continuing to stroke her back with his other hand.

"Seriously, I'd never forgive myself if something were to happen to you," he sighed.

"You'd forget all about me in a hundred years or so," Sharon whispered with no change in expression.

"Don't talk like that, Sharon. Without you there would be no point in living."

"It's a reality, Derek. Eventually we are both going to have to face the inevitable. I'm getting older every day. Some day you will drift away from me."

Derek recalled Sharon's wrinkled old face from the dream about the carousel. The gold ring had turned into Sharon. He wasn't sure what the angel was trying to express to him other than "the prize" and Sharon may somehow be related. He moved the hand rubbing his eyes back down to stroking her back.

"There's other magic at work here, Sharon," he speculated. "Let's just take it a day at a time for now."

Sharon knew that there was nothing she could do about it except to trust Derek. She was also determined that Derek could do nothing about stopping her from going with him.

"Juan and Anne are going with you, aren't they?" she inquired.

"They have a bone to pick with Sara about getting fired," Derek reiterated. "So they say, anyway. Actually, they are both great friends. They don't need to risk their lives to do this."

"Free will, right?" Sharon smiled. "Isn't that what Werner said?"

Derek rolled her around until he was back on top.

"How long are you going to be quoting that guy?" Derek teased.

Sharon felt Derek rub up against her inner thigh. She squeezed her legs tight and trapped him in between them. Sharon flexed her supple quadriceps starting with her right thigh and then alternating with her left thigh. She continued in this manner kneading his manhood.

Derek closed his eyes and soaked up the pleasurable waves. In a few moments, he was rock hard. Sharon relaxed and opened her legs. Reaching down, she guided him inside.

"I may not be able to grant you an out of body experience," she whispered, "but after seven years I know exactly how you like it."

"Amen," was all that Derek could say.

The four of them walked out of the Brazilian consulate in Frankfurt, visas in hand.

"Juan, are you sure that Stamos will allow us to see him when we get there?" Derek asked his friend.

"I telephoned him just as you asked," Juan answered. "Lucky for me he spoke Spanish. Professor Stamos believes that we are American journalists interested in doing a story about the legendary Amazon warriors."

"I guess the only thing left to do is to purchase our airline tickets," declared Anne.

"Juan, do you want to take care of that for us while we pick up some maps and travel guides?" Derek suggested. "We'll also make a trip to Deutschebank and exchange our dollars into some Brazilian Reals."

"Sure, Derek. That was Varig Airlines, right?" Juan asked, wanting to make sure.

"A late flight leaves every night from Rhein Main to Sao Paulo. That's where we get the connection to Manaus. It would be great if we could leave tonight if they have seats available," Derek told him.

"I'll see what I can do," Juan assured them.

"Is it okay if I go with you, Juan?" Anne asked in a meek voice.

Juan was surprised and delighted. "I'd be honored if you would keep me company," he told her with a twinkle in his eye.

As they walked off, Anne turned and winked at Sharon.

"What's that all about?" Derek asked her.

Sharon grabbed his arm and started Derek walking in the opposite direction.

"It means that Anne will not be coming on to you anymore," she said with a smile. "That's one less pretty woman that I have to worry about."

Derek looked out of the passenger lounge at the nose of the Varig jet as it was being prepared for the flight. He felt guilty about not being more adamant to his friends about the danger in making this journey. At least Sharon was privy to what Werner had disclosed, but Juan and Anne had no clue that they were caught in the middle of a clash between two immortals. He dared not tell them. Although he didn't discuss it with Sharon, Derek sensed that she also realized the threat to his kind if this secret were revealed to an ever-increasing number of people.

"Are you sure that you want to do this thing?" Derek addressed the three of them as they stood there with him. "You still have time to change your minds. I will not think any less of you. You made your original decision in the heat of the moment. I'm sure you've had some time to reconsider the risks."

Sharon tipped the novel she was reading, peering out over the top at Derek. She didn't say anything but gave him a look that suggested, "Don't even think about trying to leave me behind."

Juan lowered his head with shame. "With no job, Derek, I have no place to go."

Anne shook Juan's arm so that he looked her in the eyes. It was her silent attempt to boost his spirits. Juan marveled at how he never tired of looking into those lovely green pools.

"We're all in this together, Derek," she said resolutely while maintaining eye contact with Juan. "Besides," she added flirtatiously, "girls like a little adventure once in a while."

Derek sighed. He was grateful to have his friends by his side but knew they didn't fully understand what they were about to face.

From his window seat, Derek watched as the lights from the city of Frankfurt grew dimmer during the climb to a cruising altitude. He looked at his watch an hour later and noticed that it was midnight. Sharon was sleeping with her head resting against his shoulder. Derek chuckled as he noticed a track of drool bubbling in the corner of her mouth. He reached over with a napkin and wiped her face. Sharon stirred but didn't wake up.

A true pilot at heart, Derek began to mentally calculate where they might be at this point in the flight. *An hour out of Frankfurt should put us over the water*, he figured. *We probably just cleared French air space. Seven more hours and we should be home.*

It was then that Derek suddenly remembered, *Of course, we aren't going home, are we?*

CHAPTER 28

The next morning as Gonzalo rose and got dressed, Friar Gaspar met him. Gaspar slept very little that night thinking about his friend and how he would react to the news. He was conflicted about whether he should tell Gonzalo immediately, or if he should wait until Gonzalo discovered that Sara was missing. Actually, the friar wasn't sure that he had the courage to face Gonzalo. He had allowed Sara to leave without raising an alarm. Would Gonzalo ever forgive him? In the end, Gaspar realized that being a friend to Gonzalo meant that he was obligated to see this through. Sara would have wanted it this way.

Gonzalo noticed Gaspar's forlorn expression and thought it to be peculiar. "Good morning, Gaspar," he mumbled still half asleep. "Why such a long face?"

"I didn't sleep well last night," Gaspar responded.

Gonzalo stared at himself in a looking glass and began to fuss with his hair. After he was satisfied with his appearance, Gonzalo set a wide-brimmed straw hat in place on his head.

"It was humid all night, wasn't it?" Gonzalo asked rhetorically, not expecting an answer. He looked over at the friar and noticed that Gaspar rocked nervously on his feet. His head was down staring at the ground.

Gonzalo thought of a way to cheer up the friar. "Come, Gaspar," he motioned with his hand for the friar to follow him. "Let's see if Sara is awake. If we can convince her to have breakfast with us, it will put a smile on both of our faces."

"She's gone," Gaspar told him abruptly.

Gonzalo allowed the words to reverberate inside his head for some time before their meaning was clear. Even then, he would not permit himself to believe the words.

"A cruel joke, Friar," Gonzalo reproved him. Noticing that Gaspar's expression did not change, he felt a panic rise up inside.

"No, Gaspar, she's just below us," Gonzalo fidgeted as he put a hand over his eyes to survey the area in the direction where Sara was supposed to be. "I think I can see her tent."

"Gonzalo, she's really gone. Her time came, just as she foretold to us that it would."

"No," Gonzalo expressed frantically as he pointed. "She's right over there." He began to run toward her bivouac.

"Wait," Friar Gaspar shouted and began to run after him. He caught up to Gonzalo standing at the spot where Sara had camped.

"She loves that pool and the waterfall," Gonzalo said gasping for air. "That's it. She must have moved her tent near the water. Come on, Gaspar, we need to find her." Gonzalo began to run once again down the trail toward the pool.

"Sara is gone," Gaspar spoke softly to himself. He sat at the spot of Sara's camp and waited. Gonzalo returned in about an hour, disheveled and disheartened.

"I need to find de Vargas," Gonzalo sighed heavily. "If Sara left at first light, she could not have gone far. We'll get her back."

"She left last night with the rising of the moon," Gaspar informed him. Gonzalo stared with disbelief. "You know of this?" he inquired.

"I was with her, Gonzalo. I was the last man to see her."

"Why?" Gonzalo expressed with hurt and incredulity. "How could you let her go? Why didn't you come and get me at once?"

"Gonzalo, Sara perceived that you would not let her go. She also wanted to spare you the pain of watching her depart."

"No," Gonzalo blurted out shaking his head. "I will not allow this." He ran away yelling for General de Vargas. Friar Gaspar followed close behind.

The general was inspecting the progress made on the second brigantine as the two men burst upon him. Gaspar told him the story of Sara's departure.

"Round up your best men," Gonzalo barked. "We are going after her."

The general felt pity for Gonzalo but realized that this was meant to be. "Let her go, Gonzalo," de Vargas counseled him. "Sara is a creature far removed from us. Just as a cool breeze caresses us for a time as a respite from this heat, it eventually departs. So it is with Sara. I will never forget her."

"No," shouted Gonzalo. "You and the friar were both witnesses to what the Emperor spoke. I am governor of this land. He gave me the authority to do with her as I wished. I order you to immediately gather your best men. We are going to bring her back."

General de Vargas resigned himself. Gonzalo had a point. Emperor Charles had provided Gonzalo with the charter to lead this expedition. He had the authority.

"As you wish, Gonzalo, I will call my youngest and fastest officers. We need to keep the team small so that we can travel quickly. I would say no more than half a dozen men."

"Very well," Gonzalo muttered approvingly. "With you and me in the party that will make eight of us. Call them now, General. We are leaving immediately."

Before an hour had passed, the men crossed the great pool and followed the false trail cleared by Cora and her soldiers. The ambush was staged in an area where the trail dead ended, surrounded by tree-lined hills. From a promontory, the women waited for their quarry.

"They are coming!" one of the women whispered excitedly to Cora and the others. "The great sun queen spoke with wisdom," Cora replied. "The children cry for their missing mother. Prepare to send them back."

Cora and the women in her party nocked their arrows.

The attack was swift and decisive. It was totally unexpected by the men. Cora and her party were in their element. They had all of the advantages and were proficient warriors.

General de Vargas, in the lead, was the first to fall. A sharp, stinging pain in the calf of his right leg dropped de Vargas straight to the ground. As the others stopped to react to what had happened to their general, they, too, felt the stings.

Gonzalo took an arrow to his left shin. It shattered the bone clean through. Determined, he continued to crawl on his knees up the side of the hill toward the attackers.

"Sara," he screamed. "Sara, help me. It's Gonzalo."

With little emotion, Cora nocked another arrow, aimed, and let it fly at Gonzalo. It penetrated the meat of the same wounded left leg and pinned Gonzalo to the ground. He shrieked in agony and lost consciousness.

General de Vargas was one of the least wounded. The arrow that penetrated his right calf missed the bone. With the assistance of one of the other men, they managed to pull the arrow free.

"I can travel," de Vargas told one of his still-conscious lieutenants. "If they wanted to kill us, we would be dead by now. Help each other as best as you can. I'm going to make my way back and send others to carry the rest of you."

"Did you see them, General?" the lieutenant inquired, misty eyed with pain. "Women, they were bare-chested women!"

"I saw them," de Vargas confirmed. "They are gone."

"Was the maiden with these women?" the lieutenant asked gasping for air.

General de Vargas shrugged his shoulders, "I don't know. I didn't see her."

A few days later, General de Vargas, Friar Gaspar, and General Orellana met to discuss the future of the quest. Gonzalo was unable to attend. His wound was not healing well, and he had a fever.

"Sara seemed certain that the location of El Dorado and his gold is up a mysterious tributary of a great river," Friar Gaspar related to them.

"Maybe so," Orellana contemplated. "There may also be other treasures waiting our discovery. If this great river is the same that Captain Pinzon goes on about, it bisects this continent. This theory alone is worthy of pursuit. If gold or cinnamon can be found along the way, it would be an added bonus."

"One thing is for sure," de Vargas hissed as he poked at the bandage on his leg. "Gonzalo Pizarro can no longer lead this quest. His wounds render him ineffective."

"What about you, Sanchez?" Orellana asked.

"I'm not good either," de Vargas admitted. "That leaves you, Francisco."

Orellana was afraid it would come to this. The timing couldn't be worse.

"As you know my wife is with child," Orellana reminded them. "I need to get her home."

"We are well enough to make the return trip," de Vargas pointed out. "I'll protect Juana and will personally escort her to Guayaquil. You are the senior officer now, Francisco. The Emperor expects us to see this through."

Friar Gaspar remained mostly silent during this conversation, but he realized that General de Vargas was right. "I will go with you, General Orellana," he volunteered. "Maybe we should abandon all but one of the brigantines and float down the river with a smaller party. The rest can escort Juana home along with General de Vargas and Gonzalo."

Orellana gave in to them and agreed that a smaller, more manageable party of about sixty men and one brigantine could cover a great deal of territory in a shorter period of time.

Two days later, General de Vargas and his men broke camp and started the return journey back to civilization. Gonzalo was still delirious and had to be placed on a litter. Juana feared for her husband, but she bravely parted with him. Orellana promised that he would be especially careful and looked forward to seeing their child.

"Sanchez, it may be a year before I see her again," he confided to his colleague. "Promise me that Juana will be well taken care of."

"Don't worry, old friend," de Vargas assured him. "I will watch out for your child as well."

Friar Gaspar said a prayer for the departing group. General Orellana and his men began to prepare the brigantine.

The Shuhar warrior women lived traditional lives with their husbands in the seven tribal villages. Here they remained in subjection to the patriarchy and under the rule of the tribal elders. They bore children and cared for their families in the same manner as the other non-warrior females.

As young Shuhar girls reached puberty, the tribes scrutinized them. Those that were able to pass a series of rigorous physical and mental tests were nominated by the elders to become Shuhar warrior women. This was considered a great honor to both the parents of these chosen ones and to the corresponding tribal village. Once appointed, these women remained soldiers until they reached an advanced age, usually at the end of their childbearing years. After retirement, the tribes cared for them for the rest of their lives as honored elders.

During the time of the month for four days leading up to the full moon, the warrior women left their husbands and families to gather for battle training and for meditation. A parcel of ground was set aside for this purpose and remained off limits to the rest of the tribes. It was located in a meadow near the summit of a hill overlooking the Napo River.

Sara waited in this sacred place for three weeks and for the time when all of the warrior women from the seven combined tribes would finally meet with her for the first time. In those three weeks, Sara completed her plan for the conquest of the Shuhar people and her eventual monarchy that would someday sweep the planet. She would set up a fortress queendom in the deepest, most remote location of the continent.

It was the fourth day before the full moon, and they began to come. Slowly and cautiously, the women trickled into the camp, nervously glancing around for any sign of the great daughter of the sun.

As part of her plan, Sara remained hidden from view further up the hill. She wanted them to speculate about her and waited until the appointed time for a grand entrance.

At dusk, all forty-one of the Shuhar warrior women assembled around the ritual bonfire. They began to argue among themselves.

"Do you entertain us like you would your own child?" mocked Fero, a youthful girl, as she directed her question toward Lani, her chieftain. "These stories of a goddess come to earth have kept me awake for weeks in anticipation. Is she here, or have you been lying?"

Just as in a male-dominated warrior clan, open acts of insubordination among the women were regarded as a direct challenge on the authority of the female chieftain. A disrespectful outburst such as this one from Fero could not be allowed without an appropriate response.

Lani glared at the outspoken youth and bared her teeth. She drew a hammer from a scabbard around her belt.

"A goddess comes and goes as she wills. She will come to us when ready. A chieftain rules as she wills until unseated by a challenger. Do you challenge my leadership, young sapling?"

"I see you in front of me," Fero stated. "As to this goddess, I hear only stories."

This time Cora spoke up.

"Calling Lani a liar is the same as calling half of your sisters here liars who also have cast their eyes on the holy daughter. Do you call us all liars?"

Fero felt shame as forty sets of eyes burned after her.

"I did not have the privilege of traveling with you to meet the holy daughter and her sons," she stated, trying to back herself out of her mistake. "Surely it is understandable to you that one would be skeptical."

Lani approached Fero and savagely punched her in the cheek beneath her left eye. Fero yelped and fell to the ground sobbing.

Lani stood over Fero and scolded her. "A warrior woman has better control over her tongue, young one. We are not like our gabbing male counterparts."

As Lani walked away, Cora and several other women helped Fero up and tended to her wounded face.

Lani glanced up at the almost round moon as it hung in the eastern sky and began to think a silent prayer. *Do not forsake me, great daughter of the sun. My rulership hangs on the words I spoke to them.*

One of the women shrieked and Lani jerked her head around. She saw the woman pointing in the direction of the hill. Lani looked in that direction.

All of them watched as a figure approached the bonfire. The figure moved slowly and purposefully until it reached the rock platform beside the fire.

They witnessed a woman dressed in a strange garment tied around her body. A hood attached to the garment covered her head. The warrior women moved away as this strange one climbed onto the rock platform. All eyes followed her hands as the woman reached up and pulled the hood down from around her face.

They gasped as Sara shook her head and tousled her long dark hair about her shoulders. She smiled at them. Mesmerized, they observed as Sara loosened her cape and let it slip down around her ankles. She stood there in front of them completely nude. To these dark women, Sara's skin seemed white as the snow on the tops of the great mountains. The proximity of the fire caused her body to shimmer in the reflected light.

Sara took her dagger, raised it above her head in both hands and let loose with a mighty scream. The women fell to the ground cowering in fear.

Lani crawled over and kissed Sara's feet. Sara motioned her to rise. As she stood, Lani turned and addressed the gathering. "Behold, Sara, daughter of the sun." She started to chant, "Sara, Sara, Sara."

Soon the rest of them joined in. Their drone drowned out the rest of the creatures of the jungle night.

"Sara, Sara, Sara."

Great introduction! Sara thought to herself and smiled.

The Shuhar warrior women eagerly listened as Sara guided them. She had not yet completely mastered the spoken language, but where the words were unclear, she was able to communicate through Lani who understood her better.

"Your husbands and the other men of your tribe dominate you, Why? It is not because they are smarter. It is not because they are more skillful in battle. They are not better hunters or fishers."

"They are stronger," spoke Cora. "There are a far greater number of men warriors."

"Are they stronger?" Sara posed to them. "Look at you, the mightiest of the women in your tribe. Are all of the men who are warriors as strong as the least among you?"

The women began to murmur among themselves.

Fero stood holding healing herbs to her bruised face and made a motion to be recognized. Sara pointed and asked for the young lady to approach. Lani allowed her to pass but eyed her suspiciously.

"Great daughter of the sun," she said. "I am one of the least among this assembly, yet I know that many of the men could not defeat me in battle."

Sara gave her a hug and commendation. "Well spoken, my child." Then she commented to the rest of them.

"All men are expected to be soldiers, yet only a select few of you are granted the right to fight along side of them. They do not allow women to fight, because they are in fear of you. Keeping your numbers small allows them to remain strong."

"It has always been this way," Cora reminded them.

"No longer will it be this way," Sara challenged. "My father is angry. The Shuhar should be a great nation by now. Instead of seven tribal villages, there should be seven hundred great cities dominating this great land. Your men have been lazy and disobedient to the will of their god, the Sun. He has sent me to remove them from the seat of power, and turn it over to you. This is the dawning of the age of women."

"What does your father command in how we should go about doing this?" asked Lani.

"They must be made to fear you," Sara instructed. "A great and decisive victory will stun them into submission. On the night of the full moon, we will divide and enter the seven tribal villages. While they sleep, we will kill the seven tribal chief elders. I will appoint seven from among you to replace them. As is your custom, we will sever their heads and shrink them. You will wear these on your belts as a symbol of your power."

Lani shuddered at Sara's feet and begged. "My father is Goma. He is the tribal elder of Napo. Can he at least be spared?"

"No," Sara stated coldly. "They must all die. As a test of your loyalty to my father, the Sun, you will be the one to kill him, Lani."

A lump welled up in Lani's throat and she began to plead. "Please release me from this burden, Queen Sara. I cannot strike down my own father."

"You refuse my command?" Sara challenged her.

"Please," Lani groveled.

"Stand," Sara beckoned her.

Lani stood and faced Sara with her head bowed.

"You ask me to release you from the burden of killing your father?"

Lani nodded her head.

"Look at me," Sara ordered.

Lani looked her in the eye. Sara smiled.

"I release you from the burden of this thing," Sara told Lani and gave her a hug. In a loud voice she looked out over all of them and boomed, "I also release you as chieftain of these, your sisters."

Sara continued, "Who among you will now accept the challenge of leadership?"

Immediately, Fero shouted out, "I will lead. I will kill Goma, father of Lani."

The warrior women were stunned by her boldness, but Sara was pleased.

"So you have spoken, so it will be," confirmed Sara.

Fero stood beside Sara and looked out over them defiantly. All of the women bowed down low.

"I cannot allow you to kill my father," Lani snapped at Sara and Fero.

"Do you challenge your new chieftain?" Sara questioned.

"You wouldn't dare," Lani glared at Fero.

Fero glanced at Sara seeking approval. Sara nodded, acknowledging what she read in Fero's face and handed her dagger over to her.

"I no longer serve you," Fero sputtered. "Your insubordination is a direct affront to our queen."

With a quick motion, Fero thrust Sara's dagger into Lani's bosom and sliced her open in an upward direction until her chest bone stopped the blade. Blood flowed out staining both Fero's and Sara's legs. The gathered warrior women sank to their knees in abject fear.

Sara kneeled and curiously stared into Lani's face as the life force ebbed from her body. She listened as Lani's breathing grew labored. Lani's eyes went dull.

"Do you think I have a soul now, Gaspar?" Sara shouted at the top of her lungs.

The warrior women continued to cower unable to understand this strange rant.

Sara motioned them to rise.

"To those of you who obey me and my father, great gifts will be given," Sara preached. Looking down at Lani's lifeless form, she pointed. "To those of you who disobey." She did not have to finish her thought.

"This one was unwilling to kill her earthly father, while failing to consider the wishes of her heavenly father, the Sun. Women, listen to me. This is your moment. It is no time to be soft."

Sara continued her speech. "You will dominate men as they have dominated you," she bellowed. "You will keep them herded into villages. You will maintain control by spreading your legs for them only after they have served your wishes. We will turn back boy children into their care when they reach their twelfth year. Girl children will always remain with us."

298

They listened with rapt attention to her instructions.

"We will become a mighty nation and spread throughout the land. The bravest and best among you will become my special servants. I will call you 'Shadow Women,' because our enemies will always fear that you will spring on them from the shadows."

The next day, Cora found Sara and grabbed her by the arm.

"Mistress Sara," she breathed excitedly, "come and see, please."

Cora led Sara to the edge of the hill overlooking the Napo as it snaked its way toward the horizon. Cora pointed down to an object immediately below them. It was a square-masted brigantine floating gently downstream with the current. It was far away, but Sara could make out the familiar shape of Friar Gaspar as he knelt in morning prayer and of General Francisco de Orellana as he strutted about on the aft deck.

"Your sons," Cora said with a smile. "The obedient ones that go to avenge the Sun."

Sara patted Cora on the head.

"The obedient ones go," Cora repeated.

"There go the dreams of humankind," Sara told Cora. They watched as the men floated away past them.

Sara dropped her harsh facade and reverted to an innocence from deep within her. Cora was startled to hear the voice of a young girl emerge from Sara's mouth.

"Sail away," she chimed. "Sail away safely home."

CHAPTER 29

"Who is this Eduardo Gomes anyway?" Anne asked of no one in particular. She was looking at the large sign hanging over the exit to the baggage claim area.

"Heck if I know," Sharon answered her. "Apparently he's important enough that they would name the airport after him."

Juan yawned and growled, "I'm too tired to care. That was the longest flight I've ever had to struggle through."

"Grouch!" Anne exclaimed as she playfully punched him in the arm. "It's only been twenty hours since we left Frankfurt." She set her wristwatch to 1:50 p.m. local time.

All of them felt the stark contrast as they emerged from the air-conditioned building and into the clutches of the tropical heat and humidity. After only a few paces carrying both Sharon's and his own luggage, Derek felt the shirt begin to cling to his back.

"This is going to take some getting use to," he told them, trying to hold a positive attitude.

"I thought Baltimore was hot and humid in the summertime," Juan complained, "but this is ridiculous."

"It's not that bad," Anne maintained while her black leather valet with its stiff left wheel whined, "eek, eek, eek."

Sharon was the most cheerful of the bunch, as she slept well during the long trip. "I studied the Varig route map," she bubbled. "The equator goes almost directly through Manaus. It's probably torrid here all year round."

"Great," Juan groaned as he allowed the shoulder strap of his bag to slip free. He set the load on the curb.

All of them looked at Derek with stupid expressions as they waited for him to tell them what the next move would be.

"We get a cab and find a place to stay," he answered after reading the anticipation in their faces.

Exactly at that moment, a rusted out taxi screeched to a halt where they stood. The driver threw the passenger door open and motioned them to get in. Juan asked the driver if he could recommend a decent place for them to stay.

"American tourists?" the driver queried. "Let me take you to a very fancy treetop hotel sixty kilometers north of here. It is very exotic, and you will love it."

Juan frowned and objected, "We need to stay in the city. Take us to a reasonable place and there will be a nice tip in it for you."

"American dollars?" the driver asked in wide-eyed excitement.

Juan nodded in confirmation.

The driver dropped them off at a small inn called, Brasil Velho Casa Do Convidado.

"The Old Brazil Guest House," Juan translated for them. "Three rooms please," he informed the proprietor.

Anne jumped in front of Juan and held up two fingers. "Dos," she corrected him.

Juan looked at her with questioning eyes.

"Come on, Juan," she said with a blushing smile. "I feel a bit insecure in this strange place and don't really want to be alone."

Juan blushed when they got to the room and noticed that it had only one double bed. Anne started unpacking and acted as if it was no big deal.

In the adjacent room, Derek threw open the shutters covering the unscreened window and turned on the ceiling fan.

"I'm surprised that it isn't hotter given this place isn't air conditioned," Sharon observed. She glanced out of the window on her way to the closet. "What river is that over there, Derek? Are we getting this nice breeze from there?"

Derek plopped onto the bed and closed his eyes. "It's the Rio Negro, and I'm tired. Juan and I have a meeting later with Professor Stamos." He patted the bed signaling Sharon to join him.

"Down boy," she snickered. "I have a few more things to unpack first." Sharon was rooting through the bottom of the bag and grabbed up all of her undergarments in one arm. As she bent over to plop them into the drawer, the dagger slipped out between two of her panties and thumped as it struck the floor.

"This thing is such a bother," Sharon groused. "I should have left it at home."

Derek caught a quick glimpse of the object as Sharon threw it unceremoniously into the underwear drawer. "Let me see that?" he asked her while pulling himself into a sitting position.

"It's the dagger that psycho, Blaze, used when he came after me in Baltimore," Sharon explained. "It fell to the floor when Juan tackled him. I grabbed it just before Katy and I ran away. I thought that maybe I would need it if Juan was overpowered."

Sharon handed the blade to Derek, and he recognized it as the same one — the beloved Nino — confiscated from Blaze by airport security. Holding the dagger, Derek felt a strange force enter into him.

"I must not be caught with this thing," he chanted while letting it slip through his hand onto the bed.

"You don't have to worry about that," Sharon reassured Derek. "I kept it hidden away inside my luggage and not in my carry-on bag."

Derek snapped out of his trance but grew fearful about physically handling it, shuddering as he suspected this inanimate object to be somehow sentient.

"You hang onto it, Sharon," he told her. "It might be a good idea if you kept it on your person. In fact, I would feel more at ease about your safety if you did so," Derek admitted.

Anne wore a frown as she thought about what Derek was asking. "You want Sharon and me to buy a car? We don't know a lick of Portuguese. How do you expect us to do this?"

"American dollars, it's the universal language," Derek laughed as he held out a wad of bills. "Believe me, they will understand."

"The language closely parallels Spanish," Juan counseled. "Use your phrase book."

"This chic is a gringa. I'm no good with Spanish either," Anne mentioned backing away.

Sharon grabbed the wad from Derek. "I thought you were the adventurous one," she challenged Anne. "There are a few vehicles with signs on them just down the street. Let's try it."

"Well, when are you guys going to be back?" she asked Juan, still unsure of herself.

"We can meet for a late supper," Derek chimed in. "Sharon and I didn't get a chance to eat yet. I'd say that I would call you, but I don't know how."

Juan laughed. "We'll get here when we get here. Hopefully our business with Stamos will not take long."

As the ladies walked off, Juan asked for an explanation. "Are you really sure we need a car, Derek?"

"Probably," he replied. "It just doesn't feel right, Juan. I don't believe what we are looking for is anywhere around here. It may end up being a long visit unless Stamos can keep us on course."

Juan heard him and added, "Are you sure that you're not just thinking about what Elyria told you? She could be leading you astray by mentioning that Manaus is a dead end."

"I don't know for sure, Juan. Werner seemed confident that Stamos could know something."

They recognized the same rusty cab as it pulled up to the curb. The driver honked.

"Americanos!" he waved at them wildly. "Where to?"

Juan looked at Derek and laughed. "I believe this poor guy hasn't moved since he dropped us off. We may have a personal chauffeur."

"Just how much of a tip did you give him the last time, Juan?" Derek begged to know.

"The universal language, just like you told Annie," Juan responded as he crouched to slide in. "Teatro Amazonas, obrigado," he told the man.

"Sí," the driver said with excitement and bolted away. A few minutes later, he stopped in front of a massive pink structure resembling a rococo cathedral.

"What is this place?" Derek asked with astonishment.

Juan enjoyed watching the driver's eyes grow huge as he pealed off four American five-dollar bills as a gratuity. He answered Derek's question. "It's the Manaus opera house. For some reason, Professor Stamos picked this place to meet with us."

As they passed through the entrance, a smartly-dressed guide met Derek and Juan. It was a young lady, probably in her early twenties.

"Você Fala O Inglês?" Juan inquired.

"Most certainly I speak English," the young lady replied while bowing to them. "How may I be of service?"

Juan continued with the lead, "We are supposed to meet a man here named Professor Stamos in the Nobel Room."

"Ah," she nodded with approval. "Good choice, that room is very posh. You will like it. Follow me."

As they walked along behind her, the young guide seemed enthusiastic about her job. "Have you men been here before?" she asked them.

Juan shook his head.

"Let me tell you a little about our history," she dutifully drifted off into her spiel. "The opera house was built in 1896 during the rubber boom…"

Derek allowed his mind to wander while they walked and she spoke. *Sharon would really dig seeing this place*, he pondered, recalling her background in architectural design. *Am I doing the right thing?* he began to doubt himself. *I could be chasing shadows with Stamos, while Elyria was my best lead. Should I have spent some more time trying to get answers from her?*

They entered a large room and stopped. Derek snapped back to attention as he heard the guide conclude her discourse. "Italian artist, Domenico de Angelis, painted the ornate ceiling. Do you have any questions?"

The two men looked at each other and shook their heads. Juan handed her an American $5.00 bill and politely thanked the young lady for her services. She walked away with a smile.

"Are you always such a big tipper?" Derek joked.

Juan was about to respond when they heard a faint voice drift across the large open room, "Americans?" They watched as a bent, old, white-haired man began to saunter in their direction. He wore a white shirt, dark trousers, and white dress shoes. The man's right hand held a cane. Using it as a third leg while moving toward them, the chamber echoed rhythmically to the footfalls. First, it was a sharp tap as the cane touched down, then a shuffle as his right foot dragged behind, and then a muffled thump as the left leg planted itself in front of the right. The process repeated itself. Tap, shhh, thump, tap, shhh, thump.

"That can't be Stamos, can it?" Derek asked in a whisper. "I wasn't expecting someone that hoary."

Tap, shhh, thump. The old man stopped and raised his cane into the air pointing at the four corners of the ceiling. "It's an opera house you know," he screeched, "with perfect acoustics. Yes, young man, I am Doctor Stamos."

Derek was embarrassed and quickly apologized. "I meant no disrespect, sir. That was just idle thinking."

Tap, shhh, thump. "You meant it," Stamos corrected Derek as he got closer to them.

"I didn't know you spoke English," Juan stated somewhat perturbed. "We conversed in Spanish to set up this meeting."

"I have a lot of secrets you don't know about, amigo." Tap, shhh, thump. "Besides, you were the one that started the conversation in Spanish."

"Well, I assumed," Juan began.

"Assume isn't a word in my vocabulary," Stamos interrupted him. "A scientist deals in facts, not assumptions." He was now standing beside Derek and Juan and shook hands with them.

"Then you are the man we need to see," Derek quickly jumped in on the tail end of Juan's sentence. "We are looking for hard facts buried deep within legendary tales."

A twinkle appeared in the man's dark eyes. "Amazons," he breathed. "They exist, you know."

"Where?" Derek shot back interested in getting right to the point.

The professor narrowed his eyes and stared at Derek with suspicion. "I'm not so sure I like you," he voiced. "Americans are always so hasty."

Juan jumped to Derek's defense. "Please excuse the two of us. We arrived here only today and are weary from the long journey. It affects our better judgment."

Professor Stamos looked around at the walls acting oblivious. "America has so many beautiful buildings. This magnificent structure from an era long ago is the only jewel in the crown of Manaus," he related to them with an air of sadness. After a few moments, he looked at Derek, and the twinkle returned to his eyes. "You haven't come here to interview me about architecture, have you? You are here about anthropology."

Derek learned from his previous conversational blunder and quickly fell in line with what he thought was expected of him. "If you would be so kind as to share some of your knowledge with us, we would be most appreciative."

Stamos glared at Derek. "Don't patronize me," he warned.

Derek shook his head. "I can't win with you, can I?"

After an awkward pause, Derek and Juan saw the professor smile for the first time. "I tell my first-year students that anthropology means understanding the culture of the people that you are dealing with. Apparently you haven't done your homework very well, Mr. Dunbar."

Tap, shhh, thump. "Come, come," Professor Stamos motioned as he began to walk away.

"Where are we going, sir?" Juan inquired.

"To my office," he answered. "I have some things to show you."

Derek was afraid to ask how far away the office was or how they were going to get there. *The way this old man walks, it could take us all night,* he thought to himself.

"My favorite graduate assistant brought me here," Stamos told them in anticipation of what they were thinking. "She will drive us to the university."

A dark-skinned young woman waited for the professor in the parking lot. She was short, typical of the indigenous people in the area, but pretty with a powerful, muscular build.

"Hello, my name is Derek," he said extending a hand.

The girl smiled, took his hand, but didn't say anything.

Juan discerned the reason for the silence. "My friend thinks that since the professor is fluent in English that you are too," he explained in broken Portuguese. "Juan Sanchez is my name, and this is Derek Dunbar."

"Juan and Derek," the girl said with a continuous smile.

"Ah, yes," Professor Stamos chimed waking up from a daydream, "and this is Gem, one of my graduate students."

"He told us that you were his favorite," Juan told her.

"I hope so," she opened up and put an arm around the old man. "Nobody else totes him around town whenever he needs to go somewhere. He's a good friend as well as my professor."

"They're very fond of each other," Juan explained to Derek.

Derek nodded. He wondered why this woman seemed oddly familiar to him.

She drove them across town. The university was Spartan by American standards. The main office building and classroom facilities resembled cheap apartment complexes familiar to urban America.

"Please join us, Gem," the professor offered to her as they exited the station wagon. "These gentlemen are here to learn about Amazons. They represent, uh…" He turned to Juan and asked, "What publication did you say that you represent?"

Juan lied, feeling bad about doing so. "TransGlobal magazine. Our editor wants us to do a travel feature about this region. The legends of the Amazons are about as exciting as they come. We should be able to attract a lot of visitors doing this story."

"I don't recall TransGlobal being a carrier at Manaus airport," the thought suddenly dawned on the professor.

Derek jumped in without skipping a beat. "TransGlobal has a new partnership with Varig. The transfer point is Rio."

"Uh, huh," the professor mumbled.

His office smelled musty because of the many old books and manuscripts scattered about. A human skull served as a desk paperweight holding down the myriad of loose papers. Reaching up with his cane, the professor grabbed hold of a loop attached to a wall map. As it unfurled, Derek and Juan recognized the print as a relief map of Brazil.

Gem picked up a well-worn map pointer. The rubber tip at the end was gone exposing the wooden stub. She tapped the map at a region west of Manaus. "Tefé," she articulated to Juan. "Doctor Stamos's research is conclusive that Tefé is the gateway to the old Amazon queendom."

Turning to the old man, she sought confirmation. "Isn't that right, Professor?"

He woke again from a daydream. "Yes, dear, of course, Tefé," he repeated. Juan translated for Derek.

This isn't right, Derek thought and began to grow suspicious. "Can you share the results of some of your research with us?"

Gem spoke for the professor, but Derek didn't understand.

"Excuse me," he interrupted. "I'd like the professor to explain it to me. No comprende," he shrugged and held out his hands at his side with the palms turned up.

Gem stopped and smiled, but just before she did so, Derek thought he detected a brief look of contempt cross her face.

"Although I have some hard physical evidence, the majority of it is anecdotal," Stamos began. "Descendants of the ancient Shuhar tribe speak of a beautiful young woman that dropped from the sky, a daughter of the sun."

He started to root around in a desk drawer. "I have a sketch of her somewhere that I traced from an old rock drawing."

Juan watched the professor with eager anticipation. Derek kept studying Gem until it dawned on him.

"You know, Juan, she looks a lot like Elyria."

"Here it is!" Stamos cried and pulled an old leaf of paper from the stack in his drawer.

Gem didn't understand Derek's English, but he noticed her twitch on the mention of Elyria's name.

Juan heard Derek's comment and briefly considered it, but he became enthralled with the professor's drawing. It was a crude pencil sketch of a naked woman standing on the shore of a small lake or pond. Sunrays emanated from her body as she held out her hands. Dark-skinned native women bowed down to her on the opposite shore.

"Do you know where this lake is?" Juan asked with interest.

"I've been there," Stamos answered with excitement. "It was years ago when I could get around better," he said tapping his bum leg. "The lake is near the source of the Napo River in Ecuador, but the ancient Shuhar migrated east, further inland and established their civilization near Tefé."

The professor pointed out the various locations on the map to Juan. Derek hung back holding his forehead in his hand.

No, this is wrong, his head kept nagging him. There was more. "Professor Stamos?" he broke into the conversation. They stopped talking and all three of them issued a gaze at him.

"Professor Stamos?" he repeated. "Could this civilization over the course of centuries follow the Amazon and reestablish itself further east of here?"

The room fell silent.

Gem didn't comprehend Derek's question, but she grew uncomfortable after observing the professor's demeanor. Pain shown across his face.

"Tefé," she said softly.

"Of course it's possible," Stamos admitted, struggling as if trying to conjure up a long lost memory, "but there exists no evidence."

"Professor?" Derek went on. "Aren't there even stories or legends?"

Gem dropped the map pointer. "Tefé," she repeated in a more vehement tone.

Derek walked over and closed the gap between himself and the professor. "There's something east of here, Professor."

Stamos folded into the seat at his desk. His face once again grew pained. "Something east of here?" he murmured.

"Tefé," insisted Gem.

"East," repeated Derek.

"There is something in the east," Stamos said holding his head as if in pain. "Think, man, think," he pounded on his temples.

"Tefé," Gem shouted. It was nearly a scream.

Derek reached down and grabbed the professor's wrist.

"Tell me about Amazons east of here," he insisted.

In a flash, Gem shot between them grabbing Derek's arm, wrenching his hand away from the professor. Derek was stunned at her strength. The force of Gem's movements almost knocked him down.

"Whoa, hey," Juan shouted.

"This man is hurting the professor," Gem expressed to Juan. "I think you both should leave now."

Stamos stood and pounded his cane on the floor to get their attention. "All of you, stop it," he shrieked.

The room fell silent.

"I'm fine, Gem. It's fine," he told them. "My memory is not what it once was, Mr. Dunbar. I will try to recall what evidence exists about Amazons in the east. Suddenly I have a headache. Come back tomorrow morning around ten."

"But," Derek began.

"Derek," Juan broke in. "Let it go for now," he whispered.

The two of them reluctantly headed for the door.

"Would you like Gem to drive you home?"

"Uh, no," Derek told him. "We'll get a cab."

"Wow, that was weird," Juan admitted shaking his head.

"Elyria has native blood. Do you think that Gem could be related to her?" Derek speculated.

"Now, Derek," Juan laughed. "You gringos deride us wetbacks for all looking alike. Don't you think this is the same thing?"

"Maybe," Derek considered it, "maybe not."

Professor Stamos lifted a flask of rum from the bottom left drawer of the desk and poured himself a glass.

"Care to join me, dear," he held the flask aloft in offering to Gem.

"No, thanks. I'll clean up this mess," she told him. "Imagine that rabble trying to change your mind about the Amazon culture in Tefé."

"They didn't mean it that way, Gem. This Derek merely believes that over the centuries they could have possibly migrated further east. Actually it's an interesting theory."

"You don't really believe it, do you?" she probed.

"Probably not," he said and downed the drink.

As Gem flitted about the office, Stamos tried desperately to clean the cobwebs from his mind. *Why can't I remember?* he thought. *There's something about this.*

The professor stood and hobbled over to the map. Placing a finger on Tefé, he traced the route on the map eastward along the Amazon River until it paused at Manaus.

Gem watched the old man out of the corner of her eye.

His finger began to quiver. It resisted his next impulse. Although his head throbbed with pain, Stamos concentrated and forced his digit to trace eastward again following the route of the mighty Amazon. It stopped at the Xingu River's confluence and veered south along that tributary, finally coming to rest over a small dot on the map.

"Altamira," he breathed.

Gem stopped what she was doing and turned her total attention toward the professor.

Stamos wandered trance like to the bookshelf and removed a yearbook. Fumbling through the pages, he picked out a tattered newspaper article that marked a specific spot. Opening the folded yellow page, the professor glanced at the headline.

"Two students vanished in the jungle now presumed dead."

Setting it aside, his eyes wandered to the picture in the yearbook.

"Doctor Stamos's graduate students," the caption read. There were only nine students in the picture, all of them grinning for the camera. Gem's image graced the center of the print as the professor's only female graduate student. The eight men surrounding her included two faces that he hadn't seen in six months.

"Pedro and Luis," he whispered. "What were you doing there?"

"Professor Stamos?" Gem asked him in a sweet voice. "Those two went camping, remember? They disappeared. I miss them, too," she consoled the old man giving him a hug. "Sometimes bad things happen," she suggested.

"I know that," his voice cracked. "I'll be okay."

Professor Stamos carefully placed the open yearbook on his desk and poured another drink. His head continued to ache.

"There's something strange about this, Gem," he insisted.

"I think you're just tired," she told him. "Why don't you retire for the evening?"

"I will soon enough," he remarked, waving at her.

Stamos looked up at the ceiling. In his old eyes, the lights appeared to be blurry. Closing them, the professor tried to imagine a time when his vision was clearer.

Gem watched.

The old man slumped into his chair and opened a file cabinet drawer. At the very front, he found a red binder and flipped it out onto the desktop. Stamos stared at it for a long time, but he didn't open it.

To Gem, it appeared as if the professor was mentally boring holes through the binder.

"What is it, Professor?" she asked him.

Stamos ignored her, and rested his head inside of his cupped hands. Reaching deep, the professor fought through the pain. It had been so long ago, and the spell was wearing thin.

"I can almost see it, Gem," his meek voice struggled.

"You don't want to do this," Gem warned him sternly.

In his mind's eye, a fire was burning his brain. The flames hurt only when he tried to think about her. "Who is she?" the professor groaned. It was an old fire and almost spent. *I can punch through this,* he insisted to himself. Groping from within, Stamos doggedly fought on. The flames faded to mere embers while a face began to form in his mind. He almost had it!

Screaming, Professor Stamos slumped back in his chair. He wasn't strong enough to break through the flames to remember the face, but a name popped into his head, a single word.

"Sara," he whispered.

Gem bent over and smiled at him.

"The Mistress perceived that your blindness would soon fade. That's why she sent me."

Gem picked up the map pointer from the top of the professor's desk and began to tap it against the inside of her palm.

"Too bad," she told him while walking around to the back of his chair. "I really would have liked to finish my studies, but now you are a threat to us."

Grasping the pointer in both hands, Gem slipped it under Professor Stamos's chin and violently jerked it upwards. Her strength pulled the old man out of his chair. He started kicking, but since the chair was wedged between them, his kicks didn't find their mark.

In desperation, the professor reached out and was able to grab his cane. With his back pinned against Gem's chest, Stamos wasn't at the proper angle to swing it around to defend himself. With each down stroke, the silver tip clicked harmlessly against the desktop.

As Gem choked the breath of life out of him, Professor Stamos remembered.

Click, click, click, click, click, click.

"Was it good for you, Professor?" Sara laughed in his face. "Mmmm, so refreshing."

Click, click, click, click, click.

"You're a lucky duck, so I will not use you up!"

Click, click, click, click.

"You followed my trail all the way up the Iriri, but it was a dead end, wasn't it?"

Click, click, click.

"You'll tell everyone that the trail ended in Tefé, won't you?"

Click, click.

"You were never here, were you?"
Click.

CHAPTER 30

"Ole!" Sharon shouted as the van screeched to a stop in front of the Brasil Velho Casa Do Convidado. The passenger side window was down, and Sharon was hanging out of it banging a shoe against the side of the door.

Anne blasted three long beeps of the horn.

"Ole, ole," Sharon yelled while banging her shoe. "Señor Dunbar, Señor Sanchez, come and see what your amigas have done."

Derek and Juan were sitting on the porch enjoying the view over the Rio Negro when the ladies burst onto the scene.

Anne struggled to get out. The door was sticking and made a sickening creaking noise as she forced it open. She overcompensated and fell out onto the ground as the door came unstuck and flew open.

Sharon crawled over the seats on the inside and lay on her stomach while peering down at Anne.

"Whoa, Annie," Sharon sang with enthusiasm. "Are you okay?"

Anne pulled herself up into a sitting position and started laughing. Sharon joined in. Neither one could stop laughing.

Juan was flabbergasted as he observed this show. Derek looked at Juan. Juan looked at Derek. "They've been drinking," both of them said to each other simultaneously.

"Should we rescue them or act like we don't know them?" Derek joked with Juan.

Juan glanced around and noticed the expression on the desk clerk's face. The man was not amused.

"I think we should rescue them this time, Derek, or they may end up getting the two of us into trouble."

Juan helped Anne to her feet and took the keys from her hand. She leaned into him for support as he led her to the porch. Derek pulled Sharon out from the driver's side and closed the door.

"Ole," she greeted Derek and gave him a peck on the cheek.

"I believe it's 'Ola,'" Derek corrected her.

He led Sharon to the porch while she gabbed on, "Ole, Ola, whatever, we did good, didn't we?"

The four of them inspected their latest acquisition. It was an old panel van, the kind with no windows along the side. A double door opened at the back. It was a faded green, but looked to be in decent enough shape.

"I like it," Derek admitted. "It's just big enough so that in a pinch we could sleep in there. Good thinking."

Sharon smiled with pride.

"Whose idea was it to celebrate?" Juan asked Anne.

"Why the nice salesman," she giggled answering him. "He insisted that we drink a bottle of rum with him."

"A tradition!" Sharon added, not wanting to leave out that important fact.

"A whole bottle?" Juan screeched.

Anne put her finger and thumb together and held it up in the air. "Just a little one," she demonstrated.

"How did you boys make out with that professor guy?" Sharon queried.

"Not too bad I guess, but he's a strange bird," Derek informed her.

"Did you get the information out of him about the super bitch?" Sharon followed up.

Derek laughed and ruffed up her hair. "Not just yet, Sharon. Juan and I have another meeting with him at ten tomorrow morning."

The couples parted, and Derek turned the ceiling fan on high after entering the bedroom. Sharon plopped down onto the bed, not bothering taking off her clothes. Derek stripped to his underwear and took his place beside her on top of the sheets.

Sharon rolled on her back and faced straight up at the ceiling. The air from the fan blew onto her face. "That feels great," she sighed. "We've had a fun first day."

"I'm glad you're enjoying yourself."

Sharon placed an arm over her eyes. "Derek?" she asked him. "What happens next? I mean what are we going to do after you are done with the professor?"

"I'm not sure, Sharon. Somehow, I believe that we're going to be driving east. It's a strong feeling that I have. I hope that Stamos will be able to shed some more light on the situation. We'll be going home as soon as possible, I promise."

Derek leaned over to give Sharon a good night kiss and noticed that she already passed out.

*****

Juan lingered in the bathroom unsure of what to do. Anne waited for him until she finally had enough.

"Come on, Juan, I'm not going to bite. I'm sleepy and need someone to snuggle up to."

He looked in the bathroom mirror and sighed.

"I heard that," she scolded. "Come on, or I'm gonna start thinking that you don't like me."

No chance of that, he mused to himself. *No sireee.*

Juan gave up and took his place by her side beneath the thin sheet. He didn't even have a chance to pull the sheet over his legs before Anne pushed her firm breasts tightly into his bare chest. They lay on their sides facing each other. Anne had her eyes closed.

Juan felt guilty. "You know, Annie, I feel bad about this. You've been drinking, and I don't want to take advantage."

"Don't worry about that. I'm no good tonight, Juan. I'm too tired. Maybe in the morning..." she trailed off falling asleep.

Juan was relieved. *I didn't want our first time to be like this,* he thought. He considered to himself, "I'm so lucky, Annie. You have been my fantasy girl from the moment I first saw you." He stroked her hair with his free hand. "You're so beautiful."

Anne's rhythmic breathing and warm body created gentle undulations that flowed through him. Juan soon began to grow hard. Anne felt it against her belly and reacted by reaching down. She cradled him inside of her free hand and pumped a gentle squeeze before falling back to sleep.

The warm pleasurable wave soothed Juan. It was a contentment that he hadn't felt for a long time.

Forgive me, Bianca, it's been two long years, Juan reflected remembering his dead wife. *Let her go,* he thought and drifted off to sleep.

Derek was the only one of the four friends that had trouble sleeping. Lying on his side with an arm around Sharon, his mind raced. *Could I be wrong?* he wondered and glanced at the L.E.D. readout of the digital display on the dresser. It was midnight. *Stamos seems so sure of himself, but it doesn't feel right. Sara may have dwelled near Tefé at one time, but that's too far west. Back in Germany when I felt her call me, it seemed to be from a different place.*

Thinking about Elyria's warning to him added doubt. *She told me that*

315

Manaus is a dead end. That would confirm my suspicions, but is she misleading me?

There was one sure way to find out. Derek resisted the notion. *I'm a lot closer than before. Could I handle it when she touches me back?* Derek had respect for Sara. *Maybe Werner is right, and I am as strong as she is,* he thought, *but if she is as old and experienced as they suspect, she must sustain a great deal of control over her power.*

Derek remained fitful in his attempt to sleep.

Sharon rolled around mumbling something that Derek couldn't make out and began to lightly snore.

He glanced at the clock. It read 1:25.

How could she have managed to stay alive for so long? he questioned to himself. *Is it possible to perpetually isolate oneself away from danger?*

Derek drifted in and out of sleep. His mind remained in a fog.

While dreaming, Sharon threw a leg over Derek's thigh. It felt wet and clammy from her perspiration. He looked up; the clock displayed 2:38.

Is this real? Derek began to now have serious reservations. *It would be so much easier if I was just another normal human being. Sharon and I would have kids by now, and for sure we would be married.* Derek recalled the many times that Sharon tried to hide her pain from him about not being able to conceive. *She deserves better*, he meditated and drifted back into the fog.

This time it was the high-pitched whine of a mosquito that brought Derek back to consciousness. Instinctively he searched for the clock. The numbers displayed 3:03.

Enough of this, he stewed and became agitated. Derek slid away from Sharon and felt in the darkness for the bathroom. He wanted to find a place away from Sharon where he could more fully concentrate. Finding himself sitting on the toilet, Derek leaned forward and rested his forehead in his left hand.

Getting control of himself, Derek worked up his nerve. *I've never run away from anything in my life. If I have to face this evil alone, so be it. Bring it on.*

Derek reached within and launched a mental wave. *I have to know for sure,* he demanded of himself.

Despite Sara's status as a goddess to her people, she was satisfied with a primitive lifestyle. Casa Cobo was the name of her domain and her fortress. Only two rooms made Sara's quarters. There was a waiting area where guests could sit or lounge on straw-stuffed pillows, and there was an inner chamber, her private bedroom. Sara's most loyal and trusted friends among the Shadow Women took turns staying with her at night. They served in the dual capacity of handmaiden and bodyguard, not that she ever needed protecting in this circle of safety.

The adobe fortress of Casa Cobo was a large, three-story building nestled beneath the canopy of the rainforest. Dense forest and mountains surrounded the entire area. From above, it could not be seen. No wanderers were able to penetrate the perimeter of the camp. There were 24-hour patrols and guards strategically stationed around the area. These women took their jobs very seriously and with pride. Sara's queendom was one of total isolation and security from intruders.

Gloria tended to her Mistress that night and was sleeping in the berth a few meters away. Sara slept peacefully, resting her lovely face on folded hands. Her awareness of Derek took the form of a cool breeze as it refreshed her spirit. Sara's eyelids opened, and she gently propped herself up. In deep gratitude, she blinked back a psychic kiss.

With a warrior-like reflex, Gloria sensed that something was unusual and sprang to her feet, ready to do battle.

"There's no danger here," Sara spoke, calming her friend and protector. She sniffled and wiped her teary eyes.

"Are you crying? Can I do anything for you?" Gloria asked with concern.

Sara explained, "Tears of happiness, Gloria. I've endured for millennia in anticipation of this destiny that is upon me."

Gloria drew some water and handed a cup to Sara. "Drink this, Mistress. It will calm you."

Sara took it in with tiny sips and handed the cup back to her.

"Sleep well, Gloria," she told her friend. "Beginning in the morning, much work needs to be done. We must begin preparations for our king. He is coming!"

Derek braced himself for a reaction, imagining it to be rough and harsh like the exigent voice from his dreams. He tensed in expectation of the demon about to rip into his mind. Instead, the sound of wind chimes tinkled in his ears. A cool, refreshing breeze licked at Derek's face enticing him to relax just long enough to allow his eyes to enjoy a moment of relief as their lids gently closed over them.

"That's odd, there's nothing cool about this place, and I don't remember wind chimes," he mumbled to himself. An emotion that Derek never before sensed welled up inside of him, an extraordinary feeling of well-being and calm. Opening his eyes, Derek felt moisture tracking down his cheeks.

Tears? he wondered while shaking his head with incredulity. *Are they washing away my fear?*

Derek's anguish lifted, accompanied by a sudden weariness coaxing his return to bed. The afterglow resulting from the experience left him with renewed clarity.

"She is east of here, I'm sure of it now," Derek whispered. His last rumination before lapsing into a much-needed slumber was, "That was a gentle caress. Is Sara really an evil spirit hiding behind the light, or is she actually an angel?"

As sleep enveloped him, a tiny voice from within provided a third possibility, "Maybe both."

Juan awoke to the tap, tap, taping of water as it dripped against the floor of the shower. Anne was already awake and decided to be first in claiming the bathroom. The morning breeze blowing in from the river was only slightly cooler than the oppressive afternoon heat that they experienced the day before. The sweet smell of some flower unknown to Juan saturated the air.

Anne emerged from the bathroom wearing an oversized white tee shirt that covered her to mid-thigh. She was wrapping a towel around her head. Taking in a deep breath, Anne noticed Juan lying on his side with his head propped on an elbow as he stared out of the window.

"Isn't it glorious?" she pointed out, exhaling.

Snapping out of his daydream, Juan watched as Anne selected her clothing for the day. He saw that the white tee shirt that she was wearing was his.

"Hope you don't mind," she said guessing that he had noticed. "I didn't pack anything like a night shirt and needed something to throw on."

Juan smiled. It was a turn-on to him, her wearing his shirt. "You can keep it, Annie. I like seeing you in it." He turned his head back toward the window so that she could get dressed without the discomfort of him gawking at her.

She slipped into a robin egg blue midriff blouse and white shorts. Wondering why Juan was being so quiet, Anne sat on the bed at his side and slipped on her sneakers. The thought occurred to her that he might be brooding because nothing had happened between them during the night. *God, I was quick to get out of bed this morning,* she thought feeling a bit guilty. *Don't kid yourself, Anne,* she corrected herself while tying the sneakers. *Getting drunk last night was a convenient test. If Juan forced himself on me, he would have proven to be a jerk — just like the other men in my life.*

Anne's insecurity surfaced as she realized that getting out of bed quickly before Juan woke was a calculated move on her part. *He seems like such a decent guy,* she pondered staring out of the window in the same direction as Juan. *I'm so hoping that he doesn't blow it with me.*

Reaching down, she placed a hand on Juan's muscular forearm. "You're rather pensive this morning," she pointed out.

Juan reached over and rested his hand on her thigh. "It seems so unreal," he admitted. "I've realized that I am a completely different person from two weeks ago. I'm out of work, lying here in a hotel room at the gateway to the Amazon jungle. My reputation has been tarnished by scandal involving drugs and murder." He worked up enough courage to add, "and I'm lucky enough to be sharing a bed with a lady who makes me very happy."

Smiling, Anne started to massage his shoulder and tried, "I make you happy even though we haven't done anything?"

"Well, actually, Annie, I'm a bit relieved about that."

She stopped the massage. Juan observed her puzzled expression. It told him that she was completely blindsided by his answer.

"Don't misunderstand, Annie, I think you are wonderful," he clarified. "It's just that I have some guilty feelings. Since Bianca died two years ago, I haven't been with another woman."

Now Anne began to understand. "You must have loved her very much."

"It still hurts," he confessed. "It still feels like I would be cheating on her. Silly, isn't it?"

Anne was moved. She detected his sincerity and wondered if she could ever love someone with the same depth that Juan had loved his Bianca. She took his hand, the one that was resting on her thigh. "I'm sure she would understand," Anne told him. Leaning over, she whispered into his ear, "I'm sorry that I kept myself from you. It will not happen again."

Getting up, Anne stepped to the window and placed her hands on the sill. This time she was the one that perceived that Juan might feel uncomfortable about getting out of bed in the nude in front of her. She was right. Juan slipped away while she was standing there, and soon Anne heard the tap, tap, tapping of the shower.

A relieved smile broke out on her face. *Finally, here is a man that I can trust, a man that will never hurt me,* she knew.

Derek knocked on Professor Stamos's office door for the second time. "We aren't early, are we, Juan?" he asked.

"It's seven after ten by my watch," Juan answered him. "The guy may move slow, but he doesn't have a hearing problem."

A couple of minutes passed while the two of them felt awkward standing there. Juan finally took charge. "Let me try," he suggested and lightly turned the doorknob. It clicked open. The two of them looked at each other with expressions that read, "should we?"

Derek nodded his head in approval, and Juan gingerly pushed at the door. "Doctor Stamos, are you in? It's Juan and Derek from yesterday," he spoke out in Spanish.

Derek was the first to notice the overturned chair peeking out from behind the desk. "Over here, Juan," he motioned. "Oh, and shut the door."

The two of them peered for some time at Stamos as he lay there sprawled out on the floor. Juan bent over and felt for a pulse. He looked up and shook his head at Derek.

"Heart attack?" Derek suggested.

"Maybe," Juan shrugged.

Derek walked around Juan to the head end and closed the professor's eyelids. As he did so, he jumped up startled.

"What?" Juan inquired.

"Look at his throat."

Juan gently moved the corpse's face and noticed the huge dull purple bruise.

"Hell, Derek, someone throttled him. What do we do now?"

Derek considered the options. "We could call the police, but that would complicate things for us. I don't want to be associated with another murder."

"Amen to that," Juan agreed. He was starting to sweat. "Do you think anyone saw us come in here?"

"I don't know, we stood outside of the door for a long time."

"Why would someone want to kill him?" Derek speculated.

"We didn't know him, Derek. He could have enemies."

"He was going to tell us something, Juan. Do you think that someone wanted to prevent that from happening?"

"Who, Gem?" Juan offered.

"She did seem hostile about our probing, didn't she?"

Derek noticed the yearbook with the group photo on the professor's desk. Picking it up, he focused on Gem's image in the center. Placing it back on the desk, he looked back down at the professor's body. Derek's eyes opened wide with realization, and he quickly jerked the photo in the book back in front of his face.

"Look at this, Juan," Derek said almost shouting as he handed the book to him.

Juan studied the picture for a few moments and turned pale. "The caption says that his name is Pedro, but there's no mistaking," Juan said as he handed the book back to Derek. "That's Blaze."

"I wonder what else the good professor had here for us," Derek mentioned as he started rifling the documents on the desktop. He found the newspaper clipping and handed it to Juan.

"Six months ago, Blaze or Pedro disappeared along with a classmate named Luis," Juan translated. "They were last seen in a river town called Altamira."

"East of here, isn't it?" Derek said with a certainty.

"It doesn't say. It also doesn't say exactly what they were doing there."

"This might help," Derek suggested as he passed Juan the red binder.

Juan took a few minutes while skimming the pages. "Derek, this Luis was researching a theory based on a story he was told by an indigenous tribe. It's about a secluded tribe of women warriors, Amazons."

"Where?" Derek grew excited, almost unable to contain himself. "Where does his research say that they are?"

Juan found a hand-sketched map in a pocket on the cover. Altamira was marked with a dot. A red X was indicated south of that place along an unnamed tributary.

"Altamira!" Derek sighed and walked over to the professor's large wall map.

"Here it is, Derek," Juan pointed to the town.

Derek nodded with confidence. "East of here. I knew it all along. That's where we go now, Juan."

"Then where, Derek? Do you know?"

"Not yet, but we will find her. She wants us to find her."

For the first time, Derek noticed that Juan seemed troubled. "I'd ask you to trust me, Juan, but I can't provide any assurances."

Juan stopped him. "It's not that. I'm with you wherever it leads us. It's just that you seem to know a great deal more than what would be possible. How did you know that we would be going east?"

It was a fair question from a friend that was risking everything to blindly follow him. Derek would have liked to tell Juan everything, but he held back. "I get these feelings from time to time." Derek was being truthful, yet evasive. "Sort of like E.S.P." Derek raised his arms and made his fingers walk through the air. "Woo Hoo," he joked, attempting to deflect Juan from the subject.

"You think there is a back way out of here?" Juan questioned, still worried.

"Maybe, but if we were seen, that would draw more suspicion than if we just quietly walked out the front door," Derek counseled.

They decided to take the red binder and yearbook since the two of them had pawed these articles and left fingerprints. Wiping the doorknob on both sides, they slipped away unnoticed.

Halfway back to the guesthouse, Derek tossed the binder and yearbook but kept the hand drawn map stashed in his shirt pocket. Juan placed a hand on Derek's shoulder. "I don't think we need to be telling the girls about the professor," he forcefully suggested.

"Ditto," Derek snapped in a way that assured Juan that the two of them were definitely on the same page.

CHAPTER 31

Sharon was bewildered. "We're leaving now? We just got here yesterday. What's the hurry?"

Derek and Juan decided that the quicker they left Manaus the safer they would be. A man had been murdered and the authorities were bound to suspect two strange Americans that were last seen with the victim. Of course, they didn't want to share these details with Sharon and Anne.

"Hon, I promised that we would get home as soon as we could," Derek justified it to her. "We know where we need to go, so there's no need to tarry."

Anne chimed in, "Too bad, I like it here. The people seem friendly."

Derek ignored her and turned his attention to Juan. "Does our route make sense to you?"

"Yep, we follow the River Road to Santerem. From there we turn south to TransAmazon Highway Number 230 and straight on through to Altamira."

Turning to the girls, Derek asked them, "How long will it take you ladies to pack?"

"Hey, I'm a stewardess, remember?" Anne smirked. "I can be ready at a moment's notice."

Sharon was still disappointed, but she understood Derek's urgency in wanting to get on with finding Sara. "Give me about half an hour," she told him.

Juan grew serious and wanted to make sure that Derek had a clear idea of what was involved in this trip. "Derek, it's about 800 kilometers and that River Road isn't paved. It could take us three or four days to get there. Are you sure we shouldn't fly?"

"What?" Anne blurted out. "After we had so much fun buying our van you want to give it up already?"

"No way," Sharon protested. "It may take us a few days, but we can at least see some sights. I mean, come on! This is the Amazon jungle. When will we ever get this chance again?"

Derek felt safer with a vehicle. He suspected that as soon as the police made a connection between them and Stamos that they would watch the airports.

"We better let 'em win this one," Derek winked at Juan. He got the message.

Sharon later wished they had flown. The River Road was nothing more than a two-lane logging trail that followed the Amazon. The surroundings were barren due to deforestation, and there was nothing to see except mud and dust. After almost three days, they reached Santerem and paved roads. During the afternoon of the fifth day, they entered Altamira on the Xingu River.

"Damn," Anne uttered. "I love all you guys, but after five days cooped up in this tin can, I need some private time."

"I'd pay a hundred dollars for a long, hot shower," Juan dreamed.

"After bouncing around in those ruts and potholes, I swear it's going to take a long time for my kidneys to recover," Sharon added.

Derek tried to make the best of it and encouraged them. "You girls did a great job in picking this van. At least we had a place to sleep. Can you imagine if we were in a little car?"

"Yeah, and what's with that?" Anne complained. "Haven't they heard of hotels in this country?"

"Don't forget that we are in the rain forest," Juan reminded her. "Towns are few and far between."

Sharon laughed at that. "Rain forest! I hardly saw any trees."

"The ones along the river are the easiest to cut down and transport," Derek instructed them. "It's still plenty dense deep in." Derek nodded his head in the direction of a dark mountain range far off on the southern horizon.

"This place is no tourist heaven, is it?" Juan began to notice. "Manaus was teeming with people and thriving. Altamira seems like a seedy port town."

Derek attempted once again to remain positive. "It's much smaller than Manaus, so we should be able to more easily figure out what to do next."

"There it is," Juan pointed out the cantina in the middle of the town. "The proprietor at that last gas station told me that it is the best place to stay, clean rooms, hot water, and good food."

"Food!" Anne exclaimed. "Do you think we can get a nice juicy steak? I saw plenty of cattle ranches around here."

"Undoubtedly," Derek assured her. "After we eat, I'm going to sleep for about twelve hours. I'm beat," he added.

After checking in, the two couples agreed to meet for breakfast the next morning and went to their separate rooms.

The sexual tension that existed between Juan and Anne was excruciating for them. As soon as they latched the room door, they started pawing each other and kissing.

"I don't believe it," Anne gasped between breaths. "Four nights of your holding me in the back of that van, and there was nothing we could do."

Juan laughed at her. "Do you think Sharon and Derek would have minded the show while they lay there beside us?"

Anne didn't say anything and started to lead Juan by the belt loop of his trousers into the bathroom.

"What do you have in mind, Annie?" Juan asked with amusement.

"Showering together saves water," she told Juan while stripping him of his clothes.

After a few moments, they were sharing the warm water as it cascaded from the showerhead. They took turns lathering up and washing each other's backs. From the moment Juan climbed under the gentle trickle with Anne, he grew hard and throbbed for a release.

Anne loved it. She teased Juan by pushing her body into him and occasionally grabbing him. Finally, as they rinsed off, Anne grabbed him again and applied a mound of soapsuds. She began to massage it in. Juan could barely remain standing. He closed his eyes and enjoyed the rush as Anne stroked him toward a climax.

Suddenly, both of them screamed. The hot water abruptly ran out, and what seemed like icicles stung their skin. Laughing like little kids, Anne and Juan bolted out of the shower.

Anne could hardly catch her breath, she was laughing so hard. "Well, Juan," she snorted. "I guess it wasn't meant to be."

Juan stopped laughing. "It *is* meant to be," he protested and immediately grabbed Anne's hand. He led her out of the bathroom and pulled her down on top of him on the bed.

"We're soaking wet, Juan," Anne gasped as she placed a knee on either side of his hips. She guided him in home.

"Don't stop now," Juan begged. They locked hands as Anne started to pump up and down on top of him. Rivulets of water from her hair ran down onto Anne's breasts. Water droplets found their way to the tips of her nipples and broke free into the air as she slammed to a stop on each down stroke. It only took a dozen times until Juan exploded inside of her.

She collapsed on top of his chest and listened to his heart beating. In a few minutes, Anne felt Juan start to go soft inside of her. Some time later, she looked up into his eyes. "I love you, Juan," she told him.

"It's been such a long time, Annie," he said stroking her wet, matted hair, "and you are so beautiful."

Anne smiled and pushed herself back up. She felt Juan begin to grow hard again inside of her.

"How delightful to see you," Sara gushed while giving Gem a hug. "It's been two and a half years. You should have called the cantina to let us know you were returning." She invited Gem to have a seat in the waiting room of her quarters. It was late at night, and Gem had just arrived. Sara motioned for one of the servants to bring them a drink.

"Oh Mistress, it is so good to be home. There was no need for me to call, as I would have been only a few hours behind a messenger. My heart rejoices to be among my sisters again. I've also missed being with my designee. Has he behaved during my absence?"

"Gloria has been looking after him. I'm sure that she's kept him well. Before you go to your house, would you mind filling me in on your mission? Since you are here, I must assume that Stamos finally remembered."

"Yes, and he is now dead," Gem assured her.

A servant girl waited at the entrance to Sara's quarters with two cups and a pitcher of water on a tray. Sara motioned her to enter.

"Thank you, Anna," Sara acknowledged the young girl. They waited until she exited the room.

"She's a pretty one," Gem noticed.

"Yes, and her children should be quite handsome if we match her with the right designee," Sara noted. "Anna will never have the stamina to become a Shadow Woman, yet I have high hopes for her as a leader among the tribe."

Gem was nosy. "Has she expressed a preference for anyone in particular?"

"As a matter of fact she has," Sara supplied, "and I believe that you know him."

"Really?"

"He claims that he is one of your classmates from the university. A man named Luis."

Gem drank her water and refilled her glass. "Sorry, Mistress Sara," Gem said feeling a bit disrespectful for not acknowledging her right away. "I didn't realize that I was so thirsty. The journey has been long, and I am out of shape."

Sara smiled and waved an arm out in front of her. "No, please refresh yourself. I understand."

Gem took a few moments and continued. "After they didn't return to Manaus, I suspected that those two found their way here. What happened to the other one, Pedro?"

Sara smiled. "I satisfied myself with him. After a few times I turned him over to Elyria and sent them on a mission."

"Now I'm curious," Gem started. "Where did you send her? The American men that visited Stamos spoke of Elyria."

Sara stiffened and approached Gem. "What American men? Tell me what you know."

"Two men visited Professor Stamos," Gem began to report. "They claimed that they were reporters wanting a story about us, I mean Amazons. They prodded Stamos. I tried to put them off, but after they left, Stamos began to remember. These men were going to return, so I killed the professor before they could get any further information from him."

Sara became enraged. She slapped Gem with all of the might she could muster. The force knocked her to the floor. The cup Gem held sailed out of her hand across the room bouncing off the adjacent wall.

"Stupid fool," Sara screamed. "You might have ruined everything. Do you have any idea what you have done?" The recoil from the strike bruised Sara's hand. She put it into her mouth and began to suck on it.

Gem backed away against the wall near where her cup had settled. Both Anna and Gloria burst into the room to attend to their Mistress. Anna ran to Sara and inspected her hand, while Gloria drew a long knife. She held it against the back of Gem's neck. Although Gloria and Gem were friends, one nod from Sara, and Gloria would lop off Gem's head without the slightest hesitation.

Gem shrieked, "If I must die, Mistress, please tell me my error. I did exactly what you asked. You assigned me to tend to Stamos and to kill him when he remembered. How have I failed you?"

Sara remained agitated and shaking but realized that Gem was faultless. Waving Gloria away, she approached her. Gem cringed as if expecting another blow. Sara prostrated herself so that she was at the same level on the floor with Gem.

"Forgive me, friend," Sara begged. "Of course, you couldn't know. You have served us all with honor. A temporary madness blinded me, because you may have frightened these men away or caused them trouble. Had you known about them, I would have wanted you to bring them here."

"Who are these men?" Gem blubbered.

Sara helped Gem to her feet. "My dear, Gem," she spoke. "One of these men is your king."

"It must be the tall, virile one," Gem reflected.

Sara smiled and led her to a chair. "Tell me all about him," she insisted.

Gem explained all of the details to Sara. When done, Sara hugged her and asked once again for Gem's forgiveness. She yelled for Anna.

"Anna, tomorrow morning request a gathering of all of the warriors among the tribes. There is to be a jubilee. Our Gem has returned safely home and has completed a great mission for our people. She is to be honored and celebrated. Her name will be spoken of with great respect as one of our most accomplished Shadow Women."

Anna bowed and exited.

Gem's spirits lifted. She dismissed Sara's strange behavior as an aberration.

"Go home now and sleep well," Sara ordered her. "Satisfy yourself with your designee. Maybe he will plant a new warrior inside you."

"Thank you, Mistress," Gem grinned with pride while passing Gloria on the way out.

"Mistress Sara, may I impose upon you?" Gloria inquired.

"Of course, what is on your mind?" Sara encouraged.

"Are you well?"

"I'm fine now, Gloria. Thank you for asking," Sara lied as she speculated that Derek might have been scared away or captured.

Knowing that there was only one sure way to tell, she closed her eyes and sent out a wave. *If he doesn't answer me, I'll kill Gem myself while she sleeps.*

"Where are you going, Derek?" Sharon asked only half awake as she felt him leave their bed.

"It's okay, hon, go back to sleep. I just need to use the bathroom."

The cantina was nowhere near as nice as the guesthouse they left behind in Manaus. The rooms here were above the bar, and the noise from the rowdy clientele easily drifted through the thin floor. Derek walked over to the open window and observed that the streets were quiet. The air smelled of dead fish. The hot breeze from the river carried the stench inland.

Derek detected Sara's signature while he slept. It woke him. "She's close," he whispered to himself. Until this time, he was determined to find and demand an accounting from this mysterious woman. Now that the decisive moment was closing in, Derek began to doubt himself.

One glance and Tabitha held me in the palm of her hand, he pondered. *How much more powerful can this Sara be? Am I going to be able to survive this, then what of Sharon and my friends?*

His thoughts were further complicated as Derek recalled the content of his dreams. *I'm not supposed to kill her,* he considered. *So what am I doing? What purpose is there in leading the woman that I love and two dear friends into a certain trap?* He remembered that the angel of his dreams told him that he would not be alone.

Derek's mind raced as these snapshots of thought flashed in front of him.

Foundling freak. Is your will strong enough? Not all things are as they appear. You must choose the path to your destination. Follow the path. Her death must not occur at your hands. You will not be alone. Reach for the prize. Come to me.

Derek held his hands up to each side of his head. "Enough," he rebuked his thoughts in a voice that was a little too loud. Sharon stirred and sat at the edge of the bed.

"Are you dreaming, Derek?" she asked. "Come here and sit beside me."

Derek complied. Sharon placed a hand between his knees and kissed him. "I love you," she reassured him.

"I know," Derek admitted, "and that's what this is all about."

Sharon looked at him puzzled.

He explained it to her. "It's becoming clearer, Sharon. Sara fears me as much as I fear her. She wanted me to come to her stripped of support, so that she would have the greatest advantage. That's why she wanted you dead. It's not just me now. Four of us will be facing her down. Between us, there exists a strong bond of friendship and love. I suspect that she has endured all of these years on nothing but hate."

Derek stood and walked again to the window. "Love is stronger," he continued. "The four of us will defeat Sara if we do not allow her to come between us."

Sharon glanced down at the floor and mumbled. "You speak of victory and defeat. Does this mean that someone has to die?"

Derek considered her question. "I can't say," he confessed. "What I feel is that something cosmic is happening. A great force is at work here, Sharon. Call it God, or whatever. This path has been laid in front of me, and I willingly chose it. The outcome is not guaranteed."

He turned to face Sharon and leaned back against the windowsill. "Here is an even weirder thought," Derek pointed out. "I think that I am somehow supposed to save her. Anyway, I don't believe that I could kill her. I just can't."

"What are you supposed to save her from, Derek?"

"Probably from her hate and despair," he guessed.

Sharon returned to her pillow. "Cuddle up to me, Derek," she entreated him.

"I'll be right there," he responded without hesitation. "There's just one more thing I need to do."

Sharon waited as she watched Derek turn to peer once again out into the street. Closing his eyes, Derek mustered a sharp, powerful blast in return to Sara's wave. *Consider it a warning,* he thought. *I'm coming to you with a determination. My will is strong enough.*

After Sharon detected from his breathing that Derek drifted back to sleep, she stroked the hair on his chest. He didn't hear as she whispered, "Derek, I'm scared."

Derek's angel appeared to him again in a dream. "You seem hazy and distant," he told her.

"That means you no longer need me," she countered. "Your final confrontation is at hand."

"I do need you," he protested. "I still don't know. What am I supposed to do?"

The angel sighed and transported him to Professor Stamos's office. She pointed to the red binder on top of the desk. "Continue to follow the path," she pressed.

Derek looked at the binder. It no longer was Luis's notes. The cover showed a picture of a wooden boy, a marionette with strings attached to arms, legs, and head. Suddenly a hand reached out and removed the red binder from the desk. It was Tabitha!

She smiled at Derek. "It's his favorite story," she explained. Sitting in a rocking chair, the baby boy climbed up onto her lap. Tabitha read to him. The baby squealed with delight as he listened to her voice and studied the colorful pictures.

As the vision ended, Derek looked around for his angel. She was gone. Derek realized that he would never dream of her again.

*****

The next morning, the four of them sat at a table eating steak and eggs. Derek opened the hand-drawn map that they took from Luis's binder and set it down for all of them to study.

"According to the map of Brazil that we bought in Germany, another river, the Iriri, flows into the Xingu about 100 kilometers south of here," Derek pointed out. "The source of the Iriri lies in the mountains deep within the jungle."

"And pretty damn far away from civilization," Juan added as he studied the document.

Sharon pointed to the unnamed tributary on the hand-drawn paper. "That stream doesn't appear on the commercial map."

"I know," Derek acknowledged. "My gut tells me that is where we need to go."

Until now, Anne remained silent as she listened to the others plot out the strategy. Noticing that there were no roads in this area, she warned them of the obvious. "We're going to have to hoof it. Our poor van will only be able to take us part of the way."

"Are you sure about this, Derek?" Sharon reflected on what Anne said.

"I don't think we need to be exact," he argued. "Remember, Sara wants to be found. As we draw near, she will come to us."

"I hope so," remarked Juan. "After all we've been through, I wouldn't want to wander around lost."

Anne and Sharon didn't say anything, but Derek noticed them nodding their heads in agreement. "There's little chance of that if we stick to the river," Derek reassured them.

"I suppose we should stock up on whatever we think we need. It's liable to be a long journey," Anne observed.

Derek folded Luis's map and returned it to his shirt pocket. Sharon excused herself in order to visit the ladies' room. It was located in a hallway around the corner from the dining area. The door to the bathroom swung open as Sharon got there, and she bumped shoulders with another woman exiting. As they passed, the two of them recognized each other simultaneously.

Sharon threw a hand over her mouth stifling a scream. The other woman began to laugh. At that moment, her companion emerged from the adjacent mens' room. He was the first to speak.

"Geez, Sharon. What are you doing here?"

CHAPTER 32

The six of them stared at each other in disbelief. Derek was looking around for other government agents or police. Sharon's right hand secretly fingered the dagger that was stowed in her carry bag. Anne and Juan remained seated holding each other's hands.

Hank Kimball sensed their discomfort, but he had a few concerns of his own. "There's nothing to be afraid of, folks," Hank told them as he pulled a small vial from his front trouser pocket. Shaking it in the air, they noticed that it was full with yellow capsules. "She's no danger to anyone as long as I have these."

"What is that?" Anne asked.

Hank began to explain the situation. "The German government wouldn't grant custody of Elyria unless they had assurances that she would be returned to face murder charges. You've all heard about designer drugs, right? The Bureau has access to designer poisons to use in situations like this."

"Huh?" Anne followed up.

"Go ahead and tell'em, Elyria," Hank ordered.

While displaying a sheepish look on her face, Elyria began to explain. "I've been injected with a chemical agent. The way I understand, it will take a month to kill me. Every day I need to take those pills to counteract the effects."

"Tell them what those effects are," Hank insisted. Anne thought that there was too much glee in his voice as he prodded her.

Elyria rolled her eyes in resignation. "Right now I get sick to the stomach. Later I'm told there will be joint pain and then trouble breathing."

"She only needs one of these a day right now," Hank interjected as he teased Elyria by waving the vial in front of her face. "As time goes by, she will need more. After a few weeks, it will not matter."

"That's inhumane," Anne objected with disgust. "I can't believe that our government would be part of something like this."

Hank appealed to her logic. "Quite the contrary. It's a compassionate act that could save countless Americans. Do I have to remind you how many innocent lives become ruined by drugs? She's taking me to the source."

"That's incredibly stupid," Juan blurted. "They will just kill you."

"Not if they value Elyria's life," Hank corrected.

"You just said that she would be dead in a few weeks. What difference would it make?" Juan asked in confusion.

Hank smiled. "You didn't let me finish. There is an antidote. The poison will be neutralized if we return to Germany in time."

"What makes you think they give a damn about her?" Juan pressed.

"Really, Mr. Sanchez," Hank appeared hurt. "Have you already forgotten about our conversations on the flight from Baltimore? It's my penchant for observation. I believe that Elyria's boss thinks that she is quite valuable. She was trusted with a very important mission. Also, the Bureau's intelligence indicates that this probably is a newly established organization possibly on the verge of rolling out this drug en masse into our country. We have an opportunity to stop it now."

"How?" Juan countered with a mocking tone. He hadn't liked Hank Kimball from the first time the man sat beside Sharon on their flight. With every encounter, Juan was growing to like the man less.

"Quite simple," Hank answered. "I'm going to tell them to stop."

Juan scoffed, "Just like that. One man is going to march onto their turf and demand that they stop."

Hank clarified it for him. "Exactly. Call it a warning shot across the bow. I'll tell them that we now know who they are and where they are. I'll tell them that we would rather not waste our resources coming after them, but if they persist we will descend all over them like flies on shit."

"Uh huh," Juan derided him, "and then you just run away back to Germany with Elyria in tow."

Hank began to grow impatient. "Don't be a fool. It's not that far fetched. As a matter of fact, I've conducted this type of operation before."

"You're the fool," Elyria mumbled to Hank. "You have no idea what you are dealing with."

"Watch out, dear, or I'm going to hold that bad attitude against you," Hank said glaring at her.

"Well, I guess we don't have to worry about how to get there now. Elyria will lead us right to her," Sharon noted.

Hank Kimball's expression turned stern. "What about that?" he queried the four of them. "Now it's your turn. I'm more than a little curious as to what you are doing here. You know this doesn't look good. One would suspect that all of you are somehow involved."

Derek took up for the group. "We are involved. The woman that is the boss has ruined us. We are here to have a not so friendly conversation with her."

"That's not good enough," Hank snapped. "Four people don't visit the Amazon jungle to put themselves in harm's way. Besides, how did you know to come here?"

Sharon spoke next. She was hoping that the relationship they built on the flight would soften him. "Hank, we have nothing to return to. These three lost their jobs, and probably so have I. Is it all that unreasonable that we would want to confront the person that is the cause of it? How do we know what she wants? How do we know she will not come after us again?"

Elyria couldn't resist. "Hey, Derek. Tell old Hank what she wants."

"Sharon has already said it," Derek reproved her. "It's nothing more than that. We want to find out what this is all about. If it's something we can resolve, we return to our normal lives."

"What do you intend to do if you can't resolve it?" Hank asked him.

"I don't know yet."

"I tell you what," Hank said taking charge. "I believe the four of you should go home and leave this to me. When I return, I'll advise you."

"No deal," Derek stood his ground. "You have no authority to order us around. We can all go together, or the four of us can find her on our own. If I were in your position, I would be grateful for some volunteers." Derek nodded in the direction of Elyria and continued, "We're in her element now. We can watch your back."

Hank considered it for some time and gave in. "I'm on an official FBI mission," he told them. "Do what you need to do, but don't interfere in my business."

The waitress serving them seemed pleased to see Elyria. They had a conversation in Portuguese.

"You know this woman?" Derek asked Elyria.

"That's Teresa, the cantina manager," Elyria told him. "This place is controlled by the Mistress and her loyal friends," she boasted, telling them more than they needed to know. "It's like you said. You're in my element now."

"Will she get word to Sara that we are coming?" Derek wondered.

"No, this is the closest outpost to Casa Cobo. We will get there first."

Elyria spoke next to all of them. "We can drive some of the way, but there will be many days of travel on foot through the jungle. Allow me to have Teresa arrange for us all that we will need."

Elyria was sure that fate was being kind to her. Now that they had stumbled onto Derek and his party, she would be returning victorious to her Mistress. This is exactly what Elyria was told to accomplish. The only glitch was that Sharon was still alive.

In desperation she began to reason within herself, *Derek's woman lives, but I am going to die. I've seen the power that the Mistress has over men. If I bed down with Derek, maybe his power can root out the poison within me.* She resented again that the Mistress wanted to keep this man to herself. *I can have him first before we reach the Mistress. I will kill Sharon and sleep with Derek,* she decided. *After being healed, I will kill this pig, Kimball.*

Teresa needed most of the day to round up supplies for the group's journey. It was decided that they would spend one more night at the cantina and depart early the next morning.

That night when Hank and Elyria went to their room, she became nauseous and feverish. Hank shook the vial of pills with a devilish grin. Elyria reached out and tried to snatch it, but he jerked away.

Taking a seat on the side of the bed, she doubled over and pleaded, "My stomach is twisted up. It hurts."

He shook the vial again. "Penance first, my dear, you need to pay for the humiliation you caused me. You'll pay every day."

Elyria balled up a fist and held it against her stomach. "We're both soldiers," she tried. "I had my duty to perform. Can't you just respect that?"

Hank stood in front of Elyria. Looking down at her, he unzipped his fly. "Geez, I respect that," he told her, "and you need to respect that to the victor goes the spoils."

It was a tight squeeze, but the six of them managed to fit into the van with all of the provisions for the journey.

"It's only for one day," Elyria reminded them. "After that we walk."

Derek drove, and Elyria took the seat directly behind him. During a rest stop, she found herself alone in the van for a few moments with him. Leaning forward, she began to massage his neck. Derek bristled.

"What are you up to?" he asked.

Figuring that they had only a short amount of time together, Elyria got right to the point urging him, "Find a way that we can be alone. Being one of the mighty ones, you can cure me. Free me from Kimball."

Derek suspected to what she was referring. "I told you before it doesn't work that way. Only women have the power. Besides, it's destructive, not benevolent."

"You also told me that I would like it," she reminded him.

"Sorry, babe, it'll never happen."

Since that approach wasn't working, Elyria tried another tack. "You don't understand. Kimball uses me for sex. He denies me the pills unless he gets to do what he wants with my body."

Derek remained cold. "We're going to be in pretty close quarters from here on in. It's going to be difficult for him to abuse you without one of us knowing about it."

Elyria recognized an opening. She worked on his sense of decency. "You'd protect me from him, won't you?"

Derek laughed, "You seem like the type that can take care of herself."

All it takes now to win him over are tears, she realized. Feeling the moisture well up in her eyes, Elyria continued to lure him. "He hurts me, Derek. He makes me do things that I am ashamed to tell you. The poison within me causes great pain. He keeps the pills from me."

Now she was sobbing. Derek had a hunch that what Elyria was telling him was the truth. "Set up your bed roll near Sharon and me," he suggested. "I'll make sure he doesn't bother you in that way."

Elyria thanked Derek and kissed him on the cheek. This time he didn't flinch. *The Mistress has taught me well about handling men,* she observed, feeling validated.

Derek drove the van exactly where Elyria directed. The entire party felt uncomfortable about blindly following the directions of a murderess, but Derek sensed that she was not misleading them. Eventually the trail became impassable, and Elyria told them to park in a clearing near the river.

"Whose Jeep is that?" Sharon asked in alarm after spotting the green vehicle. "I wouldn't want to run into any trouble makers out here in this isolated place."

"We aren't completely defenseless," Hank assured her. Reaching into a backpack, he removed a shoulder holster and buckled it over his sweat-stained tee shirt. "Meet my 10 millimeter Glock. This is plenty of protection for us," he bragged.

Elyria answered Sharon's question. "That Jeep belongs to my people now.

We use it to shuttle between this place and the cantina. Teresa told me that one of my friends, Gem, used it a few days ago."

"Gem?" Juan repeated after hearing the name. Derek also perked up.

"I haven't seen her in years," Elyria admitted. "She's been on a long-term assignment."

Derek waited until Sharon and Anne became engaged in a conversation before following up with Elyria.

"If your friend, Gem, was in Manaus, we met her."

"So that's how you knew to come here," Elyria figured it out.

"She killed an old man," Derek said in a stern voice. "Why is it that wherever you people go there is a trail of death?"

"We follow orders," Elyria asserted.

"Your mistress approves of this?" Derek prodded.

Elyria was flabbergasted. "Whose orders do you think we follow?"

Hank Kimball strapped on a backpack and helped the ladies suit up. Juan swatted at a mosquito that stung him on the forearm.

"They get worse at night," Elyria informed him. "I'll keep an eye out for a certain plant that I know about that repels them. We can boil some leaves and make a lotion."

"I assume we go up river?" Derek asked of Elyria.

She shook her head as she looked at the rest of the party gathered around her. "Alone, I could make it in three days. With all of you in tow, it will probably take a good four or five days."

"Don't get any ideas," Hank growled. "We stay together."

"That's what I'm saying," Elyria snapped back.

"You're not very diplomatic, are you?" snarled Anne.

Elyria grew serious. "Listen up, all of you. We're in the jungle. There is no diplomacy here, only life and death. You may not think much of me, but remember that I grew up in these mountains. Heed my advice. This is a dangerous place for 'civilized' folk such as you."

None of them liked this, but they all understood that for now, Elyria was in charge.

"What's the next move?" Derek inquired.

Elyria scanned the sky. "We have about four hours of light. There's a hollow between two mountains where the Iriri cuts through. It's about twenty kilometers up stream. If we push, we can make it by dusk."

Anne placed both hands on her hips and threw out her chest. "Twenty kilometers in four hours is a piece of cake," she scoffed.

"Listen to me, pampered city girl," Elyria reprimanded her. "We'll be hacking our way through snake-infested vines. If you stray too close to the water's edge, you could end up as dinner for a caiman or alligator. If you stray out of an earshot, a jaguar could drag you off. If you decide to take a dip in one of the inviting side pools, you could be stripped to the bone by piranha."

Anne held up a hand and stopped her, "Enough already, I get it."

"Snakes?" Sharon demurred, looking at Derek.

"Stay close to me and everything will be fine," he assured her.

Derek huddled with Juan and Anne by placing a hand on each of their shoulders. "This is it, friends," he spoke to them. "You can take the keys to the van and head on back. We really are at the point of no return."

"Lead on, Elyria," Anne yelled to her after glancing sidelong at Derek.

The three men took turns at the head of the group hacking through the undergrowth while Elyria pointed the way. Although Gem passed this way a few days earlier, the jungle had already started to reclaim the trail. After about two hours, a small herd of peccaries startled them as they exploded away.

"Holy shit!" Juan gasped clutching his chest. "I just about stepped on 'em."

Hank was quick to draw the 10 mil. "Geez, would I be an asshole if I shot one of those pigs for our dinner?" he asked Elyria in an excited voice.

"You could, but it would mean that we would have to stop for the night," she told him. "It would take a few hours to gut, skin, and cook it. We would have to do it right away. Fresh meat spoils quickly."

Hank shouldered the pistol and groaned, "No, thanks. I'm not ready for that yet."

After they continued the trek, a family of spider monkeys in the trees above began to scold the humans for getting too close.

Sharon was amused and placed a hand over her eyes shading them from the setting sun. "Do you see anything, Derek? I can't make them out."

"I just see flashes as they scoot from branch to branch. Noisy devils, aren't they?" he shuddered while contemplating what other sets of eyes might be paying attention to their journey deeper into the jungle.

The hollow that Elyria referred to was a bench in the mountain that overlooked the river. It was a perfect spot to camp for the night, protected on three sides. When they arrived, Elyria collapsed onto the ground. The rest of them fared fairly well. Juan was the one that noticed Elyria's discomfort. He got down on one knee beside her.

"Is it time for one of your pills?" he asked.

She nodded with a grimace. "Can you ask Hank for me?"

Hank willingly gave Juan one of the yellow capsules. Juan passed it on to her along with an open water bottle.

"Thanks," she responded to Juan while casting a suspicious look at Hank.

After Elyria started to feel better, she instructed them that it would not be necessary to post a watch. "Only those unfamiliar with the jungle fear the many sounds at night. They are our watchmen," she said referring to the creatures that produced the noises. "You learn to sleep lightly and to wake up when the noises abruptly stop. That is when danger is near."

The six of them paired off, the couples sleeping a few meters away from each other. Juan kept a hand on Anne's arm the entire night, and Sharon stayed glued to Derek. Elyria maintained a good two meters between herself and Hank.

In the middle of the night, Hank stirred when he sensed Elyria walking off. She was gone for only a short time before returning. Looking in her direction, he whispered, "Bathroom?"

"Yeah," she confirmed, also in a whisper, returning to her bedroll.

Hank shifted his stuff closer to her. "Are you okay?"

"Look, Hank, don't try anything. Derek and Juan will not allow you to blackmail me anymore."

In the darkness, Hank could only make out Elyria's general form, but being this close, he could feel the heat from her body.

"I know you think I'm a shit," he continued whispering, "and maybe I am. It's just that you pissed me off. You played me, and I fell for it."

"Don't beat yourself up, Hank. The Mistress taught me that men have an easily bruised ego."

"Geez, the Mistress again," Hank complained.

After a few minutes, Elyria just about fell back to sleep when Hank started again. "It's not really the fact that you used me. I guess I'm upset at myself, because I developed feelings for you. I've been taking my anger out on you."

"Go to sleep, Hank."

"Geez, Elyria, we were intimate. Didn't it mean anything to you?"

For a brief moment, Elyria considered allowing Hank to copulate with her just to shut him up. Instead, she rolled on her side and faced in his direction.

"In your world it might have grown into something," she lied. "My world is completely foreign to everything that you know. You are entering an environment where a relationship between you and I could never work."

"Love always finds a way," Hank retorted.

"Love?" Elyria questioned. Even in this low tone, he detected the sarcasm. "Let me tell you something, Hank. You aren't going to like my world. It's a matriarchal society where we Shadow Women keep men as drugged drone slaves. The Mistress doesn't even refer to you as men. You are merely property assigned as a 'designee' to serve at our pleasure."

"You don't love your men, I mean designees?" Hank pushed.

"Of course we do. Just like in your society, we take care of each other and the children that are born to us. The dynamic is different, because women rule, and all of us are in subjection to the Mistress."

"Why do you drug your men?"

"Do I have to answer that? It's to control their aggressive tendencies — to keep them compliant."

As an agent, Hank was interested in all of this as a means to assess how much of a threat the Mistress and her clan could pose to the United States of America through the introduction of cobo. While conversing with Elyria, his mind worked on the problem.

The solution is obviously simple, he contemplated. *Find a way to stop the drugging of the men folk and nature will run its course. The Mistress will be toppled by what Elyria refers to as an 'aggressive' man.*

Probing Elyria further on the subject, Hank whispered, "What makes the Mistress so special? Why is it, for example, that you aren't the ruler instead of her?"

This touched a nerve with Elyria, but not in the way that Hank could have imagined.

With Derek Dunbar, I could rule, she considered. *I will find a way to win him and to destroy the hold that the Mistress has on all of us.*

What she told Hank was, "She is very old and very powerful."

"If she is so old, surely she no longer possesses such great power?" Hank concluded. "One of you could assume control."

Elyria considered further, *She locks herself up in Casa Cobo. The Mistress is afraid, and that is her weakness. I could kill her myself, but I need Derek to take her place. It would be very dangerous. She knows our minds, yet this thing could be done.*

"Elyria?"

"I'm tired, Hank. Why must you keep on so?"

"I told you. I have feelings for you. I just want to understand."

"Understand this: The Mistress is formidable. Our people worship her as a god. She is the daughter of the sun and as old as time. If any of us attempted to harm her, we would be torn to pieces by the others."

"You actually believe that?"

"Hank, you have no idea. Being a man, she could destroy you with a single thought."

Hank dismissed the notion as hyperbole and allowed his emotions to take over. Now he was a man again and not special agent Hank Kimball.

He reached over and lightly touched Elyria's shoulder. "I could free you from all of this. I know you are not a bad person."

In the darkness, Hank couldn't detect Elyria's grimace. *Ignorant blind fool*, she thought. *I don't want you to free me. I want to be the goddess that is the Mistress.*

"Listen," she told him. "You think that you are in love with me. Physically, I'm not pretty like Anne or Sharon. How do you possibly hope to avoid succumbing to the radiance of the Mistress?"

"Geez, enough about her. You're right. It's you that I love. Besides, you told me that your Mistress is old and wrinkled."

Elyria stifled spasms of laughter so as not to wake the others.

"Yes, she is ancient. Wrinkled? I never told you that."

Hank pulled himself closer and now had an arm around her.

"I don't mind," Elyria responded to his advance. Taking advantage of a way to end his silly questioning she offered, "You can hold me. I will not scream for Derek and Juan, but you must shut up, and go to sleep."

Taking this as a sign of hope, Hank complied and stopped talking.

Why can't this be Derek Dunbar? she grappled with her thoughts in frustration. *If I could only find a way to kill that clinging Sharon without his hating me for it.* As for Hank, she knew that the Mistress would soon deal with him. Elyria also knew that she was going to die. The Mistress would never let them return for the antidote.

My only hope is to convince or coerce Derek into sleeping with me. His psychic power can cure me. It must, she fretted to herself in desperation. *How do I get to Derek before the Mistress takes him away from me? I cannot allow her to withhold him from me.*

CHAPTER 33

The next morning, Elyria taught the group about foraging for breakfast. She prepared the roots and nuts that they were able to gather into a tasty meal by frying them in coconut oil. As they packed and made ready to resume the journey, Elyria's trained ear detected that someone was working their way toward them. It was someone human.

"Hank, one of my people is about to enter our camp. Don't be too quick with that weapon of yours."

The others jerked to attention.

"You think it's Sara?" Sharon whispered to Derek.

"No," he answered back, convinced that this wasn't the case.

A woman cautiously crept into their midst through the growth along the river's edge. After spying Elyria, the woman relaxed.

"Your fire is so large and wasteful that a child could track you down," she frowned and scolded Elyria in a language the others couldn't understand. Juan made out some slang Portuguese, but most of it was unintelligible to him. "You haven't been gone that long. Have you already lost some of your skills?"

Elyria embraced her friend and warrior-sister. "It's these outsiders. They are such a burden, worse than our children are. It's so good to see you, Gloria. Are you on your way to the cantina?"

Gloria's frown turned into a smile. "I am also happy that you are returning safely to our fold. The Mistress sent me to check on your progress. Which one of these is our king?"

Elyria nodded in Derek's direction.

Gloria admired Derek's stature and build. "I've never seen a man like this. The Mistress is eager, and she longs for him. How many days should I tell her you will be?"

"The man and the woman with him could travel more quickly without these others. Inform the Mistress that we should arrive during late afternoon of the third day."

342

"What do you mean, the woman with him?" Gloria queried.

Elyria blundered by letting this slip. The Mistress had ordered the killing of Sharon.

"Blaze failed, and I needed to keep her alive for reasons that I will explain to the Mistress," Elyria said, putting her off.

"So be it," acknowledged Gloria. "Travel safely, and we will expect you in three days."

The two women embraced again, and Gloria quickly slipped away.

"Wait," shrieked Anne. "Where is she going? Why didn't you introduce us?"

"Her name is Gloria, and you will all have a chance to meet her later. She goes to prepare Casa Cobo for our arrival."

"Why didn't she just travel with us?" Anne followed up. "Will she be okay out there by herself?"

Elyria didn't respond to what she felt was Anne's stupidity.

"What's up?" Derek queried Elyria, seeking a deeper explanation.

"Gloria is a scout," Elyria answered him. "I suspect that our arrival will be met with a great fanfare. Mistress Sara is very anxious to finally meet with you."

Progress during the second day was more difficult. The dense growth was not nearly as thick, thanks to Gloria having already trod through, but the sloping terrain impeded them.

When the group decided to make camp that night, Sharon wiped the perspiration from her brow. "This is a workout, Elyria. No wonder you are in such great shape."

Yeah, and how much of your vitality comes from sleeping with Derek, Elyria felt like responding. Before she could do so, a wave of pain passed through her insides. "Hank," she moaned, falling to her knees.

"I got her, I got her," Hank stammered rushing over.

"It comes earlier now, Hank," Elyria cried more from fear than from the pain. "Soon I'm going to need more than one pill a day."

"Here," he urged Elyria, pressing one of the yellow capsules to her lips.

Anne shrugged with disgust. "I can't stand this, Juan. Isn't there anything we can do?"

"Not right now," he replied. "We'll just make sure that Kimball doesn't keep them from her."

A tropical rainstorm threatened, so each couple erected a makeshift tent from plastic tarps to keep from getting drenched. After they all retired, Elyria listened as the water tapped against the tarp. She rested with her head on Hank's chest not meaning anything by doing so. This was much to Hank's enjoyment. He wasn't aware that she was just using him as a comfortable pillow. Elyria tried working through the different scenarios in her mind. *I could wait until Sharon gets up in the night to relieve herself. Then I could kill her. If I returned to Derek to take her place, would he notice? It's dark and he wouldn't be able to see me. I could straddle him and make him think I was Sharon. After he comes inside me, I would be free from Kimball's poison and could run away. Then I could kill them all one-by-one from a distance while they made their way to Casa Cobo. All, that is, except for Derek Dunbar. What a triumphant return to the Mistress that would be!*

Doubts crept in. *If he reached up to enjoy fondling my breasts, Derek would notice, since mine are smaller than Sharon's. What if he wanted to play with my hair? Hers is long and wavy, while mine is shorter and kinked. My body scent is different, too. If I failed, and if he discovered what I have done to Sharon, he would kill me instantly.*

Dejected, Elyria concluded that this would not work. Hank began to stir in his sleep and acted as if he was getting ready to roll over. *I'm not ready to lose my pillow yet,* Elyria considered while reaching into his shorts. She stroked him. It worked. Hank Kimball lost all interest in rolling over.

The Mistress taught us well how to get exactly what we want from a man, she told herself while thinking about how easy it was to manipulate Hank. *Why am I having such difficulty getting what I need from Derek?*

There was one other way. *Why kill her? I can detain Sharon and keep her alive. That way if I am discovered, he will not kill me. Yes, he will be angry for a while. All of them would, but after meeting the Mistress, they will forget all about it. This is worth a try.*

Damn it, Sharon bitched to herself. *Why doesn't this rain stop? I can't hold in this pee any longer.*

"Derek," she whispered into his ear. "I'll be right back."

"You'll get soaked," he told her while half asleep.

She kissed him. "You told me that I'm sexy when I'm all wet," she reminded him of a time in their past.

She's right, he thought. It had been two days since they were intimate due to the close quarters with the rest of their companions.

"Sharon," he whispered. "They aren't going to be able to hear us over this noisy rain. Don't be long. I'll be waiting for you."

Derek quickly fell back to sleep. His eyes opened during a pleasant sensation. She had taken him into her mouth and was masterfully massaging him with her tongue. Derek closed his eyes and let the waves of pleasure float through him while he grew rock hard.

Reaching down to touch her, Derek felt a hand firmly grab onto his. Derek's other hand reached down and was met with the same result. "Bondage, eh," he whispered. "Okay, I can dig it."

She lithely pulled herself up and slammed her knees down next to Derek's side, all the while maintaining a firm grasp on his hands.

"Easy does it," Derek gasped, wishing that she wouldn't have stopped what she started. In an instant, he felt himself plunging inside of her body. The slamming waves created by the up and down motion intoxicated him. He wanted to caress her breasts and tried to break away from the vice-like grips on his hands. Feeling the fight, she distracted Derek by pulling his right hand to her lips. She sucked on his fingers, moving her tongue in a darting fashion around each digit. Pushing the other hand to his mouth, Derek picked up on the cue and allowed her to insert her thumb into his mouth. Derek was going out of his mind in the bliss of this new game. Groaning, he thought to himself that he wouldn't be able to last much longer.

It's working, it's working, Elyria struggled to keep from moaning. She didn't dare utter a sound. Elyria lost all consciousness of the battering rain as it bounced on the tarp and danced off onto the ground all around her. At that moment, she remained aware only of her own pelvis as it tightened around Derek's virile shaft. The rush of her orgasm almost caused Elyria to lose control and cry out. A second wave passed over her after she felt Derek's consistency begin to change as a man always does before erupting. The third wave caused Elyria to fall onto his chest after she felt Derek's hot liquid explode into her.

Unable to contain herself, Elyria finally let loose with a squeal, "Heal me, Derek Dunbar. Absorb the poison from within me."

Derek considered the possibility that something wasn't right, but he was still self absorbed and needed a few moments to regain his mind. *Sharon isn't this heavy,* he thought feeling the full weight of Elyria on his chest. Derek felt her face and raked his fingers through her hair. At that moment, he understood what happened.

During the next few seconds, a flood of emotions swept over Derek. First came surprise, *What just happened?* Then a perverse pleasure, *Whoa, how about this!* Then admiration for Elyria's prowess, *Wow, how did she manage to deceive me?* Then fear, *Where's Sharon? She's going to discover us.* Then horror, *Where's Sharon? What did Elyria do to her?* Then guilt, "Sharon," Derek screamed.

Still inside of Elyria, Derek felt himself collapse. He roughly pushed Elyria off him and onto her back. Her voice uttered a squeak as Elyria's lungs slamming against the hard ground forced air passed her larynx.

Yanking her out from under the protective tarp, the two of them stood naked exposed to the pelting rain. Since he couldn't see Elyria, Derek kept a grip on her forearm.

"Where is Sharon?" he demanded, voice cracking.

"She is unharmed, I'll take you to her."

Derek felt relieved, but he didn't fully believe her. "Take me to her, NOW," he threatened.

With a free hand, Elyria reached around and grabbed Derek's butt. "You want her to see us like this?"

"I have no secrets from Sharon," he snorted. "Let's go."

Trying to pull away, Derek tightened his grip on her forearm. "You're hurting me, Derek."

"Move it," he snarled and kicked her in the leg with his knee.

A few meters away from the main camp, Derek began to hear Sharon's muffled cries. Letting go of Elyria, he ran to the sounds and found her thrashing on the ground. Elyria had tied her wrists and ankles together behind her back as if she was a roped steer. She stuffed leaves into Sharon's mouth and tied a vine around her face.

"Sharon, it's me, Derek," he reassured her. Feeling in the dark, Derek was able to free the vine from her face. Sharon spat the leaves from her mouth while Derek loosened her arms and legs.

"Oh, Derek, thank God," she sobbed. "Someone grabbed me from behind, I didn't have a chance."

"I know," he comforted her. "Come back with me to the tent, I'll tell you all about it."

"Was it one of those strange women, like that Gloria we met today?"

"No," Derek said, "but you aren't going to be happy with what I have to tell you."

Sharon was understandably cold after Derek confessed. "Let me get this straight, Elyria raped you?"

"Well, yes, you could say that," Derek offered.

"You expect me to believe that?"

"It's the truth, Sharon. She ambushed you, didn't she? It's plausible for you to grasp how the rest of it happened, isn't it?" he pleaded with her.

"Where is she now?" Sharon snarled, reaching around for her dagger.

"I don't know, probably back with Kimball."

Derek heard her rooting around in the dark for the dagger.

"What are you doing, Sharon?"

"The right thing," she blurted with a determination that Derek seldom heard from her.

Derek rolled on top of Sharon pinning her to the ground.

"You can't take her, Sharon. She'll kill you."

"Not the way I feel right now," Sharon complained, struggling to get free from him.

"Especially the way you feel right now," he echoed, trying to reason with her.

"Then you do it, Derek. By God, this woman has caused enough pain and suffering. She deserves to die."

"Maybe so, but not now. She has a bigger part to play in this yet."

Sharon struggled more fiercely against Derek's grip. He wasn't going to let her go. "I get it," she mocked him. "You liked it, didn't you? You want to keep her around for some more, don't you?"

"That's unfair, Sharon. I love only you."

Sharon stopped her struggling and began to cry. "Why do these bad things keep happening to us?" she sobbed.

He cried along with her. "A few more days, Sharon," Derek sniffled and laid his head on her chest.

In the morning, the rest of the party felt the tension between Elyria and Sharon. The two of them didn't speak to each other. Hank couldn't figure it out. When he asked Elyria about it, she kissed him on the lips and laughed. Juan and Anne decided to stay out of it. Derek became moody and stuck mostly by Sharon's side.

Elyria grieved that Derek didn't have the power she thought he possessed. She was sick and in pain before mid-afternoon. Hank fed Elyria the capsule and allowed her to sleep for a while. When they started walking again, Derek worked up the nerve to approach her. Sharon watched him. Her eyes were slits, filled with hate at the sight of them together.

"I told you that it doesn't work the same way with men. Why didn't you believe me?"

Elyria chuckled, "You also told me that I would like it."

"Sharon is the only thing left in my life worth living for. I love her. If you come between the two of us again, I will kill you. Even if it is directly in front of your Mistress, I will kill you."

She goaded him, "Hey, Derek, you were right. I liked it."

Derek walked away toward Sharon.

"And so did you," she added laughing.

The third day finally arrived. Scouts reported that the six travelers were one hour away from Casa Cobo.

"I'm begging you, Mistress Sara," Gloria entreated her. "Don't do this. They could easily kill you before we had a chance to stop them."

With her fingers, Sara wiped a tear running down Gloria's face and smiled. "Genuine concern. Such a precious thing. No greater gift can a person receive from another. I'm so grateful, Gloria. Thank you."

"Don't philosophize with me," Gloria pleaded.

Sara placed a hand on each side of Gloria's face. "Look at me," she asked. "You don't have to worry about me," Sara began. "Remember the things that I taught you about men? They have a need to feel superior, even if they are not. If we demonstrate to them that we are helpless, they will let down their guard. That is when we ensnare them."

"What of the women that are in their company?" Gloria asked, maintaining a panicked tone.

"Elyria is one of them," Sara reminded her. "She will watch out for me."

The tributary of the Iriri that ran near Casa Cobo was situated in a flat area. The tribe kept a thirty-meter square plot for a garden cleared of vines. The plan was for Sara to meet the visitors in this spot, alone. Her soldiers and the rest of the villagers were under orders to stay out of sight back in their villages. Sara stressed that they were to appear humble and non-threatening while in contact with the travelers.

Her heart was beating with an excitement that Sara hadn't felt since being with Leon. "So long ago," she sighed to herself while spreading a blanket on the ground. Sara set a reed basket on the edge of the blanket. It contained fruit and wine that she planned to share. Sara untied her hair that had been carefully prepared and let it hang down around her shoulders. She wore a red-dyed long shirt. The hem of it was well above her knee, and she was in bare feet. Sara plopped down in the middle of the blanket. Sitting sideways on legs bent at the knee, she leaned back supporting herself on the basket. Sara spread her legs just slightly in a suggestive posture. She was feeling radiant and beautiful. Looking up into the bright blue sky, she took in a deep, invigorating breath and let the sun bathe her face.

"It's just over this rise," Elyria motioned to the exhausted group. "We are almost home."

Derek's heart began to race. He sensed that Sara was close. "Sharon," he called out instinctively. She raced over to him. "Stay by my side," he entreated her. Sharon pulled the dagger from her pack and slipped it around her waist, tucking the business end into her shorts.

Juan and Anne joined them. "You don't need to say anything, Derek," Anne answered before he could ask. "We're here for you."

Hank stood beside Elyria at the head of the group. He patted the 10 mil under his shirt to make sure that it was still there. "Lead on, Elyria," he suggested to her.

Standing at the top of the rise, at a distance, the six of them saw her. She was a red dot in the middle of a sea of green plants.

Elyria smiled. "Brilliant," she whispered to Hank. "Deceptively simple. The Mistress always knows exactly what to do."

"I know you've been keeping secrets from us, Derek," Juan noted. "You've been protecting Anne and me. If there's anything we need to know, I guess that now is the time."

Derek agreed with him. "Okay, listen up. You girls are going to be fine. Juan, don't try to understand this, just do as I say. Try not to stare at her. If you feel yourself weakening, think about Annie and how much she means to you."

"What kind of devil is she, Derek?" Anne wanted to know.

"She's no devil, Anne, she's just a flesh and blood woman with her own needs, wants, and desires. I suspect that Sara is very lonely. The danger lies in her desperation. You can pity her, but keep her at arm's length."

Elyria overheard Derek and laughed. "What do you know?" she teased. "Look at her, everyone. Behold our queen. Consider yourselves fortunate. There awaits a goddess, daughter of the sun."

"Just a flesh and blood woman," Derek corrected her.

Hank and Elyria started down the hill together. Derek took Sharon's hand and signaled to Juan and Anne.

"Let's go," he boomed. The four of them marched forward with eyes fixed on the red dot in the grass. The dot grew larger as they approached. It began to take shape, the form of a woman. They watched as Elyria and Hank reached their destination. Elyria bowed and embraced the red form while

Hank stood frozen in place like a tree stump.

Derek, Sharon, Juan, and Anne came to a stop directly in front of the blanket on which the siren was sitting — the enigma and the contradiction, the ancient and the feared, yet the delicate and the beautiful life form known to all of them as Sara.

CHAPTER 34

He's all that I expected, and more, Sara thought while feeling herself blush.

Derek spoke first. "Sara?"

She wore a warm smile and told him, "I'm not the demon that you expected."

"Really?" Derek countered. "Even the devil has the ability to transform himself into an angel of light."

"You quote the scriptures," she said somewhat taken aback. "After such an odyssey, I was hoping you might try and impress me with a more appropriate greeting."

"Like what for example?" Derek asked, playing along.

Sara giggled in a girlish manner and kicked at the ground with her foot. "Oh, maybe something like, 'this is at last bone of my bones and flesh of my flesh.'"

"I'm afraid that distinction belongs to someone else," Derek said squeezing Sharon's hand, "or am I trying to convince myself?" he second-guessed.

Sharon couldn't believe it. "This is the source of the hell we've all been through? She's just a girl."

"Geez, Sharon, I beg to differ," Hank argued. "This is the most stunning woman I've ever laid eyes on."

Anne felt Juan convulse. He was weeping.

"Juan?" Anne asked with concern.

Ignoring Anne, he fell to his knees in front of Sara. "Bianca, by what magic have you returned to me?"

"Juan, she's not your dead wife," Anne said trying to comfort him.

Still seated, Sara asked Derek, "Didn't you tell them about me?"

"I, I had no idea you would affect us so profoundly," he admitted. Every nerve ending in Derek's body was on fire. Sharon felt him tremble.

Anne shot Sharon a puzzled look. "Why are these guys carrying on so?"

"What is your name?" Sara asked her.

"I'm Annie, this is Sharon. You already know Derek. My friend here is Juan and that guy over there is Hank."

Sara held out her hand. "Annie, let me fix this with Juan. I will not hurt him, honest."

Something about the woman convinced Anne that she meant no harm. She laid Juan's hand on Sara's.

"Juan, look at me."

"Bianca?" he stammered.

"Bianca loved you, Juan."

"She loved me," he repeated.

"She's dead now."

"No, you are here," he insisted.

"You see what your heart tells you to see. Bianca sleeps."

"She's okay?" he blubbered.

"She's in a better place, Juan. She is at peace and wants you to be at peace. Bianca is happy that Annie will be taking care of you now."

"Annie?" he repeated.

"Annie loves you now."

"I love you," Juan droned while staring at Sara.

"You love Annie," she corrected him.

"Yes, Annie," he finally admitted.

"Be at peace, Juan," she said and released his hand.

Juan instantly felt better. He hugged Anne and told her, "I love you, Annie. You know, I've been experiencing a lot of guilt that by being with you I am betraying Bianca. Don't worry about that anymore. She's at peace, and I know that she would want me to be happy."

"Is he yours?" Sara pointed at Hank while directing her question at Elyria.

"I suppose so, Mistress Sara," Elyria answered. "He is the only one of us that carries a weapon."

Sara gazed at Hank, "You're safe here, Hank. There's no need to carry a weapon. Would you give it to Elyria for me?"

He handed over the 10 mil without blinking an eye.

"Thank you, Hank. You'll be staying with Elyria. You will not mind that, will you?"

Responding like a robot, he shook his head from side to side.

"Mistress Sara, he has something else that I need."

"Is that right, Hank? Is there something else that you need to give to Elyria? She's so fond of you. You wouldn't want to hold anything back from her, would you?"

He handed over the vial of pills.

"Damn!" Anne said with amusement. "You've got to teach me how to do that."

Finally, Sara turned her attention to Sharon. "Don't worry about Derek. I'm in need of his services. That's why I brought so much pressure to bear on the two of you. For that I am truly sorry."

"Your people tried to kill me," Sharon complained.

"That would have caused me great distress," Sara lied, glaring at Elyria.

Sharon removed the dagger from her waistband and showed it to Sara. "This is what the murderer tried to use on me. Recognize it?"

Sara was genuinely surprised, "Why yes, that's mine. I didn't even realize it was missing."

"You should keep a closer guard on your things," Sharon reprimanded her.

"I promise you that I will from now on. May I have it back?"

Sharon hesitated. "If you don't mind, I'd like to keep it while I'm here. I'll return it to you on the day we leave."

"Fair enough," Sara smiled at her. "That dagger has been my talisman and companion for many years. If it makes you feel more secure, by all means I trust it to your care."

"Instead of trying to cause us harm, why didn't you just come to us?" Sharon demanded, returning the dagger to her waistband.

"That would not have been possible," Sara explained. "It's too dangerous for me to travel away from here."

"You're afraid," Sharon concluded.

This one has spunk, Sara thought. Lowering her head to Sharon as a further act of feigned submissiveness, she concurred. "As you guessed, Sharon. I am afraid."

"What now?" Sharon asked, wanting to get to the point of all of this.

Sara opened the basket and removed the wine and fruit. "You must be hungry after such a long journey. Please sit and have a bite to eat with me."

The three men and Anne didn't need to be asked twice. Sharon remained reluctant.

Pointing to Elyria, Sharon hedged, "This one tells stories about your drugging of men."

Sara stopped briefly in mid-pour. Sharon thought she detected a slight change in Sara's expression that had been so sweet and innocent until now.

"It's true," Sara admitted. "Please don't judge me, Sharon, until we've had a chance to talk about it. Don't be afraid, either. You are guests of honor and will eat and drink what I eat and drink." She took a sip out of the goblet and passed it to Sharon.

Derek felt a tingle like electricity running along his spine. He closed his eyes. "Sara, do you have the ability to turn it off?"

She understood what he was talking about. "I feel it too, Derek. It helps if you don't fight it. It's the reason why you are here."

"What's up with you two?" Sharon wanted to know. She didn't like this.

She's going to be a real obstacle, Sara considered. Wanting to evade Sharon's question, she obfuscated. "After we've had our picnic, we will go to Casa Cobo. Lodging has been prepared where all of you can rest. The journey has been a long one. Sharon, I really want you to like me, but I also respect that you want to reserve judgment. Tomorrow, after all of us are fresh, I will reveal my purposes to you."

Anne still couldn't believe that this talented girl was the source of so much grief. "Sara," she called getting her attention. "You obviously command a lot of respect from your people and at such a tender age. How did you get here?"

Sara giggled. "That's a long, long story. I'd like to tell it to you at some other time."

"I'd really like to hear it," Anne responded. Unlike Sharon, Anne felt right at home with Sara.

Three separate huts were prepared for the visitors near the center of Sara's compound. The overhead jungle canopy kept the entire area tolerably cool. Pointing to her large adobe estate, Sara beckoned, "Welcome to Casa Cobo, my village, my people, and my home. Tomorrow I'll give you the grand tour, but now I leave you to rest."

Hank walked into the hut pointed out for him and Elyria. "Mistress, I have my home to go to," Elyria reminded her. "I have a designee waiting for me there, and I miss him."

"Let's talk about this, Elyria," she said and put an arm around her. The other four gladly left Elyria with Sara and ducked into the huts assigned to them.

Out of an earshot, Sara scolded her, "It would have been easier for me if you would have killed this Sharon as I ordered."

"I knew you would be disappointed, Mistress Sara, but there was no other way. It was very difficult."

"Don't worry. I forgive you," Sara interrupted her. "I trust your judgment in this matter. The important thing is that you brought Derek to me."

Elyria was relieved, "Thank you, Mistress Sara. That eases my mind."

"Now what about my dagger? How did it come to be in Sharon's possession?"

"Honestly, I don't know. I assumed it belonged to Blaze. Sharon took it from him the night he was killed."

Sara thought back to the last time that Blaze and her were together. "He must have stolen it from me," she concluded.

"That explains why he so revered that thing," Elyria recalled.

Sara noticed that Elyria appeared melancholy. "Are you not happy to be home?"

"Mistress Sara, I have a very big problem," Elyria confessed and told the entire story about Hank Kimball and the poison within her.

Sara was pained at this news and tenderly hugged Elyria. "Soon such things will no longer happen," Sara groaned. "Do you now understand the importance of our quest?"

Elyria nodded. "I am afraid."

"I understand," Sara pitied her, "but you cannot return."

"I know."

"What can I do for you, Elyria, in the time that you have left?"

"Make Derek Dunbar my designee."

"This I cannot do. Ask me anything else."

"Why?" Elyria protested. "I will be dead in a few weeks. You will have him for eternity afterwards."

"No," Sara insisted. "I've already waited an eternity. You cannot have him. Be happy with this Hank Kimball and your other designee."

"As you wish," Elyria bowed. She knew that any further argument was pointless. When she turned to walk away, Sara called out to her. "Elyria, believe me when I tell you that I am sorry. You've been a loyal soldier and friend."

Elyria didn't want to give Sara the satisfaction of seeing her cry. After entering her hut, she could no longer contain herself. Elyria fell into Hank's arms.

"What's wrong, Elyria? Are you in pain? You have the pills now. Take one if you need it."

"I'm going to die, Hank," she choked. "We aren't going back."

"You're not going to die, Elyria," Hank reassured her, "and we are going back."

In the neighboring hut, Juan was swinging Anne through the air. "I feel so alive!" he exclaimed.

"She healed you, Juan," Anne confirmed. "I'm sure this is all some big misunderstanding. She's just a girl, not some evil witch."

Next door to them, Sharon confided in Derek, "I don't trust her."

"You are so right not to," Derek agreed. "I'm susceptible to her charm, Sharon. Watch out for me."

"What are we going to do?" she asked him.

Derek shrugged, "We see how it all plays out. Somewhere along the way I need to try and save Sara from herself."

Gloria met up with her Mistress as Sara returned to the estate. "Will you let me accompany you tomorrow while you are with them?" she inquired.

"Yes," Sara gave in. "Tomorrow it happens!"

Early the next morning, just before sunrise, Sara awoke. She bathed and asked Gloria to help in brushing her hair.

"Why do you make such a fuss, Mistress Sara?" Gloria asked between strokes. "These men would fall at your feet even if you were covered with mud."

"I need to look my best for Derek, Gloria. He is less vulnerable than other men are, but even he will be tamed by the end of the day. I also need to keep up a fitting appearance for the sake of his lady friends. The one called Anne is no problem. She has a need to be a mother figure for her man. Do you notice how she always tries to take care of everyone?"

Sara continued as Gloria brushed. "Derek's woman, Sharon, is a problem. As long as she is around, Derek uses her as a crutch in order to stay emotionally distant from me."

"I can kill her for you," Gloria offered.

"No, no, it is too late for that now," Sara impressed on her. "I need to convince Derek to make love with me, not to hate me. After that, he will no longer think about Sharon. In time, she will meet with an unfortunate accident."

"And the other couple?" Gloria pressed.

"Anne will be assimilated into our society. I need only to convince her to help me to be a caregiver or a teacher for our children. Juan's mind is easily influenced. He is a follower. Once Derek is won over, he will do whatever Derek and I ask of him."

"That leaves us with Elyria's designee, the one they call Hank. What about him?"

Sara sighed. "Poor Elyria will soon be dead from the poison that the savages planted inside her. After that, we will kill the man. I don't like him."

The six travelers ate breakfast with Sara and Gloria. It was a delicious mix of bananas and berries in cream.

"Yummy," acknowledged Anne. "Where do you get your food?"

"Gardens and groves are mixed in among the villages," Sara explained. "You will also see cattle, sheep, and goats. Our grain fields are scattered and small. The one where you first found me yesterday is a good example. Of course, there is an abundance of fish."

"Do your men hunt game for their families?" Hank Kimball probed.

Elyria and Gloria looked at each other and snickered.

"No, Hank," Sara responded. "In our society only women hunt and serve as soldiers. Men perform the domestic duties like harvesting and housekeeping."

"How do you keep them interested in staying that way?" Hank followed up.

With no change in expression, Sara told him in a matter-of-fact manner, "We keep them drugged. After our male children reach puberty we begin to administer cobo to them."

"Do they agree to that?" Anne asked in shock.

"It is our way," Sara informed them. "It has always been this way in our society, and it is all that our men know. Boys look forward to their first time with cobo. It is a rite of passage for them."

"Well, I suppose if it is ingrained in your culture," Anne gave in. "How docile does it make them?"

Sara smiled and took Anne's hand. "Come with me, and I will show you."

She led the party through a maze within the canopy. After a fifteen-minute walk, they entered a cleared out area where three-dozen huts were arranged in a small village. The place was alive with men preparing to go to work. They assembled into groups of six with one female among each group.

"Are those ladies among the men their bosses?" Sharon guessed.

Elyria piped in before Sara could answer. "You really think they could manage on their own?"

"They don't look all that lethargic," Juan observed.

"When administered properly, cobo doesn't work that way," Sara pointed out. "It just opens their minds to the power of suggestion. Physically, they are as vibrant as you are, Juan."

"They're slaves," Sharon noted.

"Not so," Sara insisted. "We love them, and they love us. We form families just like in your society. Each woman and her designee care deeply for each other and their children."

"In a civilized world, we don't denigrate our men by labeling them 'designees.' They are our husbands."

"It's just a word," Sara said, looking hurt. She flashed Derek an expression that begged him to help her.

Derek cleared his throat. "Why don't we talk to one of them, Sharon?" he suggested.

Juan grabbed the arm of one of the men walking by. The man stopped, offering no resistance. "What is your name?" he asked the man in Portuguese.

"They know only the tribal language," Elyria instructed Juan. "Only girls that are candidates for Shadow Woman status are taught Portuguese."

"How convenient," Sharon mocked.

Anne thought this was interesting. "Why is that?" she asked.

"Only women leave this place. Only women can be trusted to do the bidding of the Mistress out in the world," Elyria explained further.

"Allow me to translate," Gloria offered. "The man says his name is Ekon and that he is very happy serving the Mistress."

"Obviously!" Sharon shot back with disdain.

Derek whispered to her, "Come on, Sharon, let's not jump to any conclusions."

"No, that's quite all right," Sara jumped in. "All of us here find your world strange and difficult to understand. Our customs would likewise seem unusual to outsiders. It will take some time for you to absorb our ways."

Sara led them beyond the village to where the land began to rise in a gentle slope. They watched for some time as a squad of athletic young women practiced their archery skills.

"Shadow Women?" Juan asked.

"Some of them may eventually attain that status," Sara informed him. "These are my soldiers."

Sara led them further up the slope to a particularly dense section of the canopy. "There is something here that I want you to see," she pointed out.

Hank was the first to see the sight. "Geez, those vines are beautiful," he observed. "Each one has different colored flowers on those hairy tendrils," Hank continued to marvel.

Sara pointed and moved her arm in an arc in the direction of the plants.

"The cobo vine," she said with authority. "Indigenous only to this region of the world as far as I know."

"Lovely," Anne squeaked. "Can we touch them?"

"Sure. The plant is harmless to touch. The active ingredient is in the petals. We harvest the flowers and dry them. The sun bleaches the petals and starts a chemical reaction. We grind these processed petals into a white powder."

"How did the plant come to be named cobo?" Anne quizzed her. "Is that the Latin name for the plant?"

Sara paused and reflected. "Nobody has ever asked me that before. It is Portuguese, short for 'colores bonitos.'"

Juan whispered the English translation into Anne's ear.

"That's fitting," Anne agreed.

"There are well over a hundred villages in our network," Sara changed the subject. "We are mostly agrarian, but the most physically strong of our girls are trained as Shadow Women. They defend our society and venture into your world."

"To what purpose?" Hank appeared interested.

"I send them on various missions, Hank. They are trained to speak your language and to learn about your cultures. This keeps our entire society educated as to what your world is doing."

"What was Elyria's mission?" Hank asked her.

"To bring Derek to me."

"What do you need Derek for?"

"That's between Derek and I. Don't get ahead of me, Hank. It will all be made clear to you in time."

"I'm concerned about Elyria, aren't you? Time is her enemy."

"You will have most of your answers before this day is over," Sara assured him.

"What about the girls that don't make the cut as Shadow Women or common soldiers?" Derek queried.

"They serve in other ways, Derek. Elyria told me that you met Teresa, our cantina manager. Others are teachers, weavers, and most are busy raising their children."

"Sara, I asked you a question yesterday," Anne remembered. "Please don't get cross with me for repeating this, but how did you come to be the leader of this place?"

"Mistress Sara is our queen," Elyria reminded her.

Sara smiled warmly at Anne. "I'm not upset at your questions, Anne. The fact is I am different from these people. Different from all of you, except Derek."

"You mean that power of suggestion thing that you showed us with Juan and Hank?"

"Yes, that and much more. Now is not the time to speak of such things. When you and I get to know each other better, I would be honored to share some of my secrets with you."

Anne smiled. "I'd really like that."

"Then maybe you can tell me what this is all about," Juan quipped at Anne. "I'm still clueless."

The group returned to the main village where Sara showed them through the adobe structure beneath her domicile.

"It's mainly a storage area for processed cobo," she told them. "Some of these rooms are food stores, and some we use for meetings. I'd show you my quarters, but they are really quite simple, almost exactly like the huts you are using."

Hank noticed a door at the end of the structure that was guarded by an especially fierce-looking Shadow Woman. "What's that?" he asked.

"I'm glad you asked that, Hank. All of you are my guests and can wander about freely. The only thing I ask is that you do not try and enter that room."

Sara changed her voice to a more serious tone. "All of you please understand. This is my only restriction. I will be very angry at anybody that attempts to get in there."

Smiling, she turned on her charm again and continued. "Later on we will have a fine evening meal in celebration of our meeting. It will be a grand party. I have some business that needs tending. In the meantime, visit with our people."

Sara turned her attention to Anne and Juan. "The two of you might like to visit one of our village schools. The children would love to hear about your world, Anne. I will send Gloria with you as a guide and to translate."

"Let's do it," Anne pleaded with Juan. Gloria herded them off.

"Elyria, show Hank how we process the cobo. He seems really fascinated with the subject," Sara suggested. Elyria understood it to be an order.

"As you wish, Mistress," she bowed and led Hank away.

Sara turned to face Sharon. "I don't suppose you would allow Derek and me to pair off for a few hours."

"You got that right," Sharon groused and grabbed the waist of Derek's shorts.

"The quicker he and I have our conversation, the sooner we can get on with our agenda."

"Your agenda?" Sharon snorted.

Sara turned to Derek.

"We need to talk, don't we?"

"We need to talk," Derek parroted.

"We have important things to discuss, alone, right?"

"We need to be alone."

Sharon jumped in. "Don't rattle off your hocus pocus at him. The rest of them aren't aware, but I know what the two of you are. You want to feed off Derek like some kind of parasite. You'll have to kill me before I allow you to seduce him."

"Look, Sharon. You've been up front with me. I like a woman that is strong willed and direct. In return, since you know what we are, I'm going to drop my pretense and be brutally honest with you. I need to talk with Derek about things that only he and I understand. Talk first, and only talk. Yes, Sharon, later on we are going to make love. There is no way that you are going to be able to stop that. You can accept it, or you can make yourself miserable."

"You hearing this, Derek?" Sharon prompted him. "Straight from the mouth of your innocent, wide-eyed girl."

Derek stopped them before it escalated. "Stop it, both of you. Sara, excuse us. Sharon and I are going to return to our hut for now. She and I need to talk about this. I will call on you later." Taking Sharon's hand, he moved quickly in the direction of their hut. Sharon glared at Sara as they walked away.

CHAPTER 35

"No way," Sharon protested vehemently. "You're charmed and can't see through it, Derek. I know what she has planned."

"So do I, Sharon, but it will not get that far."

Sharon worked herself between Derek and the doorway leading out of the hut. "Think it through," she prodded him, her voice was quaking. "The psychic pheromone stuff that Werner told us about is real. I've seen it work for myself with you and Juan and Hank. She's a bitch in heat, Derek. My god, your heart rate doubles now just talking about her. If that woman is laid out naked on her bed waiting for you, how many seconds would it take until you are in her arms?"

Derek felt himself grow annoyed. "Come on, Sharon, give me some credit. I'm walking into this with eyes wide open. I know what her intentions are, Sara will not be able to fool me."

"Elyria fooled you easily enough," Sharon slammed it back at him.

"That was different," he snorted. "You know that I couldn't see her."

"And you are even more blinded in Sara's presence," she shouted.

Running his fingers through his hair, Derek turned his back on her. He walked to the back of the hut and sat on the dirt floor. Derek buried his head in his hands in resignation. After waiting a few moments for the air to clear, he changed his approach.

"Sharon, why are we here?"

"To convince a mad woman to leave us alone."

"Why does she want me?"

"You know why, Derek. She needs you to rejuvenate or some sort of bullshit like that."

Derek sought common ground with Sharon. "You're right. I fully agree with you. I heard her admit that."

"That's why I'm not leaving you alone with her."

"If that's all she wants, Sharon, and if I am incapable of resisting her as you say," Derek stopped here, removed his face from his hands, and looked at her. "Then why didn't she just have you killed the moment we arrived?"

Sharon pondered his question and found that she didn't have a logical answer. "I can't say. My death was important to Sara when I was back in Baltimore. For some reason it is different now."

"What's different is that Sara knows that if anything happens to you, I would snap her neck. You see, Sharon, her power does have limits." Derek hugged Sharon and kissed her. "Sex with me is only part of the picture. She is going to reveal all of her schemes, and that is what I need to find out."

Sharon realized that she was going to lose this battle, but it wasn't going to happen without a warning to him. "Derek, tell her that if she succeeds in seducing you, I'm going to hold her responsible and not you. I'll kill her, Derek, I swear it." Unconsciously, Sharon found the dagger with her right hand and held on to it.

Derek could see in her eyes that Sharon meant it. He kissed her again. "You're a different person now, stronger and determined. A fire has grown within you. I like this new Sharon," he told her.

Derek crossed out of the doorway of the hut and into the sunlight dappled by the tropical canopy. "Don't even try to hide it from me, Derek," Sharon yelled after him. "I'll know, you hear me? I'll know."

Hank Kimball learned all that he needed concerning cobo. *Small time*, he convinced himself. *One more meeting with Sara to tell her to shut it down, or else.* Looking over at Elyria, he was disgusted with himself about having to put her through so much pain. *One final thing to find out about, just to make sure*, he told himself, *and then we're out of here, back to Germany and the antidote that will free her.*

"Enough, Elyria," he told her. "I don't need you to show me anything else about cobo. Tell me about the guarded door."

"Do you want to die, Hank?"

"Do you want to live?" he reminded her. "I've been sent here to assess how big a threat your Mistress could be. Now, what's behind the door?"

"Believe me, Hank, there is nothing of consequence in there. It is something important to Sara and represents no threat to your country."

Elyria started to feel the beginning of some pain. It was happening now with increasing frequency. "Hank, let's return to the hut. I'm tired."

Even without my gun, this can't be difficult, Hank thought. He waited until Elyria slept and stole away from the hut. *There are plenty of places to hide. Geez, I'll just wait until the guard is distracted. There's only one woman.*

One quick peek to satisfy my curiosity. No one will be the wiser.

During the heat of the afternoon, there was little activity. The few villagers that noticed Hank's passing nodded and smiled at him, as ordered by the Mistress. He passed unmolested to the base of Casa Cobo and peeked around the corner at the forbidden door. Much to Hank's surprise, nobody was there.

He tried the door. It opened. Carefully entering the room, he shut the door behind him.

This was Gem's first day back on duty since her return from Manaus, and it was her turn to guard the forbidden room. Ordinarily the room was unguarded, but these special precautions were set up to discourage the visitors. It was no big deal that Gem left her guard post for a few minutes to get a drink of water. It was hot. There was no chance that anyone would dare bother this place. The Mistress told her that the guests were all preoccupied elsewhere, yet here Gem discovered shoe prints outside of the door.

With great stealth, Gem gently unlatched the door and entered.

Hank was glad that torches lined the wall. He found that it actually wasn't a room at all, but a corridor that led underground. It sloped down under the roots of the great trees above for a distance of about 50 meters before opening into a cavern.

His mind had trouble absorbing what he saw piled up in front of him. *Can this be what I think it is?* he wondered. Hands on his hips, Hank studied the pile.

Gem sneaked down and found Hank standing in that position. *This is not the one the Mistress desires,* she thought, knowing that it wasn't Derek.

Hank never heard Gem approach from behind. Instead, he was preoccupied in pondering the meaning of his discovery. *I've been burping those bananas all morning,* Hank thought as he coughed. The phlegm tasted strangely salty, and he wiped his mouth with his arm. *What's this?* he thought. *Blood?*

The pain finally caught up to him. Hank fell to his knees and felt the arrow that protruded out the front of his chest. Falling the rest of the way to the ground, he glanced up at Gem standing over him.

"Geez," was his last word.

Although Sharon feared it to be so, Sara wasn't naked. The white shirt hung loosely about her form ending at mid-thigh, similar to the red shirt worn the previous day. The two of them sat in Sara's inner chamber.

"It wasn't very tactful the way you spoke to Sharon," Derek told her starting the conversation.

Sara handed him a cup of wine provided by her attendant, Anna. "We were wasting time," she explained. "Besides, I didn't tell her anything that she didn't already know." Sara sipped at her cup.

"Okay," Derek countered and took a sip. "Let's not waste any more time. What is it that you want to tell me?"

Sara's eyes grew a bit larger. She gulped down the rest of the cup and refilled it before starting again. "The one that started the rebellion didn't believe that men were capable of governing themselves. He was right. How easy it was to play them. One simple indiscretion, and they were cast out of paradise."

Derek picked up on the conversation. "As I remember it, so was he, along with all of the others that gave up their station as spirit creatures."

"Our fathers have been misjudged," Sara tried.

"Misjudged!" Derek exclaimed. "Sara, who are we to sit in judgment of God's arrangement?"

"Don't give me that. Humans don't deserve to rule themselves. I escaped to this place of seclusion to avoid the suffering they cause one another. Derek, if you could feel the pain that I've lived through, if you would have witnessed the horror, it's always the same. Men seek power, and they kill."

Derek pitied her. "Granted my thirty-three years of experience pales in comparison to your long life, yet I've seen a lot of kindness in my time."

Sara scoffed, "How do those kind ones fare in life?"

"Mostly they do well," Derek reported to her, drawing on his own observations. "Anyway, they usually derive a great deal of satisfaction and fulfillment from their kindness."

"The cruel ones fare better, don't they?" Sara responded.

"Yes, in a material way and in the acquisition of power. That has generally been my experience," he admitted.

Sara stood and grew more animated. "You do understand. We can change that. We can set conditions so that the kind ones benefit."

Derek also stood and walked to one of the windows overlooking the village. Waving an arm toward the outside, he explained to Sara, "You miss the point. All of us, all of them out there, we have free will to choose good or evil."

"They always choose evil," Sara whined.

"Not always," Derek assured her. "You've alluded to the pain in your life. Wasn't that the result of your love for the very people that you now condemn?"

"Yes, I've been badly hurt many times," Sara confessed.

"What you are telling me is that there is much good within you, Sara."

"I could live comfortably for thousands more years anonymously, Derek. Maybe it's because I love them all that I want to change things for them."

"How?" Derek wondered.

Sara joined Derek by the window and took his hands. He shuddered as a result of feeling her intoxicating warmth.

"Don't be afraid," Sara breathed. "Look into my eyes and dream with me."

She's so pretty, he thought. *I can do this and still stay in control,* he deluded himself.

In his vision, Derek observed the Earth from outer space, a shining blue ball spinning silently against the blackness. Suddenly, a flash of light entered Derek's peripheral vision. He watched as it slammed into south Florida.

"An asteroid strike!" he shrieked.

"Shhh," he heard Sara's comforting voice. "It's a dream, Derek. Watch it unfold."

He watched as more of the lights rained down at regular intervals striking in various lands scattered around the globe.

"Where do they come from?" he asked.

"They come from the heavens, Derek."

"What are they?"

"Don't ask me what you already know. Watch it unfold."

The Earth grew closer to him, and Derek was swept down to the surface. He saw a woman standing at a podium giving a speech.

"You're good people, aren't you?" she spoke to the crowd.

"We're good people," they parroted back.

"You want to free yourselves from the evildoers, don't you?"

"We hate the corruption of the present administration," they all chanted back.

"You will vote for me, right?"

"We will vote for you."

Around the world, Derek was carried off to a Middle Eastern land. Fire and thick smoke rose from the center of a burning city. People were dancing in the streets. Derek noticed the fire emanating from a mountain of charred bodies. A woman waved a torch high above her head as she addressed the revelers. Although she spoke a foreign language, Derek understood the words.

"We're free now, aren't we?" the woman yelled.

"We're free, we're free," the crowd screeched.

"No more suffering, no more pain," she shouted.

"No more, no more," they cheered.

Once more Derek was transported. He recognized the place. It was Altamira, but not the run down, poor town that he experienced. It was a majestic city with large white marble buildings. Derek found himself standing in a magnificent assembly hall. It reminded him of the ornate Manaus opera house.

Derek looked out over a sea of people. They were cheering and applauding. Most of them were also crying with joy. It was then that he discovered that the people were applauding both him and Sara. She raised his hand into the air in a sign of victory. The throng cheered ever louder.

Sara is so lovely and radiant, he heard himself think. She whispered to him, "We did it, Derek. You and I did it."

"What have we done?" he heard himself ask.

"Look, Derek," she pointed to a mural behind them.

He saw his own and Sara's image painted on the larger than life canvas. The words at the bottom read, "Our saviors, King and Queen of Earth."

"No more suffering for them, Derek," she uttered. "No more pain."

A few seconds later, Derek felt the dream fade as Sara released him.

He swooned, and Sara helped him to sit. She handed him another cup of wine and sat beside him.

"How did you do that?" he asked in amazement.

"Oh, in a millennium or two your powers will sharpen, too," she giggled.

Is your will strong enough? he heard a voice inside of himself ask.

"It's suicidal," he uttered. "A roll in the sack is not worth eternal damnation. Are they mad? Why do they continue to do it?"

"The final purge is in progress," Sara informed him. "What you saw is the remnant of the rebellious ones being cast out. The 'roll in the sack' that you so eloquently spoke of is them reasoning to themselves, 'What the heck, we're already damned. Why not?'"

"How do you know all of this?" Derek groaned in alarm.

Sara spoke gently, "Derek, you and I are the children of Seraphs. We're the only ones — ever. We have greater powers than the children of the other angels. I know these things, because I can feel them. Open your mind, and you will also feel these wonders."

"You can reach out to all of the others?" he asked. Sara's designs were becoming clearer to him.

"I can control all of our fathers' children right from here," she revealed, "but I can't do it without you. I need you to support me with your infinite energy."

Derek became distressed. He stood and walked once again to the window. "This is wrong, Sara."

She joined him at the window. They both looked down over the village.

"Derek, when you and I join, I can tap into your great strength. It will give me the power. I can guide and direct all of the others. Together we can save humanity from themselves. It's not evil. Think of the greater good this will accomplish."

"Sara," was all he could utter at the moment. Derek shook his head. He felt Sara's hand slip into his. His spine began to tingle. He could feel Sara turning on her great power.

"Derek," she breathed into his ear.

He turned and faced her.

"Make love to me, Derek," she begged.

He filled his mind with Sharon's image.

"The saving of humanity is bigger than your thoughts of her," she gently chided him. Sara wrapped her arms around Derek and rested her head on his chest. Her energy enveloped him. "Doesn't it feel nice?" she asked.

"It feels so good, Sara."

"I'm so warm and moist, Derek. Come inside me."

From deep within, Derek summoned up his last measure of resistance.

"Sara, you are conflicted. I sense that in your heart you have a sincere desire to do good. It's what you've always wanted to do. Now you've allowed yourself to become twisted in your way of thinking. What you propose is in direct opposition to the way things have been designed. Redemption of humanity is based on individual choice. We must all choose. You can't take that away. Search your heart, Sara."

Derek felt Sara loosen her psychic grip on him. *I may be getting through to her,* he hoped.

"I can't live with any more pain, Derek," she sniffled. "I'm sorry. This is the only way."

Derek felt Sara's power once again envelop him. She placed both of her hands on the sides of his face. He saw that she was crying — begging him for help with her eyes, desperately yearning for Derek to show her another way, a release from her pain, the direction toward forgiveness.

"If I press my lips to yours, Derek, your resistance will vanish. I can make you do this, but I don't want to. Look at me, Derek, and make the

368

choice that is in your heart. Kiss me."

Derek sensed Sara's anguish. The centuries wore her down. She no longer had the will to resist carrying out her perverted plan, and he could no longer resist her. Derek had no answer for her and didn't know how to save her. He felt betrayed and abandoned by the angel of his dreams, the one that alluded that he had the strength to endure. He felt helpless and impotent. As Derek felt the gap between their lips close, he shut his eyes.

I'm finished, he concluded. *Forgive me, Sharon, in the end, my will was not strong enough.*

Juan and Anne dropped in on Sharon after their visit to the village school. "How long has Derek been gone?" Anne asked Sharon.

She thought about it and answered, "Too damn long. I'm going to get him." Sharon sprang from the hut.

"We'd better go with her," Juan urged.

"Wait up," Anne yelled.

All of them saw Elyria rubbing the sleep from her eyes as they adjusted to the afternoon sun. "Have any of you seen Hank?" she asked of no one in particular. From their blank stares, she assumed that none of them had.

At that moment, they heard a scream coming from Sara's quarters. In unison, all of them broke into a dead run toward the structure.

Anna screamed as she rushed into Sara's room. Derek and Sara felt the connection between them rip just as he was about to give in to her. Sara turned on Anna in a rage, but before she could say anything, Gem appeared, covered in blood.

"You!" Derek shouted as he recognized her.

She ignored Derek and spoke to Sara and Anna in a language that he couldn't understand. Sara turned pale and put a hand over her mouth.

"All of you better hope to God that this isn't about Sharon," Derek warned.

"No, not Sharon," Sara spouted and grabbed his hand. "Come with me."

The rest of the travelers caught up to Derek, Sara, and Gem as they found their way to the door of the secret room.

"Are you all right, Derek?" asked an anxious Sharon.

"I'm okay," he answered, "and I'm so relieved to see your face."

Sara tried to stop them from entering, but the visitors burst through the door and ran down the underground hallway.

"Gem and Elyria, come with me," Sara ordered. "The rest of you stay here."

Hank Kimball's body lay in a curled heap. Anne screamed.

Sharon stood numb. "So much blood," she observed while leaning on Derek.

Sara, Elyria, and Gem caught up to them. When Elyria saw the body, she fell on it and sobbed. "Hank, who is going to take me back? Who is going to save me now?" she wailed.

"What happened here?" Derek demanded an answer.

Sara was crying. "I'm so sorry, Derek, he had no business down here. Gem was just following orders."

"What's so damn important about this underground room?" Derek followed up.

"It's all I have, Derek," Sara answered him. "This is the only way I can send my Shadow Women into the world. It's how I finance them. We also used some of it to buy the cantina."

Elyria filled her mind with hate. Her only slim chance for life was now gone. The Mistress could grant her some comfort by allowing her to have Derek Dunbar. It was denied her. Nothing was left.

As Derek's eyes adjusted to the darkened room, he discovered what lay beyond Hank's body.

"It's gold, Derek," Juan sputtered. "A great pile of gold."

As Elyria looked up, she saw the hilt of Sharon's dagger exposed above the waistband of her shorts. *Maybe Derek has the power,* she thought in her desperation. *I just need him to make love to me a few times more.* Thinking about the Mistress, she knew that it would never happen.

Derek looked back at Sara. He didn't say anything, but his eyes asked the question.

She sighed. "One of our kind lived here a long time ago. He amassed a great fortune and hid it from the Spanish invaders. I followed the legends told among the native peoples. They led me here."

Derek and Juan started walking around to the backside of the pile to check it out.

"This is incredible," Juan gasped.

As they made their way toward the rear of the horde, Derek thought about Hank. "This isn't worth a man's life, Juan."

She denies me life, because she fears me, Elyria rationalized. *With Derek Dunbar, I could become the new Mistress.*

In a rage filled with despair, Elyria reached over and plucked the dagger from Sharon's waist.

Sharon reached around to stop her but caught only air as Elyria wheeled around and jumped at Sara. Gem was quick to react and deflected Elyria. The blade made an ugly gash in Gem's forearm. Anne immediately ran over to Gem after she screamed with pain.

Sharon jumped on Elyria's back. "Drop the dagger, you bitch," she snarled and punched at her.

Derek was horror-stricken. Screaming Sharon's name, he ran toward the struggle. Sara stood frozen with fear.

"Let me kill her, Sharon. It's what you want, isn't it?" Elyria barked.

Sharon persisted, but Elyria threw her off. When Sharon got back up to her feet, she found herself between Elyria and Sara.

Hearing that Derek was almost on top of her, Elyria knew that she had little time. "I'll kill you both," she snorted. "Then Derek sleeps only with me."

Elyria started her charge toward them.

Sara noticed the helpless fear in Derek's eyes as he realized that he wouldn't be able to stop Elyria in time. She recognized it as the same helpless fear that existed in her own eyes when Leon was killed in front of her. Sara flashed back to the terrible pain of that moment so long ago.

"No, I will not let it happen again," she screamed and rushed at Sharon. Sara pushed her away and felt the cold bite of the dagger as it plunged into her side.

It bought enough time for Derek to catch Elyria. Before she could strike again, Derek smashed his knee into her back. They tumbled down on top of Sharon.

The dagger slipped out of Elyria's hand. As she wrestled with Derek on the floor, Sharon reached out and grabbed it. Derek and Elyria rolled toward Sharon again.

Sharon cried out forcefully, "No more, you bitch," and buried the dagger up to the hilt in the middle of Elyria's back. She didn't feel guilt or remorse about this thing she did. In her mind, Sharon considered Elyria as a rabid dog. It was just something that had to be done.

Derek gingerly picked Sharon off the ground. "I'm okay," she indicated and then glanced over at Sara. Derek's eyes followed Sharon's.

Sara was slumping in a sitting position, holding her side. Blood seeped from between her fingers.

"Why?" Sharon appealed to her. "I was ready for Elyria. Why did you push me away?"

Sara's mouth moved, but no words would come. She motioned for Sharon to approach. With a weak voice, Sara told her, "He loves you. I couldn't take the chance."

"Everybody out," Derek roared. Sharon understood that this also meant her. Nobody dared protest. Anne helped Gem, while Juan walked back up the tube with Sharon.

Derek fell to his knees in front of her. "How do I help?" he sobbed.

Sara smiled, "I'm no longer afraid to die."

"Don't leave me," he begged.

Sara whimpered while trembling, "You're right, Derek. I've been allowed to live all these centuries so that you could help me to overcome my bitterness — to return me to the proper path. It wasn't meant for me to save all of humanity."

Derek banged his fists against his forehead. "You saved Sharon."

"And the two of you saved my soul," she whispered, barely able to get it out.

Sara choked, and her expression turned urgent.

"Derek?"

"I'm still here, Sara," he reassured her.

"Thank you for coming to me, for my rescue. Forgive me for the suffering I caused you — all of you," she breathed, her eyes now looking distant.

"Sara?" he yelled in frustration.

She mustered enough of her remaining strength to smile.

"Kiss me, Derek. Send me home."

She reached out to him with blood-stained hands. It didn't matter to Derek, he clutched them. Her warmth still intoxicated him. No more blood was coming from her side. Tenderly he held Sara's head in his lap. Derek closed his eyes and pressed his lips to hers.

At first, Derek was disoriented, but then the vision came into focus. From outer space, the Earth sat atop the giant carousel. The wooden horses wheeled around never stopping, never resting as they spun the blue ball forever. The moon shown on the opposite side, its silver beam guiding the way.

He watched in his mind's eye as Sara walked the silvery path holding a baby boy in her arms. A woman was waiting for them up beyond the stars. Smiles and tears showed on both of the women's faces as Sara handed the boy over to her. Sara never looked back. The two women and the boy entered a door of sorts, and it closed behind them.

The vision faded for Derek as Sara surrendered her spirit.

Derek held Sara in his arms gently rocking her lifeless body until Sharon came back for him.

CHAPTER 36

"It's Luis, our anthropology student," Sharon yelled from the outside into the hut. "Derek, are you available to see him?"

"Of course!" he answered delighted. "Come in Luis, I'll pour us a drink." The two of them shook hands. The bright white smile on Luis's face lit up the place. "So, how did it go today?" Derek asked him.

"You wouldn't believe it, Señor Dunbar. It's only been three days since we stopped taking cobo and already there have been four good fist fights."

Derek laughed while handing a cup to Luis. "Now that's progress," he chimed.

"To progress," Luis toasted.

Hoping that all would end well, Derek grew pensive and quizzed the young man. "You're the cultural expert, Luis. Most of these men have been on cobo their entire adult lives."

Luis waved him off, "They can handle it, Señor Dunbar. Besides, their wives keep them in check."

Derek laughed again. "Even without cobo, the women still have the power, don't they, Luis?"

"Sí," he replied while gulping the drink. "Sara's Shadow Women are now simply women, but they always get their way."

"Speaking of women," Derek reminded him. "I understand that you return Anna's affections, eh?"

The white smile reappeared on Luis's face. "She's a lovely girl. I can't wait to show her around Manaus." He grew sullen. "The professor would have liked her."

Derek put his hand on the young man's shoulder. "Gem will soon be well enough to travel. The men of the village will escort her back to civilization and turn her over to the authorities."

It didn't seem to cheer him up. "I'm afraid it will not be the same without Pedro. He was a good friend." Looking up at Derek, he asked, "Señor Dunbar, did he really try and harm your Sharon?"

Refilling Luis's cup, Derek reassured him, "The Pedro you knew died long before he turned into Blaze. It wasn't the same person. His mind was gone."

"What's next for us to do?" Luis changed the subject.

"We need to make sure that the rest of the cobo stockpile gets dumped back into the forest from where it came."

Luis agreed with him. "Sí, Señor Dunbar. There will no longer be a need for such a thing."

The hut flap lifted long enough for Anne and Juan to pop in. Sharon followed behind them. They were drenched. "It just started to rain buckets," she pointed out.

Luis hurriedly finished the last of his drink. "Yikes, Anna will be expecting me. I better go." All of them smiled as he made a quick exit.

Derek noticed how Anne's green eyes sparkled while she held on to Juan. He was happy for them both. "You two sure about this?" he asked them. "Sharon told me what you guys have been thinking."

"There's nothing more to think about," Anne told him matter-of-factly. "We're staying here with you."

"It isn't going to be easy rebuilding this culture," he warned. "They have a lot to learn."

"That's okay, Derek. I like my new job being a teacher."

"And, you know me, Derek," Juan added. "I can fix anything mechanical."

"There's nothing around here mechanical to fix," Sharon chuckled.

"Not yet," Juan defended himself. "A few trips back and forth from civilization will soon change that." He directed a question to Derek. "What about you two?"

"Sharon and I still have a lot of work to do accounting for all of the gold," Derek informed them. "These people don't understand what it is, or why it is so valuable. It's Sara's legacy to them. I want to make sure that nobody takes advantage."

"Then what?" Anne asked with curiosity.

Derek shrugged, "I don't know." He began to clarify the statement when Sharon cut him off.

"Then we have a wedding to plan," she admitted beaming.

Anne jumped up and down. "Finally!" she squealed.

"Congratulations, Derek," Juan praised him and extended a hand.

Derek blushed.

It rained most of the night, and the air grew damp. Oddly, Derek felt cold.

He woke once during the night, shivering. It was soon forgotten as he delighted in cuddling close with Sharon. Her warmth neutralized his discomfort. Early the next morning, before sunrise, Derek got up to check the sky.

"The rain clouds have moved off to the south," he observed talking to himself. "Good, we have a lot of work to do today and could use some sun." As he looked up at the waning crescent moon, Derek suddenly felt a strange sensation, a kind of seizure that at first he didn't understand.

"Sharon!" he yelled her name.

She quickly rushed to his side. "Derek, what's wrong?"

Sharon noticed his face turn pale as it happened again.

Derek Dunbar coughed.

EPILOGUE

Guayaquil, New Andalusia — Summer 1544

From the estate high on the hill at the end of the boulevard, General Francisco de Orellana sat at his picnic table near the top of the staircase and observed the activities on the street below. It was late afternoon. Huaorani children played ball side-by-side with their Hidalgo counterparts. The street merchants were shutting down their stands for the day. The smell of cooked meat and pastries floated on the air.

Friar Gaspar emerged from the estate and took a seat next to the general.

"They adore you, Francisco," he told the general while nodding his head in the direction of the throng below. "You've brought peace and prosperity to this place. There is no more deserving person than you for appointment as Governor of the Amazona Territory. Emperor Charles chose well."

"Maybe so," Orellana speculated. "Maybe it was a twist of fate. This honor was supposed to go to Gonzalo. If he hadn't been wounded, we would be celebrating his success and not mine."

"You speak of his physical wounds," Friar Gaspar corrected him. "Don't forget about his emotional affliction. Gonzalo would never have been able to keep his mind clear of her. He would never have willingly left the jungle."

The general drank some wine and seemed lost in thought for a while. He reached a moment of clarity. "I would never have willingly have stayed. My desire to be with Juana drove us, Friar. I couldn't get down that cursed river fast enough. Knowing that my wife and baby were waiting for me was all the incentive that I needed."

"Look where it led you," Gaspar reminded him. "Under your command we discovered both the source and mouth of the great Amazon River. El Dorado eluded us, but think of the other riches that opened before us. You're a hero, General."

Orellana laughed. "No, Friar, I'm just a simple man. I yearn for the same things that they do," he said while pointing to the citizens below. "Give me my wife and children and every once in a while a bit of adventure."

"I hope that you had your fill of adventure for a long time," Juana said sternly as she walked toward the table and heard the last bit of the conversation. She was carrying their baby. "Little Sara just celebrated her second birthday. I wouldn't want her to be without a father again so soon."

As she sat, the general held out his arms and made a motion for the baby to be handed to him. Sara smiled and cooed and eagerly struggled away from Juana toward her dad.

Following closely behind Juana was General de Vargas. He was helping Gonzalo over to the table.

"I apologize for my tardiness," Gonzalo uttered and pointed down to his leg. "I don't think I'll ever be able to walk on it again."

"Don't you believe a word of that," de Vargas joked. "Just tell him where the wine is and watch him sprint to it like a stag."

They all laughed.

"I'm grateful that you could come, Gonzalo," Orellana told him. "The reunion would not be complete without you."

"It's still not complete," Gonzalo mumbled and looked off far away into the mountains.

General de Vargas broke the moment of discomfort. "I'm humbled to be in such company," he said with a smile. "Here I sit as a lowly general with two governors and an Archbishop."

"None of this would have been possible without you," Orellana praised the general. "Thanks again for seeing Juana safely home."

"Yes, thank you," Juana seconded what her husband said. She rose and took the baby from him. "I need to get her to bed," she told them. "Don't stay away from me for too long, Francisco."

Juana gave her husband a kiss and whispered something into his ear. She disappeared with the baby into the mansion.

"It's too bad that old salt, Captain Pinzon, couldn't be here," de Vargas pointed out.

Friar Gaspar agreed, "I miss him, too. He was one of a kind."

"Passed away about a year ago, right?" Orellana asked.

"Made it back to Malaga and retired. Within two months he was dead," confirmed Gaspar.

"I believe there is a lesson in that for all of us," de Vargas observed. Raising his wine goblet, he bellowed to the men, "To Captain Pinzon."

"Here, here," they said in unison and clinked their drinks together.

The four of them drank wine and talked together relating many tall tales until well after dark. Finally, Orellana rubbed his eyes and confessed to them, "You know what Juana whispered to me, don't you?"

Of course they did.

"I guess you'll be leaving us until tomorrow," Gonzalo chuckled.

"Until tomorrow," Orellana parroted and raised his goblet for the final toast.

"I'm also ready to retire for the evening," General de Vargas announced. "Hold up, Francisco, and I'll walk with you."

After the two of them disappeared into the mansion, Gonzalo and Friar Gaspar were alone. Both of them fixed their gaze on the bright full moon as it rose above the tops of the mountains. Its brightness was not powerful enough to obscure the brightest of stars. Gaspar studied the Crux asterism as it showed through almost directly overhead.

"Well, old friend," he began. "It all started with us, didn't it? Way back there in Trujillo in what seems so long ago."

"Aye, Friar," Gonzalo acknowledged. "That is where it began, but where will it end?"

"For us?" Gaspar considered. "Only God knows."

They watched the white disk for some time. Gaspar understood that his friend had a troubled soul. Similar to his leg, this wound would also never completely heal. Finally, Gonzalo spoke up.

"Not a day, not even an hour goes by that I don't think about her," he remarked. "Was it all a dream, or did she really exist?"

"The essence of Sara lives within all of humanity, Gonzalo," the friar consoled him. "She lives on."

THE END

Printed in the United States
1336400002B/43-63